THE
HIDDEN
PALACE

ALSO BY HELENE WECKER

The Golem and the Jinni

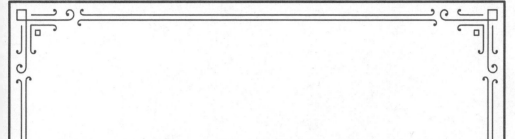

THE
HIDDEN
PALACE

– A Novel of *The Golem and the Jinni* –

HELENE WECKER

HARPER

An Imprint of HarperCollins*Publishers*

THE HIDDEN PALACE. Copyright © 2021 by Helene Wecker. All rights reserved. Printed in the United States of America. No part of this book may be used or reproduced in any manner whatsoever without written permission except in the case of brief quotations embodied in critical articles and reviews. For information, address HarperCollins Publishers, 195 Broadway, New York, NY 10007.

HarperCollins books may be purchased for educational, business, or sales promotional use. For information, please email the Special Markets Department at SPsales@harpercollins.com.

Art courtesy of Shutterstock/Vasya Kobelev

FIRST EDITION

Library of Congress Cataloging-in-Publication Data has been applied for.

ISBN 978-0-06-246871-0

21 22 23 24 25   LSC   10 9 8 7 6 5 4 3 2 1

For Maya and Gavin

Prologue

Of all the myriad races of thinking creatures in the world, the two that most delight in telling stories are the flesh-and-blood humans and the long-lived, fiery jinn.

The stories of both humans and jinn are known for their changeability. A tale told by either race will alter as it spreads, the versions multiplying into a family of stories, one that squabbles and contradicts itself like any other family. A story will seem to pass out of telling, then suddenly resurrect itself, its old bones fitted with modern garments. And there are even tales that spread from one race to the other—though the versions are often so different that they hardly seem like the same story at all.

Consider, for instance, the story of the fisherman and the jinni. The humans tell it many ways, one of which is this:

Once, long ago, a poor fisherman stood at the edge of a lake, casting his net. His first two casts brought him nothing, but on the third he pulled from the water an old copper flask. Rejoicing, for the copper was worth a few coins, he pried the iron stopper from the flask—and out exploded a gigantic and rageful jinni. The jinni explained to the man that King Sulayman himself had caged him in the flask and then tossed it into the lake, knowing that even if the jinni should manage somehow to escape, the water would extinguish him at once. For hundreds of years the jinni had brooded upon his misfortune, until his hatred of humanity had grown so large that he'd vowed to destroy whoever released him.

The fisherman pleaded for his life, but the jinni refused to spare him. At last the fisherman begged the jinni to answer a single question first. Reluctantly, the jinni agreed. *How*, the fisherman asked, *did you fit into that tiny flask? You stand before me an enormous specimen, and even your smallest toe would be enough to fill it. I simply won't believe your story until I'm convinced you were inside the flask all along.*

Furious at this doubting of his word, the jinni promptly dissolved into his insubstantial form and crowded himself back into the flask, saying, *Now do you see, human?*—whereupon the fisherman replaced the stopper, trapping the jinni once more. Realizing his mistake, the jinni begged the fisherman from inside the flask, promising endless jewels and riches if the man would only release him. But the fisherman, who knew better than to trust him, threw the flask and its inhabitant back into the lake, where it lies undiscovered to this day.

When told among the jinn, however, the tale sounds more like this:

Long ago there was a cunning human wizard, a many-times descendant of Sulayman the Enslaver, who learned of a lake where a powerful jinni lay trapped inside a copper flask. Rejoicing, for the wizard wished to bind a jinni as his servant, he disguised himself as a poor fisherman, cast a net into the lake, and drew the flask from the waters. He pulled out the stopper, and the gigantic jinni emerged before him.

Exhausted from his long years inside the flask, the jinni said, *Human, you have released me, and I shall spare your life in gratitude.*

At once the wizard cast off his fisherman's rags. *You shall serve me for all your days!* he shouted, and began to cast the binding spell.

The jinni knew that if he flew away, the spell would only follow. So, quick as a flash, he shrank himself back into the flask, pulled the stopper in after himself, and used the flame of his body to heat the copper until it scalded the wizard—who unthinkingly hurled it away from himself, into the middle of the lake.

Nursing his burnt hand and his wounded pride, the wizard declared, *Clearly this jinni would have been nothing but trouble. I shall find a better servant elsewhere.* And he stalked off, leaving the flask beneath the waters—and inside it the clever jinni, who'd decided that even a cramped and solitary prison was better than a life as a slave.

There is another story shared by humans and jinn, one that also concerns iron and magic, vows and bindings. It is known by only a very few of both races, and guarded among them as a secret. Even if you were to find them, and earn their trust, it's still unlikely that you'd ever hear the tale—which is told as follows:

PART I

1900–1908

I.

MANHATTAN, FEBRUARY 1900

A man and a boy exited the Third Avenue Elevated and walked westward along 67th Street, into the wind.

It was a frigid, blustery morning, and the weather had driven most of the city indoors. Those few who remained on the sidewalks stared at the man and boy as they passed, for they were an unusual sight in this Upper East Side neighborhood, with their long dark coats and broadbrimmed hats, their side-curls bobbing above their scarves. At Lexington, the man paced back and forth, squinting at the buildings, until at last the boy found what they were looking for: a narrow door labeled *Benevolent Hebrew Aid Society*. Behind the door was a flight of stairs, at the top of which was another door, the twin of the first. The man hesitated, then straightened his back and knocked.

Footsteps—and the door swung open, revealing a thin-haired man in rimless spectacles and a trim American suit.

If circumstances had been otherwise, the visitor might have introduced himself as Rabbi Lev Altschul of the Forsyth Street Synagogue, and the boy at his side as the son of a congregant, employed for the afternoon as a translator. The man in the suit, whose name was Fleischman, might've thanked the rabbi for coming so far, in such dismal weather. Then the two might have discussed the task that had brought them together: the disbursement of the private library of one Rabbi Avram Meyer, recently deceased. Mr. Fleischman would've explained that the late Rabbi Meyer's nephew had chosen the Benevolent Hebrew Aid Society because they specialized in book donations—but that once the Rabbi's collection had arrived, and crate after crate of Talmudic esoterica was unloaded into their office, it had become clear that, in this case, they would need to summon a specialist.

In response, Rabbi Altschul might've outlined, with something approaching modesty, his own qualifications: that he was known among his peers for his Talmudic scholarship, and had spent his entire life, first in Lithuania and then New York, surrounded by books such as these. He would've reassured Mr. Fleischman that the Benevolent Hebrew Aid Society had made the right choice, and that under his stewardship, Rabbi Meyer's books would all find new and appropriate homes.

But none of this came to pass. Instead the two men faced each other balefully over the threshold, each staring in clear distaste at the top of the other's head: the one garbed in Orthodox hat and side-curls, and the other, in the Reform manner, as bare as a Gentile's.

Then, without a word, Fleischman stepped to one side, and Altschul saw the enormous library table beyond, its scarred wooden top buried beneath stacks and rows and pyramids of books.

Rabbi Altschul's sigh was that of a bridegroom catching a glimpse of his beloved.

At last Fleischman broke the silence and delivered his instructions. The rabbi, he said, must sort the books into groups, based on whichever criteria he felt appropriate. Each group would then be sent to the synagogue of Altschul's choice. The boy translated these instructions in a nervous, whispering Yiddish; the rabbi grunted and, without a word, went to the table and began his examinations.

Thus dismissed, Fleischman retreated to a nearby desk, picked up a newspaper, and pretended to read it while surreptitiously watching his guest. The boy, too, watched the rabbi—for Lev Altschul was a commanding figure, and a man of some mystery, even to his own congregation. He was a widower, his young wife Malke having died from a fever after childbirth—and yet the loss seemed to have changed him little. All had expected him to remarry, if only to provide a mother for the baby, a daughter he'd named Kreindel; but the year of mourning had long since come and gone, and still he showed no interest in finding a bride.

The truth was that Lev Altschul was a man with little patience for worldly considerations. He'd married Malke in order to fulfill the command to be fruitful and multiply, and because she, too, had come from a respected rabbinical family, which he'd thought would dispose her to the role of a rabbi's wife. But the unfortunate Malke had been completely unsuited to the task. A mouse of a woman, she'd cringed at her husband's every utterance, and had lived in even greater terror of his congregants—especially the women, whom she'd suspected, quite rightly, of mocking her behind her back. Altschul had hoped that motherhood might strengthen his bride, but the pregnancy had turned her even paler and more querulous than before; and at the end, she'd seemed to embrace the killing fever with a certain gloomy relief. The entire experience had been so off-putting that, having fulfilled the commandment once, Altschul had no intention of doing so again. To solve the problem of a mother for little Kreindel, he now paid an assortment of young mothers in their tenement to look after her—one of whom had just arrived for the squirming girl when he received the request from the Benevolent Hebrew Aid Society that morning, asking for his help.

He'd nearly rejected the letter out of hand. In Lev Altschul's mind, the Reform movement and their uptown charities were an enemy second only to the Russian Tsar. He held a special contempt for their settlement workers: young German Jewesses who knocked on tenement doors, offering the ladies who answered free milk and eggs if they agreed to endure a lecture on modern hygiene and nutrition. *You're in America now,* their refrain went. *You must learn to cook properly.* Lev had instructed Malke that no settlement woman was ever to set foot in their apartment, that he'd rather starve than accept the worm that dangled from their hook. And now that Malke was dead, he was even warier than before: for all knew that the settlement women were also agents of the Asylum for Orphaned Hebrews, the gigantic Reform orphanage uptown that stole poor Orthodox children into its bowels and made them forget their families, their Yiddish, and their traditions. In short, he was as likely to venture inside a serpent's pit as spend an afternoon at the Benevolent Hebrew Aid Society—but in the end, the lure of an abandoned Talmudic library had worked its magic, and the rabbi had reluctantly agreed.

Now, as Altschul walked up and down the book-lined table, the character of the late Rabbi Meyer began to take shape in his mind. The books themselves were well thumbed and well cared for, the library of a true scholar. The titles, however, told him that Meyer's theology had been far more mystical than his own, even edging toward anathema. In fact, if the two had ever encountered each other in life, Altschul might've had harsh words for him. But standing in this cold and alien office, with the dead man's precious library laid out like the grubby contents of a bookmonger's cart, Altschul felt only a deep and sympathetic grief. In this room, he and Meyer were brothers. He'd overlook their differences, and disburse the man's legacy as best he could.

He began to sort the books into piles, while the boy waited nearby in nervous boredom, and Fleischman turned each page of his newspaper with a rattle and a snap. Altschul wished the man would stop making so much noise; it seemed a deliberate insult—

He paused, his hand upon a book that was considerably older and more worn than its neighbors. Only shreds of leather were left clinging to the boards; the spine, too, had flaked away, revealing narrow bundles of pages bound with fraying catgut. Carefully Altschul opened it—and his frown deepened as he turned the pages, skimming formulae, dia-grams, pages of close-written Hebrew. He could barely read most of it, but the fragments he understood told of theories and experiments and the sorts of abilities that, should the tales be believed, were forbidden to all but the holiest sages. What, in the name of God, had Meyer been do-ing with a book like this?

He closed the cover, his hands trembling with unease—and now he saw that the next book in the stack was just as worn and ancient-seeming as the first. And so was the next book, and the next. Five in all he found, five books of secret knowledge that most scholars thought had vanished into legend. These were sacred objects. He should've prayed and fasted before even touching them. And now here they were, in America—in a Reform charity office, of all places!

Heart pounding, he carefully moved the books to one side, away from their neighbors. Then, as though nothing had happened, he went on to the next, blessedly ordinary volume. He imagined he could feel his hands tingling, as though the forbidden writings had leached through the tattered covers and into his skin.

It had grown dark by the time all the books were sorted. At last Altschul summoned the boy and then traveled down the table, the boy translating his instructions while Fleischman grimly wrote them down. *These* books—Altschul outlined with his hands one large group of stacks—were to be given to Rabbi Teitelbaum at Congregation Kol Yisroel, at Hester Street. *These* books—another swath of small towers—must go to Mariampol Synagogue, on East Broadway.

"And these," the boy said as Altschul gestured to the final, solitary stack of decrepit-looking volumes, "must be sent to Rabbi Chaim Grodzinski, the Rav of Vilna."

Fleischman's pen hovered above the paper. "I'm sorry, who?"

"Rabbi Chaim Grodz—"

"Yes, yes, but Vilna? In *Lithuania*?"

Man and boy explained to Fleischman that the Rav was the chief rabbi of Vilna, and a holy and important personage. In return, Fleischman informed them that the man could be Elijah the Tishbite for all he cared—*Lithuania*, for heaven's sake! Did they think he had a pet Rothschild to pay for the shipping? No, the books would have to join their brethren in one of the other stacks, or else Altschul must deal with them himself.

The rabbi stared at him in silent anger, and then back at the tattered relics. Without another word he snatched up the books and stalked out the door and down to the street, the boy following behind.

That night, when the boy's mother asked her son what had sent their rabbi uptown, he described for her the charity office, and the countless books, and the man who'd turned his newspaper pages with a rattle and a snap. But he made no mention of the books that Rabbi Altschul had carried home on the Elevated. He didn't want to remember how the rabbi's eyes had gleamed with a terrible fascination as he'd gazed at them, how he'd neglected to stand for their stop until the boy tapped him on the shoulder. The boy had never liked Rabbi Altschul, not quite—but until that day, he'd never been afraid of him.

Rabbi Altschul did not send the books to the Vilna Rav.

Instead, he wrapped them in a prayer-shawl, placed the bundle inside an old wooden suitcase, and pushed the suitcase beneath his bed, far out of reach. Then he resumed the usual course of his life: synagogue, prayer, and study. Months passed, and not once did Rabbi Altschul touch the books, even though they tempted him greatly. Neither did he make inquiries into the circumstances of Rabbi Meyer's death—although he couldn't help wondering if the books had played some role in it. He imagined how it might've happened: the excited discovery, the heedless blundering through their pages, an attempt at some spell thoroughly beyond Meyer's abilities—and then, the inevitable consequence.

His intuition was correct, to a point. The books had indeed hastened Rabbi Meyer's death, slowly draining his strength as he studied them—not out of a naive, hubristic desire for their knowledge, but in an attempt to control a dangerous creature, one that Rabbi Meyer had discovered and sheltered and grown to care for. The creature was a golem, a living being sculpted from clay and animated by holy magic. This particular golem had been made in the form of a human woman—one who was somewhat tall and awkward, but otherwise entirely ordinary to all appearances. The golem's name was Chava Levy. She worked at Radzin's Bakery at the corner of Allen and Delancey, not seven blocks from Altschul's own synagogue. To her colleagues, she was indefatigable Chava, who could braid an entire tray of challahs in under two minutes, and who sometimes seemed to reach for whatever a customer wanted before they'd even asked. To her landlady at her Eldridge Street boardinghouse, she was a quiet, steady tenant, and an expert seamstress who spent her nights performing repairs and alterations for pennies apiece. She was so quick with these tasks that her admiring clients sometimes asked, *Chava, when do you find time to sleep?* The truth, of course, was that she never needed to.

SYRIAN DESERT, SEPTEMBER 1900

In the desert east of the human city of ash-Sham—also called Damascus—a pair of jinn chased each other across the landscape.

They were young for their kind, mere dozens of years old. For millennia, their clan had dwelt in the shelter of a nearby valley, far from the human empires that grew and shrank and conquered one another in turn. As they flew—each of them attempting to steal the wind that the other rode, a common game among the young—one of them spied something puzzling: a man, a human man, walking toward them from the west. He was tall, and thin, and wore no head-covering. In one hand he carried a travel-stained valise.

The young jinn laughed in astonishment. Humans rarely traveled alone in this stretch of the desert, and never on foot. What insanity had driven this one so far astray? Then their laughter ran dry, for he'd drawn close enough for them to see that he was no human at all, but one of their own kind. He came closer still—and a sudden, instinctual terror seized them both.

—*Iron! He brings iron!*

And indeed there it was, a close-fitting cuff of beaten iron, glinting from his wrist. But—how was such a thing possible? Did he feel no fear at its presence, no searing pain at its touch? What *was* he?

Bewildered, the youngsters fled back to their habitation in the valley, to tell the elders what they'd seen.

The man who wasn't a man approached the valley.

The youngsters had seen the truth: he was indeed a jinni, a creature of living flame. Once, like them, he'd been free to take the shape of any animal, or fly invisible through the air, or even enter dreaming minds—but he'd lost these abilities long ago. The iron cuff at his wrist was the work of a powerful wizard who'd captured him, bound him to human form, and sealed him inside a copper flask for safekeeping. He'd languished in that flask for over a thousand years—which he'd felt only as a single, timeless moment—until, in a city on the other side of the world, an unsuspecting tinsmith had broken the seal and released him. He could no longer speak the jinn language, for it was a thing of flames and wind, unpronounceable by human tongues. Inside his valise was the copper flask that had been his prison, now home to the very wizard who'd bound him—a victory that had come at great cost. And now he'd returned to the very habitation that once had been his own, to hide the flask away from the human world.

He reached the edge of the valley and paused, waiting. Soon he spied them: a phalanx of jinn, coming to investigate. The jinn youngsters returned as well, but they were not so bold as their elders. They took the form of lizards, and hid in the scrub near the stranger's feet, small enough to go unnoticed.

—*What are you?* the elders asked.

And the stranger told them his story.

Word of the stranger spread.

Before long, hundreds of jinn had gathered upon the ridges to peer down into the valley where he knelt, digging a hole in the desert floor with his bare hands. The two youngsters, meanwhile, flew among their fellows, eagerly spreading the tale they'd heard at his feet.

—*He is one of us, born from this very habitation, bound by a wizard over a thousand years ago . . .*

—*The iron is enchanted, it chains him to human form . . .*

For hours the stranger worked in the growing heat. At last he opened the valise and removed the flask, its copper belly glowing in the afternoon sun.

—*There, you see? That was his prison! And now the wizard himself is caught inside!*

The flask disappeared into the hole, along with a tattered sheaf of papers.—*The wizard's spells*, the youngsters said; it was a guess, but an accurate one. Then the stranger replaced the dirt and sand, built a cairn of rocks over the spot to mark it, and stood, wiping his hands.

The elders, too, had been watching. They descended and spoke, their voices echoing to the ridge-tops.—*But how will you live*, they said, *bound and chained as you are? What will you do, where will you go?*

"I'll go home," the iron-bound jinni replied. And without another word he walked out of the valley, and vanished into the desert.

The tale of the iron-bound jinni spread from jinn-child to jinn-child.

All agreed on the main elements: the stranger, the iron, the flask and its burial. But from there, the story fractured and diverged. Some said that he was spotted near the invisible remains of an ancient glass palace, its walls and spires worn to tatters. Others spoke of watching a jinni in human form cross into the Ghouta, the dangerous oasis along the eastern edge of Damascus, where the marsh-creatures liked to snare passing jinn and drag them into the waters, which soon extinguished them.

—*But why would he go there?* the listeners asked.

—*Perhaps to end his unhappy life,* some guessed.

But others remembered his words: *I'll go home.* And their thoughts turned to the land beyond the Ghouta, the world of men and iron. Was *that* what he'd meant? Did he dwell among them now? It seemed impossible. To live as a human, constantly trudging upon the ground; to shelter in their buildings from the killing rain, and speak to them in their languages—how long could one bear it? How long before the waters of the Ghouta began to seem like a welcome relief?

Thus they speculated, and argued, and told the tale over and over amongst themselves. And through their workings, the tale soon gained enough weight and shape to break free of the valley and travel, like its own strange protagonist, into places where it wasn't expected.

In truth, the iron-bound jinni made it easily through the Ghouta, for the marsh-creatures there were just as frightened of him as their desert cousins had been. He had no inkling at all of the story he'd set into motion, the legend now growing behind him. He only knew that he had a ship to catch.

In Damascus he caught the train over the mountains to the docks at Beirut, where he placed an overseas cable at the telegram office and then joined the line for his packet ship. The line advanced slowly. He tried to remain patient. A year now since he'd been freed from the flask, and patience was still a daily struggle. He suspected it always would be. He closed his eyes, felt the ticket in his pocket, listened to the calls of the seagulls and the waves lapping at the harbor walls. It was a humid day, and his skin tingled where the air touched it. He kept his mind on the voyage ahead: first to Marseilles, where he would change to the steamship *Gallia*, and then the Atlantic crossing to New York. It would be long and trying and uncomfortable, but then it would be over. He refrained from remembering the feel of the desert, the sight of his kin on the breeze, the sound of the windswept language he could no longer speak. He'd wanted to stay longer, to beg the elders to keep talking to him for hours, days, about anything at all. But what good would it have done? Far better to finish his errand and leave quickly. To return to New York and fulfill the promise he'd made.

At last he reached the front of the line and handed the uniformed agent his ticket.

"Name?" said the agent.

"Ahmad al-Hadid." Not his true name, of course, but his nonetheless. He'd chosen it himself: *hadid* meaning "iron," and *Ahmad* simply because he liked how it sounded.

The agent waved him through, and he started up the gangplank—just as a boy from the telegram office ran up to him, bowed quickly, and handed him a folded cable.

The Jinni read it, and smiled.

A tall woman in a dark cloak walked a tree-lined path in a Brooklyn cemetery, a small stone nestled in the palm of her hand.

It was October now, a crisp and beautiful day. The trees had long since turned, and their burnished leaves lay so thick upon the ground that they obscured the path. The woman turned at the correct spot regardless, walking between the rows of headstones to a grave whose sod had barely taken root. *Michael Levy, Beloved Husband and Nephew.* Rabbi Avram Meyer, his uncle, lay only a row away.

Beloved Husband: it was a well-meaning fiction. Not the marriage itself; she had every right to call herself Chava Levy, though she'd been married and widowed in the space of a season. But love? She'd kept her nature a secret, had built their union upon her husband's ignorance, and it had been a failure from the start. And then, at last, he'd learned the truth—not from her own lips, but through the workings of Yehudah Schaalman, a villainous man. It was Schaalman himself who'd created her, a clay bride for a businessman named Otto Rotfeld who'd wanted a new life in America and a wife to go with it. But Rotfeld had died halfway across the Atlantic, leaving her confused and adrift, utterly ignorant of humanity—knowing only that she must keep her nature hidden at all costs. Then Schaalman, too, had come to New York, and learned his own hidden truth: that he was the deathless reincarnation of a desert wizard who, a thousand years ago, had captured a powerful jinni, bound him with iron, and sealed him away in a flask. In the end, Schaalman had been defeated—but not before he'd murdered Michael, a tragedy that she couldn't help feeling was on her own account.

She crouched down, plucked the stray leaves from the headstone. "Hello, Michael," she murmured. She'd spent the streetcar ride to the cemetery considering her words, but now they felt self-conscious, inadequate. She went on anyway. "I'm so sorry I lied to you," she said. "Your uncle told me once that I'd have to lie for the rest of my life, and that I'd find it hard to bear. He was right, of course. He usually was." She smiled sadly, then sobered. "I'm not asking for your permission, or your blessing. I just want you to understand. If you'd survived, I would've been a true and faithful wife, without any lies between us. But I don't think it would've lasted."

Was she only telling herself what she wanted to hear? Would he have been willing, even happy, to stay with her? She would never bear children, never age, never change. She gazed down at the stone she'd brought, cupped inside a hand formed from the clay of a Prussian riverbank. If she wanted to, she could close her fist and squeeze until rock dust sifted from her fingers. No, Michael wouldn't have wanted her for a wife. Not once he knew.

She couldn't stay long. She had an appointment at a Manhattan pier, a promise to keep. She placed the stone atop the smooth-carved granite: a token of her visit, like she'd seen on other Jewish graves, more sober and lasting than flowers.

"I hope you're at peace," the Golem told him.

The *Gallia* approached the Hudson docklands.

The pier was crowded with men in autumn hats and overcoats, and here and there a few women, cloaked like herself. They were waiting for fathers and mothers, wives and children, distant cousins, business partners; for those whose faces they knew by heart, and those they knew not at all. The crowd stirred around her, filling her mind with their fears and desires:

Is that Mother at the rail?—

Please, God, don't let him find out what happened while he was gone—

If he didn't make that sale, then we're sunk—

It was a strange and dubious gift of Rotfeld's passing, this power of hers. Without the wishes and commands of a true master to follow, her seeking mind instead found those of everyone else. At first the compulsion to obey them had been overwhelming; but time, and training, had weakened their pull. They still harried her on occasion—when she was anxious or upset, or simply at the limits of her mind's endurance. But for the most part they were only whispers, dimly overheard.

And threading through those overheard fears and desires, neither louder nor softer: a simple sound, an elongated note, the frozen scream of Yehudah Schaalman, who lay trapped in a flask on the other side of the earth. He'd be with her always now. A small price to pay when she'd come so close to losing everything.

At last the gangplank lowered, and the passengers began to emerge—and there he was. Tall and handsome, hatless as always, his battered valise still streaked with desert dust. His features glowed as though lit from within: the proof of his true nature, visible only to those, like herself, with the power to see it. From one wrist glinted the iron cuff that trapped him; it also veiled his mind, making him the only person in the crowd—perhaps the world—whose thoughts she couldn't sense.

He must've spied her from the deck, for he angled toward her unerringly. They stood together as the crowd rushed around them and the air filled with greetings in a dozen languages, a Babel of reunion. They smiled at each other.

"Well," the Jinni said, "shall we go for a walk?"

They went to Central Park, he still carrying the valise.

They kept to the main paths and spoke little, though there was much they might have said. She considered asking about his visit to the desert and the jinn—his own people, of whom he spoke so rarely. What had it felt like, to be in their presence again? She imagined pain, joy, regret—how could it be otherwise? But perhaps he didn't want to talk about it yet. She had no wish to cause him pain, to start an argument, when he'd only just returned. There'd be time for all of that later. For now, she merely wanted to be with him again.

He, too, had questions he might've asked. How had she fared these last weeks? He couldn't help thinking of Michael, the husband he'd never met. She mourned him, surely, but he saw no outward sign of it. Perhaps he was meant to ask—but he knew next to nothing about the man, let alone the specifics of their brief marriage, and felt a half-guilty reluctance to learn. Far easier to leave it alone, for now, and simply be glad of her company.

The shadows lengthened; the crowds dwindled. She drew closer to him now as they walked the Mall—and belatedly he remembered that she'd been forced to stay indoors each night that he was gone, a hostage to the societal rule that no woman of good morals went out alone after dark. He smiled now, watching her gaze up at the elms, strangely proud to be the one whose presence meant she could walk the lamp-lit cobbles, and enjoy the cool and misted air. And she smiled, too, to feel the Park's life-force all around her, the earthly strength so like her own.

They left the Park through the Columbus Circle gates, walked south along Broadway's thoroughfare. Each passing sight—Madison Square with its tidy paths, the Washington Square Arch awash in electric light—was a landmark of their relationship, the spot of some discussion or confrontation. They'd discovered each other in these places, over those nights. Now, in silence, they listened to the echoes of their past arguments—but fondly, without rancor, their eidetic memories in perfect agreement.

They reached the Lower East Side, and her boardinghouse. She looked up at her own dark window, then at his glowing face.

"Until tomorrow?" he asked.

"Tomorrow," she agreed, and they parted.

Alone, he walked west. He crossed the Bowery—a brief burst of noise and light—and continued through the Cast Iron District with its facades of painted metal. At Washington Street he turned south again, passing shuttered markets, tobacconists' shops. To his right was West Street and the river; he heard shouted orders, the thumps of barrels, laughter rising from a cellar shebeen. To his left, the blocks narrowed and grew angular, the streets pulling together as the island thinned, drawing him along to Little Syria, the neighborhood at its tip. Here the street was dark and quiet, save for a solitary light that glowed from a half-subterranean shop window. *Arbeely & Ahmad, All Metals*, read the sign above the steps. Through the window he could see a man at a wooden workbench, his head cradled upon his arms, his back rising and falling in sleep.

The Jinni opened the door carefully, reaching up to still the bell— but Arbeely woke anyway. The man sat up, rubbed his eyes briefly, and then smiled. "You're back," he said.

"I am," said the Jinni, and set down his empty valise at last.

2.

E ast of Central Park, inside a Fifth Avenue mansion that reigned among that street's many splendors, a young woman named Sophia Winston was readying for a journey of her own.

Were it an ordinary voyage, the servants would have been in an uproar of last-minute preparations. Instead, they crept past the half-open door to her bedroom as she bustled about filling her trunks herself, her back to the fireplace that she kept at such a blaze that one could feel it down the hall. The girl's mother had informed the household in no uncertain terms that they were to provide no assistance, nor were they to speak of the matter. They weren't even told where Sophia was going. Driven to desperate measures, the maids had picked through the girl's wastebasket and uncovered a crumpled list. *Split skirt for riding, short-heeled boots, three sets of long woolens. Canvas duck, waxed twine. Aspirin tablets in water-proof tins. Six dozen hairpins of good quality steel.* It all seemed to point toward a Subcontinental expedition, not a young woman's holiday, but their snooping yielded nothing more. And so they did their best to pretend that the girl was not, in fact, preparing for a secret voyage of some kind, when—if all had gone according to plan— she ought to have been embarking on her honeymoon.

In a private study elsewhere in the mansion, Sophia's mother, Julia Hamilton Winston, sat at her small, elegant desk and surveyed the middle-aged couple across from her. They were man and wife, or so they said, with matching sturdy builds and coarse, sun-lined features. In all, a drab and unremarkable pair—which pricked at Julia's sensibilities, but in this case, she had to admit, was entirely the point.

"Your task will come in two parts," she informed them. "First, as Miss Winston's staff. You will be the entirety of her household, as well as her chaperones and companions."

The pair nodded along, as though it were entirely unsurprising that a young woman of twenty should go abroad without a single friend or relation, only two strangers for servants.

"She has arranged her itinerary, and I have approved it," Julia said. "You will be overseas for roughly six months." She slid a piece of paper across the desk. They took it and read it over together.

"Never been to India," the woman said.

"But you *do* have experience traveling abroad?" said Julia.

"Yes, ma'am," the man said. "Mexico, mainly."

Julia frowned at this—she could only imagine what two such as they had been doing in that country—but went on. "My daughter was recently ill," she said. "She has fully recovered except for a lingering anemia. Her hands tremble occasionally, and she is often cold. She may need help to dress herself—but do not coddle her, especially in public."

They nodded again, placid, unquestioning.

"As to the second part of your duties." She shifted, uncomfortable. "Last year, my daughter, through no fault save her own innocence, fell under the sway of a dangerous foreigner, a man I believe to be the ring-leader of an international gang. He invaded our house one morning this spring, along with a handful of his associates. Thankfully they were persuaded to leave—but he may still have designs upon her."

"Can you describe him?" the man asked.

"Tall, olive-skinned, perhaps thirty years old," Mrs. Winston said. "She called him Ahmad, though I have no idea if that was his real name. You will protect her from this man, and from others like him. You'll report to me regularly, describing her health in general and her comportment in public, especially around members of the opposite sex. And so far as is feasible, you will never let her out of your sight." She paused. "I hope I needn't explain that Sophia will only be told the first half of your duties."

"Of course, ma'am," the woman said smoothly. "No explanation necessary."

The interview ended; the man and woman were shown out.

Alone, Julia rubbed her eyes. She could only imagine what the pair had made of her carefully crafted story. She'd left out Sophia's failed engagement entirely; it had little bearing on the matter, and there was only so much humiliation she could endure in the face of strangers. Nor had she mentioned the feats of mesmerism that this Ahmad had performed—for she had no desire at all to report that her own husband, one of the most powerful men in America, had sworn to her that he'd watched the man burn alive in their fireplace and then emerge without a scratch.

And then there was the matter of Sophia's "illness." Julia had been there when it began, on a trip to Europe; for weeks afterward she hadn't been able to close her eyes without picturing her daughter unconscious on a parquet floor, her skirts soaked through with blood. The doctors had dismissed it as a variant of the usual female affliction, distressing yet benign. And then, when the girl's shaking and chill had refused to improve, they'd suggested to Julia that the girl's troubles rested not in her body, but her mind.

At the time, Julia had rejected this suggestion out of hand. But after the foreigners had burst into their home—and Sophia, taking full advantage of the scandal, had broken her engagement with the relief of a woman spared the guillotine—Julia had begun, for the first time, to wonder if they were right. There was no sensible reason for Sophia to act so outrageously against her own interests and willfully destroy every advantage she'd been given; it seemed a sort of self-violence, like a murderous coachman who drives his passengers off a cliff knowing that he, too, must perish. What else would one call it but a kind of madness?

A knock at the door startled her from her thoughts. It was a maid, her face apologetic. "A message from Mr. Winston, ma'am. He's been unavoidably delayed, and will miss supper."

Julia dismissed the maid with a sigh. Ever since Sophia had settled on her plan, her husband had found countless excuses to stay away. A fine thing, when the blame could be laid squarely at his feet! Would Sophia have even contemplated such a thing had Francis not allowed her to linger in his library for hours at a time, reading travel memoirs and archaeological journals? He might as well have opened their door to the gang himself!

Alone in his office above Wall Street, Francis Winston stared out the window at the evening traffic, the day's business ignored upon his desk.

His message to Julia had been a lie, and he despised himself for writing it—not out of any particular distaste for lying to his wife, but for playing the part of a weaker man, one who must bend his own schedule to fit another's. But neither could he stomach returning to the mansion where his once-vibrant daughter now sat trembling before the fire, and his wife accused him for it with every word and glance.

Worse, he suspected that Julia was right. Francis Jeremiah Winston was the descendant of fur traders and timber barons, men who'd measured their wealth in acreage and rainfall and sunlight, in rivers forded and traps set. Over the succeeding generations, these rough spoils had been transmuted to more civilized substances: real estate holdings and railroad shares, shipping lines, munitions factories. Francis couldn't regret the domestication that had placed the Winston name alongside the likes of Astor and Vanderbilt—and yet a certain vitality, he felt, had been lost along the way. And so when young Sophia had showed an interest in travel and archaeology, and had asked to hear the stories of his bachelor years spent hunting game and climbing ruins, Francis had been secretly pleased. The doctors all had doubted that Julia could carry to term again, and so it seemed fitting that the only child of his line would continue the family's prospecting spirit. By the time that little George came along—less a miracle, in Francis's view, than proof of Julia's determination to have her way in all things—Sophia had, in a sense, become both son and daughter to him. Natural law, he'd reasoned, would turn her mind to marriage and family when the time came.

But then his world had been upended.

He hadn't been in Paris himself to witness his daughter's collapse. If he had, he would've recalled another episode from his bachelor years: a drunken night at a California brothel, where he'd opened the wrong door and glimpsed a blood-slicked, delirious girl groaning over a chamber-pot while the madam held her upright, murmuring in Spanish. Instead the absent Francis had taken the polite fiction of *womanly troubles* at face value. And when wife and daughter returned, and he saw Sophia for himself, her pale face and shaking hands, still he accepted the falsehood—until the morning when a stranger had rolled naked from their blazing hearth to land at Sophia's feet. She hadn't gasped, hadn't run. She'd bent over him, and taken his hand. She had spoken his name.

She was misled, Julia had insisted afterward, when he demanded that she accept the clear and obvious truth. *She was taken in.* But Francis had seen, as his wife had not, the look in their daughter's eyes when he'd moved to intervene. It was not that of an innocent beguiled—it was plain defiance, the unmasking of a mutineer.

And so, when Sophia announced her wish to break the engagement and leave the country, he'd consented at once. Yes, let her go, let her disappear abroad, so that he might forget what she'd been to him. Only then could he begin to reconcile himself to what she'd become, and to his own neglectful role in her transformation.

With her back to her ever-roaring fireplace, Sophia Winston stood in her bedroom and surveyed her luggage, her notes and lists. Servants passed by in the hall, whispering; she ignored them, focused instead on the stacks of books that vied for precious space in her trunks. *The Journal of Biblical Archaeology. Turkey Ancient and Modern. Folk-Lore of the Palestine Peasants. A Beginner's Arabic Grammar. Narrative of an Expedition to the River Jordan. Syrian Traditions and Superstitions.* She'd tried to winnow their numbers, but found it impossible to choose—and so into the trunks they all went. Not for the first time, she reflected that her mother had done her quite the favor by denying her the servants' help. Otherwise, someone might've noticed that none of her books had the first thing to do with India.

Sophia Winston had never deliberately set out to rebel. She had, in fact, resigned herself to the existence her mother had planned for her: the engagement she hadn't wanted, the stultifying society life. And then, one autumn day, she'd met a man in Central Park, a stranger who called himself Ahmad. He'd come that night to her balcony, and she'd allowed something to happen—an indiscretion, a liberty. It ought to have ended there—except that the stranger was no ordinary man, but a being of living flame. And for a time, a pinprick of that flame had grown inside her until, in that room in Paris, her body had cast it out, leaving her to tremble in perpetual chill.

Sophia knew that her mother worried for her sanity; she could only imagine what would happen if she told her parents the truth. They would send for the specialists, and Sophia would then vanish into some well-appointed prison, erased neatly from the world. Better, far better, to erase herself instead, to vanish for her own purposes. She'd learned much from her father's stories and the books he'd allowed her to read in spite of her mother's misgivings. And now, under the guise of the young explorer and adventuress, she would travel to the desert where the man of flame had come from, and the lands that surrounded it— Syria and Turkey, Egypt, the Hijaz. There, she'd search in secret for a way to rid herself of what he'd done to her—and she wouldn't come home again until she'd found it.

The Winstons saw their daughter off at the pier as though it were any other sailing.

The two new servants boarded the *Campania* first, to make her stateroom ready, while Sophia and her family stood by the gangplank, no one knowing quite what to say. At last the ship's horn blew its warning. Neither parent reached for her, only watched as she knelt down and gave little George a last embrace.

"Good-bye," she told them, and walked alone up the gangplank.

George had wanted to stay a while and watch the ship depart; but within a few minutes he began to fidget in the cold, and Julia led him away, unprotesting, to their carriage. Alone, Francis watched as the tugs pushed the *Campania* away from the pier and into the Hudson. He'd given his daughter no true farewell, no private words of advice or encouragement. He'd expected, in this moment, to regret his silence—but instead all that he felt was envy, as deep and sullen as a child's.

Wrapped deeply in her woolen shawls, Sophia stood trembling at the *Campania*'s rail as the Hudson widened and became the bay, its shoreline a painter's smudge of autumn set against a robin's-egg sky. The city withdrew, narrowed to a point, and vanished.

I have escaped, Sophia thought. She wiped away her tears, and went below.

It didn't take long for Sophia Winston's new servants to suspect that their mistress was bound and determined to make their job as difficult as possible.

For one thing, the girl simply refused to leave the stateroom, not even for a brief promenade. They inquired, was she seasick? No, she replied, she merely wished to stay out of the breeze. They were certain she'd change her mind after a few days, if only out of boredom—but she seemed perfectly content to remain in the cabin, reading her trunk's worth of books, underlining passages and making notes in the margins. And so they, too, were forced to stay below, and within her hearing.

Then there was the matter of her clothing. They'd expected her to need help in dressing, but Sophia had packed neither gowns nor walking-suits, only simple wool dresses that she might button herself, even when her hands shook. These she topped with her ever-present shawls, which swamped her slight frame. And rather than putting up her hair in a fashionable knot or pompadour, she plaited it herself into a single tight braid, which she then wrapped about her head and fastened with an abundance of hairpins. She wore it this way even when she slept, which to them seemed an uncomfortable prospect at best.

"She's deliberately giving us nothing to do," the footman muttered one night, once they were reasonably certain their charge was asleep. "Are we minding her, or is it the other way around?"

"I'm as lost as you are," the maid replied. "The way her mother went on about strange men, I thought we'd have to tie her to a chair."

"Maybe that Ahmad fellow's waiting for her in India."

"I suppose we'll find out."

The *Campania* arrived at Liverpool amid a miserable downpour. The train to Southampton was damp and drafty, and the coal stove in their carriage refused to stay lit, no matter how the footman fiddled with it.

Sophia made no word of complaint, but her dismay was obvious, and her tremor grew with each passing mile. By the time they arrived at Southampton, she was deathly pale and could barely stand upright. They bundled her into an inn, and heaped her bed with blankets and hot-water bottles. Eventually her tremors lessened and her color improved, and she drifted into uneasy sleep.

"Well," the maid murmured, unnerved, "we're needed after all."

The next day, they boarded the S.S. *Hindostan*, where Sophia took to her bed at once and slept until they were nearly at the Strait of Gibraltar. The *Hindostan* was a fast ship, and the waters of the Mediterranean were calm and obliging, and before long they'd sighted the quay at Constantinople, their first stop on the way to Calcutta. They disembarked, and settled into a suite at the Pera Palace Hotel—all carved and gilded opulence, with velvet draperies and hot running water—and were about to ring the front desk to inquire about supper when Miss Winston announced that she had an errand she must run first.

The couple exchanged a glance. The footman said, "If you need the concierge to fetch you something—"

"No, I'll go myself, thank you. But you're welcome to accompany me."

Warily they trailed her to a nearby telegram office, where she wrote lengthy messages to half a dozen outposts throughout Asia Minor, many of them remote stations that the clerk had to peer for on his maps. She thanked the clerk in Turkish, and paid him in coins they hadn't known she'd been carrying.

"And now," Sophia said when they emerged from the office, "shall we take a tour?" And without waiting for an answer, she hailed a carriage and told the driver to take them across the river, to the Hagia Sophia.

"Like your own name, miss?" asked the maid, feeling more uneasy by the minute.

"Yes," Sophia replied with a half smile. "Except *Hagia Sophia* means 'holy wisdom,' and I'm only named after an aunt." She brightened. "Look—there it is."

An ancient-looking basilica was rising into view, its massive central dome surrounded by smaller copies arranged in rough symmetry, with minarets at the distant corners. The carriage stopped, and Miss Winston paid the driver and descended with a new and noticeable eagerness. They walked the basilica's perimeter, the maid and footman now struggling to keep up as Sophia pointed out the different domes and buttresses, listing the centuries in which they'd been added and whose rule the city had been under at the time. The basilica was a mosque now, she told them—but it once had been a Roman Catholic church, and before that a Greek Orthodox cathedral, a stronghold sacked by Crusaders and Ottomans alike. At the entrance they surrendered their shoes and went inside, treading carefully around the columns and prayer rugs, admiring the carvings and calligraphy. One of the columns bore a small depression near its base; this, Sophia informed them, was the famous Weeping Column. As legend held it, any supplicant who placed their hand in the depression and felt the tears of the Virgin Mary would be cured of all sickness. Sophia reached a hand toward it as she spoke—but then hesitated. They watched her war with herself for a moment. At last a finger was extended, and just as quickly withdrawn. "You see?" she said with a smile, and then turned away. They didn't ask what she'd felt; nor did they try the trick themselves.

They left soon after and returned to the hotel, and had barely settled into the room again when the concierge arrived, bearing a stack of telegrams. Sophia opened them one by one, frowning, until she reached one that made her brighten and sit straighter in the chair. She tapped its edge on the writing-desk, thinking—and then said, "We must speak frankly."

The maid had been in the process of turning down Sophia's bed; the footman was polishing his boots. The two blinked up at her. "Yes, miss?" said the maid.

"I assume," Sophia said, "that your loyalties lie with my mother, and not myself."

A pause. "Not sure what you mean, miss," the footman said.

"Forgive me, but—you're Pinkerton detectives, aren't you?"

The couple glanced at each other. The footman sighed and put down the boots; the maid straightened, her air of deference falling away. "Retired, miss," she said, her voice newly crisp. "And we're the Williamses, if you please. I'm Lucy, and that's Patrick."

Sophia smiled. "My mother agreed to all of this far too easily. May I ask what, specifically, she hired you to do?"

"We're to make you comfortable," Patrick said, "and keep you from harm."

"Would that include intercepting my correspondence?"

"If we thought it necessary."

"Have you?"

"Not yet, miss."

"Then here." And she offered them the telegram.

Together they read it, their brows furrowing. Patrick said, "Ephe- sus? Where's that?"

"It's south of here, near to the coast," Sophia said. "The ancient Greeks built a temple there to Artemis, the goddess of the hunt. It was called one of the seven wonders of the world. The site's under excavation, and I've been offered a tour." She dug an atlas from her trunk, found the correct page, and pointed. "Here."

They gazed down at the atlas, judging the town's considerable dis- tance from the Golden Horn, the dearth of other cities nearby. "I'm sure this wasn't on the itinerary," said Patrick.

"You must know by now that I never had any intention of going to India," Sophia said.

The man nodded. "But what *are* your intentions, miss, if we're all being honest with each other?"

She regarded them, and then said, "I'm sure my mother told you tales of my wanton disobedience. I won't ask you to repeat them," she added, as their expressions turned guarded, "nor will I call them lies. I dreaded the future she'd arranged for me, and in my unhappiness I turned to the wrong quarter for comfort. I've paid the price for that deci- sion, and it won't be repeated. My intention now is to explore the Middle East for as long as I can, and not return until . . . until I can do so on my own terms."

They took this in, weighing it between them. "And there's no chance of you changing your mind?" said Patrick.

"None. You'd have to force me back, I'm afraid."

She was trembling, they saw—not with cold, but fear. "There won't be any of that," Lucy said gently. "But we can't just give up and sail for home, either. We signed a contract. And besides, miss, you'll need protection. Traveling alone, you'd be a mark for every bandit and kidnapper in the East."

She thought. "Would you be willing to adjust your roles? Bodyguards, instead of spies?"

Patrick pursed his lips. "I'd wager your mother'd be against it."

Sophia considered this, then nodded. "We'll tell my father instead."

In his library, Francis Winston read the cable three times over, then wiped a hand over his eyes and blew out a frustrated breath. *Pinkertons*, for God's sake! Didn't Julia have any sense at all? Of course Sophia would see straight through the pair! He folded the telegram away, and asked a footman to fetch his coat and stick. No, he wouldn't be needing the carriage—he merely wanted to walk.

North he went, past neighboring mansions, and entered Central Park along the East Drive. The last stubborn leaves shivered and clung to the branches above him, while their fallen siblings hissed past along the cobbles. He brooded as he went, his midday meal souring in his stomach. He was habitually dyspeptic these days—the victim, according to his doctor, of an overrich diet. *That which wealth provides may not be the most natural for the body*, the man had said. Francis had laughed at that.

He was puffing slightly by the time he crossed the Transverse and arrived at the tall, sharp-edged incongruity of Cleopatra's Needle, jutting upward among the trees. He chose a bench and sat, planting his stick between his feet. This was where he came when anger threatened to rule him, when he must sit with his temper and wrestle it into harness, yoke it alongside reason and will. He'd spent countless hours here, gazing up at the carvings and imagining the labor, the sweat and sinew, that had gone into the Needle's making. He'd seethed with jealousy at Vanderbilt's coup when the Needle had arrived in New York, had watched from his bedroom window, far above the crowds, as the obelisk rolled along its trestles on Fifth Avenue: a captured queen, a stone Zenobia paraded through the streets in golden chains. And now look at the wretched thing. Pitted and crumbling, its hieroglyphs fading from view as the seaboard climate destroyed what centuries in the desert had preserved. Powerful men had made it; powerful men had spelled its doom.

He was growing chilled; he felt old and maudlin and foolish. The indifferent Needle rose above him, an arrow set to pierce the heavens. A line from Homer came to him: *I sing of Artemis whose shafts are of gold, the pure maiden, shooter of stags.* At last he stood heavily and walked home again, where he confided to his valet that he'd need his private bedroom readied for the night—for once he'd spoken to Mrs. Winston, she'd be in no mood to admit him into hers.

```
SOPHIA WINSTON, PERA PALACE HOTEL,
CONSTANTINOPLE

AGREE TO CHANGE OF CONTRACT AND ITINERARY.
WILL WIRE ADDITIONAL FUNDS. GO FORTH ON YOUR
HUNT AND MAY YOUR AIM BE TRUE.

FRANCIS WINSTON
```

3.

The excited whisper went out among the children of Little Syria, flying from mouth to mouth among alley games of hopscotch and marbles:

Mister Ahmad is back! Mister Ahmad is back!

And so it was, for there was the particular sound of his hammer on the anvil, issuing from the shop window: *clang-clang, clang-clang*, a different rhythm than Mister Arbeely's, slower and stronger, like the heartbeat of a giant.

The children all loved Mister Ahmad. He was a figure of some mystery among them, being a desert Bedouin—or so he'd told them—and not a Christian born and baptized, like their own fathers. The children liked to invent rumors about him, saying that he could perform feats of strange magic, and whistle birds down from the air, and survive for months without food and water. Whenever one of these rumors reached the man's ears, he'd say nothing to either confirm or deny it—only raise an eyebrow and put a finger to his lips.

Little Syria's adults took note of the man's return as well. They wondered, had he come back with a bride? Or an aging mother, ready at last to sail to America? But neither bride nor mother appeared. Nor did he throw open the shop door to visitors, or hold court at one of the Washington Street cafés, to spread the latest news and stories of home. They were disappointed but unsurprised; the man plainly cherished his privacy to an almost insulting degree. He took little part in their community life, based as it was in the various churches; nor did he side in the usual sectarian disputes between Maronite and Orthodox, a fact he seemed to revel in. He had a reputation for arrogance, though it was softened somewhat by his association with Mr. Arbeely, whose own solitary oddness had a much more amiable quality, like that of a favorite uncle.

But even those who most distrusted the man they called "the Bed-ouin" had to admit that his talent was a boon to the neighborhood. Once, Arbeely's shop had turned out pots and pans and peddlers' wares, all of good quality but unexceptional. Now, every object that emerged was a work of art. The pots and pans had acquired elegant proportions, and etched designs upon their handles; the trivets they rested upon were woven iron lattices, strong yet delicate-looking. There were necklaces, too, of silver and stone, and even an astonishing tin ceiling that hung in a nearby tenement lobby, sculpted to look like a desert landscape. *That* achievement had been the talk of the neighborhood, and had even been mentioned in a few of the English-language city papers, which had in turn brought a new type of visitor to Little Syria: the well-dressed, well-heeled admirers of the arts.

"They stare up at the ceiling for a few minutes, and then they go away again," said a customer at the Faddouls' coffee-house, a Washing-ton Street mainstay. "The children like to beg nickels from them. It's all harmless, I suppose. And it can only mean good things for the tinshop."

Another man at the table snorted. "Don't be so sure. I've seen suc-cess ruin more than one business. Arbeely is a man of good sense, but that Bedouin confounds me. He's so . . ."

"*Strange*," said the men, in unison.

"Who is strange?" said a woman's voice. It was Maryam Faddoul, proprietress, arriving among them with her brass coffee-pot. There were few in Little Syria who weren't friends with Maryam. The woman was known for her generous kind-heartedness, her ability to see the best in even the most trying of her neighbors. Even strangers felt a near-involuntary desire to unburden themselves to her, relating their woes and their fears, their most intractable dilemmas. Maryam would then store and dispense this gossip with an apothecary's precision, matching ailment to remedy, need to need. A girl whose fiancé was in need of work might know nothing of the butcher looking for a new assistant, until Maryam suggested the butcher's *kibbeh* for the bridal banquet. The girl whose younger brothers gave her no peace in the afternoons, the elderly woman who wanted only a few hours of quiet company: these, too, man-aged to find each other, once Maryam sat the girl's father at a table next to the woman's son. Now she replenished the men's cups with a practiced hand and gave them her most encouraging smile.

"Oh, we only meant the Bedouin," they told her. "He's come back, you know."

"Has he?" said Maryam.

"Yes, and alone, just like when he arrived. No mother, no wife, no new hires for the business. Who knows why he went in the first place?"

Maryam tilted her head, as though considering the answer. In reality, Maryam knew exactly why the man had gone. The copper flask, now buried, had once sat on a shelf in her own kitchen: a gift from her mother, whose own mother had once owned it, and so on back through the generations, each woman unaware of its true contents. Maryam had taken that flask to her friend Boutros Arbeely, to see if he might repair a few of its scuffs and dents—and its invisible prisoner had at last been freed.

"Perhaps he was homesick," she said to the men.

The men raised their eyebrows at each other: *Homesick?* Of course they were *all* homesick at one time or another; but to make the voyage for no other reason . . .

"Well," one of them said, "I suppose it's possible."

"The Bedu *are* different," another allowed.

Maryam smiled at them, and moved on to the next table, as gracious as ever. But her husband, Sayeed, at his usual spot in the steam-wreathed kitchen, spied the new line of tension in her back, and guessed at its meaning: for out of all their many neighbors in Little Syria, the Jinni was the only one she'd ever distrusted at first sight.

The Golem and the Jinni went back to Central Park again and again.

They explored the various landscapes, admiring their autumn aspect: the frost-edged Meadow, the bare stalks of the cattails in the Pond, the narrow Gill a swift and crystalline flow. Then, when they'd seen their fill, they'd walk south to 14th Street and climb a fire escape to the city's rooftops: a world in itself, a place of fire-barrels and plank bridges, wayward children and petty thieves. The two were a familiar sight there, but they never failed to draw the eye: a tall, hatless man and a tall, prim woman. An odd pair of characters, if only a pair among many.

Along the rooftops they'd walk to Little Syria, and find a high corner or a water tower rail. There they'd watch the first stirrings of the day: the oyster-boats casting off from the West Street piers, the milkmen and icemen trudging toward their stables, the tavern-keepers sweeping the night's sawdust out their doors. Only when the city seemed about to wake in earnest would they stroll back along the rooftops to Canal Street. There they'd bid each other farewell; and she would descend to join the growing traffic on the sidewalk, arriving at Radzin's Bakery in time to mix the morning dough. And he would return to the tinshop, and stoke the forge, while a yawning Arbeely reviewed the day's orders.

They were discreet, in the main, and so managed to dodge the worst of the gossip. The Golem's landlady was not the type to notice every coming and going; most of her boardinghouse tenants were theater folk, and kept odd hours as a rule. And as for the Jinni, if his neighbors happened to see him in the street at sunrise, looking as though he was returning from a night abroad, they were content to ignore it—so long as he kept his scandals elsewhere.

But the children of Little Syria noticed.

They'd wake in the night, roused by a snoring parent or a restless sibling, and look out the window in time to spy the couple on a nearby rooftop. Or, they'd sit blanket-wrapped on the fire escape and overhear an argument conducted in the pair's telltale blend of languages, which changed so quickly between Arabic, English, and Yiddish that the children were left to grasp at half sentences, formless bursts of rhetoric. *They mean well, but . . . Their bizarre insistence upon . . . You give them too little . . .* Who, the children wondered, were the *they* the pair spoke of? And who was *she*, the tall woman in the cloak, who could draw so many words from their silent Mister Ahmad? They would watch, and listen; and on morning walks to school they'd trade their information, and speculate about where the couple went every night, with suggestions ranging from the prosaic to the salacious.

They go to Central Park, said one boy who had a habit of waking early to search the rooftops for lost jacks and marbles, and so had seen the pair more often than most.

The others frowned at this answer, given with the air of common knowledge. *How d'you know?*

The boy shrugged. *Because when they come back*, he said, *their boots are all muddy.*

At last the first true freeze of winter arrived, and Central Park gave itself to the cold and snow. The vining roses were pruned back to a handful of canes; the elms on the Mall grasped the sky with empty fingers.

"I'm sorry," the Golem said one night as they neared the Harlem Meer. "This will be a long walk back. And it's starting to snow again."

"Stop worrying about me," said the Jinni. "And stop apologizing."

"I can't help it, I feel like I'm putting you at risk."

"You aren't asking me to jump in a river, Chava. I can manage a little snow."

She sighed. "It's just . . . *louder* now. Or it *feels* louder. Oh, it's hard to explain." She hugged herself as she walked, clearly miserable. With the onset of winter, her clay body had grown stiff and uncomfortable: an expected effect, and manageable as long as she walked often enough. But now, like arthritic joints that ached with the rain, the scream in her mind—her trapped creator, in his endless anger—had grown sharper, more distracting. She'd begun to make careless mistakes at the bakery, such as forgetting the raisins in the challah dough, or doubling the baking powder in the cookies so that they swelled as large as biscuits. Thea Radzin thought it a lingering effect of her widowhood; with each mishap she cast a pitying look at her favorite employee, thinking, *And who could blame the girl if she came unhinged?*

"Do you think I'm coming unhinged?" the Golem asked suddenly.

"Do I think *what?*"

"That I'm coming unhinged. It's what Thea thinks, though of course she doesn't say it. And no, she doesn't understand—but you do. So you must tell me. Please."

He blew out an impatient and unnecessary breath. "Chava, you aren't 'coming unhinged,' whatever that means. The winters are difficult for you, we knew this. It's all of a piece. And you're handling it far better than I would, were I to hear that man screaming in my head all the time."

"You make it sound like he's hurling curses at me," she muttered. "It's simpler than that. Like . . . a tinnitus, I suppose. Just louder lately."

"Better here, though?"

She gazed about at the dark tableau of the park, felt with her distant senses the earth below them, its warmth banked and waiting. The seasons would turn, she reminded herself; her body would lose its stiffness and unease, and her mind would quiet once more.

"Yes," she said. "Better here."

Spring arrived as promised. The rains began, forcing them apart and indoors: she sewing in her room each night, he working in the shop. Without him, she grew restless. Her mind strayed toward the couples who hurried by outside, laughing beneath their umbrellas, their thoughts full of what might happen when they reached their warm apartments, their inviting beds. He, too, became tense and distractible, full of unsettled longings, uncertain of their welcome. He, who'd once sauntered up Fifth Avenue so confidently in search of Sophia Winston's mansion! And she, meanwhile, reviewed every conversation they'd ever had upon the subject of faithfulness, his opinions ringing in her mind like a punishment. *Humans and their ridiculous rules.*

But she also recalled something that had happened before the rains had separated them: a night when they'd passed a Lower East Side synagogue just as two women, clear at a glance as mother and daughter, emerged from its basement stairwell. The daughter's hair had hung down her back in damp coils; she'd shivered in the night air, nervous and excited, her pale face glowing. The older woman had put a comforting arm around her, and they'd hurried down the street together, mother whispering to daughter, the daughter nodding.

It's late for a bath, isn't it? the Jinni had said as they disappeared.

It's a mikveh, a ritual bath, she'd told him. And then, at his confusion: *By Jewish law, a woman mustn't lie with her husband during her menses. Once it's ended, she immerses herself in the* mikveh *and recites a blessing. Brides do it, too, before the wedding ceremony.*

Ah. And the younger one . . . ?

She marries in the morning.

She'd waited for him to call it absurd, or superstitious, or any of his other usual complaints. But he'd only nodded as though half listening, his expression entirely opaque.

Perhaps, she thought at her window, watching the rain. *Perhaps.*

At last, the rain ended.

That night, he arrived at her boardinghouse at their usual hour, and they walked north together in a charged silence. He could feel the barely perceptible mist that she always carried about herself, like the lightest touch upon his skin. And she wondered, had he always been so *warm* at her side, a heat that she could feel from an arm's length away?

They entered the Park, and walked through the Ramble, quiet and alone, making only the most inconsequential of comments. *I've never noticed that path before. Look, the hillside's washed away.* They followed the Gill to where it calmed and widened, and the Jinni wondered why, for what felt like the first time in his hundreds of years, he found it impossible merely to say what he wanted. "I'd expected the river to be higher, after so much rain," he said instead, helpless, cursing himself.

"It's controlled by an aqueduct," she told him, "so the rain doesn't affect it."

"Oh," he said, nonplussed. "I'd assumed it was real, and they built the park around it."

She smiled at this. "Of course it's *real,*" she said—and then, before he could protest, *You know what I meant:* "Here. I'll show you."

She unclasped her cloak, letting it fall to her feet. He nearly asked what she was doing—but lost his voice in surprise as her shirtwaist and skirt followed the cloak, and then shoes and stockings, too. Not once did she glance his way, only calmly rid herself of clothing, then walked down the bank and into the current, disappearing beneath the water.

For long moments he was alone. Dumbfounded, he glanced at the clothing that lay on the bank, as though to reassure himself that he hadn't imagined it all—and then the Gill rippled as her head broke the surface. She emerged onto the bank, water running from her skin in rivulets as she came to stand before him. She didn't smile, but her eyes were alight; her expression was one of challenge, and expectation.

He raised a hand, traced a finger along the edge of her cheek; the clinging droplets vanished into steam. "What would you ask of me, Chava?" he said quietly.

"A promise," she told him, "that you will have only me."

He realized he'd expected this; what surprised him was his willingness. "And you'd promise the same?"

"Yes." A whisper.

"Then I will have only you," he said.

"And I will have only you," she replied.

They smiled at each other then, tentative, wondering at what they'd done. He took her hands—they were freezing cold—and drew her closer.

A few hours later, the Syrian boy who liked to wake early was once again on his rooftop, practicing his aim with a slingshot. He'd just brought down half a row of paper soldiers when he spied the couple walking toward him. He stopped to watch, wondering why there was something different about them this morning. Then he realized: they weren't arguing. They seemed, in fact, almost shy with each other. He pretended to busy himself with his soldiers as the pair neared—then glanced up again as they passed, and saw that the woman's cloak was dotted here and there with blades of grass and tiny twigs, as though it had been used as a blanket atop the ground.

The boy's eyes widened as, once again, he reached the correct conclusion.

The woman paused suddenly, then turned back to peer at the boy, her expression a mix of embarrassment and incredulous exasperation. She muttered something to her companion; he chuckled, and she shushed him. Together they walked on, and reached the fire escape—and just before they descended from view, the man turned and gave the boy a quick, conspiratorial wink.

Spring became summer—and in July of 1901 the heat fell upon the city like a hammer.

Horses dropped dead in the streets. Ambulances raced from building to building, collecting the stricken. The city parks became haphazard dormitories as all searched for somewhere cool enough to sleep.

In a stifling basement room near the Bowery, a young washerwoman named Anna Blumberg tried to comfort her baby boy, Toby, without success. She had no pennies left for ice, not so much as a chip, and Toby's cries were growing weaker. Anna, numb with fear, was about to seek out the building superintendent—he'd made his desires clear enough, and his willingness to pay—when a knock came at the door.

An iceman stood in the hall, water dripping from an enormous block on his shoulder. "You got an icebox?" he asked.

She stared at him dumbly.

"Look," he said, impatient, "some lady give me five dollars to come here. You want the ice or not?"

The ice filled Anna's icebox, and a washtub besides. Wrapped in cool flannels, Toby calmed and took the breast at last. "A tall girl, on Eldridge," the iceman said when Anna asked, between sobs of relief, who'd paid for the miracle. "Didn't say her name."

But Anna knew. She'd known it even before she asked.

Little Syria at midday resembled an open-air hospital. Men sat half asleep beneath awnings and on shaded stoops, shifting by inches as the sun moved. By unspoken agreement the neighborhood mothers had done away with propriety, and now the children ran about in their underclothes, boys and girls alike. The offerings at the Faddouls' had switched from coffee to seltzer, which Sayeed sold at a penny a glass while, in the nearby tenement halls, Maryam traveled from door to door, asking after the littlest children, the sick and the elderly. In her wake, those with ice to spare sent it down the hall to those without; impromptu meals, too, were organized to share what might otherwise spoil. Her rounds finished, she went down to the street, thinking to catch an ice-wagon on its next trip to the warehouse at Cortlandt. Perhaps she could convince the driver to come south—

"Careful," called a man on a nearby stoop.

Maryam stopped, startled. The man pointed at the open door of *Arbeely & Ahmad, All Metals*, whose threshold she'd been about to pass. And now Maryam could feel it: a wave of punishing heat that poured out of the shop's interior and onto the sidewalk in front of her.

Maryam winced and peered inside. Arbeely was nowhere to be seen, having abandoned his post rather than faint on the spot—but there was his partner in front of the anvil, wielding hammer and tongs against a glowing steel ingot. The very air sizzled around him. He looked to be enjoying himself immensely.

She shivered, despite the heat. It felt indecent to watch him so closely, even through an open door. More than once she'd overheard the children whispering, trading sightings of his rooftop jaunts with his lady-friend. *Who is she? I dunno. I think her name is Chava.* Maryam had stayed silent—but she could've told them all about the tall, quiet woman, with her own formidable powers. It unnerved her, to keep the pair's secrets. Sometimes she'd glimpse him in the street, and a nameless fear would steal across her heart—as though he were bent upon some terrible mischief, and not, contrary to all evidence, merely running an ordinary errand. Would she ever grow used to his presence among them? Did she truly want to?

"Bedouins," said the man on the stoop, with grudging admiration. "They've got the desert in them."

Maryam frowned. "He ought at least to close the door," she said, and went on her way.

The weather broke that night, descending at last from its unearthly broiling. A grateful cheer went up at Battery Park as a fresh breeze pulled at the flags. All gathered their pillows and counterpanes from the lawns, and went home.

In her slowly cooling apartment, Anna Blumberg sat in a dilapidated rocking chair, her baby asleep in her arms.

Chava Levy. It had to be. No one else in the city would've thought of Anna in that moment, certainly no one with the means to spend half a week's wages on a block of ice. Anna imagined her standing outside in the alley among the sweating vagrants, listening for Toby's cries, for Anna's panicked thoughts. Chava Levy, who'd been Anna's colleague at Radzin's Bakery, until the awful night that Anna had learned the truth.

It was over a year ago that Anna had invited her shy new friend out for an evening at a Broome Street dance hall. They were supposed to rendezvous there with Irving, Anna's new fiancé and the father of her unborn child—but when Irving had arrived, there'd been another girl on his arm. Anna had confronted him in an alley outside; Irving, drunk and furious, had attacked her, knocking her to the ground. And then—

His body, thrown against the bricks.

His assailant's blank, inhuman eyes.

The tall, strange man whom her friend had brought along—*Anna, this is Ahmad*—pulling the woman off her victim and *burning* her, with his bare hands, to bring her to her senses.

In mere moments, Anna's entire life had fallen apart. There'd be no returning to Radzin's, not pregnant and unwed; and besides, how could Anna work next to such a woman, day in and day out? Monsters, the pair of them—yet already her life and theirs were enmeshed. Soon Anna had fallen afoul of their enemy, an evil old man named Schaalman who'd taken her prisoner and used her as bait to draw them in. She had no true memory of it, only a slippery half-recollection of standing in the middle of that same Broome Street dance hall on a sunny afternoon, unable to move, while the old man held her by the wrists and grinned. Afterwards, she'd been terrified that he might have hurt the baby in some way—but Toby had arrived squalling and kicking, the very picture of health.

Sometimes, she tried to persuade herself that she'd imagined it all. The woman's strength, the man's burning hands, the ancient wizard who'd held her in place with a touch: all an invention of her over-romantic imagination, a beguiling fantasy to distract herself from the fact that she was now disgraced and penniless, a Bowery washerwoman with a baby to feed. She couldn't afford to believe in such fantasies. Not anymore.

Except . . .

She looked at the washtub full of impossible ice that sat beside her, quietly melting, and then at the baby asleep in her arms. Her living, breathing boy.

Toby startled awake and began to cry, little limbs flailing about. She shushed him and nursed him back down into sleep, set him carefully in his cradle. Then she found pen and paper, and wrote:

Dear Chava,

Thank you for the ice. I think it saved Toby's life. I know we haven't spoken lately but maybe that ought to change.

In the cradle behind her, little Toby's eyelids twitched as he returned to his dream.

It was a strange dream, especially for one so young. In it, Toby—no longer a baby, but full grown—stood frozen in a vast, sun-drenched hall while a grinning old man held his wrists in an unbreakable grip. The dream would visit him over and over again as he grew, becoming his oldest memory, his deepest fear. It would be years before Toby could even speak the words that might describe it—but his mother would've recognized the hall, and the man, at once.

From tribe to tribe, jinn-child to jinn-child, the tale of the iron-bound jinni continued upon its journey through the Syrian Desert.

Northward it spread, growing and changing as it went, until it reached an enormous tribe of jinn who, in strength and abilities, were very similar to their cousins in the valley where the story had begun. They, too, could raise the winds with a gesture, and change their shape to that of any living animal; and, when formless and insubstantial, could choose to enter the sleeping minds of flesh-and-blood creatures and roam among their dreams. Their lands sprawled in a wide swath, bordered by two forbidding human obstacles: the city of Homs to the west, and the oasis of Palmyra to the east.

Once, the city of Homs had been of little consequence to the jinn. They had no use for its territory, formed as it was around a deadly river called the Orontes; nor were they bothered by its inhabitants, who were occupied in farming the fertile banks and occasionally warring amongst themselves. But all that had changed with the arrival of the railroad.

It had begun as a double line of iron ribbons that stretched from north to south, following the contours of the desert's edge. Then, the engine: a screaming creature of steam and steel that rode the iron faster than a jinni could fly. Terrifying explosions racked the air as the humans blasted tunnels out of ancient rock. Even the skies themselves became mazes, as railway trestles stretched between the cliff-sides and telegraph wires rose alongside the tracks.

With the trains to transport their harvests, the Homsi farmers now pushed outward, cultivating new fields of wheat and cotton. Safe, rocky soil turned damp and treacherous. The jinn at the desert's eastern edge were herded inward, forcing rival clans into close quarters. Old feuds were resurrected, new ones invented—until even at the habitation's center one could see the dust and sand clouding the air as they waged their petty battles.

But as troublesome as Homs had become for the jinn, it couldn't begin to compare to Palmyra.

The oasis city of Palmyra had featured in the legends of both men and jinn for millennia. In ancient times, the stories went, a young human king named Sulayman had come to a palm-shaded village at a dusty crossroads and declared, *This shall be a part of my kingdom.* He demolished its brick huts, and commanded that edifices of shining stone be built in their place—all the work of legions of jinn who were bound into slavery by Sulayman's magic. It was they who quarried the stones and lifted them into place on powerful winds, who roamed the desert in search of rare metals to gild them with. The tribes of men came to revere Sulayman, and told tales of his great deeds and greater wisdom—but in the stories of the jinn he was a despised tyrant, a figure of terror and hatred.

Even Sulayman was mortal, though, and when he died, the scourge of his rule died with him. Centuries later, the Romans would conquer Palmyra and make it a polyglot capital of commerce, a city of temples and amphitheaters and soaring colonnades. Then they, too, were conquered, and Palmyra shrank in significance as the trade routes shifted, becoming merely another oasis again. At last the local Bedu tribes reclaimed it, raising their tents beside the crumbling temples, herding their sheep among the columns.

But the memory of the jinn was long, and those who lived within sight of Palmyra's foothills avoided them as a man might avoid a notorious abattoir. They called Palmyra the City of Sulayman, or simply the Cursed City, and it figured in many an elder's threat:—*Be careful, young one, or you will be banished to the City of Sulayman, and his ghost will rise from the stones to bind you.* Or,—*If you do not behave, I will take you to the Cursed City and cast you into the deepest, darkest well, then fill it to the brim with angry ghuls.* No such threat was ever carried out, but the youngsters were cowed nevertheless.

Among this innumerable population of jinn there lived a young jinniyeh of fifty years or so who seemed, to all appearances, to be an ordinary member of her tribe. She'd spent her childhood in the usual way: learning to ride the winds, and fighting in the mock battles of the young, and listening to stories of brave jinn and dastardly humans, the tales that belonged to all her kind and those of her tribe alone. She heard the tales of the recent battles at the habitation's western edge, and of the Homsi farmers who had caused them, and grew more and more curious—until finally she decided to see for herself.

—*Come with me,* she said to a young jinni, one of her usual playmates.

—*Where are we going?*

—*To look at the humans.*

Together they flew west. The habitation passed below them, bearing the signs of battle: sands swept clean by the winds, rocks cracked and scattered. At last they approached the outskirts of a farm, where green rows of winter wheat grew in soil dark with water. The air held traces of it, and prickled at them like a warning before a storm.

—*It goes on forever*, the young jinni said in nervous fascination.

—*Look*, said the jinniyeh.

A man was walking among the rows. In one hand he carried a curved metal blade fixed to a wooden handle. He stopped here and there to examine the soil, then chose a few of the stalks, sawed them carefully with the blade, and squinted at their cut ends.

The jinniyeh pointed at the blade.—*Is that iron?*

—*Don't go any closer*, warned her companion. But she crept forward, and he followed, until they were directly behind the man, close enough to touch. The faint breeze they rode stirred the wheat and sent it shaking.

Suddenly the man whipped around, his scythe slicing through the air, its blade missing them by inches. Fear, involuntary and instinctual, seized the jinniyeh's companion. In the next moment he'd turned and fled.

But the jinniyeh felt nothing.

Warily the farmer scanned the rows, scythe at the ready. At last he decided it had been a bird or an animal, not the bandits he'd feared. He set down his scythe and walked to the end of the row, to drink from a water-skin that waited beneath a tree.

The jinniyeh watched him go, then peered down at the scythe. What had happened? Why hadn't she felt the fear? She came closer, closer—but still nothing. At last she changed to human form, lifted the scythe by its wooden handle and examined it. Rust bloomed here and there along the flat of the blade. Wheat-sap stained its edge. She braced herself, and touched it with a finger-tip.

Nothing. No terror, no cold and searing pain—only metal, faintly pitted.

She looked up at the sound of a human's indrawn breath. The farmer, his rest over, stood at the row's end, staring at the girl who'd appeared among the wheat. She was naked, and beautiful, and holding his scythe.

They gaped at each other. In the space of a blink the girl vanished, and the scythe tumbled to the ground.

Her companion was still shaking when she caught up with him.

—*I wanted to be brave*, he said, his voice low with shame. *I thought I could ignore the fear.* He glanced at her. *Did you touch it?*

—*No*, she said. *Let's go home.*

She told no one what had happened. The fear of iron was shared by all jinn, lowest to highest; it kept them separate from the humans, and went to the very heart of what it meant to be jinn-kind. To not feel the fear, to touch the metal without consequence, was unnatural, unheard of. And so from that day forward she curtailed her curiosity and remained at the heart of the habitation, where she might listen to the tale-tellers and let their words distract her from her secret, which she kept locked deep inside.

And then, one day, a new story reached their lands: the tale of the iron-bound jinni, who'd captured his own master in a copper flask and then disappeared into the human world.

It was an instant favorite. Jinn old and young begged to hear it again and again—but the jinniyeh listened most intently of all. It thrilled her to think that the story might be true, that out there, hidden among humanity, was a jinni who believed—quite reasonably, but so wrongly!—that he could never come near any of his own kind again.

It's only a story, she told herself. *He doesn't exist.*

And yet she couldn't help wondering.

4.

The months stretched onward, the seasons passing each in turn, completing their circle, beginning again. And as they changed, New York changed, too, the city reveling in its constant newness, its own unending cycle of reinvention.

Automobiles began to dot the streets. At first they were only playthings for the wealthy, and everyone stopped to look when one went by. Thomas Maloof, the richest man in Little Syria, bought a canary-yellow roadster that he liked to be seen in—although he was more often seen in front of it, either struggling with the crank or fanning the engine with his hat. And then, seemingly from one day to the next, they were everywhere: tearing through intersections and rocketing around corners, blaring their horns at wagons and pedestrians.

"Perhaps I'll buy one," said the Jinni.

"All that noise and smoke," the Golem said, "just to sit in traffic with everyone else."

The long-awaited subway opened at last, and the pair descended into the station beneath the ground at City Hall. Together they rode the juddering train all the way to 145th, where the Jinni all but ran up the staircase in his haste to get out.

"That was unbearable," he said. "All that earth above us, pressing down."

"I quite liked it," the Golem replied.

Telephones appeared, fascinating the Jinni, who couldn't believe such a thing was possible without sorcery. He persuaded Arbeely to buy one for the shop—but Arbeely hated shouting into the receiver, and soon avoided it entirely. The Golem's landlady installed one in the boardinghouse parlor, but the Golem never used it. There was only one person she would call, and the operator might be listening at any moment.

At night the pair walked for miles together. They ventured across the Williamsburg Bridge and past the Brooklyn Navy Yard, and marveled at the half-built ships in the dry-docks. They admired the fashionable theaters on Long Acre Square, but never went inside, not even to see the latest sensations—for she was leery of crowds in such numbers, their emotions all pulled about by the performers.

"What if I lose myself and run onstage?" she said.

"I'll hold you back," he replied. But she shook her head, and they walked on.

At Coney Island they rode the Helter Skelter and the Trip to the Moon, and stood beneath the Electric Tower's shining minarets. The Golem fed peanuts to a trained elephant while the Jinni stood some distance away, afraid of startling it. The elephant ate the peanuts, then sniffed in confusion at the woman who'd held them. Soon it was feeling her all over with its trunk, trying to decide what she was.

"He likes you, miss," said its trainer.

She patted the gray trunk fondly, and went back to the Jinni, a sad smile on her face. "What's the matter?" he asked.

"I think he wants to go home," she said.

They learned the nighttime aspects of all the neighborhoods. Greenwich Village was a mix of laughter and furious discussion, of immigrants and dilettantes who drank champagne and talked gaily of anarchy. Riverside Avenue was calm and inward-turned, the stately apartments populated by safely dreaming minds. They tended to skirt the most contentious places—Hell's Kitchen, the Tenderloin, San Juan Hill—in case they should be caught up in an altercation or a raid. The few times they cut across one of the slums, they were stopped by policemen who scolded the Jinni for bringing his lady among such rough characters. The Jinni found it darkly amusing—but the Golem didn't, not at all.

"They're right, Ahmad," she said. "We shouldn't come here."

His contrary nature rebelled against this. They roamed all over, so where was the difference? And so he went alone to the slums and the stews—where all took note of the handsome man in well-made clothing, and tried to fleece him, or rob him, or sell themselves to him. One night, a poor young mother, her baby tied in a filthy sling, pulled on his sleeve to beg for money. Before he could answer, a stocky man materialized from a doorway and slapped her across the face. The woman didn't even cry out, only slunk away, one hand to her cheek.

At once the Jinni thought of everything he might do to the man, and how powerless the man would be against him. But then he recalled another night, and another alley: the sound of bones snapping beneath the Golem's fist, and the terror on Anna Blumberg's face. Nothing good had come of it, and certainly no satisfaction, only misery and peril. And so he held himself back, and stared down his opponent until the man retreated back into the doorway, muttering words of false bravado.

The Jinni never went back again, after that.

Months turned into years. Each winter brought distress, each spring its relief. Summers were a private glory. They spent the long, warm nights walking together along the Harlem River Speedway, then across the river into Highbridge's quiet hills. They returned often to Central Park, retracing the familiar paths. When the first inevitable signs of autumn arrived, she'd resign herself to summer's loss, and brace once more for winter.

The colder months were difficult for him as well. He endured the rainy nights in his apartment or the shop, growing ever more restless and morose, and at the end of a wet autumn had to be cajoled into better humor. He felt less constrained in winter—but now he must be a help and a support, and go out even on the nights he'd rather stay inside so that the Golem could walk away her discomfort, and quiet her mind.

She, meanwhile, spent the winters wheedling and snappish. On the worst nights, she had a tendency to forget her words in the middle of a sentence and stare at thin air. When he tried to coax her into the bed he'd built—wrought iron, well soldered, with globe-topped finials—she either spurned him with a frown of annoyance, or agreed with startling urgency. She had no bodily warmth of her own, and at times, holding her in winter, he had to keep from flinching away from her chilled touch. He was always grateful for the forge the next morning.

"How is Chava?" Arbeely would ask on the days that the Jinni seemed particularly distracted, rolling and smoking his cigarettes with rare ferocity.

"Fretting, as usual, about everything she can't control," his partner would say; or else simply, "I am counting the nights until spring."

But in the summer the Jinni often strolled through the shop door in a fine mood, smiling or whistling to himself. Then Arbeely would merely sigh, irritated and not a little jealous.

"You need to find yourself someone," the Jinni might say on these ebullient mornings.

And his partner would scowl and reply, "I'm far too busy, and some of us need to sleep."

The Golem, however, did not have the advantage of working among those who knew her secret. It was most difficult on winter mornings, before the ovens' heat could warm her; she might move clumsily, or fail to hear a customer's order, or fall into a mesmerized trance while kneading the dough. And then, in the summers, she had to hide her happiness: an easier subterfuge, but one that carried a greater portion of shame.

"Thea wants me to come to supper," she told the Jinni sourly one winter night, as they walked the Mall beneath the snowy elms. "She's planning, in secret, to invite a neighbor of hers, a man she thinks of as 'poor lonely Eugene.' You can guess her motives."

"I see," he said gravely. "A rival. Shall I challenge him to combat?"

"Ahmad."

"If you like him, I suppose you can see him on alternate Thursdays."

She responded to this with an Italian phrase they'd heard near Mulberry Street; it translated to "misery pig," an image so evocative that they'd added it at once to the lexicon of borrowed human idioms that now peppered their conversations. The Jinni's particular favorite was *don't bite my head off*, overheard on a summer night when they'd walked beneath a couple arguing on a fire escape. The phrase itself, and the plaintive anger with which the man had yelled it—*Sweet Jaysus, Bernice, don't bite my head off!*—had struck the Jinni as indescribably hilarious, and he'd laughed so hard that the Golem had been forced to grab his elbow and half drag him down the street before the furious man could come after them. Her own favorite idioms tended to be terms of frustration, and she was given many opportunities to practice them.

"I know you think it's amusing," she told him, "but it'll be such a terrible strain." A thought occurred to her; she turned to him, suddenly worried. "You *do* know that I'd tell them about you if I could, don't you? Only it would cause so much gossip and whispering, they'd think about nothing else, and I'd never hear the end of it—"

He took her hand and squeezed it. "I know, Chava. Don't worry. I'm content to be your clandestine lover."

She smiled at that, slightly mollified, but the worry remained. *Was he content?* She never quite knew for certain. Were all lovers so opaque to their partners? Or did he only seem so in comparison, given that his thoughts alone were hidden to her sight? She had no true wish to know his every desire or fear; she'd long since learned that some amount of privacy was necessary in a relationship. And yet there were nights, on the rooftops and on the Park's familiar paths, when a dark and faraway look would steal across his face, and the quiet would stretch too long between them; and in those moments she'd give everything she owned just to know what he was thinking.

He made her feel so young and inexperienced sometimes, so very unsure of herself. He'd lived for centuries, but she knew next to nothing of his earlier life, only a scant handful of facts. Likely he could tell her tales to fill a year's worth of nights—so why didn't he? Did it pain him too much? Or did he think that the stories would pain *her?* She knew that he'd had lovers, knew that he'd lived in a manner that humans would call immoral; that much, at least, he'd made clear. Did he think her too naive to hear the details? Worse, was he right to?

The Jinni looked across at her. "You've been quiet," he said. "Is something wrong?"

Ought she to say what was truly on her mind? No, he'd only reply with one of his vague flippancies, or begin an argument to distract her, and she had no wish for either at the moment. "I was only thinking of poor, lonely Eugene," she said instead. "I ought to tell Thea that I've sworn off all romance, but she'd only take it as a challenge."

"Have you considered," he said, "that poor, lonely Eugene might have a clandestine lover of his own?"

She smiled at the thought. "I hadn't! What a relief that would be. But really, we ought to find a better phrase than *clandestine lovers.*"

"You don't think it suits us?"

"Do *you*?"

She'd expected an arch or teasing comment—but instead he slowed to a halt, gazing at her as though truly considering it. She held herself beneath his appraising eye, refusing to shrink or simper, wishing she'd stayed silent.

"You're right," he said at last. "It doesn't fit." And then, to her surprise, he cupped a hand to her cheek and kissed her, there on the open path. It wasn't a lengthy kiss—her lips must have been uncomfortably cold—but when he pulled back, a touch of his warmth remained for a moment, before the winter air stole it away.

Pleased, a bit puzzled, she said, "You're in an odd mood. Did something happen at the shop?"

He made a show of thinking. "Yes. Our new shipment of wrought iron came in."

She rolled her eyes at that, but couldn't help smiling.

They walked on together, up the path to the Ladies' Cottage by the skating pond. The door was always locked at night, but she tried the knob anyway. She was stiffer than usual, and her legs ached. She would've liked to get out of the cold, for a few minutes at least.

"Look," the Jinni said. A pair of ice skates lay next to the door, abandoned in the snow. He picked them up by their leather straps and inspected them, held one to his shoe, then peered out at the frozen pond, considering.

"You wouldn't," she said.

"Why not?" He walked to a nearby bench, sat down, and began strapping them to his feet.

"You know exactly why not," she said, irritated. "What if you fell through?"

"Chava, the pond's been frozen for months. It's not even particularly deep. Besides, you'd rescue me."

"Oh, really? If the ice doesn't hold you, it won't hold me, either. I'll sink to the bottom and freeze solid. And you don't even know how to skate." She paused. "Do you?"

"Not as far as I know." He stood from the bench, wobbling on the blades. "It might be like the languages, though. Perhaps I can skate perfectly well, only I don't know it yet. I ought to try, at least." And he began a precarious, stiff-legged walk to the pond's edge.

She followed after him, resigning herself to the spectacle. At times like this she felt he was taking advantage of her instinct to caution, needlessly racking her nerves so he might feel he'd done something daring. If she could tell him, *Yes, go ahead and skate, I think it's a lovely idea,* perhaps he'd lose interest. But he knew her better than that, and she had no talent at all for bluffing.

She stood on the shore, hugging herself as he stepped out onto the ice, his arms outstretched, tilting this way and that. If she weren't so annoyed, she might've laughed: instead of his usual graceful self, he looked like a drunken stork, all limbs and joints, none of them quite behaving. "I don't think it's like the languages," she called.

"Apparently not. How does one move forward on these things without—" A foot slipped out from under him, and he came crashing down on the ice.

She flinched, though she'd tried not to.

Out on the ice, the Jinni ignored his embarrassment and stood again, feeling for his balance on the thin blades. It ought to be easy; he'd seen children do it . . . He scowled, shifting his weight, trying to ignore a small, uneasy prickle of guilt.

Did something happen at the shop?

He wondered, as he often did, if his thoughts were as hidden from her as she believed. Yes, something had indeed happened at the shop. He hadn't mentioned it because it was a minor thing, insignificant really; it was only his own mind that insisted on magnifying it out of proportion. He'd been at his workbench, examining one of the newly arrived bars of wrought iron—he had ideas for a line of decorative goods in wrought iron, andirons and fireplace screens and the like—when Arbeely, perusing a catalog at his desk, had said, *Any idea how much solder we have left in the back?*

Not off the top of my head, the Jinni had replied—and then had stood there in shock, utterly aghast at himself.

Don't bite my head off. She's coming unhinged. A fine kettle of fish. Oh, go threaten the geese. To trade these phrases with the Golem was one thing; it was knowing and deliberate, a shared amusement. But his reply to Arbeely had been so absentminded, so natural-sounding, that one might've thought he'd spent his entire life talking about the tops of heads. And in that moment it had struck him—for what felt, absurdly, like the very first time—that he'd never speak his own language again.

The sense of monstrous loss confused him. After all, he rarely even thought in his own language anymore. He'd resolved to do so for the rest of the day, to reassure himself that he still could fill his mind with words that mimicked wind and fire, the sounds of the natural world—and only then had he realized how much of his life refused to be translated. *Newspaper, ledger-book, automobile. Money, cigarette, customer, bank, catalog.* In vain he'd hunted for equivalents, metaphors, but they were all wrong, either too vague or too poetic. Even worse, every phrase that had to do with iron was pejorative. His chosen profession, turned to an endless stream of obscenity.

And as he'd examined his unspoken language, forgotten sayings had begun to surface, the proverbs of elders, childhood taunts. *Angrier than a ghul's mother. Stop stealing my whirlwind. Give them a storm-cloud's welcome.* With each one came the thought: *I must tell this one to Chava.* But translation was no simple matter. The words themselves were many-layered, contingent on the season, on the time of day, on any of a host of circumstances. He imagined stumbling over the explanations, going back to add some crucial detail he'd forgotten, as he tried to show her how each phrase was a small tale in itself. He would never succeed to his satisfaction; he would only sadden and frustrate them both. And even if he could find the words, then what would be laid before her? A dictionary of lusts and caprices, avarice and recklessness; a vocabulary made for wandering where one pleased, and taking what one wanted. A language suited to the ways of the jinn—which were everything that she abhorred.

He lived a different life now. He followed rules and conventions, as far as he deemed himself reasonably able. He guarded his speech, and checked his desires, and tried, at all times, to remember that his actions had consequences. He was Ahmad al-Hadíd, born by accident in a Manhattan tinshop, neither jinni nor human but a thing half between. That was who she walked with. That was who she'd promised herself to.

Grimly he pushed himself forward on the blades. One snagged on the ice; he wobbled, overcorrected, and toppled backward, landing on his shoulder. He stood back up, ignoring the Golem's stifled groan behind him. He was doing it all wrong; he was trying to propel himself forward like a sledge—but the blade needed resistance. If he pushed one foot sideways, *against* the ice . . .

He glided forward, an arm's length.

From the shoreline came a note of surprise, small but edifying. He pushed with the other foot, and then again, moving outward from the shore, curving slightly to the right; he leaned left, found his balance, and swerved to an upright halt. He looked around, pleased with himself, then took off again: one foot and then the other, finding a rhythm, building speed, the wind whistling past him as he curved out toward the center of the pond . . .

"Be careful!" the Golem called. "It's thinnest in the middle!"

Irritated, he shouted back, "Stop fretting, Chava, I know enough to hide from the rain!"—and then drifted to a stop as, for the second time that day, his words echoed around him.

Silence, from the shore.

He began again, gliding away with long strides, wanting to curse himself. He'd gone rummaging through his mind as though it were an abandoned cupboard, stirring up memories instead of leaving well enough alone. He slalomed about, turning curlicues, feeling trapped, dreading the return to shore. *What you said before*, she would ask, *about hiding from the rain—what did that mean?* The metaphor was obvious, it meant she was treating him like a child; she only wanted to hear *him* say it so that she could ask another question, and another. She'd pry him gently open and it'd be his own fault, he'd just handed her the lever—

A distant voice called his name.

He looked up. The Golem was a small, dark figure silhouetted against the Ladies' Cottage. The frozen pond stretched between them. He'd skated clear to the other side.

"Ahmad," she called again, her voice thin and odd-sounding. "I'm going to *freeze*."

He skated back as quickly as he could. She stood immobile at the pond's edge, hands slowly opening and closing as she tried to keep her fingers limber. Her face sparkled with frost.

He yanked off the skates and tossed them into the snow. "There's a stove in the cottage, I'll break the lock—"

"No," she said firmly, through clenched teeth. "Let's just walk back, please."

Slowly, like a moving statue, she turned and started toward the path. He kept to her side, placed her stiff hand on his arm and covered it with his own, as though they were a courting couple. She threw him a half-annoyed glance, but kept her hand where he'd left it; and by the time they reached Washington Square, her face no longer collected stray flakes of frost. But his own guilt hadn't yet ebbed. He couldn't help picturing Sophia Winston the last time he'd seen her: pale and subdued, trembling beneath her layers of shawls. She'd never explained, never blamed him. Not in words.

"Shall I take you home?" he asked at Grand Street, thinking she'd want to be rid of him for the night.

"No," she said, surprising him. "Your apartment, please."

And so they continued south, instead of turning east. Neither spoke, though she'd drawn closer to him. Her hand felt softer now, more pliable on his arm. They reached Washington Street, keeping to the sidewalks—it wouldn't do, yet, to climb ladders and walk makeshift bridges—and soon were at his building. It was three in the morning; the frosted windows were dark, the hallways silent.

He unlocked his apartment, brought her inside, and set about warming her through.

"Ahmad?"

She lay on her side facing him, one arm tucked beneath her pillow. The locket she wore rested on the mattress-top, its long chain pooling beside it. She never took it off, though he wished she would. He'd opened that locket once, had unfolded the paper inside and come within a breath of speaking the words that would destroy her. He disliked touching it, even by accident, but had long since resolved to ignore it. She lived with a trapped wizard's endless scream in her mind. He could manage a brass locket.

"May I ask you a question?" she said.

"Of course." He tensed inwardly, waiting.

"When you kissed me in the park, what were you thinking about just then?"

He blinked in surprise. A kiss? He reviewed his memories of the evening. They'd talked of poor, lonely Eugene, and the possibility that he, too, might have a clandestine lover . . . She'd objected to the phrase, saying it didn't suit them—

And he'd pictured her, suddenly, with another man.

He was no one true to life, just an anonymous figure, his face shadowed. But her own face was clear, with its particular expression of pleasure taken in secret, in a darkened room or a hidden bower. The very image of a clandestine lover—and it had transfixed him with jealous anger.

It made little sense. He'd always thought of their promise as *his* constraint, not hers; and yet in that moment he'd been glad that she'd made the promise too, glad that, in this one sense, she was his and his alone. It went against his nature, and his principles. Nevertheless, it was true. And so, not knowing what else to do, he'd put his confusion aside and kissed her.

She was waiting, patiently, for an answer. "I was thinking," he said, "of how lucky I am to have you."

She considered this, and then nestled more closely against him. He laced his fingers to hers. *This is my life now,* he thought, holding her. *This is my happiness. It suits me. It will be enough.*

As it happened, there was to be no dreaded meeting with poor, lonely Eugene, for greater events were about to overtake Thea Radzin and her matchmaking schemes.

"You want to *what?*" said Thea to her husband.

"Expand the bakery," Moe Radzin said slowly, his tone that of a man suffering a simpleton.

The family's Sabbath supper was on the table, Thea's chicken soup cooling in bowls before them. The children, Selma and Abie, well trained through years of their parents' altercations, exchanged glances as Moe explained that the owner of the shoe-shop next to Radzin's had decided to move uptown. "It got me thinking. We can take over his lease, break through the wall. We'll more than double our space."

Thea was aghast. "What do we want with more space? What's wrong with the shop we have?"

"What's *wrong?* We outgrew it years ago! With the line stretching out the door in the mornings, and everyone going to Shimmel's instead of waiting in the cold—"

Thea's expression darkened. "Oh, I see. This is about you and Frank Shimmel. You want to blacken his eye once and for all, is that it?"

"Frank's got nothing to do with it! Just the other day you were complaining about the display case, and how small it is—"

"Oh, stop your tongue! Don't we have *enough?* With a roof over our heads and food on the table, two healthy children, may God protect them—"

The children in question slurped the last of their soup, stuffed their pockets with challah slices, and disappeared.

"—and you'd risk everything we've built so you can be the biggest frog in the puddle!"

But Moe refused to be dissuaded. He'd started the bakery as a terrified young man with ten dollars to his name, and over the years had built it into a finely tuned instrument, a watch you could tell the time by. Now he felt stultified by his own success. He wanted a new challenge, something to prove that his best years weren't all behind him. "We'll need three more bakers," he told Thea.

"I won't lift a finger to train them," she said, waspish in defeat. "I'm too old and tired for your nonsense."

"Fine," said Moe. "I'll get Chava to do it."

The plan had come so suddenly upon Moe that his best worker was, for once, caught unawares.

"You'll be in charge of hiring and training," he told her. "That's in addition to your usual duties. I'll have my hands full with the landlord and the bank. Think you can manage it?"

The Golem looked between him and Thea, who stood stiffly at the register, pretending not to hear. *God strengthen the girl, we're in her hands now,* Thea was thinking.

"Yes, Mr. Radzin," she told him. "I can manage it." But in truth, she didn't feel nearly so certain. How on earth did one go about choosing a new baker, let alone three? She gathered her courage, set a sign in the window—and the flood of young women began. All were eager, but for different reasons. Some imagined it would be just like baking at home with their mothers; others, as Anna Blumberg once had, relished the thought of standing on view before the neighborhood, thinking it would bring them the right sort of attention. Many sought escape from a wretched family life, or from a boss whose hands liked to travel. At first the Golem worried she'd be swayed by the most desperate and impoverished, regardless of their abilities—but soon she found herself facing an entirely different challenge.

Is Mrs. Levy always so serious? Working with her must be deadly dull—
I assume this one's the widow, she certainly looks the part—
What an odd woman. I feel like she's looming over me—

Would it be unfair of her, the Golem wondered, to turn away those whose opinions of her had been the least charitable? She strove to judge others by their actions, not their thoughts, as Rabbi Meyer had taught her; on the other hand, she could hardly be blamed for not wanting to hear mockery all day long. To her relief, there were so many suitable applicants that she could give herself the luxury of choice. She settled on three young women who seemed capable and energetic, and whose thoughts hadn't plainly ridiculed her.

"Congratulations," she told them. "You start tomorrow."

Moe, caught up in his negotiations, hadn't set foot in the store for days. The Golem's three new protégés arrived, and she presented them proudly to their new employer—only to see a look of dismay pass across his face. It lasted only a moment. He recovered, smiled, shook their hands in welcome, told them, "Listen to Chava, she's the best baker we ever had." But she'd already heard the thought, plaintive and rueful: *Would it have killed her to hire a single pretty face?*

At first she was stunned, and hurt. Then she wondered how she could've been so slow to realize. Perhaps Moe hadn't hired his bakers solely for their looks—but he, too, had allowed himself the luxury of choice.

"You never noticed?" said Anna Blumberg, incredulous. "Moe Radzin and his baking beauties?"

They were walking together at Seward Park, on the circular path around the playground, as they had every few months since the summer of the ice. Anna had chosen the meeting-place; she was still frightened of the Golem, and the public setting helped calm her nerves. It also gave Anna the rare chance to be seen in the company of a well-respected woman. Mothers pushing perambulators noticed them walking together, their voices low and serious, and wondered what such different women might have to say to each other. Some speculated that the widowed Mrs. Levy, denied a family to fuss over, had taken it upon herself to act as a social worker for the unfortunate Miss Blumberg. And indeed Anna had begun, if slowly, to reclaim a small amount of respectability. She'd found a job at a new laundry, which set her up well enough for a third-floor apartment, one with working windows and a fire escape. A few of her old acquaintances even acknowledged her on the street when they passed.

"I suppose I noticed the customers staring, but that just seemed to be the way of things," the Golem said. "And I was the sole exception, wasn't I? Moe didn't choose me, he hired me as a favor to Rabbi Meyer. He would've passed me over, given the choice."

Anna huffed. "More fool him, since you're the reason for his success. Well, think about it," she said at the Golem's dubious frown. "That tiny store turning out all those pastries? How many trays go into the ovens on an average day?"

"Thirty-five," the Golem said at once.

"It was two dozen at most before you came along. Same storefront, same lines out the door, only now they sell half again as much. You're the difference." She glanced sidelong at her companion. "Has he given you a raise for all this extra work you're doing?"

"Fifty cents a day."

Anna snorted her opinion of Moe's generosity—and then they turned a corner on the path, and the woman's attention was caught by a small figure on the boys' playground: a dark-haired, cherub-faced boy who'd clambered up to the top of the swing-set and now perched there, legs dangling, a dozen feet above the half-frozen ground.

"Oh, that boy will be the death of me," Anna muttered. And a worried image rose in her mind: Toby waking in panic in the early hours, unable to hold still, tearing himself from his mother's arms in his fear.

"Oh, Anna," said the Golem. "The nightmares?"

Anna nodded. "He won't talk to me about it. Or he can't, maybe. It's not right, Chava. He's too young for such unhappiness."

"Perhaps he'll grow out of them, in time," the Golem said. "Or he'll tell you about them, when he's old enough."

"You're only saying what you know I want to hear."

"But that doesn't make it untrue."

"Maybe, maybe not," Anna muttered, and the Golem could sense her resolving to change the subject. "And you? How are you handling the winter?"

"Better, now that the weather's warming." She glanced up at the trees, the first buds of green misting along their branches.

"And Ahmad?"

The Golem wanted to smile at the woman's studied neutral tone; Anna and the Jinni's brief interactions had been abrasive at best. "He has his moods. I think the winters are nearly as hard for him as they are for me, only he doesn't want to admit it." She wondered if she ought to tell Anna about the ice-skating incident. The phrase *I know enough to hide from the rain* had drifted through her mind at odd moments ever since, like a secret she wasn't meant to overhear.

"He's behaving himself, though?" Anna said. "No broken promises?"

The Golem cast her a quizzical glance. "None that I know of. What makes you ask?"

"That look on your face," the woman said. "Like you're trying to convince yourself of something."

"Oh, it's only that he seems unhappy lately. Not with me, or at least I don't think so. I just worry that he misses his old life, and that he's judging what he has by what he lost. I want him to be content, but I don't know what he *needs*."

"Well, of course he's still judging by his old life—he's centuries old, isn't that so?" She said it lightly, as though speaking of anyone's age, but the Golem could feel her struggle: *Think of it, to live so long!*

"Two centuries, I think."

"Well, there it is. Five years must be like the blink of an eye to him. So let it lie, for a while, before you go trying to fix things."

The Golem sighed. "You're right, it's just so hard to be patient. Oh, and that reminds me—I managed to avoid another of Thea's attempts at matchmaking. It was the expansion that put it out of her head."

Anna's mouth twisted. "No cloud without a silver lining."

"I wish I could send her bachelors your way instead," the Golem said tentatively.

"If they'd have me, I wouldn't want them."

"Anna."

"I'm only teasing, Chava."

"No, you're not."

Anna sighed, acknowledging the lie. "It doesn't matter anyway. They're a risk I can't afford." The woman looked again to Toby at the top of the swing-set, who now hung from his knees, grinning as his face turned purple. Her boy, in constant motion. There was so much she wanted to give him: clothes that fit him properly, food enough to fill their icebox, the silver Schwinn bicycle he'd set his heart upon. *It's the one the Western Union boys ride, Ma.* And yes, a father, she wanted that for him, too—but more than anything, she wanted to end his nightmares. She would never forgive herself if she added to them instead, if she made another mistake like Irving, out of loneliness or a need to be desired. She wouldn't let it happen, even if it meant an empty bed for the rest of her days.

The Golem glanced at her, startled by her thoughts. As a coquette of eighteen, Anna had believed that a life without love wasn't worth living. That woman was gone now, all romantic notions burned away in the Bowery's crucible—and yet she was still, in some ineffable manner, the same Anna. *I wish that everyone could know you like I do*, she wanted to say, or maybe, *I'm glad we're friends again*—but she held back. The night at the dance hall still lay between them, along with Anna's wariness and her own guilt. Perhaps they'd never be close enough for true friendship, but the Golem had resolved to be whatever Anna needed.

"Anna," she said, "may I buy that bicycle for Toby this summer, for his birthday? You can tell him you found it on sale."

Anna glanced at her, startled, then shook her head ruefully. "I swear, I can't have a stray thought around you. You're not my charity-box, Chava. The ice was enough."

"Please, Anna. I can afford it far more easily than you, and if it would make him happy . . ."

"All right, if you insist. But that's *it*. I don't want him thinking I can make whatever he wants appear out of thin air. So no surprises, please."

"No surprises," the Golem agreed, and felt a little better.

"I'd better put supper on," Anna said. "Next month?"

"Next month."

On the playground, Toby swung himself upright on the crossbar, grinning with giddiness as the blood drained from his head. He looked around, scanning the path below. There: his mother, in her hat with the faded rosettes, and the tall lady beside her, whom he knew only as Missus Chava.

Missus Chava was a puzzling figure in young Toby's life. His mother had told him that they'd worked together at Radzin's Bakery—but that was strange in itself, because his mother was a laundress, not a baker, and her few friends were all laundresses too, women whose hair was stiff with starch and who couldn't laugh without coughing. And they only ever saw Missus Chava at Seward Park, where the two women walked their somber loops around the playground, their heads bent together like a couple of rabbis. If Toby tried to overhear, his mother would tell him to run off and play, her cheery voice lined with steel. It was the same tone she used whenever he asked about his missing father. What was his name? What did he look like? *When you're older, boychik. Now go outside and play.*

Toby loved his mother deeply; he was a little afraid of her, too. He feared her darker moods, her angers and sadnesses, the way she'd come home from the laundry and sit on the sofa and stare at nothing. He feared the pain in her eyes when he woke from his nightmare of the old man's wicked grin, the dreadful paralysis. He'd burst out of bed, desperate for movement, and she'd try to catch him in her arms, saying, *Tell me, sweetheart, I can't help if you don't tell me!* But it felt important that he keep the nightmare to himself; if he told his mother about the old man, maybe he would come for her, too. So Toby could only struggle free of her and go dashing up to the roof, to run in circles until he'd shaken the terror loose.

His secret and his mother's secret, his nightmare and his missing father. They felt linked somehow, the facets of a mystery too large to grasp.

He watched from his perch as the two women parted, his mother approaching the playground, Missus Chava turning toward the park exit. He scrutinized Missus Chava as she receded, the only solitary woman in a sea of mothers and children. Whoever Missus Chava was, it seemed clear that she was a part of the mystery, too—for what could they possibly be talking about every month, except for everything he wasn't supposed to know?

As he watched, Missus Chava stopped suddenly, and turned as though hearing her name called. A small thrill ran through Toby as their eyes met across the expanse of the park.

"Toby!"

Startled, he looked down. It was his mother, her arms folded in impatience.

"Toby, I called your name twice. Don't make me wait, please, it's supper-time."

He shimmied down the swing-set and took her hand, and they returned to their dim apartment. And he did not think about Missus Chava again until his birthday, when he woke from his nightmare, already scrambling off his pallet in panic—and nearly collided with the bicycle that waited by the door, balanced patiently on its kickstand.

The panic fell away in his shock. He reached out and ran a hand along it: the glinting metal frame, the leather seat, the rubber handgrips. Too big for him, but that hardly mattered; he was tall for his age and growing fast. A bicycle, a Schwinn, the real thing. *His*.

His mother, already dressed for work, smiled at him from the sofa. "After supper," she told him, "we'll take it down to the alley and give it a try."

He didn't ask where it had come from. Even at his age, he wouldn't have believed any story she might tell about finding one on sale, or a kindly shop owner who'd made an exception for a boy's birthday. He merely expanded the mystery to include the bicycle, trusting that someday—when he was old enough, when he'd learned enough—he'd understand how it all fit together.

That night Anna walked homeward on aching feet, debating what to buy at the butcher's for Toby's birthday supper—brisket ends maybe; she could hardly afford them, but he loved them so . . . Had she made a mistake, she wondered, in allowing the Golem to buy him the bicycle? God forbid he should think she'd stolen it . . .

Sunk in her thoughts, she didn't notice the startled squawks on the sidewalk ahead, or the wobbling shape that had caused them, until suddenly the disturbance was upon her: a small boy teetering atop a too-large bicycle, moving inexpertly but at considerable speed, and grinning at her as he passed.

She froze in shock. "Toby?" she said weakly. But he was gone already, scattering pedestrians right and left.

She didn't scold him for the near miss, or for the scuffs and scrapes he'd accumulated during his self-administered lessons. *I wanted to surprise you*, he said at supper, between bites of brisket, and then told her how he'd wheeled the bicycle back and forth in the alley for hours, how he'd stood on a vegetable crate so he could swing his leg over the seat without falling. Listening, Anna felt her love for him gather to a painful fist in her chest.

They washed the supper dishes together, and then Toby curled himself upon his pallet, across from the bicycle. He'd positioned it so that it would be the first thing he would see in the morning, when he woke. Anna tucked the blanket around him, brushed his hair from his forehead. He was exhausted but happy, already half asleep. The aching weight hadn't subsided; it felt like a warning, a premonition of some future grief, and on sudden impulse she said, "Toby, if you're ever in trouble—terrible trouble, a matter of life and death—and I'm not there, then go find Missus Chava."

Toby smiled sleepily at this. "All right, Ma."

"Look at me, boychik."

The boy rubbed at his eyes, opened them wider.

"Missus Chava lives in the boardinghouse at the corner of Eldridge and Hester. Say it back to me."

"Missus Chava lives in the boardinghouse at the corner of Eldridge and Hester." A touch of fear now, in his voice; she realized how she must look to him, a looming face in a darkened room. *Good*, she thought, even as her heart twisted. *Maybe he'll remember.*

"I love you," she murmured, and kissed him on the forehead, and left him to sleep.

In December of 1905, on a cold, wet afternoon, Kreindel Altschul stood beside her father outside the doorway of the Forsyth Street Synagogue as over a hundred thousand Jews marched silently past, all of them dressed in mourning black.

Onlookers crammed the rooftops and fire escapes, women sobbing into handkerchiefs, children clinging to their legs. Kreindel, on the sidewalk, could barely see over the men in front of her. The air seemed to press upon her ears, and she realized belatedly that even the construction pit at the bottom of Forsyth, for the new bridge across the river, had gone silent. Surprised, she looked southward, to where the anchoring tower rose above the East River slips. Sure enough, the gangs of riveters had vanished from its girders.

She stole a quick glance at her father, wondering if he, too, had noticed. His hat shaded his eyes, but there were tear tracks on his cheeks, and the edge of his beard trembled. The sight unnerved her; and so she looked away, back to the marching men and their banners, all announcing their various affiliations—the Unionists, the Progressives, the Zionists, the Orthodox. All brought together, if only for the moment, by the news from the Russian Empire: over a thousand Jews murdered in the city of Odessa, victims of the latest pogrom.

At last the final banner went by, and the crowd began to disperse. Men from the synagogue gathered around her father, wiping their eyes, exchanging murmurs. *Such anguish, what is to be done.* Kreindel stood in the doorway, unsure of her role, until her father happened to glance her way. He looked puzzled for a moment, as though he'd forgotten she was there.

"Go home, Kreindel," he told her, not ungently, and then disappeared inside.

Kreindel Altschul was now eight years old. Her father flatly refused to send her to public school, despite the truancy laws, which meant that she still spent her days in the care of the mothers of her tenement—except they could never be certain of whose turn it was, and in the confusion Kreindel often managed to escape their notice altogether. Alone, she'd wander the hallways, listening through the thin walls and peering into open doors. She scavenged the hallway dustbins for copies of *Tageblatt* and *Forverts*, and used these to teach herself to read. Sometimes the Reform settlement ladies, tall and pink-cheeked and spotless, would drift past with their baskets of milk and eggs, knocking on doors as they went. Some doors would open to admit them; others slammed shut in their faces.

When she was hungry, she'd sneak into an apartment and take a place at the table. A woman would turn from her stove and see Kreindel eating bread and schmaltz next to her own children, and wonder just how long she'd been there, and what she'd overheard. They couldn't begrudge her the food—they all pitied her, the poor motherless child with a holy man for a father—but she unsettled them all the same. No matter how much she ate, she remained a tiny thing, quiet and watchful. And whenever she asked an inconvenient question, gleaned from her silent observations—*Why does that boy on the first floor always have a black eye? Why does Mrs. Weintraub spend so much time in Mr. Litvak's apartment on the second floor, even though she lives with Mr. Weintraub on the fourth floor?*—their harried reply was always the same: *Go and ask your father.*

This was a more difficult prospect than they realized. For the most part, Lev Altschul was a silent presence in his daughter's life. In the mornings, he was a pair of feet walking past her pallet as he left for the synagogue; in the evenings, he asked a few perfunctory questions during their supper—*Did you behave yourself today? Did you study your letters?*—and half listened to her answers, then studied Talmud in the parlor while Kreindel washed the dishes and swept the floor. The only time that father and daughter truly shared each other's company was during the Sabbath hours of rest, when Lev would sit Kreindel beside him on their horsehair sofa and read to her. The book was always the same: the *Tsene-rene,* the "women's bible" of scripture and commentary in Yiddish—written for those who, owing to their youth, sex, or some other impairment, could not read Hebrew. The copy had been Malke's, and it was the only possession of hers that Lev had kept for their daughter. When he was young, Lev had watched his own mother take his sisters into her lap and read them the *Tsene-rene's* stories of the patriarchs and matriarchs, the years of slavery and wandering, the laws and their divine origins. In his refusal to remarry, Lev had denied his daughter her rightful Sabbath teacher—and so, to remedy the loss, he'd taken on the duty himself.

Neither Kreindel nor Lev was ever fully comfortable during these Sabbath recitations. For Kreindel, to be so close to her father—to smell the soap on his skin, and see the hairs on the back of his hand as he turned the pages—felt overfamiliar, impolite. For Lev's part, reading the *Tsene-rene* was a weekly exercise in patience. He found the language mundane, the teachings dull and vaguely depressing, focused as they were on tales of womanly forbearance and resignation. But Lev recalled how his own father, who'd been known to debate any point of law no matter how fine, had always kept a respectful silence while his mother read from the *Tsene-rene*. From that silence Lev had taken the lesson that women's knowledge was different from men's, the one serving as foundation and support for the other—for without women to focus on worldly needs, men would be unable to devote themselves to the divine.

And so Kreindel learned the story of Eve's fashioning from Adam's rib, and its accompanying lesson: *Thus a woman is strong by nature, for she was created from a bone, while a man, created from earth, is weak, and quickly dissolves.* She learned of Sarah's modesty, and the love between Rachel and Jacob, and the heedlessness of Dinah that led to her ravishment by Shechem. She absorbed the bits of lore and legend that Lev suspected were there to keep the attention of the young: the *shamir*, the magical substance with which King Solomon had cut the stones that built his Temple; and the Ziz, the enormous bird that liked to stand with its feet in the ocean and its head in the heavens, singing for the pleasure of the Almighty. She wished she could enjoy the *Tsene-rene*, since it was the only book she was allowed—but she was too observant not to notice her father's subtle impatience with it, his relief when he put it aside. It was clear to her that there was other, better knowledge to be had.

Alone in his synagogue office, Rabbi Altschul sat at his desk and stared blindly down at his half-finished sermon. He'd begun it that morning: a denunciation of the Tsar and his lackeys, and all those who'd joined in the pogrom's violence. They were the words of a powerless man, a man helpless to do anything but shout.

But you are not powerless, a voice inside him whispered.

He picked up the pen, put it down again, closed his eyes and saw the parade banners passing before him, each the herald of a different ideology, a different argument. *Send arms to the most vulnerable. Settle in the Holy Land. Educate the workers, start a revolution.* All of them were doomed to failure. Evil could not be cured by the flawed plans of misguided men; it required the strength and presence of the Almighty. And Lev could no longer deny that he, and he alone, held the true solution.

That night, after Kreindel fell asleep, Lev washed quietly, prayed at length, and at last drew the old wooden suitcase from beneath his bed.

5.

I t was a warm spring morning in the desert west of the Cursed City.

A group of young jinn flew together, stealing each other's winds in teasing play. Among them, hanging slightly back from her fellows, was the jinniyeh who feared no iron. Ever since the incident with the farmer's scythe, she'd been careful to cultivate the appearance of timidity, never exploring on her own or flying out ahead—for what would happen if she led them too close to iron without realizing it?

—*Look*, one of them called. *Humans.*

Three travelers had appeared on the road leading east: one man and two women, all on horseback, with a pack-laden donkey following behind. Two wore head-coverings meant to keep away the sun. The third, one of the women, went surprisingly bare-headed. She was younger than the others, and pale-skinned, with sparrow-brown hair that she wore woven about her head, fastened here and there with points of metal that glinted in the sunlight. The woman's companions rode ahead of her, as though on guard—and indeed, even as the jinn watched, another group of humans rode into view from the north. These were black-robed Bedu, a scouting party come to decide whether the travelers were worth raiding.

—*Let's see what happens*, one of the jinn said.

They flew toward the converging groups of humans, the jinniyeh maintaining her cautious distance as the trio on the road wheeled about to face the oncoming Bedu. The man placed a hand near the rifle at his side. The fair-haired woman pulled one of the dark scarves she wore from around her neck and draped it over her head. The jinniyeh saw that she was trembling, and thought it was out of fear—but then the woman called out, "Blessings upon you, O Sheikh!"

The leader of the Bedu party reined in his horse, and the others followed; he was smiling, an expression more amused than glad. "Miss

Williams!" he called back. "I had wondered if we'd see your family this spring."

"May we beg your hospitality for the night?" The woman spoke slowly, as though still learning the dialect. Her companions sat easier now; the man had moved his hand away from the rifle.

"You will be my honored guests," the sheikh replied—and the trio turned north, and joined host.

The group of young jinn watched them go. There was no question of following them: a lone human might be tricked astray and sported with, but not a village's worth. There'd be iron amulets in every door-way, and exorcists armed with herbs and chants. And so the jinn turned away, to search for entertainment elsewhere.

But the jinniyeh dawdled behind, lingering to watch the humans disappear northward. Something about the pale woman had piqued her interest: her odd appearance, her tremor, but also the amusement in the sheikh's voice as he'd answered her hail. As though he, too, thought her strange and out of place.

She turned away from the humans and flew back to rejoin her fellows.

It was nearly evening when the Bedu and their guests arrived at their destination: a village of mud-brick huts, built in two long lines that faced each other across a central alley. Children playing in the alley quickly abandoned their games to cluster around the riders and call out to Sophia, who smiled and returned their greetings. She couldn't help but notice that the crowd was smaller this year than before. For generations this village had served as a way-station for caravans on the road to Homs, men and animals bedding down between the twin lines of huts—not so elegant as the palatial caravanserai in Damascus and Aleppo, with their marble fountains and potted palms, but nonetheless safe from raiders and the elements. Now, though, the caravans were dwindling, their routes usurped by rail and sea. Families in the village had begun to drift toward Homs, where they might find work in the fields and markets.

The sheikh led the Williamses to his hut—beehive-shaped like all its neighbors, an ancient design that stayed cool in the summer heat—

and they sat on the floor around the fire while the sheikh's wife prepared tea and supper. Their host asked after their travels, and learned
that they were on their way to Palmyra for a brief visit before heading
north, to spend the summer months among the fairy-chimneys of Cappadocia. Sophia inquired about the local politics—traveling the tribal
regions was not unlike wandering across a chessboard, and it paid to stay
abreast of the latest maneuvers—and the sheikh told her which of the
warlords were lately ascendant, and which had overreached. He also told
her of a large, slow-moving group of Westerners who had passed on the
road the day before, an exorbitant train of palanquins, pack animals, and
armed guards. He'd taken them for British, and kept his own men well
away; to demand payment for their passage would only rouse their ire,
and perhaps that of Syria's Ottoman governors. "They'll be at Palmyra
by the time you arrive," he told Sophia, and watched as her expression
soured. He enjoyed the novelty of this strange girl and her wardens—
they professed themselves to be her parents, but nothing on earth could
convince him of it—though at times he wondered who, exactly, he was
entertaining.

He wouldn't hear of them sleeping in the alley, and directed them
instead to a pair of empty huts. The sun had dipped below the hills, and
the air was cooling quickly. Lucy built a fire for Sophia, and made certain she had enough blankets, and then joined Patrick in the other hut,
leaving the young woman to herself.

Sophia spent some time writing in her journal as the village quieted
around them, detailing the day's journey and the sheikh's gossip. In her
five years of adventuring with the Williamses, she'd seen no evidence to
suggest that they read her journals; still, she wrote nothing in them that
she wouldn't want her parents to hear. At last, when she'd judged that
the village was asleep, she donned a sheepskin-lined coat, lit her lantern,
and left her hut, heading in the direction of the latrine.

A child's face loomed into her path.

She nearly gasped, though she'd been expecting it. The child beckoned, and Sophia followed him to a hut set slightly apart from the rest.
The woman who crouched inside by the fire was in her twenties, barely
older than Sophia.

Sophia looked about, but the woman was alone. "Peace be upon you, Umm Firas," she said, suddenly wary.

"Welcome, Miss Williams," the woman said, her voice subdued. "I must tell you that Umm Salem is dead."

Sophia's heart sank. She bowed her head, swallowing back tears that felt entirely too selfish to show. "I grieve for you," she said. "When did it happen?"

"In midwinter, from an infection in her lungs. At the end, she tried to teach me many things quickly. But your medicine . . . I apologize. There wasn't enough time."

Sophia nodded. She imagined the elderly healer on her sickbed, deciding which portions of her knowledge to pass to her apprentice. Of course she'd choose the most important cures, the ones that strengthened newborns or healed broken bones. Not the powder that she mixed once a year for a stranger.

"I can give you this." Umm Firas handed Sophia a small packet of waxed parchment. "Take it in the same dose as the other. It won't be as effective, but it will help."

"Thank you, Umm Firas." Sophia took the packet, hoping that her gratitude showed on her face, and not her disappointment.

"Did you sleep well, Sophia?" asked Lucy.

It was morning, and the village was behind them. They'd paid the sheikh in grain and coin for the night's rest, and made their good-byes while the sun was still low. The elder Williamses had long since dropped the *miss* when addressing their supposed daughter, though in private they all still spoke with near-formal courtesy, as though to remind themselves of the truth.

"Well enough," Sophia said lightly, not wishing to lie. She'd tried a dose of the new powder after returning to her tent; as Umm Firas had warned, it was far less effective, and she'd lain awake shivering half the night. How, she wondered, would she manage now? It had taken years of secret inquiries to find Umm Salem, and now she must begin over again. She still had a small store of the more potent medicine; she could stretch it out, take it only on the coldest nights, but that would gain her little more than a month or two. At last she resolved to put it out of mind for now, and enjoy her visit to Palmyra as much as possible.

The trio rode steadily, eating their meals in the saddle, pausing only to feed and water the horses. By midday the sun had soothed away Sophia's tremor. Lucy and Patrick, meanwhile, sweated beneath their riding clothes, and drank often from their water-skins. Sophia knew they were looking forward to Cappadocia, where the sun wouldn't broil them alive. Sophia had grown genuinely fond of the Williamses, who seemed eternally willing to ride horses and camels and vertiginous mountainside rail-cars, and to eat whatever unfamiliar foods were placed before them. And the Williamses, for their part, had grown to trust Sophia enough to loosen their vigilance here and there, bestowing her an hour to browse alone at a souk, or a solitary morning at a café. Sophia used these brief spells of freedom to make quick inquiries among the local healers, or to ask in the spice-stalls about rare ingredients and rumored cures. To her knowledge the Williamses had never caught on; still, she disliked risking their trust. Even now, they must send their regular reports to New York, describing Sophia's general behavior and her continued eschewing of male company. Demeaning, for a woman of twenty-five to be written up like a girl at a finishing school—but the funding of her travels depended upon the Williamses' good opinion, and Sophia never let herself forget it.

It was nearly evening when they passed over the ridge and down into the Valley of the Tombs, at the western outskirts of Palmyra. In the distance stood a lattice of columns and low walls, the stone ribs of a toppled city. They rode along the Great Colonnade, past towering groups of pillars and the half-crumbled amphitheater, and Sophia tried, as always, to imagine how it once had been: the wide, palm-lined avenues, the market-stalls where merchants traded in half a dozen languages.

At the end of the Colonnade stood the largest of Palmyra's surviving buildings, and the city's still-beating heart: the Temple of Bel, its high, fortresslike walls now home to a sizable Bedu village. And here were the British tourists, only just arrived: a dozen uniformed officers and their wives, all clustered before the temple gate. Nearby, their retinue of Punjabi servants was setting up camp, unpacking the provisions and raising silk-trimmed tents while a herd's worth of camels grazed and napped. The officers stood with a dark-robed sheikh who'd come out to meet them, displaying for him the gifts they'd brought; Sophia spied a stag-handled carving set, and a china teapot painted with Scottish thistles. One of the officers had a camera, and was coaxing the sheikh to pose with the gifts when Sophia's horse nickered. As one the group turned to gape at the approaching trio: the older pair with their holstered rifles and dust-stained leathers, and the pale young woman in her split skirt and dark shawls.

The sheikh, however, brightened at the sight of them. He abandoned the delegation and approached the riders, calling out greetings. The trio dismounted, Sophia smiling and answering in kind. The sheikh motioned to a boy loitering near the temple gate, and the boy hurried to take their horses' reins and lead them toward grazing ground. The sheikh gestured toward the gate—and with barely a backward glance at the indignant officers, the three were ushered inside.

"So she told you nothing," Patrick said to Lucy.

The two lay together in their tent, which they'd pitched in a corner of the temple courtyard. Sophia's tent was some distance away, in a spot where the stones were still warm from the day's heat. Lucy had checked on her before retiring, and found her deeply asleep.

"Only that she'd slept 'well enough,' whatever that means," Lucy replied. "Nothing about wandering off alone in the dark, and then having herself a good cry afterward."

"I asked about the old healer-woman," Patrick said. "She died this winter."

Lucy sighed. "Can't say I'm surprised. She had to be eighty, at least."

Silence, for a moment. Then Patrick said, "Whatever the old woman was giving her . . . do you think it truly helped?"

"You mean, or is it all in her mind?"

Patrick shrugged, uncomfortable.

"I think," Lucy said, "it doesn't much matter in the end. She suffers either way."

He considered this. "True enough. And I suppose we're making it worse for her, dragging her north to Cappadocia for the summer."

"Just like Ankara last summer, and Armenia the summer before," Lucy murmured. "She ought to stay here instead—but how would you and I do our jobs, half dead from the heat?"

"Well, maybe it's time we stopped."

A long pause, as each took careful stock of his words.

"You mean, quit?" A glimmer of hope had entered Lucy's voice.

He smiled. "You've been thinking it, too?"

"Of course I have. She's twenty-five, Patrick. You and I were married younger than that. It isn't natural, what her parents are making her do, and I'm starting to hate myself for being a part of it."

He nodded. "And here's another thing. The two of us aren't getting any younger, either. These are the best years we've got left, and we're spending them eating in the saddle and sleeping on stones. We've enough money in the bank to retire for good, and I'd say we've earned it."

"So what do we do? We can't just leave her. She needs *someone*."

He thought a minute. "Remember that guide in Homs, the one who showed us around the mosques and the citadel? Used to be a dragoman?"

"Abu Alim," Lucy said. "I liked him."

"So, someone like that, maybe."

"And if we're wrong?" Lucy said darkly. "Who'll protect her then?"

"We'll teach her what we know," Patrick said. "And then, she can protect herself."

A few months later, the Williamses sent word to their employers that they wished to be released from their contract. In their estimation, they said, Sophia had matured into a steady and intelligent young woman. She'd taught herself Arabic and Turkish, could get by in a number of dialects, and had accumulated a detailed knowledge of the local politics. In fact, at this point, they wouldn't be surprised if she was one of the West's foremost experts on the region. They had never seen her behave inappropriately with any man, nor had they spotted the gang-leader her mother had described. As for her personal safety, they'd taken the liberty of drilling her extensively in both rifle and pistol. Her aim was imperfect, owing to her tremor—but on a warm and windless day, she could shoot a tobacco tin off a fence-post at thirty paces.

Francis Winston read the report with his usual mix of jealousy and pride. The truth was that he missed his daughter terribly. He wanted to bring her home, to hear firsthand her tales of Cappadocian fairy-chimneys and Palmyrene temples—but there were other considerations. In Sophia's absence, the mood of their household had improved considerably. Julia had, at long last, allowed him back into her bed. And there were several delicate matters of business approaching; he must go to Washington, and court the good opinions of dull and odious men. Sophia's return, he decided, would have to wait for a more opportune moment. In the meantime, if the Williamses were to find a reputable native guide for her, then Francis would declare himself satisfied.

Julia, however, was horrified, both at the thought of Sophia traveling unchaperoned—a native guide hardly counted!—and at her daughter's transfiguration into a Wild West showgirl. On the other hand, there was no good way to enforce the contract if the Williamses wished to be elsewhere. She might convince Francis to cut off Sophia's funds and order her home for good—but *then* what would she do with the girl? Jail her in her room, and resume their battle of wills? The thought alone made her inexpressibly weary.

And so Julia, too, agreed to the severing of the contract—but with one condition. If Sophia wished to make a spectacle of herself among heathens and savages, then she must do so under her assumed identity, and leave her family's reputation untouched. The Winston name—and all the duties and expectations that it encompassed—would wait for her at America's shore.

This must be a sin, Kreindel Altschul thought.

It was the summer of 1906, and Kreindel lay stretched upon the bare stone floor of the women's balcony at the Forsyth Street Synagogue, watching the dust motes that floated past in the light from the high windows. She'd had no trouble at all sneaking into the synagogue; the women's door was in the alley off Hester, far from the main entrance, and from there it was a quick walk down a dim hallway to the balcony staircase. A small notebook and a sharpened pencil waited in her skirt pockets. Now she only had to stay out of sight, and wait for the boys to arrive.

Which sin in particular was it? she wondered. Could it really be called trespassing if she belonged to the synagogue, and her father was the rabbi? Then again, her father thought she was in their apartment, tending to her chores. If he were to ask at supper what she'd done during the day, she'd have to lie—and *that* would be a sin. Except he never asked her questions at supper anymore, only said the blessings and ate as quickly as possible, then shut himself in the bedroom, the key scraping as it turned in the lock. Left to herself, Kreindel would wash the dishes and put them away, then lie down on her pallet and watch the glow from beneath his door. Sometimes she could hear muttering in what sounded like Hebrew, but was nothing she recognized from the prayers she knew. She'd watch and listen, waiting for him to blow out the lamp, but she always drifted off to sleep before it happened.

On Saturday mornings she walked with him to the synagogue and chose a seat in the front of the women's balcony, the better to hear him. His sermons had taken on a new ferocity, of late. Angrily he'd denounce the Tsar for his wickedness, the Reform movement for its faithlessness, the Bundists for their atheism, the Zionists for attempting to usurp the role of the Almighty. *It is up to Him alone to send us the Messiah and restore Jerusalem, and gather all the exiles of Israel into the Holy Land,* he'd thunder—and she'd listen, entranced by the voice he'd hidden from her all week, and the certainty in his words.

Then, back across the street to their apartment for the Sabbath afternoon—but now Kreindel could read the *Tsene-rene* on her own, and so they spent the hours apart, in silent study. At last the sun would set, and they'd light the braided Havdalah candle and extinguish it in the wine—and then he was gone again, into the bedroom. He always managed to open and close the door when her back was turned so that she never caught sight of the room itself.

What are you doing in there, another child might have asked, or even, *Why don't you talk to me anymore?* But Kreindel was trained in her own ways, and she knew that one couldn't solve a mystery by merely asking questions. Nor could she simply pick or break the bedroom lock, for that would be a betrayal. And besides, she didn't merely want to see what her father kept beyond the door. She wanted to *understand* it. And so she had come to the women's balcony, heart pounding, waiting to learn.

At last, from the sanctuary below there came the shuffle of unwilling footsteps as a dozen young boys took their places in the front pews. And then, her father's voice, brisk and businesslike: *Open your primers, please, to lesson four.*

The boys hated their Hebrew lessons, each and every one. It felt like a punishment they hadn't earned to sit in the uncomfortable pews, picking their way through the Hebrew, while their friends played games of alley stickball, or snuck into the construction pit beneath the unfinished bridge. For Kreindel, though, it was a new and secret pleasure to listen as her father conjugated verbs and corrected mistakes, all with a patience and calm that surprised her. Her pencil flew across the pages of her notebook, capturing his words. *The particle* lo *preceding a verb negates its action.* Lo qatsar Ya'acov etz—"*Jacob did not cut down a tree.*" *The verb* shamah, "*to hear,*" *gains the suffix* ti *to indicate the first person singular.* Vayomer et-kolecha shama'ti bagan va'ira—"*And he said, 'I heard your voice in the garden and I was afraid.'*"

For a solid hour he taught, until the light in the balcony grew so thin that Kreindel's nose nearly touched the paper as she wrote—and then at last the boys were dismissed, and she was left alone, her head spinning with rules and particles and suffixes.

She went back the next day, and the next, learning bit by bit. On Saturdays she listened to the Sabbath prayers with new concentration, unraveling them as they flew by. At night, on her pallet, she'd pull her notebook from inside her pillow and review her lessons while her father muttered behind the locked door, seemingly a world away.

It wasn't long before she noticed the toll that her father's secret work was taking. Dark circles appeared around his eyes, and hollows in his cheeks. Their suppers had always been small, mainly knishes and pickles from the pushcarts, but now he barely ate anything at all. One morning Kreindel found a scrap of leather in the garbage and recognized it as the end of his belt, trimmed away to disguise his growing emaciation. Alarmed, she stole a handful of pennies from the jar he kept in the kitchen cabinet and bought eggs and noodles, herring and potatoes. She'd never cooked before, knew only what she'd seen from the tenement mothers—but through trial and error, she taught herself to make simple meals for them both. Her father was surprised, and a touch abashed; yet he still had no appetite, and could only manage a few bites before excusing himself to the bedroom and locking the door behind him.

By the beginning of 1907, Kreindel had learned enough Hebrew to translate every word of the Sabbath service, and yet her father's nighttime mutterings still eluded her. Sometimes she recognized the various names of God, or exhortations to the angels, or the words for different body parts, *arm* and *head* and *finger*; but often it sounded as though he was saying the words back to front, or scrambling their letters about. And there were other, stranger happenings. A strong, earthy smell had begun to permeate the apartment, reminding her of something she couldn't quite place. One night, she woke in the dark to see her father standing before the bedroom door, a heavy coal-sack over his back. His sleeves and trouser-cuffs were dark with what looked like mud. He whispered something, and her eyes went heavy with sleep. In the morning, the memory had the tenuous, half-faded quality of a dream.

Seasons passed. At the synagogue her father struggled to conceal his ill health. One Saturday in autumn he seemed particularly affected; he rallied himself for his usual sermon, but after the final benediction his vigor left him, and he stood pale and wavering on the dais. The synagogue men seemed not to notice, gathering around him as always— but Kreindel, afraid that he might collapse, ran down from the balcony, pushed through the men, and grabbed his hand, saying, *Papa, you promised to tell me a story this afternoon.*

He looked down at her, eyes clouded with confusion, and in that moment she thought he'd forgotten who she was. But then his brow cleared. *Of course, child,* he said, smiling. *Excuse me, gentlemen.*

They left the sanctuary and walked across the street, his thin, dry hand in hers. Together they climbed the tenement stairs, and by the second floor he was leaning on her shoulder, gripping it tightly. At last they reached their apartment, where he collapsed upon the parlor sofa and was asleep within moments.

His counterpane was locked behind his bedroom door, so Kreindel tucked her own blanket over him, though it was too short to cover him completely. She sat down at his writing-desk—it felt presumptuous, but there was no room on the sofa—and listlessly thumbed through the *Tsene-rene*, casting occasional glances at the bookcase lined with Talmudic volumes. Finally she put the *Tsene-rene* aside, gathered her courage, and plucked one of her father's books from its shelf.

At first, reading it was like listening to a group of people all shouting at one another. There were words she didn't know, but she could guess at their meanings; she fetched a sheet of butcher paper, and wrote them down. Before long she was outlining, in Hebrew, her understanding of the competing schools of thought. She continued onto a second piece of paper, and then a third. She felt as though she were peering through a keyhole into a different world, one whose story could only be told in its own language—a language her father had handed her, piece by piece.

She stopped only when the room grew too dark to read. The sun had set; the Sabbath was over. Exhausted, exultant, she put her head down on her father's desk, and fell asleep.

When she woke, her father was watching her from the couch. In his hands were the notes she'd written. His eyes held a look of fondness that Kreindel had never seen there before.

"I fear I haven't been a good father to you," he said, his voice hoarse. "I've allowed you to become something that you weren't meant to be. But I also wonder if the Almighty has given me another gift, one I never expected."

From around his neck he removed the key to the bedroom. "Come," he said, and unlocked the door.

The bedroom was dark and close, the scent of earth overwhelming. At once, as though the key had unlocked the thought, Kreindel realized why it was so familiar: it was the smell of the construction pit beneath the unfinished bridge, where the tenement boys liked to play.

Her father put a match to the lamp, and at last the room was illumi-nated.

There was a man lying on her father's bed.

She jumped back, and might have screamed, but her father's hand clamped over her mouth. "*Shhh*," he hissed. "No one must know." She nodded, heart pounding, and he removed his hand.

The man was only partly there. One leg was missing, as well as the accompanying hip. He had two arms, but only one hand, and the arms themselves were like thick noodles, without joints or muscles. His face had depressions for eyes, a rough triangular nose, and a lipless line where a mouth ought to be. But he was, unquestionably, a man: tall and thick-chested, his solitary hand more than twice the span of Kreindel's own. She crept to the bedside as though afraid of waking him, placed a hand on his chest, and felt the cool, firm clay beneath her fingers.

"Do you know what this is?" her father asked.

"A golem," Kreindel breathed.

"Thea asked for my opinion on fur stoles this morning," said the Golem.

It was a clear winter night, cold and crisp. They were walking west along Broome Street, with the aim of heading north into Chelsea so the Jinni could see the enormous construction site at Seventh Avenue, the one destined to become a new train station. Four blocks of the Ten-derloin had been razed for the purpose, their residents, most of them Negroes, forced to find shelter elsewhere. The Golem had been angered at the unfairness of it; and while the Jinni agreed with the sentiment, he couldn't help but be overwhelmed by the scale and ambition of the proj-ect. He didn't want to argue about it, so he'd decided to keep quiet while she went on about Thea's quandary regarding mink versus ermine— were those colors or animals? Safer not to ask . . . Apparently the train station was to be entirely steel-framed, and the Jinni was intrigued by the possibilities—far more so than by the cast-iron facades here on Broome, which were poured and cooled in giant molds, a technique that bored him beyond measure. Why put all the artistry in the mold, and not in the iron itself? What was the point of working with iron if one did not truly *work* it?

Something the Golem had said managed to pierce through his musings. "Wait," he said. "An award? What award?"

"The Man of the Year, from the Lower East Side Merchants' Association," the Golem said again. "'For Enlarging Our Vision of Tomorrow's Bakery.' It's why Thea wants a stole, for the award luncheon. She thinks her usual coat is too dowdy, even though Selma said, and I agreed, that the—"

"But do you mean that *Moe* won this 'Man of the Year'?"

The Golem sighed. She'd tried to sneak Moe's award into the conversation when his attention was elsewhere, knowing that otherwise it was bound to start an argument—because the truth was that the startling success of the bakery's expansion was her own doing just as much as Moe's. Yes, the new ovens turned out twice as many goods as before, and the gleaming new display case gave the customers a full and tempting view of the day's selection—but it was the Golem's new hires who'd pushed the endeavor into greatness. She'd trained them in record time, and along the way they'd absorbed something of her manner as well, rolling and mixing with a crisp precision that was mesmerizing to watch. Once the Golem had noticed this effect, she'd suggested placing their worktables in a row at the front of the shop, so that all the customers could admire their skills as they waited. Moe had agreed with little thought, not caring at all where the tables went—and then, like everyone else, had been shocked by the result. Simply to watch the women work was an entertainment in itself. Passersby who'd never set foot in Radzin's would spy them through the plate-glass windows and be lured inside. A simple trip to the baker's, once a dull and ordinary errand, now had the feel of an exhibition, an event—and the customers, their spirits brightened, often bought more than they'd planned.

"Chava, that should be *your* award, not Moe's!" the Jinni said.

"Oh, that's not true," she replied at once. "The expansion was all Moe's idea, I never would've dared. And the girls deserve credit, too, they're such diligent workers—"

"Yes, because you trained them to be! You don't want to go about bragging, I understand—but if there are more customers per hour, *and* each customer is spending more—"

"Yes, I've done the calculations," she said, growing irritated.

But the Jinni wasn't finished. "Maybe Moe could've succeeded without you, but not like this. He certainly wouldn't have won that award. *You're* the one who 'enlarged their vision,' Chava. Not him."

"Oh, stop *needling* me. Why does it matter if he should win an award or not? It's not as though they'd make *me* their Man of the Year."

"But does he understand? Does he know that you're the reason?"

"He's begun to wonder," she muttered, "whether he simply has a natural talent for these things."

The Jinni snorted angrily. "Idiot."

"That's easy to say when you know something he doesn't. But why do I feel it's *me* you're angry with?"

"Because you seem content to let him think he's . . ." He waved his hands, searching.

"The 'cock of the walk'?"

"Yes, that. And perhaps you can't go to this association and say, *Excuse me, you're mistaken about Mr. Radzin.* But don't you wish that you could? Aren't you the least bit angry?"

She shook her head. "What good would my anger do?"

"None whatsoever! But it would be true, and honest, and understandable!"

"But I *can't!*" The words came out louder, sharper than she'd meant, echoing from the painted iron storefronts. She winced; then she said, "I can't wish that they knew the truth, or that I could show them what I'm capable of. I don't want to go to work every day resenting their ignorance. In the end, a man has given me less recognition than he ought— and that makes me no different from all the women who stand in line thinking about their own employers, how miserly they are with compliments and how quick to take the credit."

He shook his head. "It's not the same at all, Chava."

She was growing annoyed. "You're right. I'm far more fortunate. I won't get ill, or starve to death. I don't live in fear of a man's fists. I'm spared all of that."

"And in return, you only need to hide." His voice was bitter.

"Many of them are hiding, too, Ahmad."

"*I am not talking about them!*"

He'd shouted it loud enough that a nearby night-watchman, asleep on his stool behind a window, woke with a start and peered out at the street. Chagrined, the Golem put out a hand: *Lower your voice.*

"I'm talking about *you.*" He'd quieted, but he was still more angry than she'd seen him in some time. "You and me. We are different, Chava. We cannot be their drudges, or allow them to . . . to wipe their feet upon us, all in the name of 'hiding.' You let them rule you far too easily."

She'd stiffened at the word *drudges.* "That's all well and good, coming from *you.*"

His eyes narrowed. "And what does that mean?"

"Only that you have freedoms that I don't. You can choose to lock yourself away in your shop, and take no note of others' opinions, and speak as little to your neighbors as you wish, and all they will think is, *There goes Ahmad al-Hadid, that unsociable fellow.* What do you think would happen if I were to do the same?"

"They'd say, *There goes Chava Levy, that unsociable woman.*"

She snorted. "That is the *least* of what they'd call me. It's different for women, Ahmad—no, don't argue, just *listen.* If a man smiles at me, I must smile back, or else I am a shrew. If a woman mentions she's having a terrible day, I'm obligated to ask what the matter is, otherwise I'm arrogant and uncaring. Then *I* become the target of their anger, and it affects me whether I deserve it or not. If I were to act as you do, and alienate half the people I meet—how long do you think it would be before the noise grew unbearable?"

He frowned and looked away, as though trying to imagine what it would be like to hear the unspoken opinions of his neighbors as he passed them on the street. Not for the first time, the Golem wondered if it would change him in the least.

"I can't afford their anger," she said quietly. "You know that better than anyone."

He blew out an explosive breath, and scrubbed his face with his hands. Then he took a step toward her, reached out, and pulled her close. She put her arms around him; and for long and wordless minutes, they held each other.

"Have you seen the embossing hammer?" the Jinni asked the next morning.

Arbeely looked up from his workbench, already scowling. "No, I haven't," he said. "And our good rawhide mallet is missing, too. I assume they're both in the back, inside that tangled mess of wrought iron you're building."

"It isn't *my* fault if there isn't enough space—"

"If you want to go on with these experiments," the man spoke over him, "then please find another place to do it. It's interfering with our paid work."

The Jinni snorted. "Yes, our endlessly interesting paid work. Necklaces and earrings and reading-lamps, cover plates for electrical switches, the same old trinkets for Sam Hosseini to sell. I could make them in my—with my eyes shut," he said, seeming to catch himself.

Arbeely sighed, and put down his tracing pencil. "So you're bored," he said dryly.

"Yes," the Jinni said, crossing his arms. "I am bored."

"And this isn't to do with the weather, or a fight with Chava."

The Jinni shot him a contemptuous look.

"I was merely asking," Arbeely insisted, hurt. "It's been the case before."

"I know, I know." He rubbed the bridge of his nose, then dropped into Arbeely's desk-chair—the man winced as its springs let out a squawk—and rolled a cigarette, touched it, inhaled. "We went to Chelsea last night, to the construction pit for the new station," he said, through the smoke. "You should see it. They've built an entire narrow-gauge railroad just to haul the dirt up to the street. They're starting to lay the foundation, there are piles of girders everywhere, I've never seen so much steel . . . The river tunnels will connect straight to the concourse, all of it beneath the subway. It'll be a feat in itself."

"And then you came back here," Arbeely said, "to the reading-lamps and cover plates."

His partner nodded, his eyes elsewhere.

"People need such things," the man said gently. "Besides, we're tinsmiths. Not an engineering firm."

The Jinni was silent a moment. Then he got up from Arbeely's chair and disappeared into the back room, and returned a moment later with a short length of wrought iron. He sat down across from Arbeely and gripped the rod in one hand. A long pause, the familiar smell of heated metal—and the iron began to glow. He shifted his grip, the length of iron now between his palms, fingers laced above, like a gambler shuffling his deck. A quick push: and now his hands were cupped together, the iron vanished inside. A twist and a pull, and the rod stretched between his hands like glowing taffy. He brought the ends together, folded the iron and spun it, stretched it again: and now there were many strands, far thinner and finer, and for a moment Arbeely was a child in his mother's kitchen, watching her make the noodles for supper. Another dizzying series of folds, a spin—something flared inside his hands—

Swiftly the Jinni bent to the water-bucket at the end of the workbench. There was a startling clap of steam—and when he appeared again he was holding a hollow globe, perhaps six inches in diameter, made of dozens of thin and swirling filaments that all ran together seamlessly at its poles.

Arbeely took it and stared. There was a lightness to the globe, and a sense of motion, like a captured water-current. "What *is* it?" he said.

"A finial for a banister," the Jinni said. "Or for a bedpost, or a set of fireplace andirons. It could be a child's top. It might perch upon a gate. I could make all these things and more."

Arbeely laughed, suddenly giddy.

"It's time we enlarged our vision," the Jinni told him; and then he fetched his jacket, and left.

The street outside darkened as Arbeely sat in the shop, examining the precious globe by lamplight. Part of him expected it to vanish, like a fading enchantment—but it persisted, cool and real in his hand.

Enlarge our vision . . . They'd need more space. A factory floor, if possible. New equipment, a better forge. And privacy, a hidden room of some sort, for the Jinni to work his magic. They could call it a trade secret, but a landlord would grow suspicious, wouldn't he? Better to own the place outright, though of course that was impossible. Wasn't it?

From a desk drawer he fetched his private ledger, opened it to numbers that would've made his neighbors gasp: the result of long hours, simple habits, and a shining spark of luck that had burst into his life from an old copper flask. He'd spied his partner's ledger, knew that the numbers there were roughly the same as his own. But no, it still wouldn't be enough, he was letting his enthusiasm run away with himself—but *imagine* it . . .

At some point he put his head down atop the ledger; and when he opened his eyes again, the sun was shining. He stood, wiped at his eyes. His stomach growled. What was he still doing in the shop?

The swirling globe caught his eye, and he remembered.

He put the globe carefully in a drawer and went out to the street, where the morning was already underway, the sidewalks bustling with neighbors. Perhaps he'd go to the Faddouls', for a cup of coffee. And a word with Maryam, if she wasn't too busy.

He opened the coffee-house door—and Maryam caught his arm as though she'd been waiting for him. "Boutros," she said, "you play backgammon, don't you?" And before he could utter a word, she'd steered him to a table where one of her regular customers sat alone before a backgammon board, his usual opponent having succumbed to a toothache. Arbeely, an indifferent player at best, proceeded to lose three consecutive games while the man complained at length about his brother-in-law, a lazy oaf who smoked his narghile all day long and sent his wife out to earn in his stead. And now it seemed that her job was in jeopardy, for she worked at the lace-maker's in the Amherst—Arbeely knew the Amherst, didn't he? Yes, the loft building at the corner of Washington and Carlisle. Well, it seemed the owner had been ruined in the "Panic" in October, and was faced with selling a number of his properties at a loss. No doubt the Amherst would be snapped up by some faceless financier who'd see fit to raise the rents. It was a shame, the man said as he moved a checker across the bar, that so few of the buildings in Little Syria were owned by actual Syrians; it would be such a boon for the neighborhood businesses . . .

Arbeely lifted his eyes from the board. Maryam was watching him from the far corner, smiling with excitement.

In the spring of 1908, the elders of the Forsyth Street Synagogue gathered for a secret meeting to discuss the problem of Rabbi Altschul.

None of them could say exactly when their rabbi's odd behavior had begun. He was a holy man, of course, and a touch of dreaminess or self-absorption was to be expected—but lately he seemed to be coming entirely untethered. He'd developed the habit of wandering off the dais during the Saturday service, and more than once had to be guided back by a congregant. At a recent Hebrew lesson, he'd startled the boys by closing his eyes and chanting, trancelike, in what might have been Aramaic. And what no one wished to mention, but was foremost in their minds, was that their rabbi had begun to exude a terrible odor, a graveyard stench of soil and decay. No one could tell whether it was coming from his garments, or the man himself.

A delegation was sent to his apartment, to discuss matters. They knocked on the door, but no answer came. One of them bent to peer through the keyhole—and suddenly the door opened. In the threshold stood the rabbi's daughter, young Kreindel, her blouse and skirt entirely caked with mud. It streaked her face, and daubed the ends of her braids, and coated her arms up to the elbows.

"Please come in," Kreindel said. "My father wishes to speak with you."

Stunned, unsure, they crept into the apartment. The door closed behind them.

A little while later, the delegation returned to the synagogue and reassured the others that all would be well. Rabbi Altschul, they said, had indeed taken ill, but was now recovering under his daughter's care. In the meantime, he was not to be disturbed. All sighed in relief, glad that an end was in sight. Then the men of the delegation all went home and fell deeply asleep, and woke with no recollection at all of having gone to the Altschuls' apartment, or of what had happened inside.

Now, Rabbi Altschul and Kreindel could devote themselves entirely to their task. Kreindel, it seemed, had a gift for artistry, and had taken it upon herself to resculpt the golem's crude features and rag-doll limbs, giving them a more lifelike appearance. Her father recalled that Malke, too, had shown some talent for art, and had liked to sketch the view from their window, or a bowl of winter oranges. He'd often scolded his wife for wasting time in this manner, but now he silently thanked her for the gift she'd passed to their daughter.

There were limits, though, to Kreindel's abilities. The ears she'd made for their golem were slightly mismatched, and his hair was sculpted all of one piece, like a cap atop his head. His eyes, too, gave them some trouble, until Kreindel went up to the roof and came back with two abandoned marbles, one a deep indigo, the other a softer blue with swirls of white. Rabbi Altschul installed them in the empty eye-sockets, where they fit as though made for the purpose.

It was a good deal of effort for what was only meant to be a trial, their first attempt at bringing a golem to life. Still, Rabbi Altschul wanted to make it as safe and thorough as possible. He had no wish to subject their neighbors to the same fate as their medieval forebears in Prague, whose golem had turned upon the very population it was meant to protect. He would bring their creation to life, test its abilities, and watch it carefully for any violent tendencies. Once he was satisfied of their success, he would destroy the golem and take the books across the Atlantic to Lithuania, so that he might deliver his formula to the Vilna Rav himself.

"And I will come with you," Kreindel told him.

He tried to protest, saying that the voyage would be long and difficult. "I'm not afraid," she told him. "The Almighty has chosen you for this path, and placed me at your side. I will be your support, as Miriam was for Moses."

At last her father agreed. Neither of them wished to say the obvious: that Lev had grown so weak it was doubtful he could make the journey alone. The smallest exertions tired him; he could barely stomach any food at all, and slept only fitfully, consumed by dreams. His eyesight, too, had deteriorated so that he saw everything through a curtain of golden sparks. He'd forbidden Kreindel from reading the books, or even touching them—but now he copied out the command to bring the golem to life, and told her to memorize it, in case his eyesight should fail him completely. She did so, then burned the paper in the grate, and went to sit at the golem's bedside, next to her father.

"What shall we name him?" she asked.

Her father smiled. "You never met your grandfather Yossele, of blessed memory," he said. "He was a large man, like this one—but gentle, not brutish. Let us name him Yossele, and hope that he adopts my father's better qualities as well."

6.

June 7, 1908
Star of America

AMHERST BUILDING CHANGES HANDS TO SYRIAN
BUSINESSMEN.

Ironworks Opens on Ground Floor.

For evidence that the tradesmen of Little Syria are at last
gaining a well-deserved foothold in this city, one may point
to the "Grand Reopening" of Arbeely & Ahmad, All Metals,
at its new home in the Amherst Building on Washington
Street. The partners Boutros Arbeely and Ahmad al-Hadid
are now the building's joint owners, as well as the occupants
of its first floor. Despite this increase in the shop's size, the
two remain its sole employees, and will continue to produce
their goods through the work of their own hands.

Much of the neighborhood came out yesterday for the cel-
ebration. Visitors were invited inside the shop to view a selection of the duo's creations, as well as the instruments of
the trade. After a brief speech by Mr. Arbeely, in which he
thanked his neighbors for their support, the shop's new forge
was lit by Mr. al-Hadid at noon precisely.

The Amherst sat upon the southwest corner of Washington and Carlisle, the lone loft building on a long, thin block of tenements. Five stories tall, it stood above its neighbors, square and stolid, built for utility
rather than elegance. Its front door faced Washington Street between

banks of plate-glass windows, the lone word *AMHERST* carved into the lintel.

Inside, a plaster-and-lathe partition split the ground floor roughly into halves. To the north was the showroom, where prospective clients might examine the wares and make their selection. And to the south, opposite the showroom, was the workshop: a vast, cavernous space of heat and shadows, the new forge glowing dimly at its end.

The forge was the Jinni's pride and joy. It was roughly the size of a dinner-table, and sat snugly in a bed of asbestos-lined concrete, made to measure. In place of the cumbersome old bellows was an electric fan capable of the finest gradations of air-flow. The chimney-hood was stainless steel, and polished to a blinding sheen. When burning at full capacity, the forge made a luxuriant rumbling like distant thunder, a noise that was felt as much as heard.

Buying the Amherst had changed everything. At last, the Jinni had the space and the solitude to immerse himself properly in his work. No more misplaced tools; no Arbeely constantly griping at his elbow. Now the man sat beside the showroom entrance, half a floor's length away, utterly absorbed in managing the business and the Amherst both. He'd even gotten over his hatred of the 'phone, and spent hours at a time shouting down the line to plumbers and glaziers and suppliers. In fact, there were days when the partners were kept so busy in their separate tasks that they barely exchanged words at all.

But on this warm August morning, Arbeely seemed encumbered only by a sheet of stationery that he sat frowning at, pen in hand. By the Jinni's count, this was the man's third attempt at writing the letter, the first two having been tossed in the wastebasket. As the Jinni approached Arbeely's desk, the man crossed out a line, then put down the pen with a frustrated sigh, crumpled the paper into a ball, and sent it to join its brethren.

"What's that you're writing?" the Jinni asked.

"Nothing," Arbeely said, too quickly. He ran his hand over the desk blotter, as though sweeping away the remnants of his thoughts. "Just a letter home."

The Jinni eyed his partner. Arbeely had gone home to Zahleh after the purchase of the Amherst, to see to his mother's health and his family's property. He'd returned in oddly changeable spirits, ebullient one moment and downcast the next—but had said little of the trip itself, only that his mother and aunts had fed him fit to bursting. At the time the Jinni had attributed his strange moods to the Amherst's purchase, and the general upheaval that had gone along with it. Now, though, he wondered.

I'm obligated to ask what the matter is, he heard the Golem say. *Otherwise I'm arrogant and uncaring.*

"I'm going up to the roof," he said. "Care to join me?"

The man sighed, clearly daunted at the thought of the climb in the August heat, but then nodded. He opened a biscuit tin upon his desk, and pocketed a large handful of its contents. "Can't disappoint the children," he said, and gestured to the showroom door. "After you."

They passed through the simple framed doorway, and into an iron fairyland. For weeks Arbeely had painstakingly organized the showroom into individual sections, grouping like with like: gates and folding screens, bed-frames and dressing mirrors, lamps and candelabra—only to come in the morning of the reopening and find that the Jinni had rearranged it all in the night. Now, the men walked a foot-path bordered by knee-high fleur-de-lys fencing that wound past cushioned chaises longues backed by pierced screens, all lit from above by elaborate strings of lights. An ornamented gate opened to a dining table laid with wrought cutlery; a curving bench encircled the trunk of an iron oak, its knotted branches hung with lanterns and wind-chimes. A bed-frame even sheltered beneath the oak's branches, complete with sheets and pillows and a counterpane strewn with tin-plate leaves. This last was immodest enough that Arbeely had sputtered and gone red to the ears—yet even he had to admit that, its hints of hedonism aside, the Jinni's arrangement was far more appealing than his own.

At the end of the showroom was the heavy door to the stairwell. They opened it and began their climb, passing each of their tenants in turn. The lace factory took up both the second and third floors; beyond the open doors were dozens of girls all bent over the clattering

looms, their hands moving swiftly back and forth. On the fourth floor
was the biscuit factory, smelling as always of sugar and vanilla. Here,
white-aproned workers gathered on the landing to smoke cigarettes and
fan themselves, their faces red with heat. Their foreman was among
them, and he greeted Arbeely with enthusiasm. Arbeely had endeared
himself to the man by personally rerouting a tricky gas line, and in his
gratitude the foreman seemed determined to keep his landlords stocked
with a lifetime's worth of biscuits. They reassured the foreman that
they had plenty, then bade him a good day and passed the fifth and final
floor, a cigar factory that added the spiced tang of tobacco to the already
warm and heavy air. Unlike the bakers, though, the cigar-men were a
laconic lot, and only nodded as the pair went by.

At last the door at the top opened into the sunshine—and now the
children who'd been playing marbles and jacks on the Amherst roof
sprang up and converged upon Arbeely. The man grinned, his poor spirits forgotten, and began to pull biscuits from his pockets like a conjurer.

The Jinni took up his usual station by the rooftop's edge, well out
of the way, and rolled a cigarette. He liked to watch Arbeely in these
moments. Odd moods aside, the man seemed more purposeful these
days, more certain of himself. When Sam Hosseini or Thomas Maloof
stopped in for a chat, there was a new measure of respect for him in their
eyes. Maryam, too, had watched Arbeely with pride at the Grand Reopening; but when she'd looked to the Jinni, her smile had cooled, as
always. At times he wondered what selfless deed or sacrifice it would take
to earn Maryam's regard. He suspected that whatever it was, it would
be beyond him.

Soon the children returned to their games, the biscuits exhausted.
Arbeely brushed the crumbs from his hands and came to stand beside
the Jinni, looking out over the thin row of rooftops to the docklands
beyond. Neither spoke for long minutes. The dark and faraway look had
returned to Arbeely's eyes. What *was* bothering the man? The Jinni
stubbed out his cigarette, gathered his resolve—

"How are those finials coming?" Arbeely asked suddenly.

His resolve fled like a startled animal. "Halfway done," he said. "The
last few were too brittle—the mix was wrong, I think."

The man nodded. "We'd better get to it, then." And back down the stairwell they went, to find a well-dressed husband and wife standing nervously at Arbeely's desk, as though afraid the denizens of Little Syria might eat them while they waited. Quickly Arbeely ushered them into the showroom, and the Jinni was left alone.

It was well enough, he decided. As the man had said, there was work to do. He turned from Arbeely's desk, and went into the storeroom.

The storeroom ran the length of the workshop. It was perhaps twenty feet wide, though the high ceiling made it seem much narrower, a windowed canyon. He passed racks of graded iron bars, tubs of powders, half-finished commissions, the dumbwaiter that brought up coal from the cellar below. At the end of the storeroom, a thick black curtain hung behind the shelves of supplies. If one didn't know it was there, it would be easy to mistake for the wall itself.

He slipped between the shelves, ducked behind the curtain, and entered his private dominion.

It was a small, square room set into the building's corner, its windows blackened over to keep the children in the tenement yard from peering in. Already the black paint had flaked here and there, admitting crumbs of sunlight. The forge lay on the other side of the wall, only a few feet away, sending its heat through the plaster. The Jinni had brought over a number of rugs and cushions from his apartment, along with a few old pierced lanterns, more for decoration than to see by. A stack of wrought iron bars sat nearby, along with a tub of water to douse his creations and a net to fish them out again. Arbeely had taken to calling the space *your treasure-cave*; there'd been a joke involving the word *sesame*, but the Jinni had decided not to ask. The noise of the tenement yard intruded at times, especially on Mondays, when the women queued at the pump for wash-water—but in all it was as comfortable a space as he could wish.

He sat on a cushion, drew a bar of iron from the pile, and set to work.

At Radzin's Bakery, the day was coming to a close. Moe Radzin raked the ashes in the ovens while Thea assured the line of customers that of course there were enough challahs left; her girls always made plenty for everybody. The Golem was wiping down a worktable when there came a knock at the locked front door. A young woman stood there, waving through the glass.

"Selma!" Thea cried, and rushed to unlatch the door.

The Golem smiled. She, too, was glad to see Selma Radzin; the girl's presence relieved the anxiety that had become Thea's constant companion ever since Selma's contentious move to Astoria. *She can't stay at home, like other girls?* Thea had wailed—knowing, if only dimly, that it was her own overbearing habits that had set the girl on her path. In the end, Selma had won the battle, but she still returned home for Sabbath supper every week, at her mother's demand.

The girl took off her hat, and suffered Thea's usual rain of kisses, Moe's gruff peck on her cheek. She turned to greet the Golem—and paused, a puzzled line upon her forehead. *Why,* the girl thought, *does Chava never seem to age?*

A moment later, Selma had pushed the thought away and was telling her parents the news of the week, the doings of her friends and roommates. But her brief and startled thought still echoed in the Golem's mind, the tolling of a bell that signaled disaster.

She didn't linger over good-byes, but hurried to her boardinghouse, where she fetched her small hand mirror, sat on the bed, and gazed for a long while at herself. The wide-set eyes, the nose that curved under at the tip. The waved hair, cut to brush her shoulders. All of it exactly the same as the day she was made. And now someone had glimpsed the truth, if only the barest corner of it.

At once she wondered how she could've been so foolish. Why hadn't she planned for this? Had she expected to stay at the bakery forever, without anyone noticing? Perhaps she could use cosmetics to imitate wrinkles and gray hair, as actors did for the stage—but no, that would never pass scrutiny. And now others besides Selma would notice, they were bound to. A customer might remark to a friend, *You know, that Chava never seems to get older;* and their friend would reply, *I was just thinking that myself.* Curiosity would turn into suspicion—and the longer she stayed, the worse it would grow. Would she have to leave Radzin's? But where else could she possibly go? The bakery and its rhythms were the underpinnings of her life; she'd have to uproot herself and begin again from nothing—

There was a *crunch* as the mirror's wooden handle splintered in her grip.

Quickly she set the mirror down. She couldn't stay in her tiny room a moment longer, she needed to be out and walking—but the Jinni wouldn't come until midnight at the earliest. Outside, the evening light slanted across the rooftops. These were the last acceptable minutes for a woman to be out alone. If she was going to leave, it must be now.

She fastened her cloak around her shoulders and walked to Little Syria, trying to hurry as inconspicuously as possible. Even so, a few of his neighbors glanced at her curiously as she entered his building—*That's the Bedouin's lady, isn't it?* Adding to her dismay, there was no reply to her knock, no light beneath his door. Most likely he was at the shop; he and Arbeely had spent the months since the Amherst's purchase drowning in new work. But if she marched down the street to the Amherst she'd only draw more attention to herself. She'd simply have to wait.

She let herself in with her spare key, took off her cloak, and frowned. As usual, he'd left his apartment in a shambles. His wardrobe stood open, a pair of trousers dangling from the hamper inside. Unpaired cuff-links lay scattered across a small dresser; on the bed, the pillows were heaped together, the bedclothes mussed. Sometimes she thought he did it deliberately, to set himself against her own exactitude. She would *not* tidy up, she told herself; it was his apartment, and his mess. But the disorder grated at her agitated mind, and soon enough she was pairing the cuff-links and hanging away the trousers, lifting the heavy mattress one-handed to fold the sheets tightly around the corners. He'd be angry with her, but for now that seemed the lesser of two evils, if it allowed her to keep calm. Besides, what else was she to *do* with herself while she waited?

"Staying late tonight?"

The Jinni looked up from his work. Arbeely had stuck his head around the curtain, and now stood squinting into the darkness.

"I think I must," the Jinni said. "But I've made good progress. I'll have the rest by tomorrow." He handed one of the finials to Arbeely: an elongated twist of filaments that rose to a single thin point, a stylized flame rendered in iron.

Arbeely admired it, nodding, but his thoughts clearly were elsewhere. Watching him in the glow of the lamps, the Jinni couldn't help noticing the silver that had begun to pepper the man's backswept hair, the fine new lines that had appeared on his face. It was disconcerting to watch humans age.

"This is excellent," the man said, and handed back the finial. "Well, good night."

"Good night." And then, on impulse, "Arbeely . . ." But he'd waited too long, and the man was gone, the curtain rippling behind him. The Jinni sighed to himself, and went back to work.

It was perhaps ten o'clock when he finished the last finial. The building was silent, the street less so: it was a warm night, and the tenement yard was still half full of families, the women chatting and scolding their children while the men played backgammon by lantern-light, all waiting for their rooms to cool so they might sleep. He banked the forge and hung away his apron, then paused by the door. Arbeely's desk was bathed in streetlight; the wastebasket sat beside it, unemptied. He regarded it for a moment, then withdrew the ball of crumpled paper nearest the top, smoothed it out, and read:

> Rafkah,
>   I must apologize. I ought not to have raised both our hopes. Please believe me when I say that the failing is entirely mine. I must be honest with you now, as I was not in Zahleh, and tell you that I have decided I will never marry. There is a secret that I cannot divulge, not even to you, for it concerns another man's life and I haven't the right to tell it. You might insist that you would enter into this confidence as well, for the sake of a marriage—but it has been a difficult burden at times, one I hesitate to share with someone I

Here the sentence, and the letter, had been abandoned.

The Jinni crumpled the paper again and replaced it in the waste-

basket, wishing fervently that his curiosity hadn't gotten the better
of him. What was he supposed to do with the knowledge that he'd
spoiled Arbeely's chances at love? No, he hadn't failed to notice the
man's perpetual bachelorhood, or the way that he seemed to pile work
upon himself, leaving room for little else. He'd merely decided that it
was Arbeely's life to live, and left it at that. Now he wanted to shout
at the man: *I didn't ask you to free me from the flask! Tell the world if you
like!* Unfair, he knew, and uncharitable. He'd stop at his apartment,
he decided, and change into a fresh shirt, and go for a long and solitary
walk before he reached the Golem's boardinghouse. It would give him
time to calm himself, and consider what he might say to the man in the
morning.

He reached his building, and was nearly at his door when he heard
a flutter of eager footsteps from the apartment opposite. He cringed as
the door opened—and yes, there was his neighbor Alma Hazboun,
wearing a satin dressing-gown and what looked to be little else beneath
it. Her hair was loose and mussed, her pupils enormous in the dim
light.

"Oh," she said, making a poor show of surprise. "It's you."

"Good evening, Mrs. Hazboun," he replied warily. He'd complained
about Alma to Arbeely, and learned that she was notorious in the
neighborhood. *Your bad luck to live across the hall from her,* the man had
said.

She stepped into the hall, blocking his path. "I've told you, call me
Alma." Her words were slurred. "Won't you come in?"

"No, thank you."

"My husband is away." Her mouth curled into a smile. "I'll cook you
a hot meal."

"I'm not hungry," he said.

"You *always* say no." She attempted a coy pout. "But you like that
other girl well enough, the one in your apartment."

The Jinni frowned. "Beg pardon?"

"*She's in your apartment,*" Alma said, more loudly. "Your Jewess, the
tall girl who dresses like a schoolteacher. I saw her go by earlier."

She'd come alone, at night? What crisis had driven her to such lengths? He shouldered past Alma—she made a noise of protest—and put a hand on his doorknob. It was unlocked. The Golem was mere feet away. She had, of course, heard everything.

He braced himself and opened the door.

She was at the far window, staring down into the street as though she'd been standing there for hours. It was her skirts that betrayed her: they still swayed at her ankles, as though she'd rushed to the spot only a moment before.

He closed the door, took a few careful steps toward her. "Chava?"

"I'm sorry," she muttered. "Something happened at the bakery, and I wanted to see you. I didn't mean to . . . I oughtn't have come." She still hadn't turned around.

"She's an opium fiend, Chava," he said. "And she has a considerable reputation."

"I know." There was a touch of impatience in her voice. Of course she'd sensed the opium, along with the woman's lust. Likely she'd also realized that this was only the latest installment in their frequent encounters. He stood braced for accusations.

She turned at last to face him. "Do you also know that her husband refuses to divorce her?"

He blinked, confused.

"She's desperate to get away from him. She hopes that if she can lower herself enough, he won't want anything to do with her. And you're an unmarried man, without a family to tear apart."

He recalled, now, the hints of old bruises he'd seen on Alma's arms. He'd assumed it had to do with her habit. Puzzled, he said, "Are you defending the woman who just tried to bed me?"

"Of course not, she shouldn't have done that. But she's trapped, and she's in pain."

He felt blindsided, off balance. "Then what exactly are you accusing me of?"

"You refuse to see the people around you," she said, anger in her eyes. "This woman is your neighbor, yet you consider her nothing but a nuisance with a *reputation*. You, who don't even believe in monogamy!"

Now he, too, was growing angry. "And what would you have me do,

Chava? I'm supposed to be a member of this society, am I not? Everyone else considers her a nuisance, and therefore so do I!"

She folded her arms. "Who lives on this floor, other than the Hazbouns?"

"I beg your pardon?"

"Your other neighbors, this 'everyone else' who sets the example for you. Name five of them, please. No, three."

This was growing ludicrous. "Elias Shama, next door," he said. "Marcus—" No, he realized, Marcus Mina had been the prior tenant. The young man who lived there now was . . . who? The Jinni could picture him, but had never learned his name. He thought harder. The man next to the Hazbouns had married and moved to Brooklyn and been replaced by an elderly couple who only called each other *habibi* and *habibti* in his hearing. The family two doors down was the Naders, but they must've left; he hadn't heard their piano in quite some time. Finally he remembered the boy at the end of the hall whose mother was constantly yelling, *Rami, come back this instant!* "Rami," he said.

She raised an eyebrow. "*Rami?*"

Exasperated, he said, "I am barely ever here! And can I help it if they move so often? I learn a name, and they vanish!" It was the truth, he realized: at some point he'd grown inured to the ever-changing faces, and had simply stopped asking. And yet they all seemed to know who *he* was. *The Bedouin. Arbeely's strange partner. The one who walks the rooftops, with his lady-friend.* "You wish impossible things of me, Chava," he told her. "I don't have your talents. I have no doubt that Alma leads a troubled life, but when she offers herself to me in a hallway, all I see is a woman who wants something I'm not allowed to give her."

The Golem's eyes widened. "'Not *allowed*'?"

He closed his eyes, fighting back a curse. He knew he ought to reverse track, to correct his poor choice of words—and yet he couldn't. He'd had enough of being shamed for one night. "Is that not so?" he said. "If I've mistaken our promise, please tell me, and I'll seduce every woman on this street."

"That's not amusing, Ahmad."

"When I came in," he said, "I had the distinct impression that you'd been standing at the door, listening."

Her chin lifted. "I came to the door because I'd heard your voice in the hallway."

"So you were coming to greet me? Unaccompanied, in my apartment, in full view of a neighbor who stood only feet away?"

"Of course not. I only wanted to confirm that it was you."

He smirked. "These are thin walls, and you have exceptional hearing. There isn't a spot in this room where you couldn't recognize my voice. But what you could *not* do at a distance was look into Alma Hazboun's mind, deeply enough to be certain I'd never accepted her advances. For that, you'd need to get as close as possible."

Guilt and defiance warred on her face. "Can you blame me? Her thoughts were rather explicit. I couldn't tell if they were fantasies or memories, because of the opium."

"And if instead you'd merely waited and asked me for the truth— would you have believed my answer? Believed it *absolutely*, without her thoughts to confirm it?"

She started to speak, hesitated for only a moment—but it was enough.

He made a harsh noise and turned away from her. "I'll never prove myself to you. You'd pry my mind open like an oyster if you could. *You* are responsible for your fears and your distrust, Chava, not I. If you were a jinniyeh—" He caught himself, stopped.

Her eyes had gone wide. "Ahmad, what? If I were a jinniyeh, *what*?"

But he only stood there, radiating frustration.

She gave an angry laugh. "There, you see? You insist that I trust you, and then you refuse to speak! You dangle riddles for me to lunge at, but you tell me *nothing*!" And she strode past him and into the hall, slamming the door behind her.

This is not my fault, he thought. *I've done everything she's asked of me, but still she insists on doubting, when I am blameless!*

He looked around at the empty apartment, which now chided him with its neatness. She hadn't even told him what had brought her to

Little Syria. His gaze fell on the precisely made bed—and her cloak, lying on top of the coverlet. Left behind, in her urge to get away.

Cursing, he grabbed it and went after her.

At last the Altschuls' golem was complete.

Father and daughter made their final preparations in an air of tense excitement. Kreindel packed a small carpet-bag, light enough for her to carry. The precious books sat ready in their suitcase. There was a steamship leaving for Hamburg the next afternoon, and enough money put aside for a pair of third-class tickets. They'd wait until the tenement was asleep—and then they would test their creation.

Yet there were still contingencies to consider. The golem might not come to life on the first attempt; the synagogue elders might choose the wrong moment to visit their convalescing rabbi. And so, in his caution, Rabbi Altschul wrote a brief message to the synagogue president, requesting another week of seclusion and recovery. He couldn't risk delivering it himself, and so he gave it to Kreindel. "Return quickly," he told her. "There's still much to do."

The tenement hallway smelled of wood-smoke, and Kreindel wondered if autumn had arrived. But outside it was a summer night, warm and quiet. She scurried across the empty street and unlocked the synagogue door, then walked through the echoing sanctuary to the president's office, and placed the note upon his desk.

And then she hesitated. Here in the darkened synagogue, she felt suddenly alone and frightened. Her father was deathly ill, and she was eleven years old. How could she possibly guide him to the Vilna Rav when she'd never once left the Lower East Side? Would he even survive the trip? What would she do if he didn't?

Tears filled her eyes—but she wiped them away. Her father was a holy man, and the Almighty had set him on this course. She would not be so faithless as to doubt their purpose.

Leaving the note where it was, Kreindel crept back through the synagogue and opened the door—and only then did she see the rising smoke, and hear the cries of the gathering crowd.

The Golem was halfway home when she realized she'd forgotten her cloak.

At first she considered turning around. To be out alone this late, in only her shirtwaist and skirt, was tantamount to solicitation. But she couldn't bear the thought of going back and knocking shamefacedly on his door; and so she kept on, hurrying north on Broadway, past shuttered shops that glowed beneath the streetlights.

This is not my fault, she thought angrily. But how could she explain to him what she'd felt from Mrs. Hazboun? The swell of excitement, hope, and lust; the image of him naked in her bed; the dark despair that lay beneath it, the fear of her husband's fists—all of it colored by the opium that made her thoughts move like batter poured from a bowl. And then—

Your Jewess, the tall girl who dresses like a schoolteacher—

—she'd seen herself: a spindly, unattractive woman in buttoned boots and a dowdy cloak, her pale face pinched and querulous. A caricature, and a deeply uncharitable one—but on the heels of the woman's fantasies, it had seemed a confirmation of all her self-doubts. *He'll tire of you, and break his promise,* the image seemed to say. *It's only a matter of time.* It had wounded her; and since she couldn't lash out at Alma Hazboun, she'd lashed out at the Jinni instead.

If you were a jinniyeh. Had he ever so much as said the word before?

She turned east onto Grand, wincing as a driver whistled at her from a passing wagon. She doubted anyone would honestly mistake her for a prostitute, but the policemen must make their quotas. She imagined spending the night in a cell, and explaining her tardiness to the Radzins in the morning.

At Lafayette she heard footsteps from the south: quick and determined, timed to intersect with hers. Afraid, she reached out, but felt nothing—and thus knew exactly who it was, even before she turned and saw him there, holding her cloak.

Her first reaction was stark relief, but this only angered her further. She kept on, increasing her already considerable pace.

"Chava," he said, hurrying to catch up to her. "Wait."

"I don't want to talk to you."

A look of genuine hurt flashed across his face. It tugged at her conscience, and she might've relented—except that now a strange fear crept into her mind. She needed to get out, to wake the children and the neighbors; to grab her wedding photograph from the wall and the silver-plated candlesticks, and hurry down the stairwell—

Confused, she looked up—and saw the smoke, the glow in the sky.

"Chava?" But then he, too, came alert.

Something on Forsyth Street was burning.

The fire had begun on the second floor with a smoldering cigarette, its owner waking to find his bedroom in flames. An open window then beckoned the fire into an air-shaft, which drew it upward, toward the roof. The building was an "Old Law" tenement, built before the reforms, and so there were no iron staircases or brick partitions to slow the fire's progress—only old, dry wood from one end of the building to the other.

The Golem rounded the corner onto Forsyth, the Jinni close behind. They saw it all at once: the growing crowd, the billowing darkness, the flickers of orange and red. Residents were pouring onto the street in their night-clothes, coughing and crying, carrying children, featherbeds, dining-chairs. Their terror pulled at the Golem, straining what was left of her composure. She needed to help, but *how*—

"*Father!*"

The cry came from a small, thin girl who stood nearby in a synagogue doorway. Her fear ripped through the Golem's mind, and in its wake was an image: a bearded, emaciated man huddled in a parlor corner, surrounded by flames. He was ill, and helpless; and she had to save him.

The girl dashed across the street, slipped through the crowd, and ran into the burning building. And in the next moment, unable to stop herself, the Golem was running after her.

7.

In the stairwell, Kreindel covered her face with her smock and kept on climbing.

She was alone now, the last of the residents having run past her. The smoke grew thicker with each step, and by the time she reached the fourth floor she could barely breathe. The door to the hallway was closed, the knob too hot to touch. She grasped it with her skirt, and pushed.

The heat struck her bodily. She inhaled in shock and began to cough. She could see only a few feet ahead; beyond that was a reddish darkness. The sound of the flames was that of a nearby engine, or a crowd of men all muttering at once.

Father. She had to reach him.

She took a step, and then another.

Someone behind the Golem was calling her name.

She ignored it and kept on running, then threaded her way into the crowd. Men and women were staggering down the steps, rags clutched to their faces. A man at the top blocked her path, saying, "Lady, whatever's up there ain't—"

"Let me pass."

She barely recognized her own voice. It was too deep, and drained of all musicality, her guise of humanity slipping away. The man drew aside in fear, and she was through.

"Chava!" the Jinni called again—but it was too late, she'd disappeared into the building. He was trying to push through the crowd after her when a police wagon arrived, its siren splitting the air. The men jumped out at once and swarmed the sidewalk, linking arms to form a cordon that herded the bystanders into the street. The crowd thickened, grew solid as a wall.

Stuck among them, the Jinni craned his neck, watching. Any moment now, the Golem would emerge from the smoking doorway, the girl coughing in her arms.

Step by step Kreindel pushed her way through the searing heat.

One door, two, three: their apartment. Locked. Her father had locked it behind her, out of habit. She hadn't thought to bring her key.

She pounded on the door, then threw herself against it, but still it held. She began to sob, picturing her father lying just beyond her reach—or trapped in the bedroom, with the golem they'd worked so hard to build—

The golem. She knew the command to wake him, had memorized it. Would it work, with the door between them? She had to try.

She took as large a breath as she could, bent her mind to the figure lying on the bed, and shouted the command, her voice cracking.

The Golem climbed the stairwell, searching outward with her mind, ignoring the flames that had begun to lick at the treads. Was the girl on the second floor? The third? Too slow, no time for mistakes! *There*—the fourth floor, where the hallway door stood half open.

She walked through it, and into a roaring kiln.

Instantly her body began to dry and harden. She advanced into the hallway, pushing against a growing stiffness. The girl was ahead of her somewhere. "Hello?" the Golem called, her voice rough with smoke.

A quick flicker of red set the hallway aglow. She saw the faint outline of the girl, heard her shout something above the noise of the fire—

A strange thrill ran through the Golem. Something was waking nearby, and it felt like all of springtime arriving at once. Wood burned all around her, yet she could smell rain-drenched earth. She stepped forward, unthinking, searching for the source—

And then cried out as the floor gave way beneath her.

The Jinni watched the empty doorway, his worry growing with each passing moment. At last he pushed forward, to the cordon line. "Get back, you," a patrolman called.

"My friend is in there," he called back—just as, with a great groaning of wood, the staircase inside the doorway collapsed.

A plume of smoke and ash billowed down the stoop and onto the sidewalk. The crowd recoiled, nearly pushing the Jinni off his feet. The orderly cordon dissolved; policemen stumbled into each other, coughing and wiping their eyes.

Stunned, the Jinni turned around. The street was a churning bedlam. Neighbors along the block had dragged their own belongings outside in case the fire should spread, stacking the sidewalks with chairs and suitcases, bassinets and books. A fire engine swept around the corner, bell clanging, spectators jumping clear of the team. Firemen swarmed from the engine's side, raising ladders, hauling hoses. An axe thudded into the side of the building. Flames belched from the wound.

Standing amid the chaos, the Jinni felt the first true touch of panic.

Kreindel crouched at her apartment door, straining to listen.

Had the command worked? She was growing dizzy, her vision fading at the edges. For a moment she thought she heard a woman's voice calling out above the flames—but then there was a giant cracking noise, and the hallway shuddered as though some part of it had collapsed.

"*Papa!*" she screamed. And then, "*Yossele!*"

A thud of heavy footsteps—and the door was wrenched off its hinges.

He filled the doorway, even larger than he'd seemed on the bed. For a moment, despite everything, she could only stare at him. He gazed calmly back, mismatched eyes glinting in the firelight.

She pushed past him into the apartment, screaming for her father.

He was on the parlor floor, wheezing thinly. He'd been trying to carry the wooden suitcase to the door when the smoke and strain overcame him. The suitcase lay nearby, latches broken open, its contents spilled onto the rug: the five precious volumes and, Kreindel's heart caught to see, the *Tsene-rene*.

She crouched over him, crying. He opened his eyes, saw first his daughter, and then, looming behind her, the creature she'd awakened. His eyes widened; he gasped painfully for air.

"*Hide*," he whispered.

The light left his eyes. With a sigh, his breath trickled away.

Strong fingers grabbed Kreindel around her waist.

"Wait!" she cried—but for Yossele, the threat to his master was stronger than her command. He lifted her effortlessly, cradling her like a baby, and strode to the door. One last glimpse of her father—and then he was gone.

There was barely any air left in the hallway, and Kreindel struggled to breathe in thin sips. Yossele turned left, toward the front stairwell—but stopped almost at once. Kreindel peered down and saw the gigantic hole in the hallway floor, the flames in its depths. "Other way," she whispered. "The yard." He turned around and ran down the hallway, the floor shuddering at each step.

The back stairwell was still mercifully whole. Cinders and ash fell about them as they emerged into the yard. She could hear the sirens and shouts on the other side of the building, the spray of the water-hoses. Yossele set her down and stood, towering over her. His skin was grayish in the moonlight; she could see fingerprints, here and there, in the clay. He watched her with the eyes she'd given him, waiting for a command.

"Hide," she croaked, echoing her father. She pointed across the yard to the alley, and the construction pit for the unfinished bridge beyond. "There, in the water. Don't let anyone see you. I'll call for you when it's safe. Go."

At once Yossele turned and ran, the deep drumbeat of his footfalls echoing behind him.

She watched until he'd disappeared, then staggered out to Chrystie and circled the burning building, heading toward the crowd. Her face felt as tight as a grape-skin; her eyes were swollen to slits.

A voice shouted: "You! Girl!"

The man was so tall that at first she thought it was Yossele, come back again. Then he knelt down and he wasn't Yossele, only a man, his dark eyes full of worry. Bundled in his arms was what looked to be a woman's cloak. "My friend ran in after you," he said, his Yiddish strangely accented. "A woman, tall, like me. Did you see her?"

A woman, run in after her? The man watched her, tense and un-moving, as though his own life hung upon her answer. She remembered, then, the faint voice in the hallway. "I heard her," she whispered.

"Where? What floor?"

"The fourth. But—she—" *The cracking noise, the hole at Yossele's feet. The flames below.* She sat down on the curb and began to cry.

The man stared down at her, then drew an agonized hand over his face. Cursing, he stood and sprinted around the corner, the way that Kreindel had come.

A little while later, a policeman found Kreindel sitting alone on the curb and carried her to an ambulance, where a man pressed two fingers to her wrist and asked her questions she couldn't understand. She shook her head, crying. He went away, and brought back another man, one who spoke Yiddish. He asked after her mother and father, but she only cried harder. At last they made her lie down, and pulled a blanket over her; and the horses tugged the ambulance away.

The Golem lay on her back, trapped beneath a weight of wood and plaster.

She squirmed, trying to find her bearings, but she could barely move at all. Where had she landed? Dust and debris covered her face; the heat had dried her hands to claws. She tried to blink, realized her eyes were fixed open. The ground beneath her had the feel of packed dirt, not wood or carpet. Was it the cellar? Had she fallen all the way through the building?

She shook her head, clearing the dust from her eyes—and looked up at four looming stories of flames and wreckage. It was as though a giant had scooped a burning hole through the center of the tenement. Smoke poured upward through exposed apartments, around sofas and lamps. A kitchen table tipped crazily into the void as she watched, the wood shattering as it landed.

She twisted, trying to drag herself free—and flinched at a sickening pull in her hip. She batted at it with a stiff, clumsy hand, and found a spar of metal, inches thick, protruding from her body. She'd landed atop it, and now it pinned her to the ground like an insect.

She looked around wildly. How long, before the entire building collapsed? Would she survive intact? Or crumble apart, a thousand sentient pieces among the debris? The thought horrified her. She tried to call for help, but could barely draw breath.

There was nothing she could do. She hadn't even managed to rescue the young girl. She thought of the Jinni, and how they'd fought. How awful, that it should end this way. She wished she could apologize, and say good-bye.

The Jinni ran into the deserted tenement yard. The stairwell door hung open, a yawning darkness beyond. Ash floated on the air-currents.

He set her cloak on the ground, and went in after her.

The heat soaked into him at once, sharpening his senses. Within moments he felt stronger, quicker. His clothing caught fire as he ran up the staircase, but he paid no notice, only called her name.

If Arbeely were here, he thought, *he'd tell me to pray.*

The fourth floor hallway was a carpet of flames. He ran inside the nearest apartment, searching through the haze of smoke, but it was empty. He tried another, and another, calling her name, hearing nothing.

The walls of the next apartment he tried were already alight, and in the parlor he found the body of a man, his bearded face pale and thin. A wooden suitcase lay nearby, old books spilling from its insides. Flames crept across the rug, reaching the books as he watched, the paper combusting eagerly. Something about the sight transfixed him: ancient books, vanishing to ash . . . He shook himself and turned to go—and caught a deeply familiar scent, of earth or clay.

"Chava?" he called.

He opened the door to a small bedroom, its far wall smoldering. The scent was stronger here, but she was nowhere to be seen, neither in the bed nor beneath it. He looked around, confused.

A jolt, beneath his feet: the joists snapping, one after another. The room pitched downward, furniture sliding across the floor and through the burning wall. He tried to brace, but lost his balance—

—And the Golem watched from below as he fell through the air and landed with a crash nearby.

"*Ahmad!*" It came out as a rattling croak. Had he heard? What if he was hurt?

"Chava! Where are you?"

She wanted to laugh with relief. "I'm over here—" She dug her elbows into the dirt floor, tried to swivel around the metal spar.

Footsteps—and then he was lifting the wreckage away, shoving wood and plaster aside. He seemed on fire himself; the air around him shimmered with heat. He pushed away the last of the debris—and then stopped, stood staring. Something had horrified him—

Oh. It was her. He was looking at her.

"I can't move," she whispered.

He jolted back to himself, found the spar and broke it, pulled it free from her body. He bent to lift her—and jumped back as she shrieked at his scalding touch.

A roar came from above. The roof, giving way at last.

"I'm sorry, Chava," he said; and he grabbed her up and ran through the flames.

The tenement yard was still deserted. He carried her out and set her down beneath the clotheslines, as gently as possible. She said nothing, only lay there, as still as wood. He could see deep burns along her arm and on her hip, where he'd touched her. He had to get her home; the yard wouldn't stay vacant for long.

He searched around until he found a water spigot, nailed to a post in the middle of the yard. He turned it to gushing, braced himself, and ducked beneath the spray.

The water exploded into steam. Pain stabbed through him; he shouted out and backed away, staggering. A moment later, he was dry again. He shook off the last of the pain, then touched one of the shirts on a nearby clothesline. When it didn't smolder, he grabbed it down, along with a pair of trousers, and dressed himself, briefly wishing for shoes. He found her cloak where he'd left it, and wrapped her in it gingerly.

"Chava," he said, "we need to leave. Can you move at all?"

Her eyes flicked up at him. With slow and palsied movements she maneuvered to her knees, tried to rise, toppled over with a gasp.

He caught her and carried her from the yard, keeping to the shadows as much as possible until they reached her boardinghouse. Her landlady's bedroom lamp was lit—no doubt she'd smelled the smoke and heard the sirens, and gone to investigate. The rest of the house was dark and quiet.

He found her keys in her cloak pocket, then quickly carried her up the stairs, unlocked the door, and laid her on the bed. She was a stiffly curled bundle, her cloak drawn across her face like a curtain. He was about to switch on the light when she stirred and spoke, her voice a painful rasp. "No, don't. I'll be fine, Ahmad. I'll see you tomorrow night."

A pause. "Chava," he said slowly, "are you telling me to leave?"

"Ahmad. *Please.*"

The only chair was at her writing-desk: a bentwood rococo confection, more suited to a girlish boudoir than her spare and sober room. He placed it beside her bed and sat, folding his long legs together. The chair squeaked in protest, but held.

"I'm not moving," he said.

She seemed about to argue, but then gave in with a slump of her cloaked shoulders.

For long minutes he watched her, a dark form on a dark bed. He could smell parched earth, fissured with heat. A scent as familiar to him as her usual one—only he'd never thought to find it in this city, in this room. If he closed his eyes, he might be flying over a summer valley on the other side of the world.

"Are you in pain?" he asked quietly.

A pause. "No. Not really. Just . . . uncomfortable." Her voice was still a rasp.

Unnerving, to sit staring at her like this. He'd glimpsed her ruined features for only a handful of moments, but now he couldn't drive them from his mind. Would she heal, as she said? Or was that only a lie, to calm him? He had the impulse to lie down next to her, to take her in his arms; he held himself back, afraid of hurting her—afraid, too, of learning the true extent of the damage.

He shifted in the chair, cleared his throat, looked around for a distraction. His foot nudged something next to the bed: a large rattan hamper. Her sewing basket. He picked it up and set it in his lap, but could see little detail in the nearly pitch-dark room. He found the lamp on her nightstand, snapped his fingers above the wick. Already he missed the earlier acuity of his senses, the way the barest hints of color and shape had stood out through the smoke. Was that how he'd seen the world before the flask, and he'd simply forgotten?

She stirred beneath her cloak. "What are you doing?"

"Looking through your sewing basket."

"Why?"

"For lack of options."

She fell silent, then gave an irritated sigh and shifted again, as though searching for a more comfortable position.

The sewing basket was like an enchanted box in a tale, full of smaller boxes that all contained boxes of their own. He lifted them out one by one, inspecting their contents. There were buttons and needles and dozens of spools of thread: black and white and ivory, various shades of gray, dark blues, a few greens and yellows and one startling fuchsia. Another box held scraps of cord and trim and ribbons, feathers and flowers meant for hat-brims. Then, a box of tools: a small metal ruler with a sliding gauge, a pincushion neatly spaced with pins, a pale wedge of tailor's chalk, and an elegant pair of golden scissors in the shape of a stork. The stork's feet perched upon the two finger-loops; its long neck was the shaft, the sharp blades its beak. He held them up and admired them in the lamplight, surprised to find such whimsy in anything she owned.

At the bottom of the basket were folded squares of pale muslin. The Jinni chose one of these, then a needle and a spool of dark thread. He measured a length of the thread and snipped it with the scissors.

Another movement from the bed. "Ahmad, what are you doing now?"

"I'm practicing my sewing." He knotted the end of the thread, and, with little forethought, began a haphazard embroidery of crosses and zigzags. But the thread was too thick, and the muslin began to pucker and ripple around the stitches. Carefully he snipped out the offending thread, chose a slimmer one, and began again.

"Talk to me," she said suddenly. "Please."

"What shall I tell you?"

"Anything. I just want to hear your voice."

You'll be glad to hear that the girl escaped. He nearly said it—but at the last moment stopped himself. He didn't trust himself to keep the bitterness from his voice. She'd nearly destroyed herself, and for what? The girl had managed to live regardless. So instead he said, "Then I shall tell you the story of Mount Qaf."

He paused then, surprised by his own words. Why, of all things, had he thought of *that?* It was the scent of burnt earth, perhaps: it had taken him out of himself, and dragged him into the past.

She did not say, *What is Mount Qaf?* She only lay listening. Waiting. He cleared his throat. "In the legends of the jinn," he said, "Mount Qaf is the emerald mountain that encircles our world and holds up the sky. It is a land of exceeding beauty, where all kinds of trees and flowers grow without need of rain. Only on Mount Qaf does the *roc*, the king of all birds, allow his claws to touch the ground. For hundreds of generations, Mount Qaf was the home to all the tribes of jinn. There was no fighting then, for we had everything we needed, and were happy and content. But then one day, the jinn were cast out—all of us, down to the very last imp and ghul. No one knows why. It simply happened."

She hadn't moved, but her silence was now charged with attention. He opened the box of trims and ribbons, selected a spool of golden cord. He pondered a moment, then said, "Chava, this cord is far too thick for a needle. How does one sew with it?"

A pause. "First you lay it on top of the fabric," she said, her graveled voice betraying extreme patience, "and pin it into place. Then, sew across it with small stitches, and remove the pins."

He found her pincushion, cut a length of the cord. "We fell from the mountain," he said as he worked, "and landed in the desert, and had to contend with rain, and iron, and men and their magic. We searched for a cause, a fault. Brother accused sister, clan accused clan, saying, 'It was this wrong, it was that slight.' The first battle began, and we've been fighting ourselves ever since." He threaded another needle, and began to sew neat yellow stitches across the golden cord. "It's said that if one day we can discover the reason for our banishment, then the *roc* will gather us all and fly us home to Mount Qaf, where we'll live in peace again. But until that day, we are doomed to endless conflict."

His voice trailed away. Long moments passed; and then she said, "Ahmad, do you believe in Mount Qaf?"

He knew that she expected him to say no. It was the sort of story that, if it were told by a human, he'd dismiss as nonsense. But now he felt the need to give a better answer.

"I used to, when I was young," he said. "But then I began to question. How could a mountain encircle the earth? Wouldn't there be evidence of such a place, if it existed? I decided that the tale was invented—that all the stories, in fact, were invented, and I would give them no power over me. But yes. I believed, once."

She lay there, absorbing this, as he continued to sew. Then she said, "Rabbi Meyer gave me a book that told a story like that. Except it wasn't a mountain, but a garden, in a place called Eden. The people who lived there were Adam and Eve, the first humans. They ate the fruit from the Tree of Knowledge, the only fruit that God had forbidden them to eat."

She paused, as though waiting for a scornful comment. *What is the point of planting such fruit if one only means to forbid it?* But he remained silent, sewing, listening.

"Once they gained the tree's knowledge," she said, "they realized that they were naked, and it made them ashamed. God saw their shame, and knew that they'd eaten the fruit. So He banished them from the garden. And the humans have never been able to find it since."

He considered. "It's similar," he said, "but not the same. I'm quite certain that no jinni has ever felt ashamed of their nakedness."

"Somehow I believe you."

"And all men and women, they're meant to descend from these two?"

"Yes. But it grows complicated."

"I'd imagine so."

Silence returned. He kept on sewing, tied off a thread, snipped the ends away. "These scissors," he said. "They surprise me. They seem like something I'd make, not something you'd own."

"Why not?"

"They're too fanciful. You seem to value utility above all else."

"They're well made, and they were no more expensive than the others in the shop." Did he imagine it, or was her voice improving? Perhaps it was only the added tone of indignation. She paused, and then muttered something he couldn't quite hear.

"Pardon?"

"I said, 'And besides, they remind me of you.'"

Surprised, he smiled in the near-darkness. "Really?"

"As you say, they're something that you might make. I use the scissors, and I think of you. There, now you know the extent of my infatuation." She spoke it half defensively, as though he might think less of her for it—and suddenly it pained him that even now, lying injured and immobile, she felt the need to protect herself in this way.

"May I tell you another story?" he said.

"Of course."

He threaded the needle, began again. "Once, there was a jinni who was captured by a wizard, and bound to human form. He came by accident to a towering city, where all thought him very strange—and there he met an equally strange woman, a woman made of clay."

The words came to him as though fed from some distant source. He pulled thread through fabric, heard it whisper like flame. "Before long," he said, "it seemed to him that, in that city full of wonders, the woman was the most wonderful, the most worthy of his attention. For years they roamed together—and then, one night, they came upon a building in flames. Nearby was a child, panicking for her father. The child ran inside, and the woman ran in after. He shouted for her to stop—but it was too late, the woman was gone. And he was left to wonder: Had she heard him, calling after her? Or, because she couldn't feel his wishes, did they simply not matter as much as the child's? And more to the point, would he ever see her again?"

"Oh, Ahmad." A whisper. "I'm so sorry."

The stork's beak nipped at a thread-end. "If I'd been elsewhere, would you have died tonight?"

"If you'd been elsewhere, I wouldn't have been out at all."

It was a diversion; he wouldn't allow it. "If you'd heard the commotion and gone alone, then. Or if there'd been a mishap at the bakery, and someone was trapped inside. What then? Did you give *any* thought to your own safety?"

A hollow sigh. "No. I didn't think at all, I only acted. She was so frightened for her father, and I was . . . vulnerable, I suppose. Please, don't be angry. I couldn't help it. It's who I am."

The anger surged afresh, as though she'd called it forth. "Allow me," he said, "the same consideration that you demand for yourself. *I can't help it, it's who I am.* Yes, you could not help running after her, and in that moment I meant nothing to you. I know this, I try to accept it, but I cannot understand, and that is what angers me. Tonight might have been the end of you, Chava. Who would I remember you with tomorrow if you were to die tonight? Arbeely? Anna Blumberg? I couldn't even go to your bakery and cry with the Radzins."

"You don't cry." A whisper, from the depths of the cloak.

"Allow me the hyperbole, please. My point, Chava, is that if someday—"

He stopped talking. She'd moved suddenly beneath the cloak, and was now sitting up, patting herself with stiff motions. "What is it?" he asked.

"I can't find the locket." The cloak slipped open—and he saw the fissures that covered her body, the dark and ugly stripes where he'd held her. Remnants of her cotton shirtwaist were seared to her skin. Her hands were skeletal, the knuckles swollen. He felt dizzy, but couldn't look away.

"It's not there," she said in rising fear. "No, wait—is this . . ."

Her fingers had found something inside one of the fissures. He shuddered as she prized it from her own body: an oblong of flat and blackened brass.

"Look," she said, and held it out in one shriveled hand.

He took it gingerly and held it to the lamplight. The halves of the locket had fused together. He picked up her scissors, wedged the tip of the stork's beak into the thin seam that remained, and twisted. The locket cracked open and fell apart. Where the folded command had once been, there was now a teaspoon's worth of ash.

"It's gone," she said, her voice hollow.

Good riddance, the Jinni thought.

"Ahmad, what will I do? What if I—" She paused, then turned suddenly to face him. "But you know it," she said. "You read it once, you must remember it."

He wanted to tell her that he'd forgotten the command, ripped it deliberately from his memory, after that awful day when he'd come so close to destroying her. But it would be a lie. He couldn't forget it, any more than he could forget his own true name.

"You do," she whispered. "I know you do."

"Chava, no. Don't ask this of me."

"Please, Ahmad. *Please*, just write it down, and I'll buy a new locket—" She reached out a clawlike hand, giant eyes beseeching.

"No!" He recoiled, rose from the chair, upending the sewing basket.

Startled, she pulled back, then raised the hood again and turned away slightly. "May I ask why?" she said in a clipped tone.

"Haven't you heard a word I've said? I have no wish to be your accomplice in your destruction!"

"And if I should lose myself, and turn violent? How many others might die without that locket to protect them?"

"*Enough!*"

The word rang between them. Her face was a shadow beneath the hood, her lips an angry line.

"I tell you now, Chava, I won't give you what you ask. Find someone else to murder you. I refuse." And with that he left her room and her boardinghouse, and walked back to Washington Street, barefoot in his stolen clothes.

On Forsyth, the fire was out at last, though the gutted tenement still steamed from the pit in its middle. The crowd dispersed, the neighbors returning to their beds, grateful that they'd been spared.

The Forsyth Street Synagogue opened its doors, despite the lateness of the hour, to take in the newly homeless. Many of the survivors were members of the synagogue—but neither Rabbi Altschul nor young Kreindel were among them. No one could remember seeing them, either in the fire or its aftermath. And so the congregants drew the only conclusion they could. Their mourning, though, was tinged with guilty relief. The death of a child could only be a tragedy—but there had been something dark and unsavory, even sinister, about their rabbi at the end.

Meanwhile, the girl they mourned lay asleep in a bed at Saint Vincent's, dreaming that she was lost in a maze of smoke-filled hallways. At last she found the door to her father's bedroom, and turned the knob. A body lay on the bed: not Yossele, but the tall man from the street, the one whose friend had run into the fire after her. He lay motionless, staring at her with eyes full of grief, the woman's cloak bunched between his hands. She took it from him and shook it out, and covered him with it, like a shroud.

In the morning, kind-faced women would come to her bedside and ask questions in English. *My name is Kreindel Altschul,* she would tell them in Yiddish. And her age, they'd ask, holding up their fingers: Eight? Nine? *Elf,* she would say, eleven; but they'd mishear, and write it in her file as *eight,* an error that no one would ever correct. More people would come, asking questions, jotting down her answers—until at last they would bathe and dress her and take her to a nearby courthouse, where a black-robed judge would sigh in irritation at her lack of living relations and declare her a ward of the state.

The Golem lay on her bed and stared at the ceiling, wishing she could blink.

At last she sat up. Her lamp still glowed upon the desk, surrounded by the scattered boxes, the stork scissors, the spools of thread. Nearby was the hand mirror, with its newly splintered handle.

She steeled herself and picked it up.

In some ways, her face was better than she'd feared; in others, it was worse. Her hair and eyebrows were still intact—protected, it seemed, by the magic that had made her. But the dark and hollow cheeks, the parched lips and staring eyes, all gave her the look of a bewigged corpse.

She would heal. She *had* to. Over and over her hand stole to her ruined chest, where the locket should be. *Find someone else to murder you*—did he think she wished for death? Oh, he didn't understand at all! Angrily she shook her head, trying to loosen her eyelids. A strange sensation was rising in her, a discomfort different from pain but just as compelling: an unbearable itch for something she couldn't name, some-thing that reminded her of hot summer days, of children playing in open fire hydrants, longings for iced lemonade . . .

Thirst. She was *thirsty*.

She stood from the bed, feeling rickety and unsteady. The hole in her hip puckered uncomfortably as she hitched her way down the dark-ened stairs to her landlady's kitchen. She found a water-pitcher and filled it, then took it back to her room and drank glass after glass. Her body absorbed it all, then another pitcherful, and another. The cracks in her skin began to smooth together, the burnt scraps of cotton fluttering to the floor. Her eyelids loosened at last, and she blinked gratefully, over and over.

By morning her face had filled out again, losing its skull-like aspect. She examined the stripes on her arms and her sides, where the Jinni had carried her. Their edges were softening; they, too, would heal. The hole in her hip had closed enough to walk normally again. By tomorrow, with any luck, they wouldn't notice anything wrong at the bakery—

The bakery. Selma Radzin. She hadn't even told the Jinni about it.

Her small burst of optimism drained away. She poured another glass of water and drank it down in a single morose gulp, then roused herself to tidy away the boxes and tins he'd spilled onto her desk. She refolded the fabrics and spaced the pins evenly on their cushion, wanting to be angry, to think, *How typical of him, to make a mess of things and then leave*—but she felt too weary to argue even in her own thoughts. She fetched the basket, to pack everything away—and only then saw the square of muslin, lying on the floor where he'd dropped it.

She picked it up, smoothed it out. On the muslin was the figure of a woman, outlined in cord. Spreading from her back and shoulders were wings of golden flame.

If you were a jinniyeh . . . Was *this* what he wished for? A woman closer to himself, someone less challenging to comprehend? She folded it away at the bottom of the basket, then put everything else on top, as though to hide it from herself. She would discuss it with him, she decided, when he arrived that night. They would speak about it as rationally as they could. She would try, as always, to make him understand.

But their usual hour came and went, and the Jinni failed to appear beneath her window.

8.

The headmistress of the Asylum for Orphaned Hebrews frowned at the typed report before her.

Kreindel Altschul, eight years old, four feet two inches, 52 pounds. Mother, Malke, died of fever after childbirth. Father, Lev, a rabbi, died in tenement fire. No siblings or other relations. Child describes an isolated and neglectful upbringing. She has received no public education and speaks little to no English, but demonstrates intelligence. Plainly undernourished but otherwise no visible deficiencies.

"She's too old," the headmistress said at once. "You know that we draw the line at five."

The man who sat across from her smiled thinly. "And *you* know that you may draw that line when a child is surrendered by its parent. But Miss Altschul is now a ward of New York State, and in this instance the state requires that an exception be made. I understand," he went on as the headmistress drew breath to argue, "that it will take longer for her to adjust. But she has no relatives to foster her, and all the smaller Hebrew institutions are at their limit."

"We, too, are at our limit," said the headmistress, frost in her voice. "We've long since surpassed it, in fact. And we'll be of little help to anyone if the state insists on treating us like a warehouse for difficult cases."

"Why do you assume she'll be a difficult case? Aside from her age, she seems exactly the sort of child your Asylum was intended to help."

You know as well as I do what a girl like this would face here, the headmistress wanted to say. But that would be impolitic, a show of weakness, and she stayed silent.

"I'd hoped," the man went on, "that we might manage this between ourselves. But if you think I ought to invite Dr. Wald to deliver a verdict . . ."

Her eyes narrowed. Dr. Wald was the Asylum's superintendent, tasked with the oversight of the Asylum's thousand-plus residents. The children knew him mainly as the man who appeared in the dining hall once a week or so, for impromptu uniform inspections. The rest of his time was spent glad-handing city officials, attending prestigious conferences, and making hopeful forays among New York's German-Jewish *beau monde*. Interruptions to his schedule were rarely tolerated.

"I believe we needn't burden him," she said, defeat sour in her mouth.

The necessary arrangements were made, and the man took his leave without refreshment, citing the train schedule. The headmistress summoned her secretary. "Make a new file," she said, "and tell Matron to expect a new resident for quarantine. Kreindel Altschul, eight years old." She held out the report.

The secretary's eyes widened. "Eight?" And then, perusing the report: "Oh, dear. A true orphan."

"Indeed."

"What name should I put on the file, do you think?"

The headmistress sighed. "Let's try for Claire. I expect it'll be a struggle—but hope springs eternal."

The Jinni stood on the Amherst roof, rolling a cigarette.

It was the fifth morning since the fire, and still he hadn't gone to the Golem's boardinghouse. *Let her wonder if she'll see me tonight,* he'd told himself that first night, *just as I wondered if I'd ever see her again.* But with each passing night the thought had lost more of its conviction. Now, he merely felt like a sulking child.

Footsteps, in the stairwell—and Arbeely emerged, puffing and smiling, already pulling biscuits from his pockets as the children gathered around him like famished seagulls. Watching, the Jinni realized for the first time that his partner had forgone not only a wife but a family. Guilt panged him anew. He turned away and watched the ships in the river instead.

Soon the biscuits had disappeared, and Arbeely came to where his partner stood. After a moment the man said, "You've been scowling more than usual lately. Ought we to talk about it?"

The Jinni raised an eyebrow. "I might say the same of you. Would you like to go first?"

A surprised pause—and then Arbeely chuckled ruefully. "Well. Perhaps it would do both of us good to simply enjoy the sunshine."

"Perhaps," the Jinni agreed.

They stood together, gazing out over the bay. Then Arbeely clapped the Jinni on the arm—the Jinni wondered if the man had decided to forgive him—and turned back toward the stairwell. "Coming?"

"In a moment."

The man descended back to the shop. Alone, the Jinni finished his cigarette, and made his decision.

"Is everything all right, Mrs. Levy?"

The Golem glanced up from her work to find one of her hires watching her in confusion. "Yes, of course," she lied quickly. "Why?"

"It's just that you're making the morning bialys, and it's nearly closing time."

She looked down, chagrined. Sure enough, there were the bialys, two whole trays of them, each flattened middle awaiting its helping of chopped onion. How could she have made such a mistake?

It's Ahmad's fault, she thought spitefully. She'd spent the last four nights trapped in her room, unable to walk away her distractions. He hadn't even sent a message to ask how she was faring! "I'm just tired, I suppose," she said, and scraped each of the trays into the trash-bin, wincing at the waste.

This has gone far enough, she thought as she walked home that night, dodging children and pushcarts without seeing them. She'd go to Little Syria before sunset, and demand that he speak with her. She'd even pound on the Amherst door if she had to, neighbors or no—

"Chava," her landlady called to her on the staircase. "I was about to leave this in your room—it just arrived." She handed the Golem a small, paper-wrapped parcel, addressed in familiar handwriting.

She took it to her room and tore the paper away to find a hinged box covered in dark pebbled leather, the sort a jeweler might use. Inside it was an oblong locket that hung upon a silver chain. The locket appeared to be made of steel, not brass—but otherwise he'd reproduced it exactly.

She hesitated, then pressed her thumb against the latch. The locket popped open, revealing a square of tightly folded paper.

Quickly she closed it again. Then she put the chain around her neck, tucked the locket inside her shirtwaist, and walked in the evening light to Little Syria.

His door opened before she could knock. She stepped inside; he closed it behind her. She watched his eyes travel over her, taking in her restored appearance. What would he say? *You're looking well,* perhaps.

Instead he said quietly, "You have every right to be angry with me."

Her eyebrows went up in surprise.

"It was wrong of me to stay away," he said. "But I knew that I would give in, that you would convince me. And I had to convince myself first. I had to change my own mind, or else resent you for changing it. Does that make sense?"

She was still wary, but she nodded. This, she understood.

"So I decided," he said, "to bow to your authority on the subject. If you must have that thing to feel in control of your life, then by with-holding it, I am caging you, as certainly as this"—he held up his wrist—"cages me." He sighed. "Now, if you still want to shout at me, I promise I'll stand still for it."

Do you wish I were a jinniyeh? The question faltered on her lips. He was offering her a way forward, and to ask would only set off an argument that neither of them could win. For once, she would leave it alone.

He was watching her warily, as though she were a stick of dynamite that might explode at any moment. She stepped closer, brought her face to his, and kissed him. For a moment he only stood there, unresponding—she quailed, regretting the impulse—but then his arms came around her, and he was kissing her back, his lips searing hers.

"Did you open it?" he asked, later.

The lamps were turned low; she lay with her head cradled on his shoulder. "I did," she said. "But only the locket. Not the paper."

She fell silent, and he knew what she was thinking. She wanted some confirmation, some promise, that he had in fact written what she'd asked—that she wouldn't unfold the paper someday, in a desperate moment, to find only an apology, or nothing at all. He could feel her struggle not to ask, to show her trust through silence. It wasn't a struggle she often won.

But the silence stretched, and gradually became a more ordinary moment of quiet between them. Surprised, he let go of the tension he'd been holding. One hand brushed along her hip; his fingers found a small divot where the metal spar had pierced her. He winced, and moved his hand away. "Does that hurt?"

"No, it's only a little numb. Like there's a piece missing."

"You're well, then? Nothing . . . permanent?" Certainly she seemed her usual self. He supposed that if he wanted to, he could pretend that nothing had happened at all.

"Fully healed," she said. "And no one at Radzin's noticed anything."

"That's good. I'm glad."

"But—oh, I never told you." And she related her tale of Selma Radzin, and the young woman's startling moment of insight. "I'll have to leave the bakery soon," she said. "Or else they'll all start to notice, not just Selma."

"You can't be sure of that." Was she inventing this crisis, letting her fright run away with her?

"I can, though. It's like when a woman hides a pregnancy. First one person knows, and the next day a dozen, though no one's said a word. I don't know how they do it, but they do." She sighed. "I can't work at another bakery, everyone knows me from Radzin's. But to learn another trade all over again . . ."

He held her hand, lightly. "Well, what else do you like to do, besides baking?"

"I have no idea." She said it with defensive embarrassment. "I suppose I could be a seamstress, if I had to. But I already spend half my nights sewing."

"What about nursing?"

She thought. "Perhaps. But all those people in pain, all that need . . . I think I'd have a hard time not giving myself away. Especially in winter."

"It's a pity," he said, "that women can't be smiths, or I'd hire you as an apprentice."

He felt her smile. "You would not."

"Of course I would. Then you could tell me what Arbeely thinks about all day long."

She chuckled. "Oh, I see."

He remembered Arbeely's letter then, and his own accidental culpability in the man's failed love-affair. He knew he ought to tell her—but he felt himself shy away from the topic. Likely she'd insist that he raise the subject with Arbeely; she might even tell him that he, too, must find employment elsewhere, so the man might have his marriage. Already he could feel himself growing angry at the thought. "What about teaching?" he said, reaching blindly for a suggestion.

He'd expected her to dismiss it as she had the others. Instead she flinched in his arms.

"What is it?" he asked.

"Nothing. Just—my hip, where you're touching it."

"Oh." He moved his hand to a safer spot.

After a moment she said, "Do you think that I look like a schoolteacher?"

"I don't know. I suppose so." Something pricked the back of his memory—a conversation about schoolteachers? But he felt disinclined to search it out.

The silence went on. Then she said, "I hadn't thought about it until now, but I'm already a teacher of sorts, if you count the new hires at Radzin's."

"That's true. Did you enjoy teaching them?"

"I did, actually. And they learned more quickly than any of Thea's trainees ever did." Then, doubt creeping into her voice: "But wouldn't I have to earn a degree first? I've never been to school a day in my life, how would I—"

"Chava, don't worry about that yet. You'll talk yourself out of an idea before you've considered it properly."

"You're right," she said. "It's a good idea. It's only daunting to think about."

"I know." He pulled her closer and kissed her, his hand avoiding her hip.

There's a new girl in quarantine. Older, not a baby.

I heard she's a true orphan.

Like most institutions of its kind, the Asylum for Orphaned Hebrews wasn't an orphanage in the strictest sense of the word. The vast majority of its residents could name at least one living parent, a mother or father who'd made the terrible trip uptown and left a wailing child behind them. But every so often a *true orphan* passed through the Asylum gates—and with this distinction came a fearsome prestige. Rooms went quiet when a true orphan entered. They were chosen first for every team, and given the pick of the dining hall. To steal from a true orphan, or bully or wallop them, was unthinkable.

This hushed deference had its advantages—but it also placed them outside the Asylum's natural order. To be a true orphan was to endure a subtle yet permanent ostracism. They must put more effort into making friends; they must be cheerful and amusing and kind-hearted, and cast off as much of their status as possible—or else they would spend their Asylum years alone.

Kreindel knew none of this, only that she'd ended up in the very place that her father had feared for her, among people he'd despised.

On the first night of quarantine they stripped her and sat her in a metal bathtub, then filled it with water so hot she nearly screamed. A nurse searched inch by inch through her long, dark hair; a dentist peered into her mouth, extracted two molars, and pronounced the remainder sound. *Eight years old*, the nurses muttered, looking over Kreindel's chart. *A good height for eight, but so thin! We'll fix that soon enough.*

Kreindel, eleven, said nothing. It seemed useful to have a secret in this terrible place, something she might turn to her advantage.

They fed her soft white bread soaked in broth, but her grieving body rebelled, and everything came up again. The nurses held the bowl for her, and patted her back. At night she fell asleep listening to the distant cries of the newly surrendered babies in the nursery—but she herself did not cry, not once. If the nurses were concerned by this, as Kreindel secretly was, they said not a word. They sighed in relief that she could write her Yiddish letters—at least she wasn't entirely illiterate—and gave her an English primer, decorated with apples, bells, and cows. She leafed through it without interest, then went to the window and gazed out at the immense building across the lawn: two stories of brick and granite, a gabled Gothic fortress topped by a squat, open-sided bell tower. The peal of the bell marked every station of the day, from rising to sleeping and everything in between: when to line up for the synagogue and when to exit the dining hall, when to muster for classes, when to disperse to chore duties, when to gather for inspection or extra-curriculars or lectures or field trips. To Kreindel it seemed to ring incessantly. Sometimes she could see an answering commotion in a hallway, or a spilling of children from an open door. At other times, its effect was invisible.

You'll get used to the bell, the nurses assured her. *Soon you won't even notice it.*

Her appetite returned slowly, and before long the broth and bread stayed put. She slept poorly, but seemed to dream the moment her eyes closed: her father, and Yossele, and the tall man on the street, and the woman crying out above the flames. She'd wake, disoriented, and have to remember all over again what had happened, and where she was.

On the Sabbath she asked Matron for a pair of candles, so that she might say the blessing over them; and the nurses gathered in her doorway and wiped away tears as she lit them and prayed. Another woman watched with them, a steel-haired lady in a long, dark dress. This, Kreindel had learned, was the headmistress.

"Matron says you're a healthy young girl," the headmistress said briskly, once the others had left. She spoke her Yiddish like a German, just as the settlement ladies had. "We'll keep you for the full week, to make certain. Then you'll be ready to live in the dormitory." She watched Kreindel for a moment, as though gauging her, then said, "Matron also tells me that she explained to you how most children arrive here."

"She said that a parent brings them," Kreindel said. "And that I'm much older than usual. Since I'm eight."

The headmistress nodded. "It may feel overwhelming, at first. So let's find an extracurricular or an interest group for you, something that you enjoy doing, and that might help you to adjust. If you like to sing, for instance, you could join our Glee Club. Or, let's see—you could learn a musical instrument, or join the badminton squad, or learn Hebrew—"

"You have Hebrew lessons?" Kreindel said, surprised. "For girls, too? Not just boys?"

"We do indeed," the headmistress replied, smiling.

For the first time since the night of the fire, Kreindel felt something stir inside her, her soul rousing itself from numbness. "I'd like to take Hebrew lessons, please."

"Then I'll tell the beginners' class to expect a new student. Oh—and one more thing." The woman smiled again, as though to soften whatever came next. "We encourage our new arrivals to adopt new names, to help them fit in more easily. It might feel strange at first, but I promise you'll grow used to it. Now, what would you like to be called? Claire, perhaps?"

Kreindel stared at her dumbly. A new name? *Claire?* It was unthinkable—and yet the unthinkable had already happened. Her father was dead, and she was at the Asylum's mercy. Would the other children make fun of her, with a name like Kreindel? Yes, of course they would.

The governess was waiting patiently, wearing her down with silence. It would be so easy to say yes, here in this place where she knew no one, an orphan, utterly alone—

No. Wait. She wasn't alone at all. She would never be alone, for she had Yossele. She'd brought him to life, and now he was out there in the night, listening for her command. Her protector, and a sacred gift from her father and the Almighty both. She would prove herself worthy of him.

Her back stiffened. She glared at the headmistress. "My name," she said, "is Kreindel Altschul."

And in the waters of the East River, holding fast to a pier piling, Yossele saw what Kreindel saw, felt what Kreindel felt. Tugboats and rail barges plied endlessly back and forth above him, their shadows darkening the water. Currents and wakes pulled at him; engine oil slicked his glass eyes as he watched his master's thoughts, waiting for her to call him to her side.

They tried, nevertheless, to call her Claire.

When she corrected them, they'd smile and move on, confident she'd accept the change once she was among girls who couldn't remember being called Rivke instead of Rebecca, or Dvoire instead of Deborah. But when the quarantine ended at last, and she was taken to her new dormitory and saw the footlocker at the end of her cot with the name *Altschul, Claire* stenciled in black paint, Kreindel grew furious. *Show me where it's written*, she demanded, *that I must change my name to live here.*

But of course there was no such rule. The "modernization" of the children's names was meant to proceed naturally from the Asylum's civic values, not from an order on high. She'd backed them into a corner; the matter was quietly dropped. But already her reputation had been cemented. *Prickly, recalcitrant. A difficult child.*

She fared little better among her peers. At first, a few of the bolder girls ventured to introduce themselves to her, and invited her into their playground circles, to shoot marbles and skip rope. At eight, Kreindel might've been glad for the inclusion; at eleven, she thought the games pointless and childish, and soon the others stopped asking. Were she another girl, they would've played the usual pranks: items snatched from her footlocker, her cot short-sheeted, her dinner-tray knocked from her hands. But Kreindel, true orphan, was left alone.

Each morning, at the rising bell, she donned her uniform of white blouse and brown skirt—a baggy, horrible thing, the cotton as stiff as canvas—and marched through the halls to a synagogue that had no partition, only an aisle to divide the girls from the boys. Then, the dining hall, where she murmured the proper prayers over her bread and margarine while the rest of her table stared and giggled. The bell, again—and up the hill they marched to P.S. 186, where she was sequestered with an English tutor. She resented the lessons, but learned quickly regardless, and soon was sent to the regular classes with her peers: Arithmetic and Science, History and Literature. Then back down the hill for a dinner of meat and stewed prunes—universally detested for the way they dodged and squirted when poked with a fork, as well as for what Matron called their "healthful effects"—and then, at last, to the class that the headmistress had promised her.

Hebrew study was the sole balm of Kreindel's days. She was meant to be a beginner, of course, but it wasn't long before the instructor realized she had a prodigy on her hands. She made Kreindel her assistant, and allowed her to correct the other girls' papers, an arrangement that gained Kreindel little in goodwill.

Then to the muddy exercise yard for recess, the younger girls dispersing to their various territories and strongholds: the swing-set, the hopscotch board, the shady corner. Kreindel spent this time walking the perimeter of the yard, as close to the fence as the monitors would allow. She noted the small gate in the fence along 136th, and the path that led to a basement stairwell; and saw that the gate was held shut by a simple padlock, one that might be broken with enough strength.

At supper Kreindel once more prayed and ate, and endured the stares and quiet giggles. Then all went back to their dormitories, to wash and change and stand beside their cots for the nightly inspection. Each smudged face or dirty fingernail was announced by the monitor, and earned the miscreant a pinch or a slap. As Kreindel was fastidious about washing, it took some time for her to realize that most of these infractions were imaginary, merely excuses for the monitors to dole out punishments, and that she herself was immune.

At nine o'clock precisely everyone crawled beneath their thin cotton sheets and their blankets of gray shoddy. A final bell—and the lights went out in unison.

Coughs, sighs; the sounds of small, restless bodies, of lumpy pillows being punched into better shape. A few lonely, muffled sobs. Slowly the noises faded—but not until the entire dormitory had calmed into sleep would Kreindel at last slide out of bed and pad in her nightdress to the hallway door, crack it open bit by bit, and slip through.

The Asylum at night was a place of gigantic, moonlit proportions, where hallways stretched endlessly and ceilings disappeared into darkness. Night by night she learned her surroundings, memorizing the places where the old wooden floorboards groaned beneath her feet, staying alert for the creak of a door, the flush of a toilet. Sometimes she had to scurry for cover as, with a deafening chorus of whispers and shushes, a raiding party from a boys' dormitory passed by on their way to the kitchen, hunting for slices of bread and cheese. Capture by the monitors was a rite of passage for the boys, who'd bear the beatings and then display their bruises proudly in the morning. Kreindel, long trained in silence, was never caught.

Each night she scouted, considering her options. The dormitory floor was too well traveled, too full of children. The ground floor seemed more likely to contain an unused coat-closet or forgotten niche—but in the end she couldn't trust that what appeared abandoned at night would remain so during the day. And so, little by little, Kreindel's search took her down the wide central staircase, and into the basement.

In daylight hours, the north wing of the Asylum's basement was a place of loud and hectic industry. Clouds of steam billowed from the laundry, where the older residents spent their chore hours operating the gigantic pressers and mangles. Next door was the shoe-shop with its smells of leather and polish, its rows of iron lasts. Beyond that was the vast, naphtha-scented room where the boys of the Marching Band—the Asylum's pride and joy—kept their feathered hats and braid-covered jackets, their shining white spats.

The basement's southern wing, however, was seldom traveled: a place of custodial closets and supply rooms, boilers and pipes and valves. And it was here that Kreindel now crept in the darkness, just a little farther every night. The equipment room, the children's property room, the textbook room: she tried each door but they all were locked, one after another, all down the length of the southern wing. It was well into autumn now, the weather turning colder day by day; on some mornings, lying in her cot, Kreindel could see her breath in the air. But the basement's southern wing remained persistently warm, and grew more so the farther she traveled, as though she were approaching the building's beating heart.

In November she reached the final door. She had little hope left; there was no reason to think this one would be different from the others. Was there a prayer for success in opening a locked door? In her desperation she could recall no prayers at all. She thought only, with great fervency: *Please.*

She grasped the knob—and felt it turn beneath her touch.

An hour later she crept to bed again, shivering with exhaustion. Dust and grime streaked her nightgown; cobwebs laced her hair. But she was elated nonetheless. She closed her eyes, and thought:

You have a new home, Yossele. Come and see.

Later that night, a longshoreman hauling barrels from an East River rail barge suddenly yelped in fright and let go of his barrel, which rolled off the ramp and landed in the river with a splash. When his boss berated him for the loss of cargo, he could only reply that he'd seen a dead man in the water, walking beneath the pier.

Northward Yossele went, fording along the bottom. He moved only at night, in utter blackness, blindly contending with the refuse of the shipping channel: rusted anchors and propeller blades, lengths of rope twined with river-weeds. He spent a day resting beneath a Gas House pier, next to the chain-wrapped remains of a corpse, while the Blackwell's Island ferry plowed back and forth above him. Algae tried to take root in his body, without success. Bluefish and striped bass approached him, nibbled at him briefly, and then swam away.

The piers thinned, forcing him to walk in open water. The channel narrowed, and the currents strengthened until he had to crawl across the murky bottom, or else risk being pulled off his feet. The water grew colder, and only the friction of his clay muscles kept him warm. Now he must keep moving in day as well as night, or else he'd stiffen entirely.

On and on he crawled—until late one frosty night Kreindel was no longer north of him, only west. He surfaced beneath a narrow pedestrian bridge, and clambered to the shore at the edge of a coal-yard.

No one was about. These docklands were sleepier than their southern counterparts; here even the stevedores went home at a reasonable hour. He sidled between the coal-heaps, his joints tightening in the cold air. Nearby was a stack of crates, a canvas tarpaulin lashed atop it. He pulled the tarpaulin free and wrapped it around himself, marble eyes peering from beneath the makeshift hood.

He moved inland, slow and silent, past ice warehouses and saw-mills. Then the industrial yards turned to tenements, and he walked between the stoops, from shadow to shadow. At Saint Nicholas Avenue he crossed into a slice of parkland, up a rocky hill and down the other side, nearly stumbling from his stiffness. His frozen hands clutched the tarpaulin; his neck creaked as he turned his head to survey the way forward. He began, in his wordless way, to grow anxious.

Kreindel woke shivering on her cot, knowing somehow that he was near.

She crept out of the dormitory and down to the arched window at the end of the hallway. From here, she could see all the way to the iron fence with its padlocked gate, the thin path to the basement stairwell. A pair of apartment buildings sat across from the gate on 136th, an alley entrance between them.

There, Yossele, she thought. *Go there.*

Yossele saw it all in her thoughts: the alley, the gate, the path, the door. But first he must cross Amsterdam, and even at four in the morning that meant navigating the produce trucks and milk-wagons that had begun their daily rounds. He couldn't hide and wait, couldn't stop moving—so he clutched at the tarpaulin, sped up as best he could, and lumbered through the intersection like a drunkard.

Men shouted—horses whinnied and reared—and then he was across, stumbling into the alley behind the apartments. But he was moving too quickly now, he couldn't slow down—

He tripped, fell against a garbage bin, and toppled over.

The noise was immense. Shouts rang down from the apartments

above, from men and women startled out of sleep. He pulled himself onto his knees and elbows and crawled to the end of the alley, turned the corner, reached the sidewalk, and heaved himself to standing.

Kreindel stifled a gasp as he appeared between the buildings, huge and bent. Quickly she surveyed the street. At one end of the block, a wagon was turning onto Amsterdam; at the other, a man walking along Broadway crossed to the south and disappeared. There was no one else.

She thought, *Now!*

Across the street he ran, nearly crashing into the gate. One frozen hand lifted the padlock; the other clubbed it apart.

Open the gate slowly, it squeaks!

He did so, sidled through the gate, shut it again, and went on.

Kreindel clambered down from the window and padded to the stairwell. She couldn't afford to run to him, she'd be caught and then so would he—but oh, how she wanted to!

Doggedly he heaved himself along the cobbles, rocking from side to side. The basement stairwell was before him; he could see the door through his own eyes and now Kreindel's, too, as she hurried toward it.

He reached the stairwell, leaned against the wall, and slid slowly down the steps. In the warmth of the threshold, he sank to his knees and wrenched his arms outward to catch his master as she opened the door and fell upon him, weeping at long last.

The jinniyeh who feared no iron might've kept her secret indefinitely, bearing the strain year after year, had it not been for her new lover.

He was a jinni from the western reaches, come to the habitation's center to seek refuge from the skirmishes at the border. Their attraction was mutual and immediate; he became her new favorite, and she sought him out often. Together they flew to the foothills, changing form to whatever shape pleased them that day: a pair of rutting jackals, or falcons falling together through the air.

Then one day he said to her,—*I have an idea. Come with me, and we'll play a trick on the humans.*

Nervous, intrigued, she followed him west, skirting the battles and their telltale windstorms. At last they reached the desert's edge north of Homs. They flew along the border, her lover searching the ground below.

—*There,* he said at last.

She peered down. A team of men had gathered at a roadside, and were now occupied in digging a trench across it. A clay-walled pipe, longer than the road was wide, sat waiting in the scrub nearby.

—*They'll put that thing beneath the road,* her lover said. *Water will travel through it to the fields, and the humans will reach a little farther into the desert. I've seen it before.*

The jinniyeh watched the sweat drip from the men's faces, saw the steel flash of their shovels and pickaxes. Already they had dug halfway across.—*What do we do?* she said.

—*Just watch,* he replied, smiling.

The breeze began a moment later. Soon the men were hunched over, clutching the ends of their head-scarves across their faces as the grit from the roadway assailed them. At last they dropped their tools, and took shelter behind the scrub.

—*You see?* her lover said, allowing the wind to drop. *It's easy, so long as you avoid the iron.*

He was like one of the tales, she thought: the clever jinni who bests the humans, and makes them look like fools. Admiration and desire swelled in her, and the urge to show him that she could do the same.—*My turn,* she said, and gathered the winds again; and the men who'd begun to emerge from their shelter were forced once again to retreat.

Soon the pair was the scourge of the farmland. They scattered chickens, knocked down fences, ripped the grains of wheat from their stalks. A man might return to his plow only to find the harness missing, or the donkey gone lame with fright. It was dangerous work, for water was hidden everywhere in the farmlands, and iron, too: in the harness and the plow-blade, in buckets and grain-scales and the new telegraph wires that ran along the roadsides. And often their desires for each other overcame their plans, and they abandoned their mischief-making for other pleasures.

One afternoon, farther to the south, they found their biggest quarry yet: a crew of dozens of men, all swarming around a gigantic hole in the ground.

The jinniyeh laughed at the sight.—*Why do they dig into the earth like ghuls?*

Her lover did not laugh.—*They call it a cistern,* he said. *It'll collect the rainwaters, enough to feed their fields from here to the horizon.*

A wooden beam hung across the hole, supporting a pulley from which a platform dangled, loaded with bricks. A pair of well-muscled men held the other end of the pulley's rope, their arms straining against the weight. The men at the top shouted to the men at the bottom, the men at the bottom shouted back, and the platform began to lower.

A low breeze began, and turned to a buffeting wind that set the platform rocking. The men at the bottom shouted in fear, leaping up their ladders and pressing themselves against the cistern walls as the bricks slid from the platform one by one. The men at the top hurried to tie off the rope, then huddled coughing against the dust.

The jinniyeh laughed, watching them run back and forth in panic. She looked to her lover; he, too, was laughing. *They will tell stories about us one day,* she thought.

One of the men at the top was the son of a village shaman, and had learned in his childhood how to spot jinn in the patterns of their whirlwinds. He grabbed a shovel, took aim, and hurled it upward like a javelin, shouting, "*Iron, O unlucky one!*"

The jinniyeh didn't think, only saw the danger to her beloved and pushed him out of the way—and so the steel sliced through her body, and not his. It ought to have crippled her. Instead her flame rejoined itself at once, as though the shovel had been nothing more than an errant tree-branch.

For a moment, as her lover stared in awful disbelief, she thought she might convince him that he hadn't seen what he'd seen. But she'd allowed her shame to show far too nakedly. She knew that she was irredeemable; and now, so did he.

She tried to flee, but he was older, and stronger. He stole away the wind she rode, and dragged her back to the elders.

—*This is true?* they asked her. *And you knew of this . . . defect?*

—*Yes,* she said. *I've known for many seasons.* And even in her grief and terror, she felt the weight of her secret leave her.

The elders placed her under guard, then withdrew to decide her fate while onlookers screamed abuse at her, calling her *human* and *stormcloud.* Her lover jeered the loudest of all. The noise drew more and more jinn, and the story traveled outward among them, accumulating quick drifts of detail, splitting into variations that rode their own random currents, crashing together and diverging again. She was immune to iron, and had promised to use it against her own clan. She had injured her lover with a human weapon, and cast him into a hole in the ground. She was in league with the humans; she'd vowed to eradicate the jinn and pave the habitation with steel, all the way from Homs to the Cursed City . . .

None of them would remember who'd first uttered those words, *Cursed City,* but soon they spread from voice to voice.

—*Banish her to the Cursed City!*

—*Let the demons devour her, let shades and ifrits chase her through the columns!*

—*She is a monster of Sulayman, and that is where she belongs!*

They didn't wait for the elders; their own verdict had been reached. As one, the mob raised the winds into a funnel so fierce it nearly tore the jinniyeh apart. Eastward they herded her, all the way to the mountain range, and then pushed her over the ridge, down into the foothills, and out of sight.

Once the winds had died down, some of the jinn felt uneasy about what they'd done. Surely extinguishment would've been more kind? But no one spoke, and they dispersed in silence, shuddering as they imagined the horrors she now faced. Was she already cowering from the spirits that crawled through the ruins? How long could she possibly survive?

The jinniyeh took shelter in a small, dark cave at the bottom of the foot-hills. She was badly injured, and needed heat to heal properly—but to go outside would mean certain death. And so she hovered half delirious near the cave's mouth, where it was warmest, and waited for the mon-sters to emerge howling from their wells, hungry for flame.

But nothing happened.

For days she cowered, expecting an attack. When none came, she began to wonder: Had some mistake been made? Had they banished her to the wrong place? But that made no sense—for there, just visible from the cave's mouth, stood the lines of crumbling pillars, the scattered tower-tombs that housed the human dead. And yet she heard no awful howling, only the whistling of the wind.

Slowly her wounds healed themselves. Occasionally she'd hear the nicker of a horse, and peer out to see a handful of lean, black-robed men riding past, on their way to Homs to sell their sheepskins. As a child, she'd been taught never to approach the Bedu from the Cursed City, for it was well known that the spirits of that place liked to steal away inside the Bedu's saddle-bags, or their horses' ears.—*And if they sense a jinn-child nearby, they poke out their heads and . . . snap!*

Had the city's spirits all escaped in the men's saddle-bags? Was she hiding from nothing at all?

The spring rains arrived, soaking the thirsty valley.

Now the view from her cave grew more interesting, as each morning the Bedu drove their sheep into the grazing lands. New lambs trotted by on unsteady legs. Nettles and mallows sent their flowers forth, dotting the scrub with spots of white.

The jinniyeh watched the land grow green, watched the sheep fatten. And one morning—very slowly, floating on the thinnest of breezes—she ventured out from the shadow of the cave.

At the light's first touch, she nearly cried out in happiness. How bright the world was, how wide the sky! Let the demons come, she'd defeat them all!—*Come to me, demons!* she cried. *Come and fight!* But still they didn't appear—and she realized she no longer expected them to.

She ventured into the heart of the valley, and approached one of the tower-tombs: a tall column of rough stone bricks, its tumbled roof open to the clouds. She mustered her courage and flew inside, up past the scattered remnants of coffered ceilings and mosaics in blue and white. A face loomed from the shadows, and she nearly shrieked—but it was only a carving, its features worn away by the elements. She drifted from chamber to chamber, examining the sarcophagi and their shattered likenesses. What purpose, she wondered, did it serve to surround the bones of the dead with stones that were themselves destined to crumble?

She left the tomb and flew on, following the trail of fallen columns, until she was at the heart of the ruins, floating above a three-arched gate. *Now*, surely, the spirits would notice her!

But no—there were only stones. That was all. She'd been frightened of *stones*.

She could hear human voices now, could smell cooking-fires and camel dung. She followed these to an enormous stone citadel, only half in ruins. From above, the citadel was a maze of courtyards and covered walkways, storerooms and tents—all rife with humans of every age, all bent to their tasks like bees in a hive. And yet how little separated them from the skeletons in the tower-tomb! That man beyond the citadel gates, driving his sheep through the scrub: How many more years would he live? Thirty? Forty at most? Could he truly be said to be alive at all?

Let us see, she thought.

In the next moment, the shepherd's flock was startled by something unseen. They bleated in fear and bolted, scattering in every direction. Cursing, the man chased them up and down the edge of the city, calling and coaxing them.

Suddenly the man felt a tug at his headdress. He clamped a hand to his head—but there came another tug, this time at the hem of his robe. He whirled around, staff raised, but saw only the empty desert. An iron amulet hung about his neck; he grabbed it and pointed it toward his unseen attacker. "*Iron, O unlucky one!*" he shouted.

A strange shimmer before him—and a naked young woman appeared out of thin air. Reaching out, she ripped the iron amulet from his neck and flung it away. In the next moment she was gone.

The flock scattered again as the shepherd turned and fled.

Smiling, the jinniyeh watched him go. Perhaps there'd never been terrors in Palmyra; perhaps Sulayman the Enslaver hadn't ruled here at all. Why should it matter, in the end? The stories would keep her kin away; and the truth was that there were no monsters here, save for herself.

—*Be quiet, child,* she whispered, *or the banished jinniyeh will find you, and grab you with her iron fingers.*

The Teachers College admissions secretary was a limp, colorless woman, save for her ruddy nose, to which she applied a handkerchief every few moments. "I must apologize," she said, "I'm always ill this time of year. Now, how may I help you, Miss Levy?"

The woman on the other side of her desk had been studying the photographs on the wall nearby. Each one was essentially the same: a group of young men or women standing in rows upon a set of marble steps, all of them dressed in robes and mortarboards. The woman turned back to the secretary, hesitated for a moment, then said, "It's Mrs. Levy, if you please."

Surprised, the secretary darted her eyes at the woman's hands.

"My husband passed away a number of years ago."

"Oh, my goodness. I'm so sorry, my dear." She peered at the woman; surely she was only in her twenties? "Forgive me, but you must have been quite young."

"Yes, we both were," Mrs. Levy said. "He died soon after we were married. He was a social worker."

The secretary pictured a Lower East Side garret, the woman tending dolefully to her consumptive bridegroom. "I simply cannot imagine. You have my sympathies."

"Thank you," the woman said quietly.

"Well," the secretary said, suddenly unsure how to proceed, "why don't you tell me why you're here."

"I'm very interested in your Domestic Sciences program."

The secretary nodded. "I can give you a copy of our Admissions Bulletin—"

"I have one already." The woman removed from her purse a fat envelope, bearing the Teachers College seal. "I've studied it quite thoroughly. It says that all applicants must have completed their secondary education—but it also states that exceptions are occasionally made, on an individual basis." She opened the bulletin to the relevant page, complete with underlining.

The secretary sighed to herself. "My dear, before we can reach that point we must look over your curriculum vitae, and assess whether your experience—"

Swiftly the woman pulled a sheet of paper from her purse, and laid it between them on the desk.

"Oh." The paper appeared to be a neatly typed c.v. for one Chava Levy, resident of Eldridge Street. Born outside the Prussian town of Konin, no formal schooling of any kind—it was a wonder she could read the bulletin—and currently employed at an Allen Street bakery called Radzin's. *Head of hiring and training*, it said. "Does this mean you taught the other bakers?" she asked, pointing.

The woman nodded. "The new hires, specifically. The bakery expanded a few years ago, and my employer put me in charge."

"How did you go about it?" It was too much to hope that she'd followed a pedagogical process, of course . . .

"At first I taught them recipe by recipe, the same way I'd learned myself," said the woman. "But it was far too inefficient, especially since I was teaching three young women at once. I realized I must change my methods, and develop a . . . I believe the word is *pedagogy*?"

The secretary blinked. "Indeed it is. Please, go on."

"I decided to begin not with the recipes themselves, but with the basic techniques and principles underlying them. The fundamentals, as it were."

The secretary's eyebrows were creeping ever higher. "Such as?"

"Yeasted breads, for instance. It wasn't enough merely to say that a dough must rise for a certain length of time, and then be punched down before it's kneaded again. *How* does it rise? *Why* must it be punched down?" Mrs. Levy had been sitting rather stiffly; now she grew more animated, her hands rising to describe the shape of a loaf, the folding of the dough. "Once I explained the role of the yeast, they were much more likely to notice if the yeast refused to proof correctly. Since then, in fact, our wastage due to poor rising has been nearly eliminated." She smiled, in modest pride.

"Very commendable." There was something odd about the woman— she didn't blink often enough, perhaps, and the precision of her language clashed almost comically with her accent. Still, she was growing more intriguing by the minute. "May I ask, though—why apply to our program if you've had such success at this bakery? It sounds as though you have a natural talent for it. You might even open a bakery of your own someday." This would be a more appropriate course for her, surely? The Domestic Sciences program had its share of young Jewesses, but these were mainly the daughters of lawyers and businessmen, not girls from the tenements. It was all well and good that Mrs. Levy wanted to better herself—but far kinder, certainly, to dissuade her as gently as possible.

A troubled look had crossed Mrs. Levy's face. She seemed to gather herself, a marshaling of resolve. "May I speak frankly?" she said.

"Of course," the secretary said, a touch wary.

"You ask, quite rightly, why I would apply to Teachers College when I've found success as a baker. But it's exactly that success that compelled me to find your program. Here—I will tell you a story. When I arrived in this country, I was alone, and young, and rather frightened. But worse than that, I had no purpose. Then, one day, a friend gave me a copy of *The Boston Cooking-School Cook Book.*"

The secretary nodded in approval. "A staple in my own household."

"Then you'll understand how reassured I was by Mrs. Farmer's work. It was as though each recipe was saying to me, *Put everything else aside for the moment. Do just this one thing. Measure this ingredient. And now take the next step, and the next.* And with each step I moved forward. It seems like the smallest accomplishment now, but nothing will ever compare to the moment I took my first coffee-cake from the oven. It was a simple thing, but it gave me such confidence. And now I want to help others find that for themselves. So I promise you, if I'm allowed this chance, I won't squander it. I will give it my all."

The secretary was unexpectedly moved by this speech. She blew her nose with a bit more force than before. "Well, my dear," she said, "you clearly have the motivation. But have you given any thought to securing the means? There are scholarships, of course, but—"

"There's no need," Mrs. Levy said. "I can pay the tuition myself."

The secretary stared at her. "The *entire* tuition?"

"In advance, if necessary," the woman said. "I have a nest-egg set aside."

The secretary coughed. "Goodness. I applaud your frugality, Mrs. Levy. And yes, I expect that an entrance exam for you might be arranged."

The woman's eyes brightened. "And if I pass, can I enroll in time for the winter session?"

"One step at a time, dear." She pulled a form from a drawer labeled *Application for Exemption*, wrote at the top *Levy, Chava*, and skimmed down the page to *Extenuating Circumstances*. "Mrs. Levy," she said, her voice carefully neutral, "would you say that you were forced to leave your country for political reasons?"

The woman hesitated, an uncertain look in her eye.

Just say yes, the secretary thought.

"Yes," said Mrs. Levy.

The woman nodded, and wrote, *The candidate has escaped persecution in Europe and endured a young widowhood, appears to have considerable natural aptitude, and seems in all ways a credit to her race.*

PART II

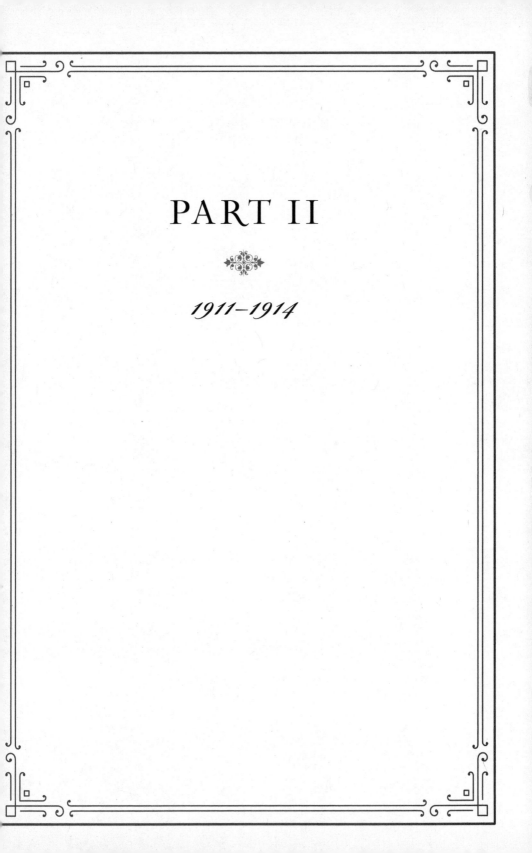

1911–1914

9.

March 20, 1911
Victoria Hotel, Damascus

Dear Father, Mother, and George:

I write to you from my usual rooms at the Victoria, having returned from Cairo only yesterday. With any luck, my letter from Egypt will have reached you by now. Father, you asked whether I will think Syria to be more plain and provincial after such majesties. It's true that there are fewer wonders here—but I can't bring myself to regret it. To return to Damascus from the Nile felt—

Sophia paused. She'd been about to write like coming home.

—instantly soothing in its familiarity. If it's possible to overindulge in grandeur, so that one's mind aches from overstuffing, then that is the condition in which I left Egypt.

I've sent a number of packages from Cairo, and hope they'll arrive without too much delay. George, the cylinder seal is from a market-stall in Beni Suef. The seller swore to me that it's an original dating to the Fourth Dynasty, but I can assure you it's only a very good reproduction. Mother, the faience vase struck me as something you might like—I remember a summer gown of yours that was very similar in color. Father, your shipment of National Geographic magazines was waiting for me here at the Post Office, for which I thank you. Also waiting for me was a telegram from Mr. D. G. Hogarth, an Oxford archaeologist whose work I've read about. He's leading the excavation of Carchemish, where King Nebuchadnezzar defeated the Egyptians. I'd sent him a letter asking if I might visit the site, and he has graciously agreed—so my rest in Damascus will *be brief after all. Abu Alim has gone to Homs to see his family, but will return to Damascus in a week's time, and that is when I hope to set out.*

Will you be summering in Rhode Island this year? Tell me if so, and I shall direct my letters accordingly.

Sophia

She put down her pen, reviewed the letter, and decided it was as bland and agreeable as she could make it. The line about the faience vase was perhaps a bit pointed. *I recall little of you,* it seemed to say, *except for that summer gown.* But really, how far was that from the mark? Her memories of her family were faded, arrested in time. George, especially: he was nearly seventeen now. She'd almost sent him a block of *halawa* from a Cairo bakery, before remembering he was far too old for a gift of sweets.

In truth, her letters home were mostly for her father. She chose the stories she thought he'd enjoy: the ruin she'd camped beside at the outskirts of Latakia, unmarked on any map; the fragments of a double-handled amphora that she'd found in Amman, near the Temple of Hercules. His responses often took months to arrive, and there was rarely any true news in their pages. *Your mother is busy as always. George is adjusting well to his school in Connecticut.* He never spoke of his own life, his own doings. Sometimes she pictured him at his desk in the library, reading her letters with an atlas at hand, tracing her journey, imagining himself in her place.

Only once had she dared to propose that the family reunite. *We could all meet in Italy,* she wrote, *or Spain, during the summer.* The answering letter said nothing of her suggestion until a brief postscript, in her mother's handwriting: *We would be very glad to see you at home, in New York.* Apparently it would happen on her mother's terms, or not at all.

She sealed her letter, addressed it to her father's Wall Street office—never the mansion, to keep it from the servants' prying eyes—and slipped it into her jacket-pocket. She had errands to run, supplies to purchase. Carchemish lay on the Turkish border, near the town of Jerablus; it was farther north than she liked to go in the springtime, but she was genuinely interested in the ruins, and could hardly pass up the opportunity.

From her trunk she took a bulb-shaped brass flask, the sort used for storing gunpowder. She uncapped the flask, measured out a spoonful of powder into a glass of water, stirred it, and drank it down. Her medicines had changed over the years, as the healers that she found moved from place to place, or simply passed away. This particular powder was her least favorite of the lot: it did nothing to warm her, only stopped her trembling so that she might move and eat and speak with no outward sign of her misery. Taking it made her feel like a living statue, a woman trapped in ice. But the herbalist who made it had the advantage of a stall in the Al-Hamidiyeh souk, only a few minutes' walk from her hotel.

She went to the lobby, gave her letter to the desk attendant to post, and stepped out into the blinding sunlight of Marjeh Square. The ancient Orontes River had been tamed here, its lazy curves narrowed and straightened into a swift channel that ran beneath a vast, unbroken plaza of red brick. The Ottoman government had built its regional offices around the square, in tall stone buildings with iron balconies. Imperial bureaucrats in fezzes and round-collared uniforms breakfasted in nearby cafés, sipping coffee over their newspapers. As always, they stared at Sophia as she went by, taking in her Western dress, her unaccompanied state.

She passed by the Citadel of Damascus with its forbidding stone parapets, and then entered the covered expanse of the souk, threading through the morning crowd, past stalls laden with rugs and teas and caged pigeons, vegetables and sheepskins. Children ran up to her, displaying scarves, slippers, sweets. She smiled and waved them away, then paused at a clothing stall to consider a thick wool tunic, thinking of the cooler weather in Jerablus. At last she went on, resolving to buy one later.

The herbalist Sophia frequented was named Umm Sahir. Her stall was toward the far end of the souk, near the Umayyad Mosque and the Old City's maze of alleys, where the market was somewhat quieter. The stall itself was set inside the low, arched entrance to an old granary, one of the citadel's many half-crumbled outbuildings that had been absorbed into the souk as it grew. To Sophia the entire structure seemed perpetually on the verge of collapse, but if it worried Umm Sahir, she made no sign of it. As usual, she'd sighted Sophia from across the alley, and by the time Sophia reached the stall was already collecting what was needed.

"Greetings, Umm Sahir," Sophia said when the woman emerged from the granary's arch, her arms laden with bottles and bundles.

"Greetings, Miss Williams," Umm Sahir replied, her sharp eyes upon her ingredients as she worked. "I'd hoped I might see you today."

"Oh?"

"I have a visitor," the woman said, with a quick nod toward the dark beyond the arch. "My great-aunt Umm Ishaq. I haven't seen her in many years. She's come from As-Suwaida to be with my cousin, who's close to giving birth."

"May it be an easy birth and a healthy baby," Sophia said, a touch confused.

The woman said, "When I was a child, Umm Ishaq was known as the most powerful exorcist from here to Amman."

Sophia's heart leapt against her ribs.

"Perhaps you'd like to meet her."

The granary went farther back than Sophia had imagined.

The noise of the souk receded as Sophia followed Umm Sahir into the depths. Herbs hung from the wall in string-tied bundles, their smell dizzying. At the far end of the granary was a split door wide enough for a cart to pass through, its top half open to the sunny alley beyond. Sophia blinked against the blinding square of light.

Next to the door, upon a low stool, sat one of the oldest women Sophia had ever seen. She was tiny, and deeply hunched, with a face as crinkled as a walnut shell and eyes that were nearly obscured by drooping lids. She saw Sophia, and her empty mouth pulled back in a smile. She waved Sophia closer, gesturing to a pallet that lay at her feet.

Nervously Sophia obeyed. She'd gone to exorcists before, had paid sizable fees to be prayed over by imams and Sufis, but none of them had helped. This woman, though, seemed different from the others. She leaned forward, her fingers at Sophia's jaw, angling Sophia's face into the sunlight from the open door. Sophia's vision swam as the woman held her eyelids open, searching. At last she drew back with a grunt. She gestured for her patient to lie back on the pallet, then placed a hand low on Sophia's stomach, pressing here and there until she found a spot that seemed to interest her. The old woman looked up at Umm Sahir and spoke briefly in an unknown dialect, her words slurred with age and toothlessness.

"She asks how long ago," Umm Sahir told Sophia.

Sophia swallowed reflexively. "Eleven years," she said.

The old woman spoke again. "A long time, for such an injury," Umm Sahir said. "It might not be possible."

"I understand," Sophia said, struggling not to hope.

A few more muttered words—and now Umm Sahir went to the dried herbs that hung on the wall, selecting sprigs here and there and tying them together with thread. She handed the bundle to Umm Ishaq, who lit a small brazier next to the pallet and placed the herbs upon it. At once the air was thick with pungent smoke. Umm Sahir filled a bowl with water from a jug, washed her hands and arms up to the elbows—Sophia was reminded uncomfortably of a surgeon—and then brought the bowl to Umm Ishaq, who did the same.

The exorcist then gestured to Sophia's head, mimed removing the pins and undoing the braid.

Sophia stiffened. "No—thank you, but—"

The old woman held out a hand to stop her, then pointed above the half door. Sophia squinted, and saw a profusion of iron amulets, dozens of them, mounted around the threshold.

"You're safe here," Umm Sahir said.

A last hesitation—and then Sophia undid the pins and loosed her hair. It fell around her shoulders, deeply crimped after so long in the braid. Without the weight her head felt too light, as though it might float away; or perhaps that was just the smoke from the brazier.

The old woman made her lie back on the pallet, then brushed thin, dry fingers over Sophia's eyes to close them. Sophia lay motionless as a warm oil was rubbed onto her forehead and then her abdomen. Umm

Sahir squatted by Sophia's head, and placed her hands on their patient's shoulders, as though to hold her in place.

The old woman began to chant in a high, thin voice. There was Arabic in the words, and other languages, too—Aramaic? Phoenician? Sophia wanted to listen, to remember, so she might write it down later; but the exorcist's warm palms rested heavily on her oiled forehead and stomach, and as though in response, the chill inside her strengthened. Her body began to shake despite the medicine she'd taken, her ever-meager warmth draining away completely. The woman was chanting more loudly now, but Sophia could barely hear her. *Stop,* she wanted to say, but her teeth were clenched so tightly she feared they might shatter. Her spine had gone rigid, her breath was locked in her throat, she was going to freeze to death—

Whiteness swept across her vision.

When she opened her eyes, the light through the door had changed from late morning to midday. A sheepskin-lined coat, smelling of hay and lanolin, had been placed over her like a blanket. Umm Sahir was no longer there; Sophia could hear her outside, instructing a customer in which herbs to steam for a sore throat.

Umm Ishaq sat asleep on the stool beside the door, her chin sunk to her chest. As Sophia sat up, she woke, and shook her head with regret.

But Sophia already knew. She nodded, and reached for her coin-purse. Umm Ishaq waved her away with a half-offended look, but Sophia said, "Please. For your grandchild." At last the woman nodded and accepted the small stack of lira. Then Umm Ishaq settled back and fell asleep again, leaving Sophia to braid her hair with cold and trembling fingers.

It was a Saturday morning in March, and the Golem was at the subway station on Spring Street, waiting for her train uptown.

"Chava Levy," cried a woman nearby, "is that you?"

The Golem turned, spirits flagging. Gittel Epstein, Thea Radzin's closest friend, was hurrying across the platform in a flurry of false warmth.

"Our very own college girl!" said Mrs. Epstein as she embraced the Golem. "I miss seeing you at the bakery! How are your studies, have you met anyone nice?"

The Golem kept a smile in her voice as she replied. Yes, her classes were going well; yes, she was heading up to campus now, to visit the library. In a year, if all went as planned, she'd have her teaching degree in Domestic Sciences.

"Domestic Sciences, my goodness!" the woman said with a fluttering laugh.

In my day, the Golem thought wearily, *we just called it cooking.*

"In my day," the woman said, "we just called it *cooking!*"

The train arrived then, pushing a damp gust of air into the station. "Take care of yourself, Chava dear," the woman called, thinking, *Never would've marked that one for a striver. And after everything Thea did for her, too.*

The Golem found a seat in the subway carriage among the clerks and secretaries, feeling as though she'd been caught playing truant. She didn't *need* to study uptown, not really; she could just as easily bring her textbooks back to her boardinghouse. But these days, even a walk to the corner pharmacist's was likely to end in an awkward conversation. Most of her neighbors and former customers were happy for her, Gittel being the rare exception; Thea had been devastated when the Golem left the bakery, and Gittel was still angry on her behalf. But even those who approved of the Golem's new path now felt wary around her, as though she herself had changed.

You were supposed to be a poor widow for the rest of your life, Anna had said when the Golem complained to her about it. *Now they're afraid you'll pity them, the same way they pitied you.*

The carriage pulled away into the tunnel, and she closed her eyes as the cool earth surrounded her. The Elevated would be quicker, but the subway never failed to soothe her nerves. She'd go to the library and finish her assigned readings, she decided, and then begin her essay on how best to instruct a classroom of mixed ages. The dean had at long last approved her accelerated schedule, so she could earn her degree in three years instead of four—but with a stern warning that he'd rescind his approval if her grades slipped. *You're a gifted student, Mrs. Levy, but you mustn't take on more than you can handle.*

It would be imprudent, she supposed, to tell him that she could "take on" twice again as much. She absorbed her lessons at a glance, grasped the underlying principles nearly as quickly. In the laboratory, she timed chemical reactions with precision, and grew multicolored molds in glass dishes. From textbooks and lectures she memorized the strange science of the human body, all of which was new to her: the digestive system and its extraction of nutrients, the roles of saliva and gastric fluids, the chemistries of blood and lymph. She could name each step in the pasteurization process and explain why it was necessary, could identify every cut of meat in a butcher's window and knew which were best roasted and which braised. She gleaned knowledge like wheat from a field, and passed all her exams handily—though she was careful to make a mistake every once in a while, so as not to be too perfect for comfort.

Still, there were difficulties. The phrase *a credit to her race* seemed to chase her around campus like a whisper. Many of the professors expected less from her because of it—and then, when she eclipsed their own favorite students, they recast her shyness as self-satisfaction, her intelligence as cunning. As for her classmates, they had little idea of how to approach her. They knew she was a widow, which was an unfathomable prospect; many of them wondered how she was not constantly in tears. The other Jewish girls turned a pitying eye upon her frugal shirtwaists and unfashionable cloak, but were mainly glad that she wasn't so provincial as to embarrass them. If she'd struggled in the classroom, they might've invited her to join their study groups and *kaffeeklatschen,* as an act of benevolence. As it was, they were terrified that she might offer to help *them.*

But the Golem had expected all of that, had prepared herself for it. Never had she considered that her own longtime neighbors might now think differently of her; and it was their new, unspoken distance that drove her uptown, where she might study in peace, instead of skulking about the Lower East Side.

One more year, she thought as her carriage raced through the thawing earth. *You can manage one more year.*

The Jinni sat on a bench at Pennsylvania Station, smoking a blissful cigarette.

He ought to have been at the shop, working on their newest orders. But Arbeely had developed a bad head-cold over the winter, and the resulting cough refused to go away. "It's your cigarettes," the man insisted. "They tickle my throat."

"That's ridiculous, I've smoked them for years," the Jinni had replied. "Besides, how can they be bothering you when you're over here"—he indicated Arbeely's desk, upon which he was currently leaning—"And I'm all the way over there?" He pointed to the far corner of the workshop.

"It's the air-currents. All of your smoke ends up at my desk."

"Then move your desk," he'd said, which had earned him a disgusted look; and the man had spent the next few hours coughing in so dramatic a fashion that the Jinni had at last decided to go somewhere he could smoke in peace.

It was as good an excuse as any to walk all the way to 31st Street in the middle of the day—for now that Pennsylvania Station was completed, he never passed up an opportunity to visit it. He always took care to approach the station in the same way, for the best effect: First, the Seventh Avenue entrance with its wide, many-columned facade. Then, the vestibule and the high, narrow barrel of the Arcade, the windowed arch at its end. Through the arch, and down the stairs—and the view opened into the soaring marble expanse of the Waiting Room, with its ornate mosaics and soaring columns, its electric candelabra that rose, treelike, from the floor. Across this shining plaza, and through another towering arch, to the Concourse: and now the ribs of the building changed from stone to steel, a framework of arches and vaults all set with glass panes like an enormous greenhouse. Even the floor was steel, and pierced like a screen so that one might gaze below one's feet, to the waiting trains.

The Jinni had gone to the station at least a dozen times since its opening, yet he always found some new detail to admire. It reminded him of a caravanserai he'd seen once outside Isfahan, in the days before his capture. From the outside, the structure had seemed merely a high-walled, rectangular fortress. But inside, it had revealed itself as a paradise of tiled fountains and potted palms, its courtyard open to the stars. On entering, the newest of the caravan guards had goggled at the sight, while the veterans chuckled at their faces. It was the same at Pennsylvania Station. To pass through its columns was to feel oneself dwindle in size, yet grow in significance; it was every traveler's splendid palace, if only for the time it took to walk from the entrance to the platform. He liked to position himself near the platform stairs and watch the arriving passengers, searching for the signs of the newcomer: the widening eye, the dropping jaw.

I ought to bring Chava here, he thought, as he always did. The station had been open for months now, and still they hadn't seen it together. It wasn't his fault, not really; it had been a long winter and a wet spring, and his mind had been elsewhere. Business was still pouring in. The shop had been featured in a few of the city's fashionable magazines; one had even sent an illustrator, who'd captured the Jinni at the anvil in mid-swing. A few of Little Syria's children had taken to scouting the train stations for tourists and charging them a nickel each to escort them to the showroom. Everyone marveled that the business still comprised only the two partners—and yet in truth all the ironwork was the Jinni's, for Arbeely was kept busy by his other duties. At one point Arbeely had suggested bringing on an apprentice smith to lighten the load—but the Jinni had turned him down. The truth was that he worked better alone. Tools stayed where he put them; supplies failed to vanish when his back was turned. He could imagine an entire commission from start to finish without having to draw tedious diagrams, and improvise if necessary without explanation or argument. The workshop was his own domain, and he was glad of it.

And yet sometimes he missed the early days of their partnership, the subterranean shop full of pots and pans, the trivial repairs—even the endless circular arguments, as Arbeely attempted to explain yet another bizarre facet of human nature. Nowadays they might go hours on end without exchanging a single word. Other Syrian businessmen would drop by, and their chuckling voices would carry from Arbeely's desk to the Jinni's ears—and something like loneliness would creep inside him. But loneliness for *what*? He had no true desire to hear the neighborhood gossip, or to listen as they reminisced about villages he'd never seen; nor did he wish to tell lies of a Bedouin childhood he'd never lived. So instead he would step closer to the forge, and allow its comforting murmur to shade out the human voices so he might concentrate.

Sometimes he felt like telling all of this to the Golem. But lately, during their nights together, he could hardly get a word in edgewise. Yes, of course he was glad that she enjoyed her studies—but *must* she tell him everything she'd learned about the human digestive system, and in such unfortunate detail? Now that she'd been enlightened upon these matters, she'd apparently decided that he, too, was in need of improvement. And for all her newfound volubility, her life seemed more opaque than before, not less. What did she *do* all day, on that campus? She appeared to him the same as ever—yet he had the sense of small, disorienting changes occurring out of sight. Then again, it had been a long winter, and a damp spring. Perhaps things would improve now that the rain had stopped.

He finished his cigarette, took a final, strengthening glance upward at the soaring trusses, and left the station for the long walk south.

In the library reading room, the Golem plumbed the depths of her Food Chemistry texts while, above her, the university regents peered down from their portraits as though reading over her shoulder. She greatly preferred the main library, with its anonymous crowd, to the more intimate Teachers College library, where she felt conspicuous among her classmates. *There goes Chava, by herself as usual . . . Should I invite her for tea? But what would we talk about? No, I won't bother her, she must want to study, otherwise she wouldn't have come all the way uptown . . .* Far better to remain here, where she might study in peace.

She'd thought to stay longer, and loiter among the back issues of *McCall's*—but it was past four o'clock, and the library's chill was making her legs ache. So instead she returned her borrowed books to the shelving desk, and went down the library steps, past the marble-fronted buildings and carefully tended lawns, and out onto the wide expanse of Broadway.

After so many years of working behind a counter from morning until nightfall, to walk alone in the daytime like this was a surprising new luxury. Her classes and lectures were scattered through the week, among various mornings and afternoons, which left entire handfuls of hours in which she was meant to be nowhere in particular. She couldn't fill them all with study, so she walked instead. The increase in exercise had done wonders for her winter stiffness, and now she could spend even a string of nights alone in her room without discomfort. It made her less reliant on the Jinni—which was probably for the best, as he was consumed lately by his work and tended to be in a difficult mood. For once, she'd seemed to have an easier winter than he had.

She went north on Broadway, past Teachers College itself, a long quadrangle of tall buildings that faced inward around a narrow lawn. On a Saturday afternoon like this, there'd be earnest discussions in the cafeterias, and giggling and gossip in Whittier Hall. She'd considered moving to Whittier only briefly, before discarding the idea. She'd have no privacy there at all, and at far greater expense than her boardinghouse.

She detoured west at 122nd, to walk along Riverside Park: a half-neglected wild this far north, its terraced lawns tangled with weeds and debris. Still, the park had its own tenacious beauty. Soon the yellow-woods would be covered with flowers, long garlands of white among the green. The air seemed newly washed thanks to the recent rains, with barely a whiff of the acrid coal-yards farther north, or the cattle-cars that ran along the Hudson below. At 129th the park ended and she turned back towards Broadway, listening to the vendors' patter in the public market—*These onions were in the ground this morning, you won't find any fresher, ten cents a bunch, but for you I'll make it eight.* Now that the weather was dry, a few of the more optimistic cafés had set out tables and chairs, as though to coax the sun into warming them.

As always, she felt vaguely guilty that she never brought the Jinni here, to the streets she'd learned in daylight. She kept meaning to suggest it—but always faltered, and changed her mind. Was it so wrong of her to keep these streets for herself? This was *her* territory, the one neighborhood she explored on her own. Besides, he'd only make his usual acerbic comments, about the very details she loved: the wide bay windows hung with curtains, the clean sidewalks and tidy stoops. Tedious, he'd call it—and perhaps he was right. But wasn't tedium a rare and precious thing in this city? How many of its citizens would give everything they had for a chance at an uneventful life?

Onward she went, until she reached 136th, where Hamilton Place sprouted east at an angle from Broadway's trunk. She glanced right as she crossed the street—and noticed for the first time the high fence of wrought iron that ran alongside a wide expanse of grass.

Curious, she turned toward it.

Bit by bit a many-gabled building appeared, surrounded by a vast lawn, and a playground where groups of children ran about. A squad of teenaged boys stood in rigid formation upon the grass, each holding a pole with a flag at its end. A whistle blew, and the boys executed a complicated set of maneuvers with the flags, waving them above their heads and sweeping them side to side.

She watched, fascinated. Was it a school? The building seemed far too large—and besides, it was a Saturday. A much smaller outbuilding sat near the fence at the middle of the block, and as the Golem approached it she felt a wave of—homesickness? Yes, from young minds full of confusion. *Where is Mama? Who are these people, and why don't they speak Yiddish?* Their agitation receded as she passed. She rounded the corner at Amsterdam, where a double gate led to a long, circular drive like a mansion's. Only then did she see the sign, mounted beside the gate: *Asylum for Orphaned Hebrews.*

So this was an orphanage. She placed one hand upon the fence and closed her eyes, ignoring the afternoon traffic around her. At this distance, she felt only a diffuse jumble of thoughts—the flag-wavers' concentration, the various victories and betrayals happening upon the playground—but underpinning it all was a loneliness that seemed to saturate the very bricks. It saddened and beguiled her, and she reached out to it, wishing she could soothe them all—

A bell rang, startling her. The boys on the lawn broke their formation and ran inside, flags whipping behind them. She looked up at the sky, which was just beginning to darken. With some reluctance she walked back to Broadway and descended into the subway. Lost in her own thoughts, she rode back through the earth to the Lower East Side and emerged onto Spring Street: and only then did she feel the galvanizing shock of tragedy all around her, the grief like lightning in the air.

10.

Anna Blumberg's brush with death occurred while the entire Lower East Side was looking elsewhere.

It began at near to closing time at the Waverly Steam Laundry on Greene Street, where Anna had now worked for eight years. The laundry took its name from nearby Waverly Place, and was meant to evoke Washington Square's stately brownstones—though in truth the laundry sat among a mishmash of lofts and tenements, and even an ancient wood-frame stable that leaned to one side like a rotting tooth. A man named Hopkins owned the laundry; he'd bought it with the aim of installing his son Morris as the manager, a ploy to keep him out of the betting parlors.

Anna was the most senior of Morris's hires. She was listed on the books as a washerwoman, but in reality it was Anna, not Morris, who managed the daily choreography of washers, carters, sorters, and pressers. This left Morris free to spend his work hours as he preferred, thumbing through the racing papers and nursing his various grudges. He'd hired Anna in full knowledge of her fallen condition, and was smart enough to give her small raises here and there, just enough to keep her chained to his side. Anna despised Morris, and longed to quit—but what else was there? The laundry had stolen her youth away. At thirty she looked a decade older, her face lined and florid from the constant steam. No one would take her for a salesgirl or a secretary, or even a baker. Waverly, she knew, was as good a deal as she was likely to get.

Sunday was the laundry's day of rest, its Jewish employees notwithstanding. Morris, however, liked to begin his own personal Sabbath on Saturday afternoons, so he might fetch a good seat at his boxing club; and so Anna had been left in charge of finishing the week's orders, as usual. She was rushing to fold a hotel's bedsheets when Daisy, one of the sorting-girls, paused at her table to peer outside the window. "Something's going on," she said. "There's a crowd of people out on the street."

"Go see what it is," Anna said, and went back to moving the stacks of folded sheets from table to cart, table to cart. She'd have to buy something for Toby's supper on the walk home, as they had nothing in the icebox. And tomorrow was her monthly walk with the Golem, which was a strange prospect these days, what with her classes on digestion and chemistry—

A scream pierced her thoughts.

She turned in surprise and stumbled into the cart, her leg colliding painfully with its sharp edge. Daisy had returned, and was speaking to another laundry girl, who stood horrified, her hand over her mouth. Without a word the girl ran out the door.

"What is it?" said Anna, walking over. "What's wrong with Ellie?"

Daisy was white-faced. "There's a fire at the factory where her sister works. Girls are jumping out the windows."

"Oh, my God," Anna murmured.

"Which factory?" another girl demanded.

"Triangle Shirtwaist, in the Asch Building."

"My friend Ida works at Triangle," someone said, a quaver in her voice.

The girls all began edging worriedly toward the door. Anna looked around at the work that still had to be done: the sheets rolled halfway through the mangle, the washers full of boiling water. "Go," she told them. "I'll finish up." They threw her grateful looks, and in a moment the laundry had emptied.

Something warm and wet was trickling onto Anna's foot. She looked down—and saw the gash. It was inches long, and carved deep into her calf. The edges of the skin were pressed inward, along with the torn stocking. Bloody footprints traced her path back to the cart.

She shuddered, suddenly dizzy. *Don't look*, she thought. *Just take care of it.*

She found a towel, tied it tight around the now-aching wound, and mopped the blood from the floor. Then she gritted her teeth and dragged the steaming sheets from the washers. Slop-water drenched her leg; the cut burned as though she'd soaked it in vinegar. She ignored the pain, loaded and spun the extractors, fed the sheets into the mangle one by one.

At last the deliveries were all tagged and sorted. She peeled away the now-sodden towel. The skin around the wound was swollen and grayish, but the bleeding had stopped, at least. It would heal. Others were no doubt hurting worse tonight. She drew the ruined stocking over her calf, then switched off the lights, locked the front door, and limped toward home.

The streets seemed quieter than usual, though more than once she heard crying. Her head throbbed in time with her leg; she remembered the empty icebox, but couldn't bear the idea of stopping at the butcher's. She'd send Toby out for something.

She climbed the tenement stairs slowly, gripping the railing tight. By the time she reached their floor, the hallway lamps had turned gray and distant, as though receding down a tunnel. With shaking fingers she fished the key from her bag.

"Mama?" Toby stood in the doorway, dressed in his new Western Union uniform. He was so proud of it that he rarely took it off.

"Hello, boychik." She smiled, hoping that it looked natural. "I'm sorry I'm late. Are you hungry?" She dropped her bag next to the couch, sat down heavily. Had he said something in reply? She wasn't sure. He, too, was vanishing down that tunnel, watching her from far away. *I'm all right*, she told him, *I just need a little sleep . . .*

The tunnel dimmed entirely, and Toby disappeared into the dark.

The news arrived at the Asylum at supper-time, and sped through the dining hall.

A fire, at a factory.

Frum's mother was there.

Who?

Max Frum, in Dormitory 1.

All craned their heads toward the table where the youngest boys ate in pale-faced silence, their eyes avoiding the empty chair in their midst.

Poor kid.

He's a true orphan now, I guess.

At her own table, Kreindel Altschul heard the whispered words—*fire, true orphan*. She shivered, and put down her fork.

Yossele, she thought. *Tonight. I'll come to you tonight.*

The storage room at the end of the basement's southern wing was known as the large-item repository, and it was the most neglected and disorderly spot in the entire Asylum. Once, it had been used exclusively for surplus furniture and old pageant props—but that had been in the building's early days, before the Asylum's population had grown so large that a second boiler had been deemed necessary. With nowhere else to put it, the workmen had carved a boiler closet from the large-item repository itself: a room within a room, accessible only from the hallway, like a slice taken from the side of a cake. Now, as one traveled deeper into the storage room, it constricted to a narrow corridor and then expanded again at the very back, creating an alcove that was nearly impossible to see from the door.

In the years following the room's alteration, its contents had become a hopeless jumble. Boxes of concert programs, dusty yearbooks, and other ancient ephemera stacked the walls, shading the feeble light from the window-wells. No one knew exactly when the lock on the door had broken—but no one wanted to replace it, either, in case the act should somehow make them responsible for the room and its contents. Few of the Asylum's current staff even knew about the alcove in the back, and none of them had seen it for themselves.

In the darkest corner of this hidden lair, shaded by a dusty length of burlap painted with palm trees from a long-ago Biblical play, Yossele the golem sat waiting for his master.

It wasn't a difficult life, there in the storage room. Instead of the dockyard tarpaulin, he wore an old theater curtain of moth-eaten velvet that Kreindel had unearthed from a box and draped around him. He might've grown stiff and uncomfortable in winter were it not for the gigantic boiler on the other side of the wall, sending out its heat day and night. He had no wish to be anywhere else, unless it was closer to Kreindel; and he had no need for visitors, for Kreindel's mind was his constant companion.

He watched, now, as she lay awake and impatient, waiting for the Asylum to grow still. More children than usual were crying in their cots, their sniffles echoing in the silence. She'd have to be careful tonight.

At last the orphanage settled into a deeper quiet, and Kreindel slipped out of her bed and down the wide staircase to the basement, the route familiar in the dark. Then, the warmth of the boiler, and the doorknob beneath her hand.

Yossele felt her grow closer, and heard the doorknob turn.

To Kreindel, the storage room was like her father's synagogue: the same smell of paper and wood and dust, the same welcome stillness of a holy place. She crept her way through the maze of stacks to the narrow corridor, knowing that he was there, that they were only a few steps apart.

He made no noise, moved not an inch. This was their ritual, and he cherished it just as she did.

Foot by foot she entered the alcove, and at last reached out, unseeing in the dark—

He reached out for her, in the dark—

—and felt his cool, solid hand grip hers, to guide her the rest of the way.

For near to an hour she sat in his arms, her tears soaking the velvet at his shoulder while his square-fingered hands stroked her hair. *Hide*, her father had said, and sometimes she wondered: Why was she still hiding? It would be easy to leave under cover of night, the iron gates being no match for a golem. But as much as she hated the Asylum, she couldn't make herself run away. She was only fourteen. Her father wouldn't have wanted her to live on the streets, or work for pennies at a factory that might go up in flames. Here, at least, she was fed, and clothed, and sheltered. Here, she could keep Yossele safe.

She kissed his cheek—this, too, was part of the ritual—and whispered, *Good night, Yossele,* and retreated again through the maze and up to the dormitory, at last to sleep.

Toby Blumberg had no reason to think that anything was wrong with his mother.

After all, it wasn't the first time that she'd dragged herself home past supper and fallen asleep on the couch. He made her comfortable, as usual, placing a pillow beneath her head and covering her with a blanket. She flinched, but didn't wake. He wondered, did she know about the factory that had burned? It was close to her laundry, it seemed impossible she hadn't heard—but it was the sort of thing she would've mentioned, even in her fatigue. *A horrible thing, boychik, just horrible.*

"Mama," he called softly, "I'm going out for a chop suey. Do you want anything?" There was no answer, only the rise and fall of her chest. Well, if she woke up starving, it wouldn't be on his head.

He carried his bicycle down to the street. He was still in his uniform, though he wasn't supposed to wear it off duty. He was proud to be one of the youngest messengers in Midtown, and one of the fastest, too. He loved his job, loved imagining the Morse operators in faraway lands sending their signals down wires and across oceans and into his hands so he might speed them the final mile. His mother, of course, lived in terror of him ending up beneath a streetcar. He took a guilty satisfaction in that fear, as revenge for her ongoing silence. *I'll tell you when you're older*—but how old did he have to be before she'd tell him the first thing about his father? Even just his name?

He rode to his favorite chop suey restaurant on Pell Street. The proprietor seemed more subdued than usual, his wife red-eyed. Toby found a spot at a table and ate, and no one glanced his way. He'd noticed that the uniform gave him a sort of invisibility, as though it turned him into a part of the city's workings, something you'd walk past without noticing, like a statue or a bench.

It was growing late by the time he finished, but he didn't want to go home, not yet. He wasn't tired enough; he'd only lie on his pallet and stare at the ceiling, waiting for the nightmare to come. So he got on his bike and rode up and down the avenues until his legs ached and his lungs burned, pretending all the while that he wasn't avoiding the corner where the Asch Building stood. At last, surrendering to his curiosity, he turned onto Greene Street, and nearly rode straight into the silent crowd.

Immediately he dismounted. Hundreds of women and men stood together in a crescent-moon sweep, all facing the building on the north-west corner. He craned his neck upward and saw the lights creeping about in the topmost floors, beyond the broken windows. Below, the sidewalks shone with puddles of water, as though recently washed.

Movement, at the base of the building. Two firemen emerged, carry-ing a stretcher between them. Upon the stretcher, draped carefully with a blanket, was something not quite large enough to be a person. The crowd exhaled as one at the sight; a woman's sob rose into the air like the call of a bird.

Toby wheeled his bicycle away.

His mother was still on the parlor couch, her breath whistling thinly as she slept. She looked sallow in the lamplight, her cheeks slack with exhaustion. He made certain she was covered, and then unrolled his pallet at last, hoping that he'd tired himself enough to sleep without dreaming.

The Golem sat in her room, desolate.

The walk to Eldridge Street from the subway had been an unspeak-able battle, each step a fight against the grief and horror that pulled at her from every direction. Dreadful knowledge had poured into her from each mind that she passed: images of the fire, and the falling women; the sight of the bodies arriving at the Bellevue morgue, more and more of them, so many that the attendants had begun to lay them out along the nearby pier. Occasionally someone had gone past her at a run, someone who'd only just heard and was now frantic for news. *My daughter was up there. My sister, my mother.* Here and there she'd passed a building where a victim had lived, where anguish now bloomed behind the walls. It had taken every ounce of her concentration merely to climb the boarding-house steps and unlock her bedroom door.

Sorrow weighted her like lead. More than anything, she wanted the Jinni. Perhaps he'd even come early. He'd take her to Central Park, where she could walk beneath the elms. They'd put their preoccupations aside, give each other their full attention.

Soon, she thought, her head in her hands. *He'll be here soon.*

"Staying late again?" Arbeely said.

At his worktable, the Jinni tightened a vise around an iron bar. "Not very," he said. "This shouldn't take more than a few hours. And Chava's expecting me." He peered at his partner. Did the man always look this exhausted?

"What is it?" Arbeely said.

If he told the truth—*You look terrible*, or the like—Arbeely would scold him for his lack of tact. "Nothing," he said. "I was only collecting wool."

The man chuckled. "Woolgathering. I'll see you Monday. Say hello to Chava for me." And the man put on his hat and left, coughing into his hand.

Alone, the Jinni fitted a hook around the iron bar and twisted, care-ful to keep the motion smooth and even. It took one's whole body to cold-twist a wrought iron bar, and he'd developed a rhythm: the waiting bars stacked to one side, the finished ones to the other, placing the hook, gripping it, bracing, twisting—

Movement, from a nearby window. A young woman, her arms burdened with groceries, had paused on the sidewalk to watch him. He met her eye, not even meaning to—and she blushed, and quickly walked on.

A wave of desire washed through him as he watched her go.

He took a deep breath and set the hook on the table. This had been happening more often lately. Not the desire itself—that had never left him—but the urge to act upon it. To follow a woman who'd caught his eye, and let the evening go where it might. To counter the impulse, he pictured a woman's face: not the Golem's, but Sophia Winston's. Pale and unwell, trembling beneath her shawls. All because she, too, had caught his eye.

I will never again take a human lover, he told himself. Lately it had become a second vow laid beside the first, a way to remain true to the Golem without resenting her for it. He told himself that, from a certain perspective, the two vows could be seen as one and the same.

He released the bar from the vise and laid it aside. He felt unsettled, in need of distraction. He'd bank the forge and then go back to his hidden workroom for a while, before leaving for the Golem's boarding-house.

He approached the forge, its warmth soothing away some of his irritation. He switched off the electric fan, bent to pick up the coal-rake . . . and stopped. Stood straight again, at the forge's edge, and inhaled the heated air. Better, even, than his cigarettes.

He turned around, peering out the windows for pedestrians. For the moment, there were none. Quickly, before he could tell himself not to, he unbuttoned his shirtsleeves, rolled them up, and placed his bare hands atop the burning coke.

Heat and strength roared through him. There was a noise like wind in his ears. His eyes sharpened, showing him infinitesimal colors and patterns in the glow of the flames. Within moments he felt more alive than he had in months.

He lifted his hands away before his clothing could ignite. Every detail of the shop's dark corners stood out in relief: flakes of plaster, strands of cobweb. He picked up an iron bar from the pile and it softened immediately, pliable in his hands. He could see the grain now, the dark striations running lengthwise through the bar, with microscopic clarity.

He went back to his hidden room and settled in to work. Before long he was surrounded by spirals and peelings and curlicues of wrought iron, an explosion of metal excelsior. He'd gotten caught up in the work; he'd be late to the Golem's apartment—she'd be annoyed, of course, but he'd weather it . . .

"Ahmad?"

The Jinni started at the sight of his partner's head poking through the curtain. "Arbeely, what are you doing here? Couldn't you sleep?"

"It's seven in the morning," the man said.

"What?" said the Jinni blankly. He went to the curtain and pulled it aside.

Sunlight assaulted his eyes.

Disoriented, he followed Arbeely out to his desk. He'd thought it only an hour past midnight, two at most—but here was morning, the tobacconist's open across the street, pushcarts and wagons vying for the spaces beside the curbs. Arbeely wore his Sunday suit and hat, and held a folded newspaper. "I went out for a paper, and I saw that the forge was still burning," the man was saying. "And—well, it worried me, given what's happened. Chava didn't know any of those poor girls, did she? Perhaps we ought to install sprinklers—"

"What poor girls?" the Jinni said. "*What's* happened?"

The man eyed him. "You don't know?"

"Just tell me, Arbeely."

The man sighed, and handed him the paper.

The Jinni unfolded it, winced deeply at the headline, read on. *Triangle Shirtwaist, where many worked from the Lower East Side . . . nearly at closing time . . .*

Chava. Where had she been when this factory had gone up in flames? Uptown, or at home?

He thrust the paper into Arbeely's hands and ran from the shop.

Toby woke at dawn in the grip of his nightmare.

He sat up gasping, ready to burst out of his skin. His eyes focused on his bicycle, leaning against the door. In the next instant he'd donned his coat and shoes and was carrying it down the stairwell.

Outside, the streets were shrouded in morning fog. Black wreaths had sprouted overnight from doorways; they blurred to smears as he rode, his tires hissing on the pavement. He passed a newsstand, read the *Times* placard: *One Hundred and Forty-One Dead in Factory Fire.* He pictured the lump on the stretcher, the rinsed sidewalks, and pedaled faster.

At last he felt calm enough to go home again. The building was quiet, for a Sunday morning. He carried the bicycle through a hallway that smelled of coffee and frying onions, past neighbors sunk in their own dismal thoughts.

His mother was still on the sofa.

"Mama," he called. She never slept this late, not even on Sundays. He went to her and shook her shoulder—and the heat of her skin made him pull back his hand. He switched on the light and saw that she was drenched with sweat, her breaths shallow and quick. He pulled the blanket from her—and only then saw the rent in her stocking, and the swollen, livid wound beneath it.

"Mama!" He shook her, urgently, but she only moaned. He had to find a neighbor, get her to a hospital—they couldn't afford it, but what if she was *dying*—

An old memory swam up through his fright. His mother, her face in shadow, her voice urgent: *Find Missus Chava.*

He grabbed his bicycle and ran down the stairs.

The boardinghouse was silent when the Jinni arrived, the windows drawn and black.

"*Chava!*" the Jinni shouted up at her window. She'd be furious at him for making a scene in front of the entire neighborhood, but he hardly cared, only *let her be there*—

The door opened.

It was the Golem, whole and uninjured. He nearly sagged with relief. But she didn't rush down to shush and berate him, or march coldly past him in annoyance. She didn't say anything, didn't even look at him. She seemed dazed, drained of life—

And it was his fault, he realized. He'd left her alone all night, with the grief of an entire neighborhood.

She sat down on the steps and put her face in her hands. For a terrible moment he thought she was about to start sobbing. He tried to think of something to say—but what excuse could he make? He'd lost track of time; he hadn't heard the news. Both were true. Neither was enough.

He decided to try anyway. "Chava . . ."

But her head came up then, as though hearing something in the distance. She stood, peering down the street. A boy on a bicycle was pedaling furiously toward them, tears streaking his face.

"Toby?" she said—and then she was rushing down the steps and past the Jinni as the boy skidded to a stop on the sidewalk. "Toby, what's wrong?"

"Mama's hurt her leg," the boy said, voice quavering. "She's got a fever, she won't wake up—"

"Toby, listen carefully. You must go back home, and keep her as cool as you can. I'll telephone Mount Sinai and have them send an ambulance to your address."

His eyes had gone round at the name. "But we don't have—we can't—"

"Don't worry, it'll be taken care of. Now go. I'll meet you at the hospital." And the boy pedaled off—though not without darting a glance at the Jinni first, as though, even in the midst of this crisis, he couldn't help his curiosity.

The Jinni stood lost, defeated.

"I must go," she muttered, not looking at him. "Anna needs me."

He nodded. "May I see you tonight?"

"No," she said, walking past him up the steps. "Come tomorrow, if you can remember."

He went to Pennsylvania Station after that. Even the Sunday travelers seemed quieter than usual, hurrying to and fro with their heads lowered. He found his favorite bench in the Concourse, unoccupied save for a newspaper whose headlines seemed to shout at him, telling of the girls dead and burned. He picked up the paper and tossed it beneath the bench. *Callous*, he could hear her say; *selfish*. And perhaps he *was* callous, and selfish, and every other failing she might list. But what did that mean, in the end? That he valued himself above others—that he valued *her* above others? Was that truly such a fault?

He knew he had no hope of undoing the damage he'd caused. She couldn't feel his remorse, so she would never quite forgive him. She couldn't sense the truth of his words, which meant she'd never truly believe him. Some part of her would always think him unfeeling, uncaring—and he'd begun to wonder whether it was worth convincing her otherwise.

He sat there for a while, looking up at the glass-set arches that divided the Concourse from the heavens. *I wish I could fly again*, he thought, to his own mild surprise.

He walked back to the Amherst, where Arbeely had banked the forge and left a note for him at the workbench, awkward with concern. *Off to church. Come by later if you need anything.* He considered going to Arbeely's apartment, possibly with a bottle of *araq*, to unburden himself— but what good would it do? The man was in no position to give him advice. He'd been a bachelor his whole life—and the Jinni hardly wanted to remind him of that fact, not when he himself was the cause of it.

He went to the forge and dug out the coals, adjusted the fan, watched the flames spread themselves the length of the bed. For a moment he stood with his hand inches from the fire, remembering that rush of warmth and strength, before he turned away and threw himself into his work.

"Toby," said Missus Chava that evening, "do you know where your mother keeps the pepper-mill?"

It wasn't Toby's fault, what had happened to his mother. Everyone had said so: Missus Chava, the nurses, the doctor, the neighbors he'd begged the ice from, everybody. Yet he couldn't tear himself free of the guilt. The pepper-mill was in the cabinet above the stove, it had been there all his life—but how could he say such a mundane, everyday thing while his mother lay in a bed at Mount Sinai? He could still smell the hospital on his clothes, still see her writhing in pain from the dressing they'd placed on her leg while the doctor marveled at the infection, saying, *I've never seen a case of septicemia progress so rapidly. Do you ever feel a tingling in your extremities? Do you spend an excess of time on your feet? Ah, yes—it says here that you're a laundress. That would account for it.* What would happen if she lost the leg? Toby thought of beggars and wheeled carts, then pushed the heels of his hands into his eyes. He should've known something was wrong, he *should've*, and if he opened his mouth to say, *It's in the cabinet above the stove*, he might start sobbing again. He struggled with himself, took a hitching breath.

"It's all right, Toby," Missus Chava said gently, from the doorway. "I've found it."

He nodded, relieved. Missus Chava had been a bustle of activity ever since their return. The icebox, so recently bare, was now packed with eggs and vegetables. A fresh-baked challah cooled on the counter; the aroma of chicken soup floated through the apartment.

"Are you hungry at all? Would you like some soup?" Her tone was neither prodding nor expectant, as though any answer he gave would be the right one.

He shook his head, and then, conscious of his manners, forced himself to say, "No, thank you."

"Will you try to eat something later, after I've gone?"

He nodded, eyeing his bicycle in the corner, wishing he could go out and ride. She must have followed his gaze, for she said, "Your mother told me that you're a Western Union messenger now." She smiled. "She also said that you're very good at it."

"She did?" That surprised him. Within his earshot, his mother only voiced worries and complaints. *You ride too fast on that bicycle, it terrifies me. Why do you have to be gone so early in the morning, can't you ask for better hours? If those gears and things aren't off my table by supper-time . . .*

"Does riding in traffic ever frighten you?" Missus Chava asked.

"Not really," he said. "It's easy, as long as you pay attention. And if I get lucky, and there's a clear street for a block or two, maybe a bit of a slope, and I can get going *really* fast . . . there's this point where everything just lifts off me. Like I'm flying."

He brought a hand up in demonstration—and then realized that, for a moment, he'd forgotten about his mother. He reddened, dropped his hand.

She came to sit next to him on the sofa. "Toby, can I tell you something?"

He nodded, not looking up.

"I've been spending time uptown, lately," she said. "Sometimes, if I don't have anything else to do, I walk around and explore the neighborhoods. If I'm feeling unhappy, or unsettled, walking always makes me feel better. I suppose it's like you and your bicycle." She smiled, briefly. "Yesterday, I found an orphanage I'd never seen before. I stood there for a long time, watching the children on the playground. It felt like a lonely place, but it made me feel better to be there, because I felt lonely, too. Does that make sense?"

Yes, Toby thought: this made sense.

"That's where I was," she said, "when the fire started. When I came back, and heard what had happened, I was angry with myself. I told myself that I should've stayed home, that I could've helped, somehow. I know," she said to his puzzled frown, "but it's so tempting to imagine. Like punishing oneself, but with wishes."

He saw now that she was talking about him, and his mother's leg. He nodded.

"And besides," she said with a smile, "it turned out that I was needed here after all. How did you know where to find me?"

"Mama told me," he said, "that if I was ever in trouble, I should find Missus Chava at her boardinghouse on Eldridge."

"Good," she said firmly. "I'm glad. It makes me feel better to know that someone needed my help. But please, don't tell your mother I said so. She'll say I'm 'going funny in the head.'"

This last she said with such an accurate imitation of his mother's voice that he laughed once, breathily—and then the sobs were upon him, and he cried into her shoulder while she held him, her touch cool and soothing.

He calmed after a while, and fell asleep. When he woke, he was alone, still on the sofa. The counterpane from his mother's bed had been placed over him. The clock told him it was nearly one in the morning. His head ached, and his stomach growled. He went to the kitchen, and found three slices of challah waiting on a plate, next to a bottle of seltzer. He ate, and drank, and felt better.

It felt strange, to be alone in the apartment. He thought of his mother in her bed uptown, wondered if she, too, was awake, and fretting about the cost. He wished he could tell her about Missus Chava at the front desk, telling them to send the bills to her Eldridge Street address, as cool as you please—

A puzzle-piece suddenly fell into place. *My bicycle,* he thought. That had been Missus Chava's doing, too. He imagined them planning the gift together, on one of their walks around Seward Park. How many secrets had they discussed together, over the years? What else did Missus Chava know?

The wet weather returned a month later, on the morning of the memorial parade.

The entire city came to a halt, thousands huddling beneath awnings and umbrellas as the squadrons of women marched from Seward Park to Washington Square and then up Fifth Avenue, their fringed banners aloft and defiant in the rain. *Ladies Waist & Dressmakers Union, Local 25. United Hebrew Trades of New York. We Mourn Our Loss.*

The Golem, though, was not among the onlookers. For her, the past month had been excruciating. Uptown, her classmates had turned newly solicitous, approaching her in the courtyard to press her hand and ask how she was faring, if she'd known anyone who'd died. *No, I didn't,* she told them truthfully—and yet, after so long among others' grief, it felt like a falsehood. And there was a grasping undercurrent to their questions, a desire to attach themselves to tragedy, that she deeply mistrusted.

So she kept to herself even more than usual, finding hidden carrels in the library to occupy, arriving at class at the last minute to avoid conversations in the hallway. Afterward she escaped as quickly as possible, often walking to the Asylum for Orphaned Hebrews, where she'd stand on the sidewalk and watch the children run about on the playground in their ever-changing cliques. She took care not to linger too long, though—more than once she'd overheard a child wondering if she was someone's mother, come uptown to watch them at play.

Then, the subway south again, to walk quickly home past theaters and lecture-halls where women shouted their anger from the stage. *They call us too weak and delicate for the vote, while our bodies burn to fuel their fortunes!* Her boardinghouse had begun to feel like a prison where she waited each night for parole. To his credit, the Jinni had arrived punctually ever since the fire—but they'd never quite patched their rift, and his mood grew ever more poor and distant. She knew that his lapse in memory had been a case of terrible timing more than anything else, yet his morose silence irritated her more with each passing night.

Then, a ray of hopeful news. Anna, through good luck and better care, had been allowed to keep her leg. The hospital discharged her, the infection in retreat.

Anna arrived home to find her apartment swept and scrubbed, and the icebox crammed with food. On the kitchen table was a basket of the biggest oranges she'd ever seen, along with a sheaf of recipes for various nutritional broths and mashes. Anna hid the oranges at once, in case the neighbors should spot them and start rumors about a wealthy admirer. She'd assumed that she no longer had a job—but, to her considerable surprise, there was a letter from Morris that said she was expected at the laundry as soon as possible. Later she'd learn that, emboldened by the new talk of workers' rights and general strikes, all the girls at Waverly had threatened to walk out if Morris so much as thought about replacing her. Within a week she was managing her charges from a rolling chair, her foot propped upon a stool. One night, the girls dragged Anna to a suffrage meeting on Canal Street, and begged her to tell the audience her story—and from then on she was a mainstay, distributing flyers and sewing banners, her limp transformed to a badge of honor. *It's something I can do*, she told the Golem as they walked slowly together at Seward Park, Anna leaning on her crutch. *I'm not good at much, but I can work.*

"I wish I could do more to help them," the Golem told the Jinni one morning near dawn, as they lay together on his bed.

"You always wish that, Chava." As was often the case these days, the Jinni's voice was tinged with impatience. "Why not be content with saving Anna's life?"

"That's different. I owed her a debt. I still do."

"It seems to me that you've paid it."

She shook her head. "You're changing the subject. This isn't about Anna, it's about all of them. How can I add my voice to theirs when I'm afraid to go to a suffrage meeting?"

"I don't understand why you'd want to go to one in the first place," the Jinni said.

She turned to face him. "I beg your pardon—do you not think women should have the vote?"

He sighed, as though already weary of the conversation. "Of course they should, it's ludicrous that they don't. But we aren't speaking of women, Chava. We're speaking of *you*."

The words hit her like a slap. She lay still a moment, and then said, "What, exactly, do you mean?"

"Only that you seem to forget, sometimes, that you are *not* one of them. There's nothing for you to fear in a factory, or a laundry. You needn't worry about the inheritance laws, as you're no one's parent and no one's child. Yes, you must live by their rules, as I do. But to 'add your voice to theirs,' as you put it, would simply be meddling in their affairs."

Her ire rose. "Are you saying I shouldn't worry about protecting the women who work in factories and laundries because I'm not one myself? That's more selfish than I would expect from you."

He chuckled. He was lying on his back, one hand behind his head, gazing up at the ceiling. "Chava," he said, "what do you think will happen when the suffragists win? Will all injustice be wiped from the land once women have the vote?"

"No, not all at once. But much of it, yes, over time."

"And what of the wives of the businessmen who own the factories? Will they, too, vote to improve the lives of working-women?"

"They certainly ought to."

"What they *ought* to do is neither here nor there. Let us concentrate on what they *will* do. The businessmen's wives will vote to keep their money in their own pockets. The Temperance reformers will vote to keep their husbands sober, and the barmaids will vote to protect their jobs. The Christian women will vote to close businesses on Sundays, and the Jewish women will vote to keep them open. The Negro women, I assume, still will have no vote at all—but the rest will divide themselves, just as the men have. And you will do exactly the same. You will vote your own interests, which are the interests of those around you, and believe yourself to be a model of compassion, when in truth your motives are just as self-centered as their own."

She lay there stunned. Had he ever talked to her like this before? Where had this tirade come from? "That's not true!"

"Oh, it isn't? What if, when you arrived in New York, you were rescued not by a penniless rabbi on the Lower East Side, but a Fifth Avenue millionaire? Do you think that you'd be half so anxious to gain the vote and save the Annas of the world?"

"Well," she said, "perhaps I wouldn't feel it quite as I do now. But I hope that I'd act rightly, all the same."

"Here is what I think, Chava. It's easy to consider yourself altruistic when you live among the poor and the downtrodden. But if you were removed from their side, it wouldn't be long before they faded from your mind."

She sat up, pulling the sheet tightly around herself. "Why are you saying these things? Why are you so angry at me?"

"I'm not angry."

"Clearly you are."

"I'm not. But if you wish to make me so, keep asking."

She stood then, and dressed in fuming silence, and fastened her cloak around her neck. "Do not come to see me again," she said, "until you can be more civil." And she left, not waiting for a reply.

The Jinni arrived at the shop that morning in a foul mood, the Golem's parting words still ringing in his ears. *Until you can be more civil.* Well, she'd placed the decision in his hands; she'd have no one to blame but herself if the result wasn't to her liking. And yet every night he stayed away was a night she must spend inside and alone. He thought of the locket he'd forged, his resolution never to become her jailer— and yet she seemed to insist upon it at every turn; it was completely maddening . . .

Arbeely was already at his desk, opening the morning mail. "Good morning," he said as the Jinni came through the door. "Here, this just arrived. You might find it amusing." He held out a small cardboard box.

The Jinni took it. Inside, nestled in excelsior, was an ordinary-looking rock. It was squarish in shape, roughly the length of his palm and nearly black in color. "Someone sent us a rock?"

"There's a brochure underneath it."

The Jinni tipped out the rock and the excelsior, and found a folded brochure decorated with a sketch of an enormous steam shovel. The words *Superior Iron from Hibbing Ironworks* were written at the top. The Jinni opened it, and read:

> This iron ore of the highest grade comes from the heart of the Mesabi Iron Range, the source of all of Hibbing Ironworks' products. Our smelting process refines it to our exacting standards, using . . .

"Imagine paying to send a rock through the post," Arbeely said. "It's a clever bit of advertising, but no wonder Hibbing's iron is so expensive—" He broke off, interrupted by a spell of coughing.

"Another cold?" the Jinni said, somewhat irritated. He'd been hoping Arbeely would let him smoke in the shop again.

"It comes and goes with the weather," the man replied, once he could.

"Isn't there medicine you can take?"

"I tried codeine drops, but the nausea was worse than the coughing."

"At least this proves that my cigarettes aren't to blame," said the Jinni, and received a scornful look in reply. He held up the box. "Can I have this?"

The man shrugged. "Go ahead, it's no use to me."

In his secret room, the Jinni lit the lanterns, cleared the bits of wrought iron from the floor, sat on the cushion, and hefted the rock in one hand. It was heavy, and jagged-edged. In the lantern-light, the sheared surfaces held a dusting of red. He brought it to his nose, inhaled its warm, sharp scent—and felt, not fear, but the remembrance of fear: childhood dares and taunts, boasts and bravado, the excitement of hovering with one's playmates outside an unknown cave, daring one another to go in first.

I ought to show this to Chava, he thought—and then remembered their fight. He tossed the rock aside, rubbed his face with his hands, then impatiently extinguished the lanterns again. He'd go to the roof, he decided, and clear his head.

"Arbeely," he called as he left the supply room, "if you feel like distributing your biscuits—"

But Arbeely lay on the floor, unmoving.

II.

The weeks that Sophia spent at the ruins of Carchemish were some of the happiest of her life.

She'd planned to stay only three days, not wanting to be a nuisance: enough time for a tour of the ruins, and to dine once or twice with Mr. Hogarth, if he was at his leisure. And indeed, the man had been refreshingly welcoming, and had answered her questions with care and attention. But the true surprise had come in the form of Hogarth's young assistant, a young Oxfordian named Thomas Lawrence, whom everyone called Ned. If Hogarth was the governing mind of the dig, then Ned Lawrence, it seemed, was its household spirit. He was a small, disheveled lad, with manners at once courtly and artless, who could talk for hours on subjects that roamed from Hittite fortifications to Spenserian verse. He'd lecture her like a professor, then turn boyish and brotherly, insisting that she come see the spot where a pack of wild boars had charged him. The excavation itself hadn't begun yet, only the surveys, so she'd arrived too early for any spectacular finds—but it was more than worth it to stand with Lawrence and gaze out at the Euphrates running high with snow-melt, and be glad at the company of this strange young man who seemed not to notice her own strangenesses.

For two weeks Sophia stayed at Carchemish, sketching the river views and helping Lawrence improve his Arabic. And she would've stayed longer still, if it hadn't been for the arrival of Miss Gertrude Bell.

For years Sophia had heard tales of the adventuress, and more than once had been mistaken for her. She'd even gone so far as to read Miss Bell's travel memoirs, and thought them well written, if typically British in their droll condescension. When she learned that the woman planned to visit, Sophia grew excited at the thought of stories divulged, opinions compared. Perhaps Sophia wasn't as experienced as Miss Bell— but surely, she thought, the woman would prove an ally.

Then the lady herself arrived, with her caravan of servants and tents and trunks—and at once Sophia realized that Miss Bell was the sort of woman who had little time or patience for her own sex. In Sophia, Miss Bell saw a cheap impersonator, a grasping dilettante. Yes, Miss Williams had purchased herself a life in Syria, but what were her credentials, her connections? What sort of company did she keep, besides her Homsi dragoman? The girl gave no good answers; and so a slender shoulder was turned to her, and there it remained.

Not once in her years of travel had Sophia so desperately longed to reveal her identity. Of course it would do her no good at all, American wealth being only a vulgar and inadequate substitute for British peerage—but in the face of Miss Bell's judgment it was the only superlative to hand, and she found herself reaching for it again and again. The reflex went expressly against her idea of herself, and she resented Miss Bell for it at once. A chilly silence fell between the women— all while Lawrence kept on about verses and fortifications in his eager, oblivious way.

And so Sophia left Carchemish with lowered spirits. Abu Alim made no comment on the change in her mood, but she knew that he saw it; knew, too, that he was glad to be gone. There'd been little for him to do while she took her walks with Lawrence, and the idleness had made him ill at ease. He was a quiet man from a farming family, a devout Muslim who'd learned English in his youth from a Protestant missionary. The skill had proved lucrative enough that Abu Alim had purchased an orchard in Homs for his sons, so they wouldn't have to squabble with their cousins over the family holdings.

Sophia had never told Abu Alim the true purpose behind her wanderings, and yet at times it seemed to be an open secret between them. After their first summer together, he'd stopped offering her a parasol in the sun; more than once she'd seen him glance at her trembling hands, before making some excuse to leave her for a few minutes so that she might take her medicine in private. Nor did he comment upon her "market trips," when she'd go alone to a local souk and return hours later with nothing more than a new woolen scarf. At times the polite silence between them seemed absurd, and Sophia longed to rip the veil away—but again and again she refrained, not wanting to upset their equilibrium.

From Carchemish they reached Aleppo, and followed the River Queiq into the heart of the city; then took the railway south, bound for Damascus. But as often happened, the railway timetable proved untrustworthy, and they found themselves stranded in Homs, the next train not expected until the morning.

"Please, go home for the night," Sophia told Abu Alim, not wanting to keep him from his family. "I'll sit up at the station. I've seen other women do it, it's perfectly safe."

But as she'd feared, Abu Alim wouldn't hear of it. He hired a donkey-cart and loaded her luggage upon it, and sent a message ahead to his wife to expect a guest; and at that point Sophia was obliged to quit her protests and accompany him through the winding streets.

When they arrived, his wife, Dalal, was waiting outside. She clapped and sang out at the sight of them, then brought Sophia inside and sat her next to the fire, and served her strong tea from a brass pot. Their sons were both tending to their orchard with their wives, and soon it was proposed that they should journey out with supper for everyone, as a surprise.

They arrived in the last light at an orchard at the desert's edge. The young men were reddened and dusty from the day's work; they shouted in joy at seeing their father, and embraced him with nearly enough force to knock him over, before bowing to Sophia and complimenting her Arabic. The orchard boasted a stone farm-house with a cushioned patio behind it, and the men disappeared inside the house to wash and pray while the women showed Sophia to a cushion and laid skewers of sea-soned chicken upon the fire.

The food was delicious, and the fire warmed Sophia enough that she could even enjoy the meal. She answered their polite questions, made the proper inquiries and congratulations—one of the daughters-in-law was visibly pregnant—and then listened while Abu Alim and his sons discussed the prospects for the harvest, and whether they thought Italy would truly start a war for control over Libya. Coffee was passed around, and dates and pistachios from the family's own trees. Sophia drew a proffered blanket over her shoulders, and watched the family before her, and found herself thinking about the dig at Carchemish. For the first time, the entire undertaking struck her as misguided, even pointless. Hogarth's men would piece together the fallen city from its stones and shards; they'd take their photographs and their measurements, and return home to write their papers and give their lectures—and they'd leave Carchemish exhumed behind them like Mrs. Shelley's patchwork creature, a bloodless thing, neither alive nor dead. There'd be no one to build new homes from its ancient stones, to plant orchards and eat the fruits, to sit around the fires and talk of crops and rain and war. To turn the city's bones to living flesh, and breathe a new future into its lungs.

The wind had strengthened, whipping the fire about. Sophia shivered once, and then realized with a jolt that she hadn't taken her evening dose of medicine. She'd expected to be on the evening train to Damascus, not at the desert's outskirts. Her powder-flask was at Abu Alim's house, with the rest of her belongings.

She looked up, and saw that Abu Alim was watching her. "It's growing late," he said. "We ought to go back to the house."

Protests, from the younger generation. It was only half past nine, the fire still burned, there were pastries to eat—

"Miss Williams and I must be at the station at sunrise," he said, overriding them.

They'd forgotten their guest; they relented at once. The women began to pack the dishes away, while Sophia felt as though she'd inadvertently spoiled the party.

"Miss Williams," said Rafik, the younger of Abu Alim's sons, who seemed the more mischievous of the two, "has my father told you the *true* reason he doesn't want to be out here late at night?"

"Rafik," his father said, with a warning tone.

"Of course he hasn't," said Alim, the older son, with a grin. "He's far too proper to tell such a story to a lady like Miss Williams."

"I suppose the task falls to us," said Rafik, clearly delighted at the opportunity to puncture his father's dignity. "Years ago," he said, "when my brother and I were only babies, Father was alone at our uncle's farm one afternoon, threshing the winter wheat, and—"

"I wasn't threshing it," Abu Alim interjected in annoyance. "It was too early in the season. I was only measuring its growth."

"Yes, measuring it," said Rafik, waving a placating hand. "He had his scythe, that's the important part. He put it down by the wheat, and went to the end of the row, for a drink of water—and when he came back—"

Sophia shivered.

"—there was a beautiful woman standing between the rows, with Father's scythe in her hand. And what was she wearing, but—"

"*Rafik*," Abu Alim said, brows lowering.

"Well," Rafik said, "I shall leave out that part of the tale. But suffice to say that Father was shocked indeed—and the woman must've been as well, for she dropped the scythe and vanished into the air."

Sophia raised her eyebrows. "A jinniyeh," she said, keeping her voice steady.

"Exactly," said Rafik proudly.

Abu Alim wouldn't look at her. "It was a silly story," he grumbled, "for a pair of silly boys."

"Ah, but Miss Williams believes," said Rafik. "I see it in her eyes."

A pause as the men turned to look at her—and Sophia realized she'd pulled the blanket close about herself, and was shivering visibly in the firelight.

"Did I frighten you?" Rafik said, chagrined.

Sophia tried to laugh. "No, of course not—I'm only a bit cold—"

Abu Alim said, "Rafik, go and help the women. I'll see Miss Williams to the cart." It was a rebuke, and the young man took it meekly; he bowed and departed.

Abu Alim gave Sophia another blanket, which she placed over the first, and then led her back through the yard. "I apologize for my son, he has never learned proper manners," Abu Alim muttered as they approached the wagon.

But the story was true, wasn't it? Sophia wanted to ask. But instead she allowed him to help her into the wagon, and concentrated on staying as still and upright as possible, while the donkey plodded back to town.

At the Amherst, the spring went by in an unseen blur.

Doctors and experts were called to Arbeely's bedside from every corner of the city. The conclusion they reached was unanimous. *A fibrous
carcinosis of the lungs, hopefully in its early stages.* Their tones were serious,
but not somber: there were new treatments, they told him, encouraging
advances. He was lucky to live in modern times, and to have the means
to afford their cures.

Arbeely took the news with his usual grumbling optimism. He
wrote letters to each of the Amherst's lease-holders, informing them of
the situation and asking for their patience while he was indisposed.
Soon his sick-room had been outfitted with paneled lace curtains and an
endless torrent of biscuits. The cigars were confiscated by his doctors,
to be smoked elsewhere.

With the Jinni, Arbeely was confident, even cheerful. *Just keep working,* Arbeely told him. *Don't worry about new customers, we've got plenty
of orders to keep you busy. You could even close the showroom, if you prefer.
Oh—but please, don't forget the children on the roof. I wouldn't want to disappoint them.*

Then the treatments began.

All that spring and into the summer the doctors assaulted Arbeely
with tinctures and syrups, injections, radium vapor baths. Before long
the man was bedridden. Maryam Faddoul came each day to his apartment, coaxing him into eating bits of milk-soaked bread. The Jinni
came, too, after Maryam left, to stand uncomfortably at the foot of Arbeely's bed and tell him the mundane details of the day. *I had to remake
that fireplace screen, they weren't satisfied with the design, even though it was
exactly what they'd asked for.* Arbeely, propped upon his pillows, would
nod, and perhaps croak out an encouraging comment—and then he'd
begin to cough, a horrible gagging sound, and the hired nurse would
shoo the Jinni away.

Every afternoon, as promised, the Jinni stuffed his pockets with biscuits and climbed the Amherst stairwell to the roof. The children still

congregated there in anticipation; but they, too, knew that Mr. Arbeely was ill, and they accepted the biscuits with a solemnity of duty that dimmed their pleasure somewhat. Then the Jinni would go back down the stairs, avoiding the sympathetic eyes along the way, and give himself over to the oblivion of his work, until it was time to leave for the Golem's boardinghouse.

This, too, had a new and unwelcome sense of duty about it. They'd never resolved their fight, merely let it fall to the side in the face of this new crisis—yet it was rarely far from his thoughts. The phrase *That's more selfish than I would expect from you* seemed to have taken up residence in his mind, and he heard its echo in her gently patronizing questions about Arbeely's treatments and his diet, his doctors, their pedigrees. *I don't know*, he'd reply. *I didn't ask.* And she'd gaze at him, mournful and disappointed, until he was forced to turn away, lest he shout at her that he wasn't her student, to be taught how to behave. He began to arrive later and leave earlier: a perfunctory walk to Central Park and back, his eyes barely seeing the summer blossoms. They still went to his apartment occasionally, according to his mood, and were mostly silent afterward. He made excuses to stay longer and longer at the shop, building fences, gates, fireplace screens, sets of andirons. He'd spend hours in a trance of movement, looking up only to find that there was some new object in front of him that he couldn't recall making, and that it was now night instead of morning, or morning instead of night.

One afternoon, a boy walking down Washington Street happened to glance through the shop window just in time to see Mister Ahmad pull an iron bar from the forge with his bare hand and carry it halfway to the anvil before he seemed to realized what he was doing. Quickly the man returned the bar to the forge, put on his gloves, picked up the tongs and began again. Baffled, the boy thought of the old rumors, then decided he must have misunderstood what he'd seen. There'd been no glamour of magic about it, no incantations or flourishing gestures— only a dejected and ordinary man lost in his own concerns.

The Golem ought to have been celebrating her achievements.

Her end-of-term exams had gone as well as she'd wished. She'd been careful not to score highest in her class, instead contenting herself with a spot in the top quarter: an undeniable success, but not a conspicuous one. And she'd performed admirably in her teaching practicums at Wadleigh High School, where she'd learned to judge by her students' thoughts whether they found the lesson easy or complicated, dull or interesting. Before long, even the girls who'd silently scoffed at her clothing and her accent were, at the very least, paying attention.

But now the city was mired in summer's doldrums. The girls of Wadleigh had all gone north to Westchester, or abroad with their families. Most of Teachers College, too, had vanished rather than brave the notorious summer session, with its stifling classrooms and shuttered cafeterias. Other than herself, the few who remained were mostly scholarship students, accustomed to making the most of their circumstances. Before long they'd organized their own roster of amusements: evening picnics in the quadrangle, excursions to the recreation piers. The Golem dearly wished to join them, and she knew they would've welcomed her. But every time she considered it, the Jinni's caustic rebuke—*You seem to forget, sometimes, that you are not one of them*—buzzed inside her like a fly trapped in a glass.

So instead she kept her distance, and tried to busy herself with other things. She asked the Jinni about Arbeely's treatments, thinking that she might help somehow, as she had with Anna—and yet every question seemed to anger him more. He'd grown unpredictable, his moods impenetrable. Sometimes, in his bed, he seemed his usual self, attentive to her desires as well as his own. At other times, she wondered if he truly knew she was there.

Walking alone was still a comfort. After class, she headed north along the well-heeled stretches of Broadway and Riverside, past apartment buildings with names like the Billmore and Saxonia Court. At Trinity Church Cemetery she wandered among the tombs and obelisks, more like a sculpture-garden than a graveyard to her eyes. But no matter her route, it always ended at the Asylum. The longer she spent watching the children through the fence, the more the orphanage seemed like a

world unto itself, one whose rules she knew by instinct. *Find your place.
Don't draw attention. If you're sad, don't let it show.*

Then she'd return to Broadway, to mingle among the currents of
pedestrians that dipped in and out of the subway stations: clerks and secretaries, businessmen and salesgirls. The women especially fascinated
her. *Ought I to buy myself a new coat?* went their thoughts. *I must remember
the flowers for Mrs. Pearson tomorrow.* Some anticipated an evening out, at
the theater or the picture-house. One, imagining a plain supper and
a cheap novel, might feel glum at the prospect; another, picturing the
same, was filled with contentment. Taken together, they seemed like a
secret regiment of the solitary, the self-sufficient. It satisfied the Golem
to walk among these women, and pretend for a time that she was one of
them—until she, too, boarded the subway for home.

At summer's end, Arbeely began to improve.

His cough lessened, and his voice grew stronger. He started to eat
again, a few bites here and there. He slept less, and sat up in bed, and saw
visitors. One August day, the Jinni came to the man's apartment to find
him at the kitchen table, sipping a cup of broth and scrutinizing a newspaper. The Jinni stood in the kitchen doorway, not truly believing, and
looked to Maryam Faddoul, who was heating more broth at the stove.
Maryam said nothing, only tilted her head toward their mutual friend:
Are you seeing this, too?

Arbeely looked up from his paper. He'd lost a good deal of weight,
and wore a scarf wrapped around his neck despite the heat. "Ahmad! I'm
glad you're here. They won't let me outside, but I'm about to tear my hair
out from boredom. Can you bring me the ledgers from the Amherst?
And the mail, if it isn't too much trouble?"

"Of course," the Jinni said. He nodded solemnly to Maryam—she
nodded back, her eyes dancing—and then went downstairs, where he
sat abruptly on the apartment stoop and took deep, shuddering breaths
of the thick summer air.

"Mister Ahmad?" A young boy was standing at the bottom of the stoop. "You okay?"

The Jinni drew in a last breath, then looked at the boy. "I think I will be," he said, and smiled for the first time in months.

Autumn arrived.

Uptown, the Teachers College students poured back onto campus, full of gossip about their summer travels. A number of the girls sported new engagement rings; the Golem admired them and offered her congratulations, her own thoughts elsewhere. Her walks with the Jinni had improved somewhat, now that Arbeely was better—yet still they said little beyond minutiae.

"It's like we've forgotten how to be with each other," she told Anna on a crisp October Sunday as they walked around Seward Park—more slowly than they used to, owing to Anna's limp.

Anna said, "Are you still . . . ?"

The Golem saw her meaning. "Yes, sometimes," she said, self-consciously. "Though . . ."

"Not like before," Anna finished.

"Not like before," the Golem agreed.

"You don't think he's . . ." The woman's mind finished the sentence: an image of the Jinni, his arms around someone else.

"No," the Golem said quickly. "It's not that. And yes, I know—"

"Every woman thinks it won't happen to her," Anna said darkly.

"I *know*, but . . . I've been thinking about it, lately." She paused. "May I tell you something in confidence?"

Anna rolled her eyes. "You have to ask?"

"Have you ever heard the name Sophia Winston?"

"I don't think so. Is she one of *the* Winstons?"

"Yes, the daughter of the family. I met her, briefly."

That earned her an incredulous stare. "Chava Levy, you've known a Winston all this time and you never *told* me?"

"I don't know her, Anna, not really," the Golem muttered, mindful of the others strolling around them. "I only met her once, years ago. She and Ahmad had been lovers, briefly."

Anna's eyes widened with images of gilded boudoirs, mussed satin sheets.

"Yes," the Golem said wryly, "something like that. But . . . I think Ahmad hurt her, without meaning to. I don't know how, exactly." She described the young woman's pallor, her shaking. "He could barely look at her," she said. "And she refused to discuss it."

"The poor girl," Anna murmured. "What happened to her?"

"I don't know. She left the country, and I never asked Ahmad for the details. But now I wonder if . . ." She paused, then said in a miserable voice, "Maybe I'm just a woman he can't hurt."

Anna gaped at her. "Chava! What a thing to say!"

"Yes, but what if it's true?"

"Well, *ask* him!"

"But how will I know if he's lying?"

"You won't," Anna said, "any more than the rest of us ever do. You'll just have to decide whether to believe him."

The Amherst's tenants didn't need to ask for news of Arbeely's health; they saw it in the lightness of his partner's step as he climbed the stairwell, his new willingness to nod hello on the landings. The showroom was still closed, the plate-glass windows hung with thick curtains—but now, anticipating Arbeely's return, the Jinni pulled them back and saw the layers of dust on the balustrades and bedposts, the cobwebs between their bars. He fetched a rag and began to clean the first piece, a headboard he'd been especially proud of. Except—here was an ugly weld, and this twist ought to be finer, and . . .

It wasn't long before he tossed the rag aside and began to pull apart the showroom in dissatisfaction. Each of his pieces seemed hobbled by flaws and compromises, spots where he'd altered the design to fit the limitations of his materials. Perhaps wrought iron was a dead end after all. Or—no, wait. Perhaps he'd been going about it wrong from the beginning.

He went to the supply room, scanned its contents. Wrought iron, pig iron, graded steel: all of it refined to standard ratios, this much pure iron to that much carbon, and then smelted without variation. All of it made to someone else's specifications, not his own. But what if he could control the entire process himself? Without human tools or methods, human notions of what was possible?

He searched through the shelves, and found the cardboard box labeled *Hibbing Ironworks*. He tossed box and excelsior aside, hefted the lump of iron ore. Would it be it enough for a definitive test? He'd need immense heat, and a good amount of pressure. Luckily, he could provide both.

He found a ceramic crucible, placed the ore inside, and carried it to the forge. Then he rolled up his sleeves, and—after a quick glance out the windows—placed his hands upon the burning coals.

The Golem stood at the Asylum fence, lost in her thoughts.

You'll just have to decide whether to believe him. And that was the crux of the problem, wasn't it? Even if she dared to ask, even if she managed to pull some reply out of him, she'd never know, not truly. She thought of all his silences large and small, all the times he'd refused to explain himself, and wondered how to weigh them against everything they'd shared. How could she possibly decide? And how on earth had they ended up in such a state?

I haven't enough apples for class tomorrow, and no time to shop, either . . . Perhaps I'll have them make a raisin tart instead . . .

The Golem looked up. There was a woman on the other side of the fence, coming toward her, deep in thought. The Golem watched as the woman unlocked the gate and went through, closed it behind herself, and turned toward Broadway, despairing that the new semester had barely begun and already her students were running roughshod over her. But it wasn't *her* fault that the girls stole ingredients out of the cabinets when she wasn't watching—and besides, who could blame them? If *she* had to eat the Asylum food for years on end, she'd pilfer as many sugar-cubes as she could! Though what they intended to do with the missing baking powder, she had no idea . . .

Intrigued, the Golem followed after her.

The woman was in a hurry, but the Golem kept pace with her as first she stopped at a butcher's—a chicken cutlet for supper, and a *weisswurst* for breakfast—and then went down into the subway. After a moment of hesitation, the Golem paid for a ticket and followed her to the south-bound platform. From a discreet distance she watched as the woman pulled a compact mirror from her bag, fussed briefly with her hair, cast a critical eye at herself, and then snapped the mirror shut as the train arrived.

The carriage was nearly empty. The woman took a spot on a bench, and pulled a novel from her bag. The Golem found a seat nearby. The train pulled away and made its slow progress south, accumulating pas-sengers here and there. The woman's thoughts became nervous, antici-patory.

At 72nd Street the doors opened to admit a dark-haired man in a brown suit, carrying a leather briefcase. He took a seat across from the woman, his briefcase upon his lap.

The woman glanced up at him and smiled shyly.

He smiled shyly back.

Stop after stop went by, he pretending to read a newspaper, she pre-tending to read her novel. In their months of riding the subway to-gether, they'd never spoken a word. He was a clerk, she'd decided, judg-ing by his briefcase and the ink on his fingers. She, he was certain, was a teacher of some sort. He'd once spied a copy of *The Settlement Cook Book* in her bag; she, an issue of *The American Hebrew & Jewish Messenger* in his. By these favorable signs their hopes had been raised. But decency demanded they have a good reason to speak to each other, and neither could ever find the proper entrée, both being rather timid in these matters. And so they rode on silently beneath the river to Brooklyn, where he departed at Borough Hall, and she at Atlantic Avenue.

The Golem took the subway back to the Spring Street station, berating herself for her voyeurism. *That was going too far*, she told herself as she walked along Lafayette with the crowd. *You all but followed that poor woman home, just to distract yourself from thinking about Ahmad—*

And suddenly, as though she'd conjured him, she spied him across the street.

He was standing in the middle of the sidewalk, staring up at an ordinary loft building, a strange look upon his face. He must have come from the shop, for he still wore his leather apron, and hadn't bothered to put on a jacket.

She crossed Lafayette as quickly as she could without drawing attention. The passersby were giving him a wide and startled berth, and when she neared, she saw why. He was radiating heat, as though he'd bathed in fire. His collar was singed, and his sleeves, too, though he'd rolled them nearly to his elbows.

"Ahmad?" she said, alarmed. "What's happened?"

"Chava, look at this," he said, gesturing to the building. He hadn't so much as glanced at her yet. From his tone it was as though he'd fully expected her to find him there.

"Look at . . . the building?"

"The *iron*."

She remembered, then: the cast-iron facades, the ones he'd scoffed at. "I thought you didn't like them," she said cautiously.

"I don't. They're ridiculous. Why make an iron building and give it columns, and capitals, and pediments? Why not let the iron be itself? And for that matter"—he turned to her now, and she nearly recoiled from the heat—"Why must a building be square?" He gestured all around. "Square plots, square buildings, boxes upon boxes. *Why?*"

"Ahmad," she said, "are you all right? Why are you so warm?"

He reached into the pocket of his apron and pulled out a fist-sized object. "*Look*," he said, and handed it to her.

Whatever it was, it was nearly too hot to touch. She joggled it a moment, then peered at it: a rounded lump of steel like a river rock, its bottom flattened as though he'd poured it on a table to cool. Along one raised side was a thick band of opaque blue-green glass. The glass, she saw, had come first; the metal had then draped itself over and around it—as though to form a low, curved house, and the glass a long and tapered bank of windows, set beneath smooth steel eaves.

He nodded, watching her. "You see it, too, don't you? Arbeely told me once, 'We're tinsmiths, not an engineering firm.' But Chava, what if we *were?*"

He didn't wait for an answer, but grabbed the steel-and-glass lump from her—she flinched, but he didn't notice—and started south at such a pace that she had to run a few steps to keep up. "Slow *down*," she urged as others stared. But he was lost inside his inspiration, talking to the air, switching languages too quickly for sense. She heard the word *or* half a dozen times before she realized it was *ore*, that he was speaking of rocks; and what, in her bewilderment, she'd taken for *schlag*, whipped cream, was—"Ahmad, what is 'slag'?"

"The glass," he said, impatient. "It forms during the smelting, it's the oxides, the impurities. I'll have to experiment with it, but I'll need a hoard's worth, more than a—"

The word that emerged next was an unformed sound, a breath of air. He startled; his step faltered. A cloud of confused anger passed across his face—and the Golem realized that, for the first time in her presence, he'd tried to speak his own language.

He glanced at her, then away again. "But that won't be a problem," he muttered, walking on. "Hibbing sells it by the train-car."

They were nearing Little Syria now, and she realized she had a choice: abandon him to his mania, or be seen walking with him in broad daylight, perhaps even up to his apartment. She gritted her teeth and stayed with him. They'd have words about this later. "Where are we going?"

"To Arbeely's," he said, as though it were perfectly obvious. "I have to tell him, it's his, too."

"*What's* his?"

"Our new business."

"Your—Wait. Ahmad, *wait.*" She hurried ahead, turned and placed herself before him, as though to stop a moving train. For a moment she thought he'd walk around her, or cross the street—but at last he halted, and folded his arms with annoyance.

"Please, calm yourself," she said, "and think of Arbeely. He's in delicate health, you can't go turning his world upside down for a—a piece of metal and glass—"

"You don't think I can build it," he said.

She gaped at him. "I *know* you can! That's the problem! You can make such beautiful, astonishing things, but—"

"But only at night," he said, cutting her off. "Behind curtains, in the dark. When and where I'm allowed."

She sighed. "I understand how frustrating it is. You *must* know that."

"No, Chava, I think you're perfectly glad to hold yourself to their limitations."

Now she, too, was growing angry. "Ahmad, don't do this. Be sensible."

He snorted at the word, and walked on.

Washington Street was crowded with men and women leaving work, running their errands, walking to and from the Elevated. He cleared a path through them all with his heat and his stride, a flaming arrow aimed at Arbeely's building. The Golem hurried fearfully behind. They passed the Faddouls' coffee-house, and she cast a desperate glance through the window and caught Maryam's eye. At once the woman put down her coffee-pot and hurried to the door. "Chava, what's happened?"

"I don't know," she said in a low voice, "but he's in a state and I've made it worse. He insists on talking to Arbeely, and I'm afraid—" She broke off, not knowing what, exactly, she was afraid of.

"I'll come with you," Maryam said.

Together they followed the Jinni to Arbeely's building, where he took the stairs two and three at a time, the women in his wake.

"Why is he so *warm?*" Maryam whispered.

"I wish I knew," the Golem murmured back.

Arbeely's door was shut. "Arbeely," the Jinni called, "it's me. Let me in, I've had an idea." The women came up the stairs behind him. His eyes narrowed when he saw Maryam, but he said nothing.

"Ahmad," they heard, faintly, "it's not the best—"

But he'd already opened the door and was through it.

Arbeely sat at the kitchen table in his dressing-gown and scarf, a letter in his hand. He looked up, startled, as the Jinni entered, followed by the two women. The Jinni placed his model upon the table, and without preamble launched into his story: the steel, the slag, his sudden revelation that buildings didn't have to be square, they were only square because everyone had decided they must be, but what if they could change that, what if . . .

But Arbeely seemed hardly to be listening. His gaze slid from his partner to the Golem. *I could've hidden it from him*, he was thinking. *Maybe even from Maryam. But not you.* And she knew, then, that the letter in his hand was from his doctors, and that it began with the words *We regret we must inform you.* She felt the flush of fever upon the man's skin, and the growing pain inside his bones. Saw exhaustion, and resignation, in his eyes.

The Jinni had stopped talking. He looked blankly from Arbeely to the Golem. "What is it?" he asked.

Behind her, Maryam had covered her mouth with a hand.

Silently Arbeely proffered the letter. The Jinni took it, read its first line—and the paper burst into flames.

Everyone jumped. Maryam rushed to Arbeely's side. The Golem grabbed the letter and carried it to the sink, smothered the flames beneath the tap.

By the time she'd turned around, the Jinni had vanished.

12.

The lace-makers were the first of the Amherst's tenants to leave.

It was November, the year stretching remorselessly toward its end. Arbeely was feverish and weak, often asleep. Doctors appeared on occasion, felt his forehead and took his pulse, and left again. Maryam came daily, and sat at his bedside whether he knew she was there or not. Others came, too, when he was lucid: shopkeepers, church members, neighbors. They spoke a few words, shed quiet tears, squeezed his hand.

One man was conspicuous in his absence.

For weeks the Jinni had been locked in the Amherst, hard at work. He'd ripped out the supply room's neat racks of bars and ingots, and in their place there stood a mountain of iron ore, delivered by truck and poured in through the window. The front door was locked, the showroom curtains closed. The 'phone, which at first had rung without cease, now sat with its receiver dangling. His forge, his tools, his plans, his solitude: everything he needed, he told himself, was here, inside the Amherst.

One morning, he was in the process of tearing down the showroom's walls when a knock sounded at the stairwell door. He ignored it—but the knock came again, more loudly, amid a buzz of female voices. "Mister Ahmad," one called, "we're from upstairs. Please, it's important."

At last he opened the door to find dozens of lace-makers gathered in the stairwell. They apologized for the interruption, but it was an hour past their starting time, and neither of the business's owners had arrived to unlock the doors. Mr. Arbeely, they said, had the only spare key.

Arbeely's desk still sat in its usual place, next to the remnants of the showroom. The Jinni opened its drawer, and was faced with his partner's life rendered in ephemera: pencils and drawing-compasses, postage stamps, cough drops, unopened packs of shirt-collars. Blindly he rooted through it all, until he'd found the key.

The lace-makers milled together on the second-floor landing as he unlocked the door and pushed it open on its track. The factory was dark, the giant looms silent. The owners' offices were at the far end, where an odor of stale smoke lingered in the air. The office safe stood open, its shelves empty. Nearby was a charred metal wastebasket, a layer of ash at its bottom.

"But it's Saturday," one girl said, disbelieving. "We're supposed to be paid today."

The women all began to talk at once. One girl, taking matters into her own hands, went out to the floor and broke open the boxes of lace curtains and pillow-cases. She rolled these into bundles, and began parceling them out to the crowd. Another girl walked the looms, cutting the cones of fine cotton thread off their spindles. The key to the third floor was found, and before long the entire operation had been stripped of everything the women could carry: spools of lace the size of cheese wheels, boxes of needles and bobbins, magnifying glasses, embroidery scissors, reams of the company stationery. The biscuit-bakers and cigar-makers gathered on their landings to watch as the women marched out the door, their arms laden with goods, scraps of lace fluttering over their shoulders. A little while later the creditors arrived and hauled away what was left: the looms and cutting-tables, the desks and chairs, even the empty safe.

The biscuit-makers were the next to leave, although theirs was a more orderly and dignified departure. There was no profit in it anymore, the owner told his workers sadly, not for the little outfits like theirs. He paid out their wages, sold the equipment at auction, and set a final tin of biscuits next to the Arbeely & Ahmad door on the way out.

The Jinni couldn't have said how long it was before the cigar-makers, too, disappeared. He simply realized one morning that he hadn't heard anyone in the stairwell in quite some time. He went upstairs to investigate, and found the fifth floor deserted, the long wooden tables still scattered with knives and cutting-boards and pots of sealing gum. Crumbled tobacco leaves littered the floor like an autumn forest.

He broke up the wooden tables and tossed the pieces down the stairwell, then heaped them out the door and into the alley, where they quickly disappeared. Before long, the rooftop fire-barrels of lower Manhattan all smelled of quality tobacco.

Alone, the Jinni walked the Amherst from top to bottom, seeing the building itself as though for the first time. Each floor was a vast expanse of wooden boards, the support columns piercing them at regular intervals. He stood in the empty stairwell, and looked up at the sharp-angled spiral that the railings made.

Then he went back to the forge, and kept working.

Eventually, the Golem stopped waiting each night at her window.

More than anything else, it was a matter of self-preservation. Winter was approaching, and with it her restlessness; she must learn to manage without him. And the solution, when it came to her, felt entirely obvious: instead of taking the subway, she'd simply walk to her classes instead.

Now she spent six hours each day in walking: three hours north and three south again, over two hundred and forty blocks in total. She learned the different patterns of morning and afternoon traffic, and which short-cuts she might take along the way. She enjoyed the feeling of moving with the crowd, of being merely one among many. When the rains began, she bought a good umbrella, and learned to angle it into the wind. On the wettest mornings she'd duck into a cafeteria to wait out a squall, and buy a cup of coffee and a sticky bun as payment for the shelter. The counters would grow crowded with others like herself, a temporary fellowship, all with their own buns and coffee-cups, their own furled umbrellas dripping onto their shoes. At last the rain would pause—and then everyone would hurry out together, umbrellas open and raised, coffee warm in their bellies. It was the most mundane of experiences, and yet the Golem found that she treasured it.

The return home was different. At Columbus Circle she'd feel the first pangs of indecision, and by the time she reached Washington Square she'd be arguing with herself. *Don't. It's getting dark. You'll only draw attention. He didn't want to see you yesterday. He won't today, either.*

But it didn't matter. She had to try.

At Grand she would turn west instead of east, and hurry down Washington Street to knock upon the Amherst door and then wait, huddled beneath the awning. She knew he was there; she could hear him sometimes, walking about in the building's depths. At first she'd slipped notes into the letterbox, but then she ran out of ways to plead with him, and it began to feel demeaning. So now, she merely knocked—and never once did he open the door.

Boutros Arbeely took his final breath on a January night in 1912, while Little Syria slept around him. The Faddouls were there, and a Maronite priest, and the friends and neighbors who'd shared the vigil. It was after midnight when the priest said the final prayer. The director of the funeral home was summoned, the arrangements made. Maryam Faddoul dried her eyes, went to the telephone, and asked the operator for a number on the Lower East Side.

The Golem heard the 'phone ringing in the parlor and rushed downstairs to answer it. "Hello?"

"Chava? It's Maryam." The woman's voice trembled. "Boutros just passed."

"Oh, Maryam. I'm so sorry." An awkward pause, and then, "Ahmad never came, did he?"

"No. He didn't." A quick touch of anger in the words. Then, "Chava . . . someone has to tell him."

The Golem heard the unspoken plea. "Don't worry," she said, "I'll do it. And I'll go now, before he finds out some other way."

It was an unpleasant night to be out of doors. It had snowed all day, and now a cutting wind began, whipping her cloak about. The streets were nearly deserted, but still she paused at each corner to listen for anyone ahead who might give her trouble. Twice she managed to avoid policemen cooping in doorways, out of the cold.

At last she reached the Amherst. She knocked, first hesitantly and then with more insistence. As always, there was no reply.

She hesitated, glanced up and down the empty street, and then gave the doorknob a sharp and forceful turn.

Metal pinged. The knob came off in her hand. Carefully she laid it out of the way, and then opened the door.

The air inside was thick with heat. "Ahmad?" she called. The murmur of the forge seemed to swallow all noise. She found Arbeely's roll-top desk, switched on the lamp—and saw that the show-room walls had been torn away, with only crumbs of plaster left to mark where they'd been. Much of the workshop, too, was gone, save for a few cabinets, a solitary worktable, the anvil, and the forge's oblong pool of glowing coals.

She gazed at it all in mounting dismay, and then ventured into the supply room. It was darker here, the windows covered or else obscured—and there was a strange taste in the air, like burning earth. Her boot nudged something on the floor. She bent down and picked up a rock, dark and glittering, the size of her palm. She looked up, and realized that she was standing beside a sloping mountain of loose rubble that reached as high as the window-tops. She peered toward the back corner of the shop, to the shelves and the curtain behind them. The faintest glow crept around the curtain's edges. Yes, of course: his secret room.

"Ahmad?" She approached the curtain—and suddenly it was flung aside and he was striding toward her, heat pouring off him like water, his face so bright in the dark that she could barely look at him. She backed away, nearly tripping over the scattered rocks as he walked past her, out of the room.

She followed, and found him standing at the forge's edge, his hands buried in the coals. She wanted to flinch at the sight. He wore only his leather apron and a pair of trousers; his shirt, it seemed, had burned away completely. The forge was so hot she could barely come near him.

"Ahmad," she said. "I'm so sorry—but I just heard from Maryam. Arbeely's gone. He passed away."

Silence. He only stood there, staring into the flames.

She frowned. "Ahmad? Did you hear me?"

"Yes," he said at last. "I heard you. Arbeely is gone." He lifted his hands from the coals, and brushed the coal dust from his fingers.

All at once she wanted to shake him. "Does that mean *nothing* to you? He was your friend!"

He smiled. "Ah, I see. You're here to instruct me on how to mourn properly. And to chide me, if I fail to meet your exacting standards."

She shook her head. "I won't let you push me away."

"Spare me, Chava. Spare me your—" And again that sigh of air, a word that was not a word. He froze—and then all at once his face crumpled. He put his hands over his eyes and swayed on his feet.

"Oh, Ahmad," she whispered. She stepped toward him—but he barreled past her and across the remains of the showroom, to the stairwell.

Up he went, past the four empty floors to the top, where the door opened onto a rush of snowflakes that vaporized before they could touch him. He walked across the roof to the farthest corner, by the platform where the water tower stood, and braced his hands on the low ledge. The ice and snow vanished beneath his fingers.

"Please." She was standing behind him. "Please, talk to me."

"Go away, Chava. Go far, far away."

"You need—"

"*You have no idea what I need!*"

She reared back as if slapped.

"You have *never* known!" He had rounded on her, and stood shouting into the wind.

"Then tell me!" she cried. "You must *tell* me!"

An apprehensive silence, as though he were about to put a match to a powder-keg—and then: "Do you know what I see, when I look at you? I see a woman who fills herself with the lives of others, who'd throw herself on a pyre if someone wished for it and then curse herself for not burning brightly enough. A woman who wears her own death around her neck, like a present she can hardly wait to open."

She stood staring, listening, utterly still.

"You are exactly like them," he said, pointing out toward the city. "You'd make me as meek and obedient as yourself, if I would only allow it. You'd make a human of me—no, you would turn me into *you*."

He stepped toward her, and she backed away, hands half raised—but he couldn't let her go now; he was growing reckless, daring himself onward. "We aren't good for each other, Chava."

"Stop," she said.

"We never were."

"*Stop!*"

"You know that I'm right. You know it's true."

Her head jerked once, either a flinch or a confirmation. She turned then, as if to go—and all at once he was furious that she'd failed to defend herself, that she'd submitted so quickly, as though to confirm his worst opinions. And on the periphery of his anger lay a terror, waiting to be acknowledged. *Arbeely is gone. Arbeely is gone.* If she left him there, he'd be alone atop an empty building, with nothing but those words for company.

"Chava—" He stepped forward and grabbed her arm.

Like the uncoiling of a spring, she whirled toward him and punched him in the face.

He skidded backward, beneath the water tower platform. She advanced on him, her expression blank, her eyes flat and empty. He'd seen her like this twice before: on the night she nearly killed a man, and on the day he'd come close to destroying her. Both times, he'd fought her until she returned to herself—but now he made no attempt to struggle. He only closed his eyes as she lifted him from the tar-paper and hurled him upward, into the girders.

Metal rang around him. He landed face-down atop a snow-drift near the roof's edge and sank through it in a cloud of steam. Dizzy with pain, he levered himself up to one knee, awaiting her. Immediately she was upon him, her hands to either side of his face. She jerked upward, a movement that would've ripped any ordinary head from its neck, but instead brought him to his feet. His hands, flailing, came to her waist—and for an instant they stood together as they had on countless nights upon countless rooftops, in the quiet moments before the dawn.

The woman blinked, uncertain. Her hands twitched to either side of his face.

"Chava?" he said.

She convulsed, grabbing at him. Unbalanced, he fell into her; she rocked backward at his sudden weight. The rooftop ledge caught her knee. They staggered, teetered together—and went over.

The Jinni looked up at the falling snow.

For long, confused moments he held himself still. The Golem lay in his arms, curled against him. The ground seemed to be cradling them together. He turned his head, and concrete rubble scraped his cheek.

The Golem stirred in his arms. Her eyes opened, and there was life in them again.

For a moment they only gazed at each other—and then she was scrambling away from him, up and out of the crater they'd made in the alley. Concrete dust coated her face and clothing. He saw horror in her eyes, and desolation. He wondered what she saw in his.

Neither of them spoke a word. After all their arguments, all their attempts to explain themselves to each other, when the bridge between them broke, it broke in silence. He stood and watched as she ran from him, her boot-heels splashing through the frozen puddles. Then he went back inside the Amherst, and closed the door.

It was nearly two in the morning when the knock came.

Toby Blumberg woke on his pallet beside the sofa. Another knock, loud and urgent; he groaned, wondering which of the laundry girls it was this time. They all liked to come to the apartment and cry on his mother's shoulder after a fight at home. He got to his feet, wiped his eyes, and opened the door.

Missus Chava stood in the hallway. Her hat was gone, and her cloak hung in tatters. A wet gray dust covered her from head to toe. She might've been a statue, save for her eyes, which were wild with anguish.

His mother's footsteps, behind him. "Toby, who—" And then, with a cry of fear, his mother pushed him aside and slammed the door in the woman's face.

Toby was aghast. "But Ma, that was—"

"Be quiet, Toby." Her voice allowed no argument. Her hands were flat upon the door, as though to brace it. "Go to the kitchen, and open the window. Get ready to climb onto the fire escape."

"What? *Why?*"

"Just do as I say!"

Frightened now, he complied, and stood shivering in his pajamas next to the open window.

"Chava!" he heard his mother call. "Are you still there?"

Silence from the hallway. After long minutes, Anna cracked the door open—but there was only a trail of sodden boot-prints, and the muddy mark of the woman's hand upon the door.

When morning arrived, the residents of Little Syria all greeted their neighbors and asked if they, too, had been woken in the night by an echoing *boom*, as though a wrecking-ball had broken free of its chain. No one could say what had caused it—but then it was forgotten, as the news spread that Boutros Arbeely had passed away in the night. A number of callers knocked at the Amherst, but there was no response. A few of the local businessmen took it upon themselves to purchase a mourning wreath and hang it upon the Amherst door. Immediately the winter winds began to tear the crepe away, shred by shred.

Weeks passed. Eventually the Jinni's landlord decided that he'd been lenient enough in the face of tragedy; the fact remained that the man was delinquent on his rent. He went to the apartment, expecting to find vermin feasting on rotten food—but the larder and icebox were completely empty. There were no portraits or photographs on the walls, only a number of candles set inside mirrored sconces. The cabinets were bare of plates or cups, save for one small glass that sat beside a bottle of *araq*. The shelf in the bathroom held neither soap nor razor, not even a toothbrush. There was only the wardrobe with its minor assortment of clothing, and a wrought iron bed, elegant and well made.

The landlord claimed the bed for himself, and the bottle of *araq*. The rest of it was put out on the street, for the tinkers and ragpickers to find.

Eventually, a crew from Public Works came to look at the strange crater that had been discovered in the alley behind the Amherst. They gathered around it and scratched their heads, wondering what could've fallen from the roof that was heavy enough to shatter the concrete, yet light enough to be carried away without a trace. At last they shrugged and patched the crater with a mixture of tar and gravel that would turn viscous in summer, and foul the shoes of all who walked across it. Soon it was the only outward sign of all that had changed that night, save for the circle of bare and tattered branches that still hung upon the Amherst door.

The staff of the Beirut Deutscher Hof, Sophia decided, must be the most industrious and overworked in the entire city. Every room in the hotel was kept neat as a pin from top to bottom, the bedsheets boiled and ironed to a crisp, the mirrors polished daily. Merely to inhabit one of the rooms felt like a discourtesy to the maids. *It's the sea air, miss,* one of them said when Sophia commented upon their labors. *If you let the salt take hold, there's no getting rid of it.*

Sophia had come to Beirut for neither cures nor artifacts, but to recover from a mortifying disappointment. She'd spent the spring in Jerusalem, traveling with Abu Alim to the ruins outside the Old City's walls. There she'd dipped her hand in the Pool of Siloam and drunk the water from the Well of Job, and had felt no effect from either—but she hadn't really expected to. The most necessary ingredient for a Biblical cure was not water, but faith; and for all that her eyes had been opened to what was real and what was possible, she'd never once felt the sort of faith that the Bible demanded.

One afternoon, they'd traveled to a nearby village, where a number of Yemenite Jews had recently settled. She'd thought she might look in their market for a healer; but instead, she'd found Daniel Benbassa.

Daniel was a Sephardic Jew, the youngest son of an old Jaffa merchant family. As a student in Jerusalem he'd fallen in love with the Old City, and when his schooling was over he'd turned to charity work in a bid to stay. He'd been on his usual rounds in the village, distributing

food and donations, when he saw Sophia in the market and took her
for a member of a nearby Presbyterian settlement. He'd stopped to introduce himself—she'd apologized, and corrected his misapprehension—
and the conversation had gone on from there.

Soon Daniel was leading Sophia and Abu Alim through the winding streets of the Old City, showing them his favorite sites. He had something of Ned Lawrence's natural enthusiasm, but with a greater maturity
of spirit; Sophia sensed that he'd been disappointed in life, or love, and
that it had changed him. He spoke of Jaffa with the same deep fondness
as he did Jerusalem, describing a childhood spent hiding from his chores
in the orange groves, and playing among the stone warehouses on the
quay—and before long Sophia was completely smitten. Here was a man
who neither dismissed her opinions nor was intimidated by her intelligence, only spoke and listened, as to an equal. Abu Alim soon found
excuses to stay at their lodgings or busy himself with errands, leaving
the pair to walk the Quarters together.

Don't be a fool, she'd berate herself at night, awake beneath blankets
that never warmed her through. *Of course you can't tell him, he'd never
believe. But what if . . . what if.*

Then came the morning when Daniel failed to meet her at a café as
planned. She waited an hour, then returned to the hotel, where a letter
soon arrived. In it, he apologized for misleading her. There was a woman
in Jaffa, a childhood friend, the daughter of a family whose business
strengthened his father's. Not an arranged marriage, but an expected
one. The language was tortured, self-castigating. Perhaps it was a failure
of character, he wrote—but he could no more defy his family's wishes
than he could cut off his own arm.

Humiliated, Sophia had packed her belongings within the hour.
They soon left for Nablus and the blessed train, where Sophia could
sit alone in the women's car and not have to face Abu Alim's silent
sympathy.

He would've rejected you anyway, once he knew, a vicious voice in her
mind had whispered.

Onward they'd sped to Beirut, without itinerary or plan. Abu Alim
had seen her settled at the hotel and then gone back to Homs, to return

for her in a week. In the meantime she wanted no markets, no ruins, and nothing more taxing than a novel to read, something frivolous and French.

But after only three days, Sophia had grown inordinately sick of her own company, as well as the Deutscher Hof. The hotel took great delight in its Bavarian incongruity, and the Black Forest décor of mounted stag heads and *Reichsflagge* pennants was wearing on her nerves. On the wall beside her bed was an oil painting of Hohenzollern Castle in winter, its pale battlements rising above a mountainside bristling with snow. Looking at it made her shiver, and she wished she could take it down.

She decided to allow herself a change of scenery. She'd visit the Saint George Cathedral to view the frescoes, but nothing more enriching than that. She donned her hat and her shawls, and walked north along the high-walled street, the sea a mist-blue line in the distance. At a corner she passed a newsstand, and glanced down at a stack of papers.

Her father's face stared back.

The R.M.S. *Carpathia* neared the Chelsea docks.

The city was muffled in rain and mist. Church bells rang out suddenly from the shore, the noise pulled about by the wind on the river. Likely they were meant as a gesture of respect, thought Julia Winston as she sat in the ship's dining-room with the rest of the widows. To her they sounded like the din of a crowd, come to harry the grief-stricken. *What was it like. What will you do.*

Young Madeleine Astor sat nearby, her pretty face pale and drawn, her hands draped over the visible swell of her stomach. They'd put her next to Julia in Lifeboat No. 4, while Francis stood smoking a cigarette with Jack Astor and George nervously watched the crewmen fumble with the davits. At seventeen, George had been deemed too old to be sent off with the women and children—and Julia hadn't said a word against it, hadn't begged them to let him go with her. Too afraid to hurt the boy's dignity, in front of his father.

There'd been room for a dozen more in the lifeboat when they'd lowered it. She should've screamed at the men, clawed their eyes out. *Let me have him. Let me have my son.*

The *Carpathia* nudged the dock, and the women all flinched. Looking around, Julia wondered which of them would sell their stories to the papers. She'd heard the crew murmuring that the press was inundating Cunard with telegrams, demands for interviews. They were calling the *Carpathia* the "Ship of Widows," a romanticism she found utterly vile. Her thoughts returned again and again to the empty seats on the lifeboat, the sight of Francis and Astor smoking their cigarettes while George tried to mimic their calm. Here were men who ruled empires, men whose names meant power and consequence—and if these men chose to plant their feet firmly upon a sinking deck, then George would do the same. The pointlessness of it all took her breath away.

The crew gave the signal. The survivors gathered themselves and walked out onto the dock and through the pier shed, into the rain and the gathered crowd: hundreds of reporters and onlookers, a sea of pale faces, all utterly silent. She'd expected shouting, but this was worse. Flashbulbs exploded, blinding her. Someone, she had no idea who, took her by the arm and guided her to the curb, where Francis's Oldsmobile waited. The driver seated her inside, closed the door—then seemed to hesitate, confused, before remembering that there was no luggage.

At the house, the staff waited anxiously beneath the portico, next to columns swagged with crepe. They brought her into the parlor and sat her by the fire, offered her broth and toast, hovering, clustering around her, murmuring questions: Was she warm enough? Did she want a shawl?

"Stop coddling me," she snapped, and they backed away.

Presently she became aware of a muffled argument behind her. She caught the words *unwise, her father,* and *pity's sake.* All fell silent—and then a maid appeared, bobbed nervously, and handed Julia a tray that bore an overseas cable. "There's been a good many cables and telegrams, ma'am," she said, "but we thought this one might be important."

Julia dismissed them all, and opened it.

```
BEIRUT SYRIA
18 APR


MOTHER I AM HEARTBROKEN. GREATLY WISH TO
ATTEND FUNERALS BUT CANNOT STAY LONG. WILL YOU
ALLOW IT. IN GRIEF SOPHIA.
```

Julia realized her hand was shaking. She put the telegram down, breathless with what must have been anger. *Cannot stay long.* The sheer *gall* of the girl. Any decent daughter would've been on that lifeboat, at her mother's side. Instead, Julia had watched alone as her son and husband made sacrifices of themselves rather than be labeled cowards for stealing a woman's place. And now Sophia demanded the right to come and go, to choose her place and discard it again, when and where it suited her?

For too long the girl had enjoyed privilege without its duties, freedom without its price. One way or another, Julia would end it.

```
NYC
18 APR


IF YOU COME HOME YOU WILL STAY. IF YOU REMAIN
ABROAD YOUR ALLOWANCE ENDS. THE CHOICE IS
YOURS.

JHW
```

The late-spring heat arrived on the day of the Golem's college graduation.

It was a long and tedious event. The graduates all sweltered in their gowns, the white satin sashes at their necks growing damp with sweat. Guests and loved ones fanned themselves with the printed programs. At the calling of her name, the Golem stood and walked across the stage, took the proffered diploma, shook the dean's hand, and ignored his thought: *After all that hard work, you'd think she'd look happier.*

She had no guest of her own among the onlookers, for there was no one to invite. She'd left the Lower East Side months ago, her belongings packed into a suitcase and a hat-box, a note of apology and two months' rent in an envelope on the desk. Now she lived at the Martha Washington, a women's hotel near Madison Square, in a room that was even smaller than before—but it had a desk and a lamp, and a door for privacy. She'd rent an apartment soon, if all went according to plan.

At last the ceremony ended, and the crowd dispersed for the department receptions. Domestic Sciences' was near the main library, beneath a canopy hoisted against the sun, its poles decked with streamers. The department chair gave her speech—*The Domestic Sciences, with their marriage of scientific exactitude and the nurturing impulse, represent modern womanhood at its zenith*—and then all applauded and turned with relief to the punch-bowls on the tables, their ice-rings already melting. Fiancés were introduced and admired. Girls whose hands were still bare spoke brightly of their new teaching positions in Connecticut and Massachusetts.

"What about you, Chava?" a few asked.

"I think I'll find something soon," she replied. They gave her politely puzzled looks, then allowed their attention to be grabbed by others. Their world and hers had briefly overlapped; now they were drawing apart again.

At last the Golem excused herself, and left the lawn for the cool recesses of the library. From the cloakroom she retrieved a wide leather shoulder-bag, the sort that her professors carried. She placed her new diploma inside, next to her letter of reference from the department chair, attesting to her capabilities.

In the ladies' room she removed her mortarboard, sash, and robe. Beneath them, instead of her usual shirtwaist and skirt, she'd worn a pleated dress of navy French serge and a girdled belt tied with braid: bought not from an Orchard Street pushcart, but the Montgomery Ward catalog. Off went the plain black loafers; from the bag she drew a pair made of finer leather, with curved heels and pearl buttons. She wetted her fingers at the sink, twisted her hair into ringlets, and pinned them back from her face. Then she set to work with a box of complexion powder and a small pot of rouge—she'd been practicing with them for weeks—and donned a smart straw hat trimmed with navy ribbon. She stepped back from the mirror, straightened her shoulders from their self-conscious slouch, took a deep and steadying breath. *You can do this,* she thought. *You've made your own opportunity.*

She meant it quite literally. After that final, terrible night at the Amherst, she'd decided to follow the Asylum cooking instructor down into the subway again. In the carriage, she'd watched as the woman balanced her groceries in her lap to keep them from the slush-covered floor. At 72nd Street the clerk had boarded—and the Golem had gasped, *My stop!* and jumped from her seat, brushing past him at an angle calculated to make him stumble toward the woman. In the moments before the train pulled away, the Golem had watched from the platform as the clerk righted himself and helped the woman collect her scattered groceries, both of them blushing and talking at once.

The Golem had avoided the Asylum, after that. There was too great a risk that the woman might recognize her. But at last, after weeks of scouring the *Help Wanted* pages, the advertisement had jumped out at her:

Cooking instructor to teach girls ages 8–17. Must provide reference. Apply to Asylum for Orphaned Hebrews, 672 W. 136th Street.

The Golem cast a final glance at herself in the mirror, then left the library and descended the stone steps, in full view of the lawn party— and not a single one of her classmates realized it was her.

She walked north on Broadway with the noontime crowd. The apartment building on the corner at 136th was advertising rooms to rent; she took note of the fact with interest. She passed through the Asylum's enormous front gate, up the curved drive and through the door, then down a shadowed hall to the office, her pearl-buttoned heels clicking neatly on the floor. A young woman at a desk looked up at her approach.

"I have an interview with the headmistress," the Golem told her. "My name is Charlotte Levy."

PART III

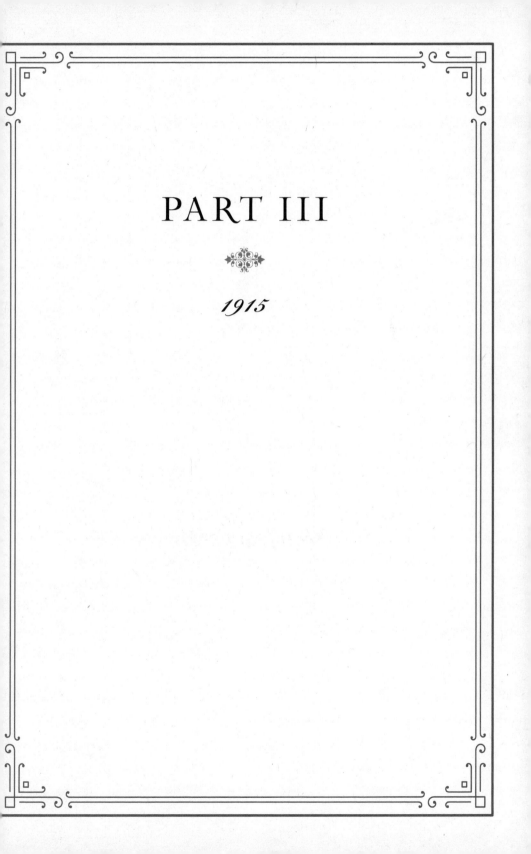

1915

13.

In the years following the jinniyeh's banishment to the Cursed City, the Bedu residents of Palmyra were forced to wage a constant and rather irritating battle.

Their adversary stole strips of meat off the drying racks, and frightened the goats so that their milk went sour. It raised dust-devils between the tents, hid the men's swords in the animals' bedding, and snipped the coins from the women's veils while they slept. It could only be a jinni of some kind—but no matter how many amulets they hung above their doorways and tent-flaps, still they woke to find their looms unstrung in the night, and the chickens gorging themselves in the granary. They began to set aside small offerings for their uninvited guest—old veils, colorful balls of wool, the best morsels of lamb—in hopes that they'd be accepted, and the rest left alone.

The jinniyeh was amused by these bribes, and took them more or less at random, hoping to confound the Bedu further. Sometimes she considered entering their sleeping minds, to watch their dreams and search through their memories—but the prospect held little true appeal. Their lives seemed to be made only of drudgery, so why should their dreams be any better? Besides, the tales were full of jinn who'd entered a human's mind at night, only to be trapped there come morning—a risk that hardly seemed worth any reward.

So each day she flew from her cave to the citadel, where she contented herself with her small mischiefs: raising winds to pull the clothing from the washing-lines, or turning into a mouse and nibbling through the ropes that held their tents aloft. The women chased after their laundry, and the men cursed as their tents fell around their ears; and she'd laugh, and fly back through the ruins to spend the night in her cave, telling herself stories in the dark. It was a lonely existence, perhaps, but far preferable to hiding among her own kind. She fully expected to live out

her centuries in this manner—until a spring evening in her fourth year
of banishment when, approaching her cave, she saw the glow and snap
of a campfire.

Shocked, she halted in midair, then flew closer. Beyond the fire, inside the cave, was the elongated outline of a sleeping camel, and a donkey beside it, its bristled back to the flames. The camel's saddle and an
assortment of packs and panniers sat nearby, against the jagged wall.

Footsteps—and a human figure emerged from the cave's depths.

At first the jinniyeh thought he was a Bedu, though they rarely traveled alone. He wore a scarf about his head, and a long shepherd's coat
lined with sheepskins, still dusty from the road. A thick assortment of
fringed shawls topped the coat, as though he'd traveled from a land still
mired in winter. The man unwound the head-scarf—and the jinniyeh
saw that it wasn't a man at all, but a woman, pale and fine-boned, her
long hair braided tightly around her head.

Intrigued, the jinniyeh flew closer—and startled the camel, which
snorted and kicked in its sleep before settling again. The woman tensed
and looked out past the fire, searching. For a moment her eyes seemed
to focus upon the jinniyeh, who felt an irrational prickle of fear.

Slowly the woman reached into a pocket in her coat, and withdrew a
slim metal case that she opened to reveal dozens of steel pins, each bent
at the middle like a miniature horseshoe. The woman held the case open
a moment, then removed a few of the pins and slid them into her braids,
which already held such an impressive number of them that the jinniyeh
wondered how she bore the weight. With a last glance beyond the fire,
the woman snapped the case shut and put it away again. Her hands, the
jinniyeh saw, were shaking.

With a jolt the jinniyeh remembered that she'd seen this woman
before.

The woman went to the camel's saddle, and from a holster withdrew a rifle like the ones the Bedu carried. She sat down by the fire, laid
the weapon nearby, and rubbed at her eyes. The jinniyeh held perfectly
still, floating only upon the air-currents that rose from the fire, until at
last the woman curled up against the camel and fell asleep. Even in slum-

ber she shivered, minute tremors that traveled the length of her body. She frowned, her mouth twitching.

Slowly, slowly, the jinniyeh drifted closer. The camel shuddered once, and snorted into the dust, but the woman slept on. Her mind was open, the way clear—and for the first time, the risk seemed worth the reward.

The jinniyeh flew inside.

Her name was Sophia.

She had been Sophia . . . Williams? Winston? The difference seemed laughably small, though to the woman it mattered immensely. But she was only Sophia now, and only to herself. The tribespeople of the desert called her Saffiyah, a different name in a different language. Saffiyah the stranger, Saffiyah the afflicted. Shivering Saffiyah.

But before that, there had been a telegram, and then a letter, written to a man named Abu Alim: With utmost sorrow I must tell you that I can no longer employ you as my guide.

Then, doors upon doors, a city's worth of them. Protestant missionary schools, écoles françaises, wealthy Damascene families who might want a tutor for their children. She knocked upon them all. She could teach English, French, history, mathematics. References? She had none.

The doors closed in her face.

You aren't a Winston anymore, she told herself bitterly. So stop thinking like one.

The souk in Damascus, the calls of the vendors. Umm Sahir, her sharp eyes spotting her customer across the alley.

You're early this month, Miss Williams. Has something happened?

She needed employment. She had no skill at healing, and was too old to apprentice. But she'd been the guest of every tribe from Aleppo to the Red Sea. She knew their sheikhs, their languages, their alliances. More than that: she knew their healers, and what they needed. Herbs, mastics, incense, salts, items too rare or too dear to be gotten easily in the desert. But here in Damascus, Umm Sahir sold them all.

You would be my . . . agent? My go-between?

Something like that, yes.

You'll be killed, sighed Umm Sahir—but she agreed all the same.

A few tried to rob her, at first. Scouts and warlords, spying a lone traveler, rushed her with rifles drawn. She put an easy hand upon the pistol at her belt, called out greetings—and to their astonishment they recognized the woman who'd once sat at their fire and talked politics. Would they be so kind, she asked, as to escort her to their encampment? She'd like to pay her regards to their healer, whom she remembered.

A Western woman, alone on the road in the noonday heat? It was shocking, bizarre. She knew their ways, but stood outside them; she ought to be dead, but she wasn't. And so, in their consternation, they did as she asked— and were shocked, again, by the healers' crows of delight when they saw what the woman offered.

She'd stay a few days, sharing their fire and food, and then be on her way again, to the next village—or else back to Damascus for more supplies, and for the powder that never warmed her, only made the cold more bearable. Once a month she went to the post office and mailed a postcard to her mother, the space for the message left blank. The card itself was message enough; and besides, she had nothing civil to say.

And then, a headline glimpsed in Marjeh Square: Archduke Franz Ferdinand Murdered by Serbian Assassin. To the watching jinniyeh, the words were meaningless, and yet they meant war.

Now the world changed. In Damascus, in Homs, in Jerusalem, men marched in the street while women stood nearby and wept. The prices in the markets began to climb, the Western tourists to disappear from the cities. The countryside was battening down, turning inward. But Sophia had nowhere to go except for the road.

Bandits grew more numerous, and soldiers, which was worse. She spent a week in an abandoned orchard at the edge of Homs, collecting fallen pistachios while tears wetted her cheeks. She traveled to the Jerusalem outskirts and bartered with the healers there, then hid behind a stall like an embarrassed child as Daniel Benbassa walked past, his new wife at his side. At night she dreamt of being dragged across an ocean and locked inside a marble tomb, of freezing slowly to death beneath her mother's gaze.

The souk grew quiet. Men disappeared from their stalls, were replaced by wives and young sons, their faces anxious. Her familiar routes between the cities turned impassable as the army built barracks and training-grounds. She needed a foxhole, somewhere safe to hide. She thought of Palmyra, deep in the desert. Would they remember her there? If she brought enough supplies, would they shelter her for a week? A month?

She went to the souk, and Umm Sahir was gone.

In her place, a stone-faced man stood beside a rack of poorly tanned hides. Behind him, beneath the arch, other men sat on wooden crates, reading newspapers. Their bodies were well-fed. Expensive cigarettes burned in their mouths.

She turned around and walked away. None of the other vendors would meet her eye.

She put on her old Western blouse and skirt, walked to her bank, and withdrew the dregs of her savings. She bought food and ammunition for the road, and then sewed the rest of the money inside a belt around her waist. She thought of the Bedu girls and their dowry head-scarves, the coins that bought them a place in the tribe. She wondered if hers would be enough.

Her powder ran out on the road to Palmyra.

She made it over the pass before the evening grew too cold for her to sit upright in the saddle. She found a cave, fashioned a fire, and took stock. She'd go to the citadel in the morning, once she'd warmed enough, and make her offer. She didn't know what she'd do if they refused.

She leaned against her donkey and closed her eyes . . .

When she opened them, it was noon, and she was walking through the Valley of the Tombs, thin grasses whispering beneath her sandals. Ahead of her, a tall, dark-haired woman stood beneath a tower-tomb. The woman was naked and holding a scythe. She ran a finger along the edge of the blade, then looked up at the tomb again.

I've never understood why you build these, the woman said. The stones will crumble, just as the bones will. So why go to the effort?

It's simple, Sophia told her. We build them to tell the stories of the dead.

The woman glanced at her. What do you mean?

History. The tale of what once was, of people and civilizations come and gone. We read the past in what remains.

The woman shook her head. But the story will fade with the stones.

Not if we tell it well enough.

The woman raised an eyebrow, amused. The expression was familiar; it reminded Sophia of someone from long ago . . . The woman's eyes were entrancing, as black and deep as wells. A distant flame glowed at the center of each.

A note of warning sounded from the part of Sophia that lay shivering in a firelit cave. But she ignored it. Here in the sun it was warm and lovely, and she didn't tremble at all.

The woman smiled, and lifted a hand to Sophia's cheek. Sophia turned her face into the woman's hand, searching out the warmth of her skin. She wanted to stretch like a cat in a sunbeam. When was the last time she'd allowed herself to be touched like this? Not for years, not since . . .

The towers and tombs faded, the sun-warmed valley disappeared. She stood barefoot on the cold granite of her childhood balcony—and in place of the naked woman was a man, tall and handsome. He leaned down and kissed her with burning intensity. She drew him closer, the wall cold at her back; his hands slipped inside her dressing-gown, the iron at his wrist hot against her skin—

Ahmad.

At last her alarm broke through to her dreaming self. Fury flooded her veins. She put her hands on his chest and shoved, hard. Startled, he backed away.

She charged toward him, caught him by the neck, and lifted. He squirmed in her grasp—and then melted back into the woman, her feet dangling above the stone.

Who are you? Sophia shouted.

The world darkened. Rain burst from the clouds overhead. It struck the woman, and she screamed. Her pain racked Sophia's mind, she was harming herself as well as the woman, but she refused to let go.

Tell me!

The woman kicked feebly, then relented . . .

The scythe fell from her hand, to land among the winter wheat.

On her lover's face, shock turned to disgust as the iron passed through her without effect.

The mob tore at her flame as they herded her over the pass, and down to the Cursed City.

Sophia watched the jinniyeh cower in her cave for months—and then felt her joy when the jinniyeh realized that there were no monsters, and the stones were merely stones. She heard the tales the jinniyeh told herself at night, the story of the iron-bound jinni, the only one of their kind who might view her with something other than loathing. And yet he was merely a tale . . .

Except that now, the jinniyeh knew otherwise.

Release me, the jinniyeh said, trembling in the grip of Sophia's thoughts, and take me to him. And in exchange, I will give you what you seek.

And what is that? Sophia said.

A cure.

There is no cure. I've been to healers, exorcists—

Human healers. Human exorcists. You ringed yourself with steel and drove away the very ones who might help you. I can feel it, even now—a cinder, a bit of ash left behind. Was it a child, once?

Sophia's hand trembled. Prove it. Prove you can do what you say.

No. Not until you've taken me to him—

A spasm of pain passed through them both.

—and if you do not release me quickly, then neither of us will survive this.

A moment's hesitation. Then, reluctantly, Sophia loosened her hand—

—and woke in a sickening rush as something withdrew itself from her mind.

She stumbled from the cave and ran a few steps before vomiting into the scrub. Her head throbbed as though it had been ripped to pieces, and she was trembling so hard she could barely stand. In the cave, the animals snorted and brayed, thrashing against their tethers, then mercifully calmed again.

A moan from nearby.

A naked woman lay on the ground near the cave entrance. With painful slowness she sat up, her head in her hands. She looked as wretched as Sophia felt.

"That," the jinniyeh said with a glare, "was exceedingly foolish. You might've torn me to shreds, along with your own sanity."

Sophia glared back. "You invaded my dreams while I slept. Was I supposed to welcome you with open arms?"

"You were in my cave!"

"I hardly knew that, did I?"

The jinniyeh frowned. "What language is this?"

"English." She hadn't realized it until that moment. She hadn't spoken English in years.

"It hurts my mind," the jinniyeh said.

"I know five others, if you'd prefer."

The jinniyeh made no answer, only crawled to the campfire and huddled miserably atop the coals.

Sophia limped back to the cave, found her water-skin, and drank. Then she sat by the fire again, keeping a body's length between herself and the jinniyeh.

"Can you truly do it?" she asked at last.

"Of course I can," the jinniyeh muttered from the coals. "It would be simple, though not without risk. But only if you take me to him."

Sophia's head swam. Her teeth were chattering so hard she could barely open her mouth. "I can't think properly," she said, with effort. "I need sleep. We'll discuss it in the morning. And if you try anything like that again—"

The jinniyeh groaned at the thought. "I'd destroy myself, in this state. Now stop all this *talking*."

I ought to make her promise, Sophia thought—but the cave was already growing dark, and within moments she was beyond her worries.

The iron-bound jinni was real.

The jinniyeh could hardly believe it. The very one whose story had given her such comfort, and he was *real!*

The woman slept on, her chest rising and falling beneath her many layers of clothing. Watching her, the jinniyeh realized she could end this encounter now, without any further dealings between them. She'd made her offer to Sophia in a desperate moment, to keep the woman from ripping her apart—but that danger was past. She could simply find another cave and go about her life. Easier, certainly, than what she'd proposed in the woman's mind.

And yet she couldn't just fly away. The iron-bound jinni was real—

and now that she knew, how could she be satisfied with her lonely exile, her small mischiefs? How could she live out her pitiful centuries, and not at least *try* to find him?

But then, what if she succeeded? Would he loathe her and reject her, as the others did? After all, he was cursed to his condition, while her own was innate. But perhaps his own loneliness would sway him. If he learned there was another option, a place in the desert where he could live as himself, safe and accepted—then wouldn't he see the wisdom in joining her there? After all, what was the point of the Cursed City, if not to shelter the cursed?

Sophia woke in the morning alone, with the remnants of her headache. She stirred the embers of the fire, half expecting her visitor to appear and snatch the stick out of her hand—but the jinniyeh was nowhere to be seen. She heaped more wood upon the embers, then untethered the camel and donkey, who wandered calmly out of the cave and began to crop the nearby grasses. Sophia frowned. It seemed the jinniyeh had lost interest—or, more likely, she'd only feigned it in the first place.

A stab of disappointment ran through her, and she shook her head at herself. How many times must she raise her own hopes, only to—

A sudden breeze whipped past, making her shiver—and the jinniyeh appeared on the other side of the fire, as naked as before. The donkey brayed belatedly, then resumed its breakfast.

"I thought you'd never wake," the jinniyeh said. "Here." She extended a hand across the fire. In her palm were three strips of dried meat. "I've noticed that humans eat food, in the mornings."

Sophia raised her eyebrows. "Did you steal these?"

"Of course."

Sophia knew she oughtn't accept, but she was ravenous, and she suspected that the jinniyeh meant it as a sort of peace offering. The meat was tough and stringy, but it filled her belly. The jinniyeh watched her intently as she ate.

"Will you take me to him?" the jinniyeh said at last, abruptly.

Sophia swallowed the last of her breakfast. "I told you, we must discuss it first."

The jinniyeh made an impatient noise. "What is there to discuss? Each of us needs something from the other."

"It isn't that simple. I can't just spirit us across the globe—there's a war on."

"Yes, yes, I saw it," muttered the jinniyeh. "But you're always at war, just as we are."

Sophia shook her head. "This is different. Imagine if every jinn tribe in the world went to battle, all choosing sides one after the other, like a flood sweeping the desert. My own country has managed to stay neutral, but it's only a matter of time. And there are new weapons, too. They have ships now that can sail entirely underwater, and destroy whoever's on the surface. No one is safe from them. And besides, I haven't so much as spoken to Ahmad in years. I have no idea whether he's still in New York—or for that matter, whether he's alive at all."

The jinniyeh's eyes had grown wide, her expression unsure; but now she shook her head, as though to scatter Sophia's objections. "You still have ways to find him. The money, in your belt."

"It's all that I have left! And I won't spend a single cent of it until I'm certain you'll heal me."

"I could simply overpower you and take it myself," the jinniyeh said.

Sophia folded her arms. "Yes, that occurred to me too. But if you want to reach him, you'll need my money *and* my knowledge. You'll even need my help just to make it through the jinn territories." She paused, then added, "Although for that, you have my sympathies. What your tribe did to you was exceedingly cruel."

The jinniyeh looked away. "Yes. It was. But it was better than the death I'd expected."

Sophia sighed, rubbed her forehead with trembling fingers. She wanted to ask, *Why?* Why leave a place of safety, and cross a dangerous ocean, for someone she'd only heard about in a story? But in truth she knew the answer already; it was the one she would've given herself: *for the chance to no longer be alone.* "You might consider," she said, "that if you heal me now, I'll be in a much better condition to help you reach him."

The jinniyeh pondered this, then said. "No, I won't risk both the healing and the voyage when I might gain nothing from them. We find him first."

"Then must I insist on a time limit," Sophia said. "I refuse to be stranded on the other side of the world, with no money and no cure, obligated to help you search until you accept that he can't be found."

The jinniyeh looked like she would argue, but then relented. "A limit, then. How long?"

Sophia considered. "A week. Seven days, from when we reach New York. At the end of seven days, you'll heal me, no matter what."

The jinniyeh gaped in outrage. "Only seven days!"

"The money might not stretch that long to begin with."

The jinniyeh paced before the fire, hands clenched in frustration. At last she huffed a sigh. "I suppose. Seven days, then."

But Sophia distrusted her tone. "Will you swear to it?" And then, unsure: "Is that something that jinn do?"

The jinniyeh looked offended. "Yes, of course we do. We swear by Mount Qaf. And if we should break our word, then we forfeit all chances of returning there, in this life or any other."

Mount Qaf. The name was distantly familiar to Sophia: she remembered a book of collected folklore, its tales of the idyllic emerald mountain where the jinn had once lived. "Then swear to me, by Mount Qaf, that you will heal me within seven days of our arrival in New York, whether we've found Ahmad or not."

The jinniyeh mulled it over, and then said, "Upon Mount Qaf, I swear it."

It wasn't ideal, by any means. Sophia knew the advantage still lay with the jinniyeh—but in truth, the advantage had been hers from the beginning. Sophia had no shelter, no friends, no medicine. Coming to Palmyra had been a desperate gambit—and now the mere possibility that she might be healed seemed as certain as anything else.

"Good," Sophia said. And then, belatedly: "Do you have a name?"

The jinniyeh looked away. "It was taken from me when I was banished. But even if it were still mine, I couldn't speak it—not in this form."

"Well, I can't just call you *jinniyeh.*"

The jinniyeh thought a moment, and then smiled. "Dima. That shall be my name, if you must use one."

"Dima," Sophia repeated. It was a common name among Arab women; it meant "the cloud that brings rain." She recalled the flashes of memory she'd seen, the mob, the taunts. Ah, yes—*storm-cloud.*

"Well, Dima," she said, "how shall we get you to Homs?"

They struck the camp and set out, up the mountainside and back over the pass.

It was a deeply uncomfortable journey. Sophia's camel spent the first few hours bucking and dancing as it tried to dislodge an old trunk, reinforced with steel at its corners, that hung in the pannier at its side. The donkey trailed well out of the way as Sophia cursed and held on, her teeth chattering. Eventually she convinced the camel that trotting might help matters, and little by little they made up their lost time.

She spent a sleepless night camped by the side of the road, and reached the outskirts of Homs the next evening. At a stable near the train station, she sold the camel and the donkey for a handful of piastres, then bought a train ticket to Damascus and sat for hours in the women's waiting room while the attendants made apologies for the delay. The usual train had been requisitioned for troop movements, they said; its replacement would be there shortly.

A *thump*—and the steel-cornered trunk at her feet lurched slightly to the left. Sophia frowned and nudged it forcefully back into place.

It was past midnight when the train arrived. There was no heat in the women's carriage; the stove, it seemed, had also been requisitioned. A group of officers' wives and their maids sat clustered in the middle of the carriage, blankets spread across their laps. They glared at Sophia as she boarded, as though to ward her away.

Reluctantly Sophia took a seat near the window, where it was coldest. A discarded newspaper lay upon the carriage floor, and she placed it inside her satchel while a porter loaded the rest of her luggage into the rack overhead. She'd need to know more about the state of the war, if they were to have a hope of reaching New York. Likely the newspaper was heavily censored; still, there might be something she could use.

By the time they arrived in Damascus she was shaking so violently she could barely stand. A porter helped her to a wagon; and by dawn she was at the Victoria Hotel. The desk attendant stared at her travel-stained clothes and dilapidated luggage, but such was his desperation for paying guests that he allowed her a room regardless.

The bellboy carried her luggage into the room, and withdrew. The door closed behind him—and at last Sophia fumbled at the trunk's latches.

The jinniyeh exploded into the room. "Two days!" she hissed. "Two days in a wretched box!"

Sophia said nothing, only swayed on her feet, then stumbled to the fireplace. There was wood, and kindling; she heaped both into the grate, then reached shaking hands for the match-box.

"Oh, move aside," muttered the jinniyeh, and lit the kindling with a touch. There was a *whump* of flame, and a burst of welcome heat.

The jinniyeh paced while Sophia huddled as close to the grate as she dared. "Why are we in this room?"

"Because," Sophia said when she could form the words, "this room has a fire in it."

The jinniyeh growled in frustration. "When do we leave?"

"We'll need a plan first. I can't get us past the blockade until I know which routes are open and which aren't."

"And how will you do that, from here?"

In answer Sophia crawled to her satchel, extracted her scavenged newspaper, and brought it back to the fire. The jinniyeh peered over her shoulder as she scanned its pages. Was there anything that might help them? Here, a report of smugglers evading the blockade; perhaps she could bribe one to take them across . . .

Exhausted, she turned the page—and the headline *American Warship Arrives at Jaffa* leapt at her like the answer to an unspoken prayer. She read the article, then said, "Here, look. A ship from my country is ferrying expatriates from Syria to Egypt—mostly settlers from the Jewish colonies, I'd expect. If we can get to Egypt, we can sail to England and find passage from there to New York, if anyone will take us." She frowned, and checked the date. "No, wait. The ship sails from Jaffa tomorrow afternoon. We'll never get there in time."

"Why not?" asked the jinniyeh.

Sophia dug her railway timetable from the satchel and unfolded it to show the map. "We're here, in Damascus. And this is Jaffa, here. The trains only go as far as Haifa, and they're unreliable at best. It'll take us at least a day and a half to reach Jaffa. Still, we ought to get to the coast. Perhaps the navy will send another ship, after this one."

The jinniyeh peered down at the map. "But why can't we simply . . ." And she drew a line with her finger from Damascus to Jaffa.

"Because that's half again the distance from Homs to Palmyra, and across a mountain range."

Dima pondered this. "I could fly such a distance," she said. "And no jinn would recognize me, this far from my old habitation. Carrying a burden would be difficult, but not impossible. The mountain winds might even help us."

Burden? Sophia thought.

"We can reach it by tomorrow morning," the jinniyeh said. "Would that suffice?"

Sophia gaped. "Tomorrow *morning*? You can't be serious!"

The jinniyeh pointed at the luggage. "But we must leave this behind. Take only what you absolutely need."

"Dima." Fear clutched at her. "I'll *freeze* up there."

The jinniyeh's expression did not soften. "And I will exhaust myself. But neither of us will perish."

Later that morning, a maid who was sweeping the hallway outside Sophia's room noticed a strange breeze pulling at her ankles. She peered down in confusion as the breeze grew, whipping her skirt about her legs.

The door to Sophia's room flew open with a bang.

Something fell over and shattered. Dust swirled, stinging the maid's eyes—and for a moment she thought she saw a whirlwind, and a figure inside it, rising from the balcony beyond.

The wind died away, revealing a room in shambles, its lamps smashed, the curtains torn from the rods. Sophia's campaign trunk lay tipped upon its side, its contents scattered. Its owner had disappeared without a trace.

The emigrants stood in a line that stretched along Jaffa's narrow quay.

For days they'd gathered at the port, waiting. Most were European Jews, citizens of the Russian Empire, the ones who'd left the Tsar and his pogroms to build a new homeland in colonies like Tel Aviv and Petah Tikvah. But the war was worsening every day, and their own position had grown more perilous. Some of their neighbors had decided to take Ottoman citizenship; others simply declared that they would put their trust in God. But many had looked to the Ottomans' treatment of their Armenian subjects—men killed village by village, women and children driven through the desert—and said, *Perhaps it will be us next.* These were the ones who'd packed their belongings and come to Jaffa to board the U.S.S. *Des Moines*, a towering wedge of steel among the wooden fishing-dhows, and now waited with their crates and carpet-bags in the morning sun.

The solitary woman who joined the end of their queue seemed to have barely survived some terrible ordeal. She wore a sheepskin coat and heavy shawls, far too warm for the morning, and carried nothing but a leather satchel that she clutched as though it might be torn from her by force. Her face was waxen pale, save for wind-burnt cheeks, and she trembled from head to toe. *Are you ill, miss?* someone asked her.

Sophia shook her head, but couldn't speak. She closed her eyes—and she was in the whirlwind again, suspended high above the mountains, the wind slicing to her marrow. She wavered and fell.

At first the jinniyeh didn't notice. Drained from her own efforts, she hung limply above the émigrés, staring at the curving, foam-capped sea and the unthinkable length of steel that pierced it like a poisoned thorn. How, she wondered, could there be enough iron in the world for such a monstrosity? Was it the only one, or were there more? And Sophia meant for them to *travel* upon it?

She heard the commotion then, and saw Sophia sprawled upon the ground. Others had gathered around her, and were stripping her of her heavy coat and woolen shawls while Sophia batted at them, her tremor worsening.

I could leave her here, and go back to the Cursed City, the jinniyeh thought as she watched. *I could forget that I ever saw her.* But the thought was feeble, fleeting. She would ride the monstrous steel ship across the killing waters; she'd find the iron-bound jinni and bring him home again. She had a purpose now, and it was stronger than her fear.

A moment later, a small green gecko landed upon Sophia's chest and darted beneath her collar, out of sight. An impossible warmth spread outwards from its tiny body.

Within minutes the woman was able to stand again. She thanked the others for their concern, and collected her coat and shawls with hands that hardly shook at all. Only when they'd all taken their places in line again did she dare peek down at the gecko that sat upon her collarbone, staring up at her with one jet-black eye.

The line shuffled forward, and at last they reached the *Des Moines'* gangplank. A navy serviceman, no older than nineteen, peered at her mussed braids and meager leather satchel and then at her passport, stained and creased from years of travel. "Winston, huh?" he said with a grin. "Any relation?" And he laughed and waved her through, not waiting for an answer.

She found a place at the rail among the others, many of whom were sobbing, or praying for safe passage. The ship's horn blasted a warning—beneath Sophia's shawls, the gecko tightened its grip—and the *Des Moines* pulled away from the dhows.

Excerpt of letter from T. E. Lawrence to D. G. Hogarth

Cairo War Office, February 1915

> *You'll have heard about the recent trouble at the Suez. One almost has to pity the Turks—all that time and preparation made for a poor showing in the end. Of course they'll be back to have another go, but no one expects anything to come of it.*
>
> *Here is something unexpected: Last night, whom should I pass in the street but Sophia Williams, the American girl you'll remember from Carchemish. She'd tried to weather the storm in Syria—I'd thought her more sensible—but gave up and retreated out of Jaffa, by the skin of her teeth. She was in Cairo for the day to outfit herself*

before sailing for home. I bought her dinner at Shepheard's, and gave her a bit of money when I left—she seemed to need it. Now she is off to Port Said—and in her wake I feel my confinement more painfully than ever, here in my stifling office with pen in hand from dawn to dusk. Currently I'm at work on a précis about the divisions in Syria's interior: race, language, tribe, religious feeling. But I doubt that many will read it, and doubt even more that those who do will learn its lessons.

T.E.L.

14.

The morning fog pressed itself upon Little Syria, sneaking through the gaps in the window-panes, weighting the air and dulling the senses. Mothers stood half asleep at their stoves, their pots of rice and lentils threatening to scorch. On Washington Street, the newsboys called out halfheartedly about Allied losses at Gallipoli, German deaths near Verdun.

In the kitchen of the Faddouls' coffee-house, Maryam warmed the day's first coffee-pot while Sayeed scooped the beans and cardamom into the grinder.

"I forgot to tell you," Sayeed said as he worked. "I stopped in at Faris and Habiba's yesterday, when I was in South Ferry. They told me they're moving to Detroit. There's a grandchild on the way."

"Oh, how wonderful! Habiba will be such a happy grandmother. But—what about the restaurant?"

"They'll have to sell it, or find someone to take over the lease. He asked if we were interested."

Maryam glanced at her husband, startled. Was he suggesting that they move to Brooklyn? "What did you tell him?"

"That I didn't know, myself—but that I'd ask you." His eyes were on his work, but she could read his worry for her as clearly as if he'd spoken it aloud: *How long can you go on like this?*

A pause. Then, "No," Maryam said. "It's a lovely thought, but no."

"It's a good location," he said quietly.

"It is. And someone will be lucky to have it." She glanced at the clock. "It's time. I'll get the door." She squeezed Sayeed's arm as she left: an acknowledgment of his concern, and a plea for understanding. Away from his eyes, she took a deep breath and crossed herself, then unlocked the door and turned the sign from *Closed* to *Open*.

The first customers trickled in, yawning and sighing as they sat.

Chair-legs squeaked against the floor. Maryam walked from table to table, pouring, smiling, listening. Gossip was shared more quietly these days, thanks to the war. Few felt comfortable bragging of success, or grumbling over a minor misfortune, when so many of their loved ones were in peril. The Mediterranean blockade had stretched the villages of Lebanon to the breaking point. The remnants of last year's harvests had all been sent to the Imperial supply lines—and now, just as the spring crops began to ripen, came news of locust swarms unlike anything seen in a generation. They flew in clouds that blocked the sun, fell upon fields and stripped them bare in minutes. It seemed clear that no matter how much money Little Syria's residents managed to send home, no matter how many coins they added to the collection plates, it wouldn't be enough to ward off starvation.

They spoke little of it, among themselves. It was too difficult to talk about, too weighted with guilt and worry and helplessness. Instead they turned to matters of the neighborhood, and vented their frustrations there—which meant that Maryam didn't have to listen for long before she caught the word *Bedouin* as it flew past her, flashing like a silver bird.

She angled toward its origin, a table in the corner, listening as she approached:

It's been three years now. How long will he let the Amherst sit empty?

It's a waste, and an eyesore, with all the windows papered over like that.

One might be forgiven for thinking he was up to no good in there—

And then Maryam arrived and refilled their cups, and asked if they'd heard that Faris and Habiba Mokarzel had decided to move to Detroit. Who, she wondered, would be left to run their restaurant? It was a good location, and it would be a shame to lose such a successful business. But then, perhaps someone would offer to buy it from them. With that, she danced away again while the men sat back, pondering the idea.

So went Maryam's vigil each day, as she sought out each whisper, deftly uprooted it, and planted something else in its place. But the strain had taken its toll. Worry and fatigue dimmed her spirit. When she looked in the mirror, she saw new creases in her brow, new threads of silver advancing through her hair. But she couldn't rest, she simply couldn't—not when the Amherst exerted such a pull on the neighborhood's imagination.

Since Boutros' death, the building had taken on a new and foreboding personality. All the windows were covered over with butcher paper, five floors' worth, from top to bottom. Groans and creaks rose at times from the depths, and the occasional muffled reverberation. The chimney-top still shimmered with heat, and snow that landed on the rooftop melted instantly, even in the coldest winter. Delivery trucks came monthly with their coal and ore, but there were no visitors, no customers—only its sole resident, a moving silhouette glimpsed occasionally at night, through the papered windows.

It was the most tantalizing of mysteries, and only natural that Little Syria should whisper about it—but what would happen if she allowed the whispers to spread? Her neighbors, powerless to stop a war elsewhere, would invent a battle nearby that they thought they could win. They'd convince themselves that the Amherst was a danger and its owner their enemy; they'd force their way inside and confront him— and then what? There was no way of knowing. No one had spoken to the man in years. The Golem, too, had vanished. Occasionally Maryam thought of the broken concrete in the alley behind the Amherst, and wondered what had happened between them—but she didn't linger upon such thoughts for long. Their world and its considerations, she'd decided, were not hers to influence or understand. She would instead concentrate on her loved ones, and protect them from the danger that they would otherwise insist on rousing.

The Amherst's owner, the man who'd caused so much consternation, stood at the forge with his hands buried in fire to the wrists, and looked up at what his building had become.

It was no longer a factory loft, not by any stretch of the imagination. The floors themselves had long since vanished, and the stairwell enclosure too: the boards ripped apart, the joists burned to ash, the plaster walls demolished, the stairs uncoupled weld by weld. In the months after Arbeely's death he'd torn down every bit of the interior he deemed unnecessary, every pipe and wire and conduit, until all that was left was the support columns, a grid of brick pillars rising through five stories of empty air. Ready, at last, for his true work to begin.

It had taken him some time to settle on a design. Perhaps he couldn't build his river-pebble of steel and slag, not yet; he had only the Amherst, and its boundaries suggested a different purpose. He thought of his glass palace, abandoned in its desert valley. The necklaces he'd once made, with their silver wires and discs of colored glass. The Pennsylvania Station concourse, its arches that shaped the sky beyond. The steel pebble, with its suggestion of a building without corners. He'd fuse them all together and create something entirely new, the first and only one of its kind.

The central column came first. He crushed the iron ore a handful at a time and reinforced the middlemost support pillar with steel, smoothing it onto the brick, building it up one layer at a time. He developed a feel for the mix of iron to carbon, adjusting its strength and pliancy as he went. The slag he set aside for later, a hill of glass growing slowly beside the forge. Inch by inch the steel ascended—and as he strengthened the column, he encircled it with a spiral staircase that grew rung by rung as he needed it. Whenever his body grew too cool to work the metal, he descended to the forge to warm himself, then went back up again, rising through the empty building.

When at last he reached the top, he began the arches.

They branched outward from the column, reaching up to form trusses that held the weight of the roof, then down again to hide the roof's corners behind their iron curves. Where the trusses met the walls, he fit hidden bolts that sent the weight of the steel down through the bricks and into the bedrock.

He worked in midair, upon a slender iron scaffold, a five-story drop at his back. Days and nights went uncounted, unnoticed. The filtered sunlight entered first one set of windows, then another. His life was heat and movement; his thoughts were in the sounds of flame and wind as much as human words. The forge sustained him, it was his companion and his storyteller, whispering to him from his past. *Once there was a jinni who was injured in a storm, and took shelter inside a Bedu's cooking-fire. Once there was an imp who tricked a wizard into falling in love with a horse.*

When at last the arches were in place, he removed the rest of the support columns, tearing them down brick by brick. It was an agonizing process, and at each moment he expected the awful shifting groan that would mean he'd taxed the building beyond its limits. But the central column and its arches held steady; the iron bore the weight.

Then, he began the platforms.

Each was a steel disc roughly fifty feet in diameter, cantilevered out from the central column and held up by curving trusses. There were eight of them in total, and they rose around the column in a helix, each one making a curved half-roof for the next. When he stood at the top and looked down, they were a series of moons that spiraled away beneath him, filling the void with shining steel.

There was still much to be done. The hill of slag, growing beside the forge: he would melt it down, turn it into panes of glass, and then fit them in the spaces between the arches, a second roof snug inside the first. He'd run electricity up the central column, hang lanterns and fairy-lights from the platforms' edges, create hanging sculptures that soared through the open air. There were any number of alterations he might make—enough to occupy his mind fully, and leave room for nothing else.

In the Culinary Science classroom at the Asylum for Orphaned Hebrews, twelve girls in pressed white coats and hats stood eagerly around a rectangular island of countertop, each at her own place.

"Your attention, ladies," their teacher said. "Today, each of you will prepare and stuff a chicken for roasting. The recipe is on the blackboard. Please take a moment to review it."

The girls all looked to the blackboard, and read:

Roast Chicken with Stuffing

1. Singe bird.

2. Cut off head and remove any pinfeathers.

3. Remove feet and tendons.

4. Cut off neck, leaving skin intact.

5. Remove entrails and giblets.

6. Melt fat and mix with crushed crackers.

7. Stuff the bird.

"The main ingredients are before you, as you can see."

The girls now turned their attention to the cutting-boards on the countertops, one for each girl, and the plucked chickens that sat atop them, stray bits of fluff still clinging to their flesh.

"You have thirty minutes to complete the recipe, and your success will depend on how well you manage that time. Which begins"—she glanced at the clock—"Now."

For a long moment no one moved. Another teacher might have reminded them of the ticking clock, and scolded them into action. But she only examined them calmly, with all her senses. They were fearful, excited, but also disgusted by the raw birds: their yellowish skins, their wrinkled, reptilian faces.

The silence stretched. Their teacher waited. She had faith in her students. They would master their fears, and begin.

At last one of the girls lit her oil burner, grasped her chicken with both hands, and hoisted it above the flame. One by one the others gathered their courage and did the same, turning the birds evenly above the burners. The room filled with the acrid smell of burning feathers.

Now their teacher began her customary clockwise stroll around the island, assessing their progress, making notes on her clipboard. She had no true need for the notes, or the clipboard, but it was a useful prop nonetheless. It reassured the girls that cooking was a skill, to be learned like any other—not some secret art that could only be gleaned in a loving home, at a mother's side.

There were scattered *thunks* as the girls took up their cleavers and unburdened the chickens of their heads. One girl already had advanced to step three; she laid one spindly orange foot across the edge of the counter, then gripped it, steeled herself, and jerked downward. There was a loud snap, and the foot came away trailing its ribbon of tendon. The girl burst into horrified giggles.

The others looked up, startled. Their teacher frowned. "Maddie."

"Sorry, Miss Levy." The girl composed herself, and removed the second foot with more dignity.

Their teacher kept her slow pace around them, judging their progress. One girl had wandered into a daydream, not realizing that she was about to slice through the chicken's neck without first pulling back the skin. Ought she to intervene? No, better to let it happen. The lesson would be useful. They moved on to the stuffing, melting yellow cupfuls of chicken fat over the burners, pouring them into bowls of crushed crackers—and now the one who'd made the mistake realized it at last. She stared down at her bird; tears welled in her eyes. "Miss Levy?"

Her teacher went to her side. "What happened, Miss Rosen?"

"I cut the skin off the neck," the girl said in a near whisper.

"And why does that make a difference?"

"The stuffing'll fall out. There's nothing to hold it in." The girl's chin wobbled.

"All right, Sarah," her teacher said consolingly. "What might you do to fix the situation?"

The girl thought. "Sew it shut?"

"Exactly. Loosen the skin around the breast and pull it forward across the chest cavity"—she demonstrated, and the girls all stared in awe at her fingers, so quick and precise—"And then lace it shut with needle and twine. It won't look as elegant, but it'll taste the same." She turned to address the room at large. "To keep an economical kitchen, you must learn to be flexible, and salvage your mistakes. If a plan falls through, then change the plan. The stuffing could also be baked on the side, as a dressing—or you might forgo roasting the chicken entirely, and make a stew or a casserole instead. Once you have enough experience and proficiency in the kitchen, decisions such as this will become second nature."

They nodded as one. *Experience and proficiency in the kitchen.* At first, these phrases of Miss Levy's had seemed embarrassingly mannered. Now, the girls relished them.

The lesson ended without further catastrophe, and each chicken was examined and declared a success. Even Miss Rosen's looked better than expected, with its neat twine stitches. In heady pride the girls washed their hands, hung their hats and jackets on their pegs, and filed into the hallway precisely at the sounding of the bell.

Alone, their teacher washed and dried the knives and cutting-boards and replaced them in the labeled cabinets, then scrubbed the island countertop. At last the scrum in the hallway cleared, and she loaded the trussed birds onto a cart and wheeled them down to the creaking elevator. A quick trip to the first floor—and then the kitchen, where the dining hall cook left off mashing a giant vat of potatoes and took the cart with a brisk and wordless nod. Come supper-time, the Asylum's monitors would have roast chicken on their plates.

The staff lounge and its cloakroom lay at the very end of the wing. Inside, a number of instructors sat chatting over tea. They looked up at their colleague's entrance and returned her polite smile with their own, but refrained from drawing her into conversation. They were not a little intimidated by this woman who'd effected so many changes among them, in ways both large and small.

Until recently, the modest aim of the Asylum's cooking curriculum had been to familiarize the girls with the basics of the kitchen so that, upon graduation, they might cook for themselves with some reasonable amount of success. To that end, the teachers had constructed a haphazard syllabus of Jewish staples—challahs and soups, noodle puddings, chopped liver, the occasional boiled vegetable. Most students sailed through easily, on little more than daydreams and half efforts.

Then, Miss Levy had landed among them.

Now, to her students' considerable shock, they spent the first week of each semester learning the fundamentals of kitchen sanitation. After that came a working knowledge of food chemistry: the interactions of acids, bases, and fats; the various leaveners and their differing roles. She set them mock household budgets, took them to the market at 125th, taught them to bargain with butchers and greengrocers. At the end of her first year at the Asylum, her classes had worked together to host a cold luncheon for the entire staff, complete with Parker House rolls, sponge cake, and three different varieties of meat salad. More than one attendee declared it the best meal they'd eaten in years.

Miss Levy's girls adored her universally. *She treats us like adults,* they said; *she knows everything about everything.* Somehow she'd requisitioned the funds to buy them all crisp white hats and jackets, which hung upon pegs on the classroom wall. She collected these at the end of each week—praising those students who'd managed to keep theirs near to spotless—and made sure they were washed separately from the rest of the Asylum laundry, to keep them from turning gray. Dressed in their "cook's whites," the girls were no longer orphanage inmates of whom little was expected, but scholars of Culinary Science. They stood taller, and spoke more precisely, their words as crisp as their jackets. In the dining hall they examined their supper plates with new interest, noting how the bubbles of grease floated atop the chipped-beef gravy, using words like *insoluble* and *emulsion.*

It wasn't long before the other teachers, inspired or else threatened by Miss Levy's innovations, strove to match them. Lesson plans that had lain stagnant for years were scrutinized and overhauled. The Telegraphy classes visited the Western Union building, watched as the messages were recorded and distributed. The Dressmaking teacher brought in guest speakers for her advanced class: buyers from Wanamaker's, a *McCall's* pattern-maker, a costumer from a Union Square theater.

Even the Hebrew department had felt the winds of change. Jolted into action, the instructors searched about for some novelty they might add to their curriculum. Their timing was impeccable, for just then a new movement had begun among the more progressive Jewish schools of New York. Called *Ivrit b'Ivrit,* "Hebrew in Hebrew," it advocated teaching the language not as a sacred, book-bound tongue, but a living, spoken language.

The idea was so new as to seem scandalous. Yes, many of the Holy Land settlers had learned to speak Hebrew—but those were pioneers and radicals, impractical by nature. Still, the notion had its appeal. Now that the future of the Holy Land colonies hung in doubt, *Ivrit b'Ivrit* seemed a way to show solidarity, even contribute to the effort. And certainly the Hebrew department couldn't be accused of letting their curriculum languish, not with *Ivrit b'Ivrit* in their lesson plans. They debated the merits, and took the plunge.

The girls in the Asylum's Hebrew classes tended toward the shy and studious, most comfortable hidden behind a book. Now, forced into Hebrew conversation with each other, they surprised themselves by loving it. They mimed tea parties, family dramas, encounters on city streets. *The weather is warm today. Pass the sugar, please. Excuse me, how do I get to Central Park?* When they encountered a word without a Hebrew equivalent, they searched for approximations, often giggling together at the results. And on the day that Susie Baum brought the entire class to a halt with her description of a dining hall dinner as *the bad brown cow meat we ate yesterday*, Kreindel Altschul at last decided she'd had enough.

"Miss Altschul is here to see you, ma'am," the secretary said.

The headmistress sighed and dismissed the girl across from her: Harriet Loeb, a habitual offender, caught pilfering ribbons from the sewing room. Harriet slunk away, unchastened. "Send Kreindel in," the headmistress said.

Kreindel stormed through the door in her usual full pique and stood to attention. "Headmistress, I request—I must *strongly* request—that I be removed from my Hebrew class."

"Really?" The headmistress had been expecting this, but it was usually better to feign innocence. "I was under the impression that you were the head pupil."

"I no longer wish to be," Miss Altschul said stiffly.

"Does the new curriculum fail to meet your standards?"

Miss Altschul pressed her lips together, said nothing.

The headmistress shook her head. "Kreindel. You must learn to *bend*, a little. Or what will happen when you leave here? The world can be a disappointing place. It, too, will fail to meet your standards. *Then* where will you go?"

But Kreindel only stared ahead, the very picture of resolve. Sometimes the headmistress wondered how such a slip of a girl managed to sustain such constant ire. Was it the memory of her revered father that kept her fighting? The headmistress could only imagine him as the most stiff-necked man ever to walk the earth. She could refuse Kreindel's request, of course—but that would only serve to punish the rest of the class.

"All right, Kreindel," she said. "If you must have your way, then so be it. What do you propose to do instead?"

"An independent study," Kreindel said. "For my Psalm translations."

"An independent study! You know perfectly well that won't do at all."

"I'll only need a table in the library, I won't bother anyone!" But her protests were feebler now. Independent studies were reserved for prodigies, the college-bound; they were bestowed with great ceremony, and rarely upon girls. Kreindel had used up her teaspoon's worth of liberty, and she knew it.

"Kreindel, when did you last take a domestic elective?"

The young woman's face fell.

The headmistress went to her file cabinet, retrieved *Altschul, Kreindel*, paged through its innards. "Sewing, four years ago. Your only such elective to date."

"But—I could double up on chore duty—"

"Out of the question." The folder snapped shut. "It's time you studied something other than Hebrew. I believe we can find space for you in Miss Levy's third-period class."

Kreindel gaped. "*Cooking?*"

"Miss Levy prefers the term *Culinary Science*, if I'm not mistaken. Oh, stop making that face, Kreindel—a little cooking won't be the death of you. You might even enjoy it."

The bell rang, announcing the beginning of chore duty. Still fuming, Kreindel joined the line at the supply closet, grabbed her rags and brush and shoe polish, and went down to the Marching Band room, to clean the uniform boots.

For an hour she worked silently amid the racks of uniforms. The boots stank of rotten cheese, thanks to the dozens of adolescent feet they'd housed over the years. From nearby came a steady *plink, plink, plink* of water dripping from the sacks of rock salt that hung from the ceiling, drawing moisture out of the air so the uniforms wouldn't rot. It was filthy, dispiriting work—but at least it gave her time to herself, which in the Asylum was a precious commodity.

The worst of it, Kreindel reflected as she scrubbed and blacked, was that, against her own will, she'd actually started to enjoy the *Ivrit b'Ivrit*. She knew that this secularization of the language was a type of blasphemy, a willful destruction of the holy mystery that had sustained Hebrew through the generations, that she might as well use a silver Torah pointer to scratch her back—and yet, when her teachers had put the Gettysburg Address in front of her and asked her to translate it, her mind had leapt at the problem. *Four score and seven years ago:* Ought she to translate that directly, or simply write *eighty-seven? Our forefathers* was *avotaynu*—that was easy—but what about *brought forth*, which was merely a poetic way of saying *created?* Which verb for *to create* should she use? *To make, to produce? To mold*, like clay? And was it best to choose one's words for precision, or to mimic the tone and rhythm of the piece? *From these honored dead we take increased devotion to that cause for which they gave the last full measure of devotion . . .* She made a first attempt, hoping they'd let her return to her Psalm translations. Instead they'd praised it to the skies, and assigned her the balcony scene from *Romeo and Juliet*—and her mind had leapt at that, too.

But Susie Baum's bad brown cow meat had been the final straw. The girls had laughed together, untroubled, and it had tempted her; she'd wanted to join in, to share in the joke, to become one of them. A step on the road to decreased devotion, to forgetting her own honored dead. So instead she'd pictured Yossele in his alcove, and marshaled her resolve, and left Hebrew behind.

It simply wasn't *fair*, though! Hebrew had been her daily source of happiness; it made the hours fly, made her heart sing like the Ziz-bird, with her feet in the oceans and her head in the heavens. And now the Asylum had managed to ruin Hebrew, too. She longed to leave—but for what? A factory job, perhaps. A husband, children, boarders in the living room. Sabbath mornings in the women's balcony, listening to prayers she wasn't meant to understand; Sabbath afternoons with her children on her lap, reading them the *Tsene-rene*'s lessons of resignation and forbearance. Yossele concealed in a tenement basement, crumbling away to dust. The most beloved parts of herself hidden out of sight.

He was just a few rooms away, watching her, with his endless patience. She paused in her work to send him a brief, wordless acknowledgment, like the squeeze of a hand. Whatever path she chose, she wouldn't neglect him. She'd make a new life for them both.

She finished the boots, then moved on to emptying the water-buckets that sat beneath the bags of rock salt. The buckets were heavy, and the water stank of sweat and mildew; she struggled to keep from spilling as she carried them to the laundry room and tipped them into a drain. All around her, the older boys worked the drums and mangles in their undershirts, the grayish cotton plastered to their backs. One of them saw her watching, and grinned. She left hurriedly, eyes averted. It frustrated her how easily a boy's grin could make her blush. No matter how carefully the Asylum separated the sexes, the boys seemed to lurk constantly on the periphery of the girls' lives, watching, looming, smiling whenever Kreindel dared to look. She couldn't understand why some girls seemed to relish drawing their attention. One might as well call out to a wolf, and offer it one's throat.

"If I am trapped on a ship with you for much longer," said Dima, "I'll go insane."

Sophia said nothing, only lay curled beneath her rough woolen blanket, too drained to argue. They were aboard the S.S. *Kansan*, a merchant steamship bound for Baltimore. On the morning they'd left England the ship had sailed into a line of thunderstorms, and Sophia had spent the journey since then in abject wretchedness. As the only woman on the ship, she'd been assigned a private cabin with a sink and toilet, so at least she could be sick out of the crew's sight, if not the jinniyeh's. There'd been no sign of U-boats, though it had occurred to her that the Germans might at least put her out of her misery.

The *Kansan* struck a swell, the bow lurching. Sophia flinched, teeth chattering, and eyed the toilet in the corner.

"Do you intend to vomit again?" asked the jinniyeh.

"Not if—I can help it."

The days since their departure from Egypt had gone by in a tense and sleepless blur. They'd sailed from Port Said on the S.S. *Persia*, a cramped if elegant passenger ship, where she'd been forced to choose between staying in her tiny cabin with the restless jinniyeh or enduring the small talk in the salon. Then, the Tilbury docks, where most of the American merchant captains had refused to take her, unhappy at the thought of a woman aboard in dangerous seas. In fact, when the *Kansan's* captain had at last agreed, she'd wondered if it was a sign that she'd be preyed upon, and had resolved to keep her pistol within reach. Thankfully the crew had their hands full with managing the cargo and watching for submarines, and had left her entirely alone.

It now seemed an age since Cairo, when she'd left Dima in their room at the Grand Continental and run into Ned Lawrence in the street. She'd been startled to see the change in him. Much of his boyishness had disappeared, though not his restless energy; in truth he'd seemed as much a pent-up spirit as the one she'd just left behind at the hotel. He'd said little of his work at the War Office—a few vague mentions of mapmaking, and of serving as a tribal liaison—and had talked of Carchemish as though it had all happened long ago, in a golden youth. And she, in turn, had recounted a deeply edited version of her own hasty departure from Syria, painting herself as the heedless adventuress who hadn't realized the danger she was in until it was nearly too late. She'd known full well the impression she was making, and hated it; hated, too, that she hadn't been able to refuse his discreet offer of folded British pounds. Were he a different man, she would've wondered what he'd expected in return—but on that matter, she had her own suspicions about Ned Lawrence.

After he'd left Shepheard's, she'd gone to the bar, elbowing her way through the drunken soldiers to ask the barkeeper if they had anything like a New York City directory. He'd pointed her to the sitting room, and a dusty shelf that held a handful of tourists' guides and street atlases— and, among them, a copy of the 1909 Manhattan *Trow's*. She'd flipped through it and found the *Metalsmithing* section, and the advertisement had jumped out at once:

Arbeely & Ahmad
Fences and Gates, Railings and Balustrades.
Vestibule Doors, Grills and Artistic Work.
446 Washington Street at Carlisle

She'd copied the pertinent information onto a napkin and tucked it into her folded passport, resolving not to say a word of it to the jinniyeh. All it proved was that he'd been in Little Syria in 1909—and much could happen in six years.

Her final stop in Cairo, after purchasing a cheap but serviceable as- sortment of Western women's clothing and a new trunk to put them in, had been at a druggist's for a bottle of laudanum, the largest that the man would sell her. *To help me sleep at sea*, she'd told him, which was the truth. He'd stared a moment at her shaking hands, but then sold it to her anyway. She had no wish to become an opium fiend, but she'd forgotten how difficult it was to sleep without Umm Sahir's medicine, and pride had prevented her from asking Dima to repeat the trick that had revived her at Jaffa. She wondered what had happened to Umm Sahir. Ought she have tried to find her? And Abu Alim—had his sons been conscripted? Were they already at the Black Sea, the Dardanelles? Tears welled in her eyes at the thought.

Dima appeared out of the air. "You're dripping water," she said, her tone somewhere between alarm and accusation.

Sophia sighed, and wiped at her eyes. "I didn't mean to."

The ship rocked. Sophia closed her eyes, and had half fallen into a queasy slumber when Dima said suddenly, "What is he like?"

"What is *who* like? Oh—Ahmad, you mean?"

"Of course," Dima said, impatient.

"I hardly know," Sophia said. "I told you, we knew each other only briefly. And it was years ago."

"He told you nothing of himself?"

"Well, he certainly didn't tell me the truth, at least not at first. He only said that he came from the desert. No—wait." She cast her mind back. "He told me a story, about a jinni who'd been captured, long ago, by a terrible wizard. I had no idea what it meant, at the time. I thought it was only make-believe. A fantasy," she said, as the jinniyeh frowned at the phrase. "Something that could never be."

"Did others know his secret?"

"Perhaps. I'm not sure." It was a lie, but a principled one. Sophia had thought often lately of his companion, Chava Levy, the woman with her own incredible secrets—secrets that weren't Sophia's to tell. How might Dima react to such a woman? Sophia had no way of knowing—and it had occurred to her that, if he and Mrs. Levy were still acquainted, the jinniyeh might prove an unwelcome party between them.

Dima looked troubled. "Do you think—" But then, as though impatient with her own thought, she stood up and began to pace. "If you were alone for years, hiding among strangers or enemies, and one of your own kind arrived—you'd be glad to see them, wouldn't you? Even if—if they had a defect, or were different in some way—"

"I would," Sophia said. "And if some part of me wished the person were otherwise, it would be to my own discredit." She hesitated, thinking of the napkin in her passport. "Dima?"

"Yes?"

But at once she reconsidered. She didn't fully trust the jinniyeh; she doubted she ever would. It made no sense to divulge information before it was absolutely necessary. She said, "I hope that he's still in New York, and that you can be friends to each other. That's all."

Dima took this in. Then, "Jinn do not have friends," she said. "We may be allies, or enemies, or lovers, but not friends."

Sophia considered this. "And I suppose a lover is not necessarily an ally."

"Not in my experience," Dima said.

"Nor mine." Sophia sat up gingerly; her stomach stayed put. "I think

I'll ask the captain about our progress," she said. She fetched another shawl from her trunk, plucked her passport with its folded napkin from her valise. "I won't be long."

Shivering, one hand to the bulkhead, Sophia walked along the passageway to the *Kansan's* telegraphy room, considering what message she ought to send. *Jinn do not have friends*, she thought. *And a lover is not necessarily an ally.* If he was indeed alive and in New York, then she must also take the lives of others into account, and proceed carefully.

Would he even remember her, and with a different surname besides? Or—as seemed entirely possible—was she merely a faded entry on his roster of long-ago conquests? A dull, resentful anger rose in her at the thought. Well, if that was the case, she'd simply have to jog his memory.

Charlotte Levy's apartment was at the corner of Broadway and 136th, only half a block from the Asylum. The address wasn't rarefied enough for a doorman, but the lock was secure and the lobby clean, its harlequin tiles polished weekly.

She took the stairs to the fourth floor, and opened her door to a welcome cloud of warmth, courtesy of twin radiators and a landlord who didn't stint on coal. She set down her satchel, hung her coat away, pulled the heavy drapes shut. The apartment was small, but more than suitable for an unmarried working-woman. Besides the radiators, there was a Pullman kitchen with an oven and an icebox, and a bed that stowed itself neatly against the wall. An electric fan hung from the ceiling, to dispel the summer heat. She had a large, cubby-holed desk with its own lamp, an armchair for reading, a bookshelf for her recipe collections and textbooks—and, most precious of all, her own bathroom, complete with a claw-foot tub large enough to stretch her legs in.

She plugged the bathtub drain, opened the hot-water spigot. Her dress she hung on the bathroom door-hook, to let the steam loosen any wrinkles. Her underclothes went into a small hamper below the sink, to be sent out to the corner laundry. The locket and its chain she took off, held a moment—

You wear your death around your neck

—and placed upon the small glass shelf above the sink. Naked, she lowered herself into the water and lay back in the tub, palms upward, fingers loose. Inch by inch the water crept up her neck and ears, then washed across her eyes. Submerged, she stared up through the ripples at the ceiling, inhaled the water, and sighed it out again. Slowly her muscles smoothed, her body softened. No need for walking anymore, not unless she wanted to: she had plenty of hot water all year round. Winter and summer were nearly the same now, the noise in her mind so minor it might truly have been tinnitus.

Her life was one of comfortable simplicity. She taught three classes a day, went to the market twice a week, spent evenings on lesson plans and grocery lists and semester reviews. She subscribed to the *New York Times*, *McCall's*, the *Ladies' Home Journal*. She went to Riverside Drive on sunny days, to sit on a bench and take in the view: the long strip of park, the Hudson beyond.

On the rare occasions when she allowed herself to look back at her previous life, she wondered how she'd managed it. To spend her days hiding in the open, and her nights telling the truth in secret: how complicated, how *exhausting* it had been. Now, she had no need to explain herself, to justify herself, to anyone. She was merely Charlotte Levy. There was no one else at all.

The bathwater was beginning to cool. She pulled the plug and dried herself, avoiding the spot of numbness on her hip. The locket she clasped around her neck—a quick motion, without looking. She put on her blue quilted housecoat, made a cup of tea at the stove, and carried it to her desk, where she began her evening's occupations: student evaluations, lesson plans, grocery lists, recipe reviews. If she was careful, and took her time, it would be enough to last until dawn.

"Pass the salt, Ma."

Anna Blumberg raised her eyebrows at her son. "I didn't put in enough salt for you?"

"I'm just asking for the salt, is all."

Anna huffed and handed Toby the salt-shaker, watched him douse his potatoes and shovel them into his mouth. Still a growing boy, her Toby. Almost fifteen, and already taller than her—though he still had his childhood habit of never sitting still, except for supper.

Toby chewed beneath her scrutiny. She was sore at him, like always; he told himself that he didn't much care. "You got a meeting tomorrow?" he asked.

"No, Friday." Her face soured, and his, too. Anna's suffrage meetings always left her in a terrible mood. She'd come home fuming about the fancy-hatted ladies who liked to stand up and make speeches: *What have we gained that we might show our sisters who died at Triangle,* and so on. It made her want to scream, she said. *Not a one of those peacocks would've worked a day at Triangle, not for all the tea in China.* But she went anyway, and spoke her mind. Toby knew she believed in the cause, and he supposed he was proud of her for going—but he couldn't help resenting it all the same. She never smiled anymore. Neither of them did.

She eyed his shirt. "You've got a spot, boychik."

He rolled his eyes, dabbed at the spot with his napkin.

"You need to take better care of your things, or the next uniform's out of your own pay."

"All right, Ma." He could afford it, easy, but didn't say so. He didn't want her to know he'd defied her orders about taking deliveries to the Tenderloin, to the addresses where young women lounged about in parlors and winked at him, and tipped in quarters instead of nickels. But how could he turn down the extra money? He'd need it if he wanted to take a girl out someday. Girls, lately, had become a point of definite and consuming interest. The city seemed to have filled up with them when he wasn't looking. They made him bashful and his body unruly; they perplexed with their mere presence. What on earth was he supposed to do about them? His father would've told him, he was sure of it. Or he might've asked Missus Chava, if his mother hadn't chased her out of their lives. She'd never explained that to him, either, not even an *I'll tell you when you're older.* Which would've been a lie, anyway. Maybe it was good he didn't have a girl yet. His ma would've chased her away, too.

He finished the potatoes, took his plate to the sink, fetched his jacket from the sofa.

"You're going out again?" his mother asked, alarm in her voice.

"Yeah, just to ride. Don't wait up." The door slammed behind him.

Anna sighed. *Don't wait up.* The man of the house now, and he certainly acted the part, with his silences and glowers, his making her worry every night. Oh, and she knew about the extra money from the Tenderloin brothels; she'd found the loose floorboard under the sofa, his cigar of rolled-up bills—or did he think he'd invented that trick? She'd resolved not to confront him about it, only checked the roll every so often to make sure it neither grew nor shrank too quickly. Either, she knew, would spell trouble. And what would happen if the war came, if America decided at last to pick a side and fight? Europe was a maze of trenches; the headlines talked of thousands of men sacrificed for gains measured in yards. Maybe he was too young to be drafted now, but it wasn't hard to imagine such a war raging on for years, and her Toby sent into one of those trenches—or even volunteering to go, just to get away from her.

She supposed it would be punishment for her sins, for refusing to tell him everything he wanted to know. And maybe she deserved it—but not for the sin of slamming the door in the Golem's face. That, she'd do a hundred times over, if she had to. She'd thought it was her own death at the door that night, and Toby's, too, the bill for their lives come due at last.

Three years, now, and not a sign of her. Had she left the city altogether? Anna had thought about making inquiries in Little Syria—but that was only curiosity, and she ignored its temptations. On the nights when her worries kept her awake, she'd stare up at the ceiling and think to herself, *Enough of the fairy tales. Chava Levy was no more a golem than I am.* Or, sometimes: *It could've been anyone in the alley that night. It was dark, and the mind plays tricks.*

But she could never make herself believe it.

Toby rode west on Canal, aiming for Death Avenue.

This was his favorite time to ride, these hours when the worst of the traffic had cleared but there was still enough light to see by. He dodged a pedestrian and then a wagon, scanning the blocks ahead for obstacles. The bike Missus Chava had given him was like a part of him now. He kept it in good repair, replaced the spokes and tubes when they needed it, never stinted on the grease. He could teach the Western Union mechanics a thing or two, if he said so himself.

The air changed as he approached West Street, thickening to a mist that smelled of brine and coal-smoke. He turned north, the pier sheds flashing by. Ferry stacks poked above their roofs, gray wisps drifting from their insides. Railroad ties rumbled beneath his tires—and he grinned, and picked up speed.

No one really called it Death Avenue anymore except for the newspapers, but this stretch of Eleventh had certainly earned its reputation over the years. With nowhere else to put the New York Central freight line as it emerged from the dockyards, the city had elected to run it right down the middle of the avenue, forcing the wagons and automobiles to either side. Every so often someone was killed trying to beat a train, or surprised by one at a crossing—but for Toby's money there was no better riding in the city, so long as you kept to the narrow channel between the tracks and the traffic, and stayed alert for the hard press of air, the cotton in your eardrums, that meant an engine was at your back.

He whisked past taxicabs and delivery wagons, searching beneath the streetlights for pedestrians who might step out in front of him. A signal-rider appeared on horseback, trotting south, hoisting the red-glassed lantern that meant a locomotive was on its way. He felt the telltale change of pressure—and a moment later the engine loomed out of the fog, dragging its reeking line of cattle-cars toward the slaughterhouses.

At 59th the tracks veered west along the shoreline, and the tenements and factories turned to brownstones. Riverside Park appeared to his left, the cherry trees barely visible in the dusk. He slowed, his heart beating. His ma would throw a conniption if she knew he was riding Death Avenue after sunset, but it was his only way of letting off steam—and there'd been a lot of steam to let off, lately. Most of it wasn't even his ma's fault. As far as Toby was concerned, the shine had long since come off the Western Union apple. He'd believed in the job, had swallowed all their nonsense about the rewards of hard work and loyalty; he'd even studied Morse code, tapping out words on the kitchen table while his mother glared at him, all in hopes of being promoted to operator someday. And then Western Union had finished their new building on Lispenard, and invited all the employees for a tour. He'd washed and ironed his uniform, polished his badge until it was bright as a mirror, even paid for the streetcar so he wouldn't arrive sweaty and mussed—only to be crammed into a line with hundreds of other boys, all similarly slicked and polished, and paraded through room after room of baffling contraptions. This here, the tour guide proudly told them, was a repeater that did nothing but fling telegrams from one wire to another! And here, a printer that could send eight messages at once over a single line! Specialists in white coats tended to the clattering machines like cherished pets, feeding them pneumatic capsules and reams of paper. Tentatively Toby had raised his hand: Was there a Morse department? Yes, over there, said the guide, pointing to a far corner where five middle-aged men sat morosely at their desks, their hands idle at the keys.

But worst of all had been the cold and gleaming cafeteria, where tall men with brilliantined hair sat at white enameled tables, eating chicken sandwiches and smoking cigarettes. As he'd peered in at them through the glass, Toby had felt all his hopes abandon him. Not a one of those men had grown up within sight of Hester or Mulberry, or the Hell's Kitchen shanties. They'd never risked their necks on icy streets for nickel tips, or driven roofing nails into their shoes to keep the soles from flapping. They'd come from somewhere as clean and shining as that cafeteria—a place that boys like Toby might glimpse, but never touch.

He'd left in deep embarrassment, angry at himself for ever having thought it might be otherwise. Most of the messenger boys his age had jumped ship years ago, but Toby had stayed the course, and for what? Sure, the money was decent, but there was no future in it. At eleven, he'd been one of the youngest messengers in Midtown. Now, nearly fifteen and looking older, he was in danger of becoming that most pitiful object, a man working a boy's job. He had no one to put in a good word for him elsewhere, no family business to join. And every night the ancient man in Toby's nightmare held him immobile and grinned at his fears until Toby woke in silent panic. Was it any wonder he preferred Death Avenue to sitting up all night in an apartment full of his mother's secrets, waiting in dread to fall asleep?

Kreindel lay awake listening to the Asylum's usual symphony of snores and sleeping murmurs, the creaks and groans as the old building settled. At last she slipped from the dormitory, descended the stairs, and crept down the basement hall to the storage room.

Her route through the room was like a convoluted dance, over theater props and between filing cabinets, reaching to feel for the next obstacle. The warmth of the boiler grew stronger; and now here was the narrow passage, and the alcove beyond, shrouded in velvet darkness. She tiptoed forward, straining to hear, fingers outstretched to find him—and at the moment when she felt his cool hand grip her own, her composure broke.

He held her close while she cried, and wrapped the velvet curtain around her to keep her warm. "Thank you," she whispered. She always seemed to breathe easier, sitting with him. Sometimes, even after all these years, she worried that he'd grow bored there in the alcove, and decide to go off exploring; that she would find him in the Marching Band room, trying on the uniforms, or in the laundry, mending the holes in the children's trousers. Now, curled against his clay shoulder, she could smile at the image.

But perhaps it wasn't a silly idea after all. A golem for cleaning, laundering, cooking? Why not? He would be swift and diligent, would never complain or wish for other work. She pictured a cozy home, the floors mopped, the clothing washed and folded, supper in the oven, and Yossele waiting at the table.

"Would you like that, Yossele?" she whispered.

And indeed he would. It was his master's own vision and desire, and therefore he desired it as well. He would please her however she wanted, and protect her however he could.

Before long, she'd fallen asleep in his arms. He had no need, now, to watch her thoughts, for they were only dreams; no need to stay alert in case she was threatened, for he was there with her. A small relief, to set aside his sentinel's tasks, if only for a few precious minutes. But to see her so unhappy! It was akin to a physical discomfort, an ache inside him. Worse still was the knowledge, flickering darkly at the edge of his understanding, that he himself was one of the burdens she carried. Yet she never resented him, never wished it otherwise, never thought, *If not for Yossele . . .* He'd follow her down whatever path she set them upon, for he had no other choice; he'd wait forever in that basement if she demanded it. But only now, as she slept beneath his gaze in the quiet of the alcove, could that involuntary devotion take on the depth of something closer to love.

15.

S *omething was missing.*

The Jinni frowned, and pushed the thought away. He was kneeling beside a long, shallow iron trough that held a thin layer of blue-tinted glass, newly made. He eyed the pane carefully, watching for bubbles or imperfections that might cause a crack, but he saw none. Good. He'd lost three panes already that morning.

The entire glass-making process had proved much more delicate and difficult than he'd imagined. He wanted broad, thin swathes, but the slag was erratic and temperamental, and nothing he could make by hand was consistent enough. So he'd constructed the trough instead: a mold that he could heat evenly over the forge and then move to the floor, where the glass might cool and harden. On the worktable nearby were the stacks of finished panes, all polished to an even shine. He'd hunted through his supplies for something to place between the panes to keep them from scratching, and at last had found a stash of gold coins, bought in the Bowery and then forgotten. He'd intended to melt them down for gilding, but as spacers they worked perfectly.

He didn't enjoy making the glass. It was dull and finicky work; it required paying attention while the glass cooled, so he might lift it from the mold at exactly the right moment. It stretched the seconds and minutes so that in his boredom he was tempted to let his mind wander, to reflect, consider, take stock.

Something was missing—but what?

The thought itself was ridiculous. As far as he knew, no one had ever attempted to build anything like this—so how could something be said to be missing? The Amherst's new form was a vision born of his own mind, and correct in every detail. And yet something was missing, and it *itched* at him.

Finally the glass was ready. Carefully he prized the pane from the trough, lifted it away, and placed it with the rest atop the worktable. Then, released at last from the tyranny of waiting, he went to the forge and plunged his hands gratefully into the coals. His irritable mood receded in a wave of sharpened sensation, his nagging thoughts collapsing into an endless, perfect *now*. He smiled, without quite realizing. He'd earned a rest from the glass-making, he decided.

He spiraled up the central column to the topmost platform, stepped out onto the steel. There was a portion of the platform near the edge that had been unevenly smoothed; he'd noticed it the day before. He walked out to the rimless edge, following the curve, searching for the spot. Below him the forge was a glowing rectangle, a pool of fire he might dive into—

He staggered against her, they teetered together—

He shuddered as a wave of vertigo passed through him.

Stop that, he told himself sharply. He closed his eyes, held still until the last of it was gone. Then he found the spot and patched it over, his back turned to the view.

The Western Union branch at Canal and Broadway was little more than an overgrown vestibule that had been crammed into the lobby of the Columbia Bank. On most days there were at least three young boys waiting on the messengers' bench when Toby arrived, all of them yawning and kicking their heels; but that morning the bench was empty, a bad sign. Behind the counter, Julius, the branch manager, was shuffling through the delivery sheets with an air of nervous dyspepsia. Toby glanced over at the bin that caught the overnight messages in their pneumatic tubes. Usually it was half full, but now it looked close to spilling over.

"What's going on?" he said.

"Some genius from Public Works stuck his axe through our conduit," Julius said. "Every branch south of here is out of commission. The rest of us are working double until it's fixed." He handed a sheet to Toby, pointed to a stack of envelopes on the counter. "Here's your share."

Alarmed, Toby glanced down the list. Sure enough, all of the messages were already hours late. Half of them were for the City Hall offices—and, even worse, the rest were overseas cables, destined for the Hudson shipping concerns. "Aw, hell! Why couldn't you give this to one of the babies?"

Julius snorted. "Send a baby to the docks with a bag full of late cables? Might as well pour catsup on him first."

"Well, why should *I* have to do it?"

"Because you're man enough to take it, and they ain't."

Toby blew out a frustrated breath. He'd started as a bench-baby, too, and had prided himself on never letting the company down. Once again it seemed he was being punished for his loyalty. But there was nothing he could do about it, save for quitting. Scowling, he grabbed the sheet and the envelopes, and wasn't too careful about shutting the door gently on his way out.

In the alley, he unlocked his bike and looked over the delivery sheet. He was supposed to start at the docklands and work his way back to City Hall—likely because, from Western Union's point of view, a cable that halted a thousand dollars' worth of cargo was more important than some bit of business from Albany. Toby, however, saw things differently. It was nine o'clock already, and once the morning barges were past Sandy Hook, it didn't matter how late the cable was. On the other hand, the civil servants of New York were a highly distracted lot, and delayed messages often worked out in their favor. If Toby went to City Hall first, he might still make a few tips for himself.

He stuck the delivery sheet and the envelopes in his satchel, and pedaled away south.

Kreindel stood alone in the Asylum hallway while the other girls of her dormitory arrayed themselves before and behind her, two by two, for the walk up the street to P.S. 186. As usual, no one wanted to be Kreindel's partner. The trips to and from school were precious opportunities to talk openly with a friend, to giggle and gossip out of the monitors' hearing—so why stand next to Kreindel, who never did any such thing?

A few final girls straggled into place, and Rachel Winkelman at last came to stand next to Kreindel. Perpetually late to the line, Rachel was Kreindel's partner more often than not. The girl glanced across at Kreindel, and took in her expression. "What's got your bloomers in a twist?"

"It's none of your business." In Kreindel's opinion, Rachel Winkelman was a fat-headed sort of girl, more interested in simpering at boys than doing anything useful. To make matters worse, Rachel was also one of the very few Asylum residents who gave no consideration to Kreindel's status as a true orphan. She thought Kreindel was a condescending know-it-all, and was glad to say so to her face. Their walks together were rarely pleasant.

The monitors took their places at the front and rear of the columns. The bell rang, and the boys began the procession, oldest to youngest. Quickly Rachel pulled a lemon-yellow ribbon from her pocket and tied it into her hair. It was strictly against the uniform code, and Kreindel wondered where she'd found it. The boys marched by, Rachel making eyes at her favorites, until it was the next dormitory's turn—at which point Rachel undid the ribbon and pocketed it again, before the monitors could notice. At last the youngest of the boys went past, and the girls were allowed into the sunshine, their double line spreading along the sidewalk.

"Heard you quit Hebrew," said Rachel once they were out of their monitor's hearing.

Kreindel's frown deepened. "Who told you?"

"Harriet. She heard you in the office." Rachel smirked. Harriet Loeb was her best friend; the two were thick as thieves. "So what'd they give you, more boot-shining?"

"No, cooking."

"Hah! Well, don't go ruining it like you always do."

"I don't intend to ruin anything," Kreindel told her. "If they'd just give me an independent study—"

Rachel burst into cackles.

Kreindel's face turned hot. "Well, why shouldn't I get one? I just want to learn Hebrew the way it's supposed to be learned! Why'd they have to go and change it, anyways?" She cringed as the word *anyways* escaped her mouth, with its crude and sibilant *s*. It was difficult to keep her English free of the Asylum vernacular, and she felt each *anyways* and *nohow* and *ah, quit it* as a small act of self-treachery.

"I thought Orthodox girls weren't supposed to learn Hebrew," Rachel said.

"It's not a sin or anything. It's just . . . not usual."

"Yeah, not usual. Just like you."

They turned the corner at 141st and approached the squat bulk of P.S. 186. "And besides, I don't see why I should have to take cooking lessons," Kreindel muttered. "It's just food, anyone can do it. I cooked for my father when I was only—"

"Aw, *my father, my father*," Rachel cut in, eyes rolling.

Another Asylum girl might've delivered a reply with her fists, monitors or no. But Kreindel said only, "He was a brilliant man, and you will show him respect."

Rachel smirked. "Or what?"

"Or I'll tell everyone what you and Harriet get up to in the toilets after lights-out," she said, and climbed the steps to the school as Rachel stood stricken and red-faced at the bottom.

The Asylum's weekly Girls' Instructors meeting was held in the women's staff room: a dispiriting place, perpetually stuffy and overheated, crammed with mismatched chairs. Charlotte Levy arrived early, found a seat in the back, and exchanged polite smiles with the others as they trickled in. At last the headmistress arrived and called for attention, and began her list of announcements. The ceiling in the sewing room had developed a wet spot, and would soon be repaired—but if the rains returned, would Miss Rothstein be willing to share her Stenography classroom? Miss Rothstein graciously agreed. A new instructor had been found to replace the girls' choir director, who had departed recently . . .

So it went, a lulling litany. The radiator hissed; eyes drooped. The woman in front of Miss Levy began to snore lightly. Miss Levy coughed; the woman straightened in her chair.

"Which brings us to a new subject," said the headmistress. "The last few years have seen a much-needed revitalization of the Asylum's curricula, and I commend you all for it. But as a consequence, we have a small crisis on our hands—namely, the state of our storage rooms."

Everyone winced.

"The rooms have gone neglected for far too long—and with the recent addition of so many old textbooks and other materials, it's become impossible to find so much as a pencil. I've decided the time has come for a good old-fashioned spring cleaning. Each of you will pick a responsibility," she said, holding up a sheet of paper. "I'll work with you to decide what ought to be kept and what thrown away. If we put our minds to it, it needn't take more than a week. Two, at most." She smiled at their resigned faces. "That will be all, thank you."

The women all rose at once, maneuvering toward the paper. Each of them hoped they wouldn't get stuck with the worst of the tasks, and more than one reflected that the male teachers would never be asked to do such work—

"Miss Levy, a moment, please." The headmistress drew her to one side. "I've placed a new student in your third-period class, Miss Kreindel Altschul. She was the top Hebrew student, but she objects to the new curriculum and asked to be transferred out. Given her utter lack of domestics, I thought your class was her best option."

Startled, Miss Levy said, "But we're already quite far into the syllabus. If she has no cooking experience, wouldn't it be better—"

"I understand your concern, but Miss Altschul is an intelligent girl." *Too intelligent for her own good,* said the woman's thoughts. "I have no doubt that she can master it, if she applies herself."

"But—"

"I'm not asking for miracles, Charlotte," the headmistress cut in, her voice firm. "Just do what you can with her."

With some irritation Miss Levy joined the end of the dwindling line, wondering why Miss Altschul had been allowed to quit Hebrew in the first place. The headmistress had seemed to consider the girl a special case of some kind, one whose idiosyncrasies were tolerated, if grudgingly. She only hoped that Miss Altschul wouldn't spoil what was promising to be a very rewarding semester.

At last the line cleared—and she saw that a name now accompanied every item on the sheet, with the exception of *Large-Item Repository (Basement, South Wing)*. This, she realized, must be the very task that her colleagues had been trying to avoid. She'd never seen the room herself, only heard it described as a hopeless collection of clutter. Sighing at her poor luck, she took up the pen, and wrote *Charlotte Levy* on the line beside it.

Toby left City Hall at ten thirty, with six new nickels in his pocket and six fewer envelopes in his satchel. He felt a little better, his gamble having paid off—but now the prospect of the docklands loomed before him, and the inevitable tongue-lashings. He stopped at a cart on Broadway to fortify himself with a frankfurter and a seltzer; and then, unable to avoid it any longer, gritted his teeth and rode West Street from pier to pier, to stare red-faced at his shoes while stevedores bellowed at him in German, Swedish, and Portuguese. He left an hour later without a single tip, and reflected grudgingly that Julius was right: any of the babies would've run home in tears.

There was only one message left in his bag, a cable to a Washington Street address. He read its origin and winced: the S.S. *Kansan*. If he'd seen it earlier, he might've delivered it first, City Hall tips or no. A full-rate cable from a ship at sea usually meant news that couldn't wait.

The address led to a five-story loft in Little Syria. The building looked strangely empty. Its windows were papered over on every floor, and there were no signs, no painted advertisements—only the word *Amherst* carved above the door.

He leaned his bicycle against the building, and rang the bell.

Reluctantly the Jinni had returned to his glass-making.

The latest pane was giving him trouble, refusing to lift free of the trough. He levered it up a hair's-breadth at a time, first one side and then another, feeling his way around the edge. He must slow down, be patient—

Something's missing—

A knock, at the door.

He clenched his teeth, ignored it, lifted another fraction of an inch.

The knock came again. *Go away*, he thought.

Retreating footsteps. Silence. Good.

Another gentle lift—and at last the pane came free.

There was no answer at the door.

Toby stepped back to examine the building again. Something about the papered windows gave it an eerie look, like it was hollow inside. He walked down Carlisle to see if there was a back entrance, and found an alley where a group of boys were crouched on their heels, playing jacks.

"'Scuse me," he said. "I'm looking for"—he peered down at the envelope—"Ahmad al-Hadid?"

He said it haltingly, certain that they would snicker at his butchering of the name. Instead they all came alert in an instant. "He's in there," one of the boys said in a tone of frightened reverence, pointing at the building.

"I knocked, but no one answered."

"He don't ever come out," the boy said.

Toby sighed in annoyance. He'd delivered to plenty of elderly cranks and shut-ins; they always griped, and never tipped. "Well, someone sent him this." He held up the envelope.

"Who's it from?" asked a boy.

"We're not allowed to peek."

The boys only stared, their helpfulness run dry. "Guess I'll try again," Toby said, and went back around the building. The boys followed, as he'd hoped they might. If this Ahmad al-Hadid tried to beat Toby with his cane, at least there'd be witnesses.

He knocked again. "Mr. al-Hadid!" he called loudly. "It's Western Union!" The boys watched from the spot where they'd gathered, clearly prepared to run if necessary. Toby glanced at them—and then, succumbing to a weary hilarity and the lure of an audience, crouched down, pushed open the letterbox, and shouted through it in Yiddish:

"Hey, old man, come and get this envelope, or I'll shove it up your ancient ass!"

Silence—and then there came a cacophonous shattering, like a baseball thrown through a cathedral's worth of windows.

Toby cringed. The alley boys clutched at one another.

Footsteps—and the door was yanked open. Toby stumbled backward as a wave of burning air rolled over him.

The man who stood in the doorway was tall and imposing, and far younger than the wizened crackpot Toby had imagined. He wore nothing but a scorched leather apron and a pair of ragged trousers. His dark eyes were thunderous with rage.

"What did you just—"

But then the man's voice died away in surprise. He looked up, beyond Toby. Toby turned to see what he was staring at, but there was nothing—only the street, and the sunshine, and the Woolworth Building's crown peeking above the tenements. The boys from the alley had vanished like smoke. Pedestrians on the sidewalk gawked at the open door, and the man in his apron.

The dark eyes focused again on Toby—and suddenly the boy was certain he'd seen this man before. He swallowed. "Western Union, sir. A cable for you." He held out the envelope.

The man reached out to take it. There was a hiss, like a match being struck—

Toby yelped in surprise. The envelope fell to the concrete between them, flames curling along its edge. For a moment they both stared at it—and then Toby lunged forward and stomped on the envelope until the fire was out. He bent down, picked it up between thumb and forefinger. "Sorry, sir," he said, panting a little. "Dunno how that happened—"

But the man was retreating through the half-open door. "I don't want it," he said sharply.

"But it's yours, sir!" There was something in the depths of the building behind the man, a silver shape of some kind . . .

"I don't want it," the man said again—and then, as though to ward boy and envelope away, he dug into his apron pocket and thrust a coin at Toby. The boy took it, then nearly dropped it: it was burning hot. Liberty's profile filled its front. *Three Dollars*, said the reverse.

Giddily Toby looked up from the coin—just as the door slammed shut and the bolt slid home, leaving him alone on the stoop, a singed cable in one hand and half a week's pay in the other.

In a daze he walked back to his bicycle. What had just happened? The man, the heat, the flames, the coin: it had all taken less than a minute. He'd have thought it all some kind of vaudeville illusion, except that the man had seemed just as confused as Toby.

He slipped the coin into his pocket, then considered the envelope. Had it been doused with kerosene somehow, at the docks? He brought it to his nose, but smelled only burnt paper. One entire side of the rectangle was gone. He squeezed the envelope a bit—and it gaped open, revealing paper that was darkened at its edge but otherwise whole.

We're not allowed to peek.

He looked around, but the spectators had all moved on. Carefully he pulled the message free—and the words *Chava Levy* leapt at him from the paper.

He took a startled breath, then read it from the beginning:

MY NAME HAS CHANGED BUT I TRUST YOU
REMEMBER THE FOUNTAIN IN CENTRAL PARK AND
THE FIREPLACE ON FIFTH AVE RETURNING TO NYC
THURSDAY PM MUST SEE YOU SEND REPLY HOTEL
EARLE URGENT CHAVA LEVY MUST NOT KNOW.

SOPHIA WILLIAMS

He remembered, then, where he'd seen the man before. The morning after Triangle; his mother on the sofa, burning with fever. The tall man talking to Missus Chava in front of her boardinghouse, falling silent at Toby's approach.

He stared up at the Amherst's facade. Then he slid the cable back into its envelope and wheeled his bike around the corner, into the alley.

Only one of the boys had stayed behind, the smallest of the bunch. He was perhaps seven, and wore what looked to be an older brother's cast-offs: a too-large shirt tucked into baggy short pants, with a rope belt to cinch it all together. The boy glanced up at Toby, then turned his attention back to the ground, where he was using a stick to poke at a dark, irregular patch that had been set into the concrete.

Toby leaned his bicycle against the alley wall. "So, that's Ahmad al-Hadid," he said.

"He's just Mister Ahmad," the boy said.

"Do you know him?"

The boy shook his head. "No one does. He's—" And then a word that sounded like *biddoo.*

Toby frowned. "What's that mean?"

"Means he ain't Christian."

"Huh." Toby wondered how to proceed. "So, you aren't allowed to talk to him?"

"Naw, we're allowed, he just *don't.* He never comes out, not since Mister Arbeely died."

"Who's that?"

"His friend. They bought the Amherst together. Now it's just Mister Ahmad's."

Toby whistled low. "He must be rich," he said, feeling the weight of the coin in his pocket.

The boy shrugged again, but his expression suggested that he shared this theory.

Toby considered a moment, then said, "You ever heard the name Chava Levy?"

The boy looked up. "I seen her once," he said.

Toby's heart leapt. "You did? Where?"

The boy gestured heavenward with the stick, and Toby realized he meant the rooftops. "With Mister Ahmad. They usedta walk up there, and talk in different languages, all twisted together. My brother said they'd done that since before I was born. They'd walk around all night and then go to Mister Ahmad's apartment, and in the morning she'd come out again."

Toby's eyebrows rose. Missus Chava had kept a secret love-nest in Little Syria? "But this was all before Mister . . . before the other fella died."

The boy nodded. "She never came around, after that. And all the people who worked in the Amherst left, too."

"When was that? Do you remember?"

The boy thought. "Ma was pregnant. And Hanna's almost three."

"So he's been in there all alone for three years?"

"Guess so."

"Huh." He would've liked to show the boy the cable, and ask what he made of it, but held back. Peeking at a message was bad enough; showing it around was worse. Still, the boy had been a surprising help. Toby reached into his pocket, past the golden coin, and fished out one of the City Hall nickels. "Here," he said, handing it to the boy. "Take yourself to the pictures."

The boy grinned his thanks, and ran off.

Toby frowned down at the envelope. He couldn't just *keep* it; it belonged to the man in the building, even if he didn't want it. For all Toby's disappointment in Western Union, he still believed in the job itself. A message must reach its destination.

He wheeled his bicycle back to the front door, slipped the cable through the letterbox slot as quick as he could, and then pedaled away, thinking hard.

The Jinni stood among the shards of his work, cursing himself.

He never should have opened the door. He should've had the sense to ignore it. But the incongruity of the boy's taunt—*Was that Yiddish?*— had wrested his attention away. He'd joggled the pane upon the stack, and they'd *all* shattered, four days' worth of glass gone in an instant, and before he could stop himself he'd opened the door—

And the world had come rushing in.

Sunlight, near to blinding. A messenger-boy in a uniform, a badge on his cap. Children running away in fright. A chemist's across the street that should've been a grocer's. The Woolworth's crown, the new copper already tinged with green. The shock on the boy's face as the envelope burst into flame.

He wiped a shaking hand across his eyes and looked down at the fragments, then up at the Amherst, his private, perfect world.

Something's missing.

No. Nothing was missing. It was merely unfinished. He would melt down the shards and begin again.

He swept up the fragments, heated himself at the forge, lost himself in his work. It was some time before he passed by the front door, and saw the singed envelope. Without missing a step, without allowing himself a moment's thought, he grabbed it and turned it to ash.

"Hollandaise," said Charlotte Levy, "is the most difficult to master of the five basic sauces."

The girls of the third-period Culinary Science class listened in rapt attention.

"In fact, given the delicate chemistry of the sauce, it would not be out of place to cook it in a laboratory. But since this would be inconvenient for our purposes, we must make do with our classroom instead."

This was as close to joking as Miss Levy ever came. She smiled at them, and they smiled back—all except for the new girl, Kreindel Altschul, who stood crammed into a corner of the island like an extra hour added to a clock. Had there been more warning, Miss Levy might've created a separate lesson for Kreindel, to smooth her way into the class. Then again, perhaps the girl would relish the challenge. At the moment she mainly seemed resentful of having to wear the cook's whites.

Miss Levy launched into her lecture: the process of emulsification, the role of the egg-yolk and the binding properties of lecithin, the need to hold the sauce at a low and constant heat to keep it from curdling. From there she reminded them of the dangers of bacterial growth, and the symptoms of salmonella. When at last the girls began to light the burners and crack the eggs, the room was so charged with trepidation that they might've been stirring up batches of gelignite.

She began her circular patrol, watching their progress. Four of the girls' sauces had curdled immediately; they stood over pans of thin, lumpy liquid, desperately whisking. "If the sauce has merely separated, an extra egg-yolk may be whisked in to improve the emulsion," she told them. "But a curdled sauce can only be rid of its lumps." The girls sighed, and fetched their strainers.

She came around to the corner where Kreindel stood beside Sarah Rosen, her reluctant partner. Kreindel was whisking their pan, her face a portrait of frustration.

"It's gonna curdle," Miss Rosen hissed.

"No, it *won't*." Kreindel whisked harder.

"Girls," Miss Levy said—and then Kreindel's head came up to glare at her, and she nearly gasped as the girl's anger struck her with shocking force, near to a physical blow.

She took a step backward. "Excuse me," she heard herself say. And then she was walking out the door, down the hall to the teachers' lavatory, as time slowed down and the world pulled away.

The lavatory door closed behind her with a calm and faraway sound. She went to the sink, gripped its sides, and stared at herself in the mirror, her sharpened vision showing her the minuscule particles of clay that made up her face, the rouge smeared atop them like paint on a wooden doll. There was a *crack* beneath her fingers. She released the sink, saw the new fracture that webbed through the porcelain—like the cracks in the concrete, the crater in the alley where—

No, she told herself. *You are not her. You are Charlotte Levy.*

She stretched her fingers out, pulled them in. Slowly, the world in the mirror returned to normal. Time resumed its usual pace.

She frowned down at the crack in the sink, and left the lavatory.

The class was quiet when she reentered. Inevitably, a few of the girls were wondering if she'd fallen pregnant, and had left to vomit in secret.

Kreindel had abandoned her whisking and now stood with folded arms, staring at her saucepan and its mess of curdled yolks.

"I *told* you," Sarah said.

"It doesn't matter anyway, it's just a sauce," muttered Kreindel, a touch too loudly.

The room stilled in shock. Didn't *matter*? Only Kreindel would dare say such a thing—an insult to their teacher, not to mention their own accomplishments! And yet she'd said it with such offhanded certainty that they were suddenly unsure of their convictions. Was Kreindel right? *Did* a sauce matter, like other things mattered?

Miss Levy took a steadying breath. "It's true," she said, "an individual sauce may not 'really matter,' as you say." She turned to address the class as a whole. "But tell me, if you would. Above all else, what is every resident's complaint about the Asylum?"

"The food," the girls groaned in chorus.

She smiled. "Exactly. And this is not to disparage our kitchen-workers, by any means. In fact, one might argue that theirs is the most difficult task in the entire Asylum. They must plan nutritious meals for over a thousand children, on a closely monitored budget, using ingredients that can be purchased in large quantities and held in storage for days—and on top of all that, they must also follow our dietary laws. Given so many restrictions, it's a wonder there's any variety to your meals at all. But—let us imagine that, one day, the kitchen staff forgoes all the rules. You arrive at your breakfast, and find that on every table is a bowl of brandied vanilla sauce, to pour over your usual eggs and toast. Or, at supper, a béchamel with grated nutmeg, for your boiled vegetables. What would the general reaction be, do you think? Would it be memorable?"

Their wide eyes assured her that it would be memorable indeed.

"An unfair example, perhaps, but you see my point. Any individual dish may not make a great difference in itself—but well-prepared food, in variety and abundance, matters greatly in the aggregate."

The girls nodded with her, their certainty restored. Kreindel stood sullen and alone, arms still folded against them.

The bell sounded then, and in a rush the girls peeled off their white coats and caps and began to file toward the door. "Thank you, ladies," Miss Levy called. And then, "Miss Altschul?"

The young woman paused, longing to leave. Her teacher waited un-til the others were out of hearing, and then said, "I'm told that you joined my class under protest. I can understand your frustration—but please do give it an honest try."

"Yes, Miss Levy," Kreindel said; but her voice was dull with resent-ment.

16.

_S_ophia stood naked in a crowded ballroom.

She tried to cover herself, mortified. She'd been wearing a dress, a wine-colored silk, but it had disappeared somehow, and now the guests were all staring. She ought to leave the party, but she couldn't; she was waiting for someone, only she couldn't remember his name . . . Oh, her mother would be furious. She tried to pretend it didn't matter to her in the least. Her nakedness was a choice and she preferred it that way, they were the ones in the wrong—but she was too cold, far too cold—

Next stop, Pennsylvania Station, someone called.

She woke with a shivering jolt. She was on a train from Baltimore to New York. And, to her relief, she was fully clothed.

She rubbed her eyes. Her head ached; her entire soul was weary from travel. She glanced up at her trunk in the luggage rack, already dreading the mood that the jinniyeh would be in when they arrived. They'd argued about it on the _Kansan_, the jinniyeh declaring she'd rather fly into the ocean than get in the trunk again. But Sophia had insisted that she couldn't go about with some animal perched on her shoulder like a witch's familiar, and that if Dima went on refusing to wear clothing, there was nothing else they could do. So at last, with much grumbling, the jinniyeh had consented to the trunk. Secretly, Sophia was relieved. It was easier to keep track of her this way, and it saved her the cost of a second ticket.

She peered out the window at New Jersey, the flashing greenery slowly acquiring streets, buildings, railyards—and then the Hudson tunnels swallowed them in darkness. The train slowed, emerged at a platform, and stopped.

I've come back, Sophia thought.

The carriage began to empty. One of the porters fetched down her trunk, and offered to carry it up to the taxi stand. She thanked him, wondering if he'd noticed her trembling, or if the porters simply carried everyone's luggage for them. She followed the man's broad back onto the platform, up the staircase to the top—

To a room of steel and marble and shining glass, and vast overhead arches that seemed to hold back the clouds.

She stopped in surprise. Her eyes widened; her jaw dropped. "Oh, my goodness," she murmured.

The porter noticed, and smiled. "First time here, miss?"

She nodded, still gazing about. "I've been away. It's beautiful."

"There was a man who used to sit there"—he pointed to a bench—"and look around for hours. Never took a train that I saw. Just wanted to be here, in the station."

"I can see why," Sophia said.

He led her through the Concourse to the Waiting Room, where she stopped to buy a map of the city, and then to the taxi stand. She tipped and thanked him as the taxi-driver tied the trunk onto the rack—she made certain it looked secure—and they were off.

It was a quick jaunt to Washington Square. The driver dodged all over the road and honked his horn at every corner—Sophia feared for the trunk, but it stayed stubbornly upon the rack—and then they were at the Hotel Earle, where Sophia paid the driver and then stared at the trees and the pathways and the Arch above, feeling as though she'd arrived inside her own memories. Fifteen years; and yet it seemed only days ago, no time at all.

They passed into a lobby—dark wood paneling, velvet couches—and Sophia signed the register at the desk. She wished her hand were steadier; the second half of *Williams* was nearly illegible. "Are there any messages waiting for me?"

The clerk checked the cubbies behind him. "Afraid not, miss."

Well, it meant little. Perhaps he'd moved the business. Or, he simply hadn't answered yet. They'd go to Little Syria tomorrow and look for him. She'd fulfill her half of the bargain. And then . . .

Perhaps it'll happen, perhaps it won't, she told herself. Promise or not, she was still at the jinniyeh's mercy. But it was difficult not to think, *Soon, I won't shake anymore. Soon, I'll be warm.*

The room they'd given her was on the top floor. It was small but well-appointed, with a radiator and—Sophia rejoiced to see—a bathtub. She tipped the bellboy, reassured him she had everything she needed, then closed the door and opened the trunk.

The jinniyeh materialized, looking ill, and sat down on the floor at once. "By the six directions," she said through gritted teeth, "I shall never do that again." She glared around at the tiny room. "And this is little better."

Sophia sighed. "At least there's a bath."

Dima shuddered. "That hardly helps *me*."

Sophia ignored this. She was exhausted, and hungry as well. First, though, the bath. She'd grown used to disrobing before the jinniyeh—it was abundantly clear that Dima thought little of it—and soon she was inside a steaming tub of water, her hair floating about her, the weeks of travel sloughing from her skin. Her shaking diminished. Before long, her eyes were drifting closed.

The jinniyeh, meanwhile, flew about the tiny room, trying to shake her sense of confinement. It astonished her how humans seemed to hate open spaces. They built their buildings and then put rooms in them, and then trunks inside the rooms, and cases inside the trunks.

She approached the window, blowing the thin curtains to the side. Outside, the twilight was deepening toward evening. She heard the growl she now knew to be an automobile, and the ring of hooves upon stone. Beyond were treetops, a space cleared of buildings—and in the middle of that space—

An enormous arch, bone-white, rising into the air.

She shot backward. The Cursed City, it was here! But how was that possible? Had it followed her somehow, were the demons real after all? Or—had she truly left the desert? Sophia had kept her in so many boxes; she'd never seen any proof of their destination, had merely trusted the woman's word—

Terrified, she raised winds to flee. The curtains whipped about, tangling her inside them.

"*Dima!*"

Sophia stood dripping wet, a towel hastily wrapped around herself, one hand shielding her eyes from the wind that spun through the room.

The jinniyeh took form; the winds stopped. "You tricked me! We are still in the Cursed City!" She advanced upon the woman, fury in her eyes.

"What?" Startled, Sophia looked to the window. "Wait—the Arch?"

"Yes!"

The woman put up her hands. "Dima, please! Look again. It's not Palmyra. It's not the same."

Was this a trick, too? The jinniyeh glared at her, but went back to the window—and saw that the woman was right. This arch wasn't old and crumbling, but new and whole. Carvings decorated its sides, undamaged by time.

"I should've thought to warn you," Sophia said. "That's Washington Square Arch. It's only a hundred years old."

The jinniyeh stared at it. "But . . . it's so alike."

"It's in the Roman style, just as Palmyra was. Here—wait a moment, I'll show you something." She replaced the towel with a dressing-gown from her trunk, then dug through her valise and found a rectangle of paper that she unfolded once, then again and again, until it was nearly too large to hold. She placed it upon the bed. "It's a map of Manhattan," she said. "Like the railway map I showed you in Damascus, but only one city, and in much greater detail. We're here, in Greenwich Village, on Waverly Place."

The jinniyeh squinted. There was Waverly Place, at the edge of a small box labeled *Washington Square Park.* Inside the box, the map's creator had sketched the outline of a miniature arch. She glanced out the window to the real thing, towering above the trees.

"I want to see for myself," she said.

Sophia considered this, and then nodded. "Of course." She unlatched the window and raised the sash. "Go ahead."

The jinniyeh was startled. Did Sophia trust her that much, to encourage her to fly free into the city? No: she trusted the promise that she had made. The vow upon Mount Qaf.

The breeze from the window smelled of green leaves and burning wood, and the dark, oily scent of human machinery. Not the desert at all. With a wary glance at Sophia, she loosed her form and flew out into the dusk.

Downstairs, the hotel was preparing for the evening. The scents of as-paragus soup and roast beef drifted into the lobby, reminding the desk-clerk that he wouldn't have anything to eat until the restaurant closed for the night and the cooks served what was left to the staff. He glanced at the clock, and then behind himself at the grid of cubbyholes, one for each room, keys dangling from the hooks of those guests who'd gone out on the town. Soon they'd drift back and reclaim their keys, and find that in their absence their rooms had grown too warm, or perhaps too cold. They'd demand a seating at the restaurant five minutes before the kitchen closed; they'd ask about nearby entertainments, and then go to exactly the same pictures they could see at home. The clerk despised the evening shift. He wished he had a newspaper, or a sandwich.

The lobby door opened. It was a Western Union boy, an oyster-pail in one hand. The boy walked to the desk, set down the pail, and pulled an envelope from his bag. "Day letter for Sophia Williams," he said, slid-ing it across.

The clerk took the envelope and peered at it, and then at the ho-tel register. Williams, Williams . . . The pail distracted him with its scent. Here she was—Williams, Room 812. He slid the envelope into the cubby for 812; and when he turned back, the boy said, "Say, do you like chop suey?"

"Sure I do. Why?"

The boy nodded at the pail. "I went to Pell Street to get this for a lady, but when I came back, she didn't want it anymore. So now I'm stuck with it."

"You ain't gonna eat it?"

"Naw, I still got deliveries to make, and it'll be cold by the time I'm done. I can't stand the stuff cold. You want it?"

The clerk considered the pail. He looked at the clock. "Sure," he said. "Thanks."

"Anytime. Hey—you got a toilet around here?"

He pointed. "Down the hall, past the restaurant."

The boy thanked him, and left in the direction of the W.C.—and the clerk, his stomach growling, took the oyster-pail to the back office and shut the door.

The Arch was closer than the jinniyeh had realized.

It stood upon an open oval of hard ground, surrounded by foot-paths. Startled pigeons scattered from its carvings as she flew closer, examining the marble. Then she pulled back, gazing out beyond the park's edges. There were no fallen columns here, no foothills in the distance, only a profusion of tall, rectangular towers dotted with glass, so many that she couldn't see the horizon. She flew higher—and now the pattern of streets began to reveal itself. Street-lamps cast their circles upon the ground; lit windows and flood-lights illuminated the sky. She flew higher still—the air was colder here—and spied the western edge of the island, the ships that plied the coastline and bobbed at the piers. The city stretched north and south below her, a patchwork of parks and buildings, structures of all sizes, carriages with horses and without, iron bridges, iron railways, iron fences and spires—

And humans. The humans were everywhere. They walked the streets and passed through the doorways; they drove the carriages, they rode the trains, they piloted the ships. They were behind every window in every building. They swarmed out of stairwells in the street, like ants from a mound. Thousands upon thousands of them, more than she'd known existed. They'd covered the land and the oceans; they'd stretched themselves into the heavens and burrowed inside the earth. They'd conquered every last element and direction.

All at once she was overwhelmed with a loneliness that bordered upon desperation. The very landscape seemed to reject her as alien, bizarre. Here, it would be easy to believe that there was no such thing as jinn at all. Was this how the iron-bound jinni felt, too?

Please, she thought, *let him be here, and alive.*

In the W.C., Toby waited.

One minute. Two minutes. Let the man eat his supper. With any luck, the clerk would be distracted enough not to notice Toby's failure to return through the lobby. The telegram he'd given the man was just a dummy, a blank—and for that, he could land in enough trouble to lose his job. But he needed to see this woman who knew something that Chava Levy was not supposed to know.

He left the W.C. and found the staircase, its steps deep and carpeted. He paused at each turning, listening, but encountered no one on his way to the eighth floor. He'd chosen the right hour, before the evening rush.

Room 812. Heart pounding, he fetched another envelope from his bag and knocked on the door.

Sophia stood by the open window, shivering.

The jinniyeh had been gone for at least five minutes. Of course Dima would want to explore; Sophia only wished she'd thought to dry herself more thoroughly first, and change into something warmer. Another minute, and another—and Sophia grew colder, and more worried. Would Dima remember which building was theirs? Perhaps she was lost out there, in the growing dark. Had she ever navigated a city before? No, of course she hadn't. Sophia hadn't prepared her at all. She'd merely opened the window and told her to fly. Sophia was shaking terribly now, the weeks of travel and sea-sickness had drained her—but this was her own fault; she'd made a mess of things and she couldn't leave the window in case Dima should be looking for her—

A knock came at the door. Was it her? Had she gotten in through the wrong window, and was now standing naked in the hall? Numbly she wrapped her dressing-gown more tightly about herself, stumbled to the door, and forced her fingers to turn the knob.

"Western Union, miss," Toby said to the damp-haired woman in the dressing-gown. "Are you"—a glance at the envelope and its invented name—"Anna Smithfield?"

He expected her to tell him, *No, young man, you have the wrong room*; to scold him for interrupting her bath instead of just leaving the envelope at the desk. Instead she only clutched the doorknob with a white-knuckled hand. She was shaking, badly. Her lips were tinged with blue.

"Miss, are you—"

Her eyes rolled upward, and her knees buckled.

He lunged, and caught her: a fumbling catch, the heel of one hand bumping the swell of her breast. He jolted with embarrassment and adjusted his grip, hoisted and half carried her inside, to a settee by the bathroom. She curled there, shaking.

"I'll call for a doctor," he said, and reached for the 'phone.

"No!" It was barely audible above her chattering teeth, but her eyes pleaded with him. "Blanket. Please. And—hot-water bottle. In my trunk."

He fetched the blanket off the bed and wrapped it around her, tucking it against the settee cushions. Then, blood climbing in his cheeks, he searched through her trunk, past the slips and underthings—and, to his surprise, a pearl-handled pistol—until at last he found the hot-water bottle. He filled it in the bathroom, and gave it to her to tuck beneath the blanket. She was small and delicate-looking, though the skin around her eyes was finely wrinkled, as though she'd spent a good amount of time squinting in the sun. He eyed the 'phone again, wondering if he should put a call in to the house doctor, despite her objections.

"I don't need a doctor," she said, following his gaze. She seemed to be warming; her lips, at least, were a healthier pink. "It's a kind of anemia. I've had it since I was young. It . . . gets the better of me, sometimes. When I don't expect it."

"I could go to the chemist's, if there's anything—"

"No. Thank you. Honestly, I'll be fine. Once I've rested." A pause. "You were looking for . . . who?"

Oh. The telegram. He'd dropped it somewhere, in the confusion. He looked around, noting the billowing curtains—the window was open, no wonder she was cold . . . There it was, on the floor. He picked it up—and froze at a familiar sensation.

There was a train engine approaching behind him.

All his instincts shouted it, though he knew it was impossible: he was in a hotel room on Washington Square, not out riding Death Avenue. But it was the same gust of air pushing at his back, pressing upon his ears. It was barreling down upon him; *something was coming*—

The pressure lessened, the breeze died away, and with a bone-deep certainty Toby knew that there was someone else behind him in the room. Hovering. *Waiting.*

The woman's eyes had gone wide. She was staring beyond him, at the window. She'd left it open . . . deliberately.

Don't turn around, he told himself.

He swallowed, and looked down at the telegram. "It's for Anna Smithfield," he said, his own voice thin in his ears. "Is that you?"

"No," the woman said. "No, I'm not Anna Smithfield."

"Oh. I'm sorry. It must've . . ." He felt faint. His skin was crawling; he wanted to scream. *Don't turn around.* "It must be a mistake. I'll check with the desk. Sorry to bother you."

"That's all right," she said. "And thank you, for your help. I'm sorry if I frightened you."

He stared at her.

"Before, when I—"

"Oh. That's all right. Do you need any—"

"No. Thank you, but no."

He took a breath, let it out. The door was to his left. He would have to turn around, a little, to leave.

He turned.

There was nothing there. A hotel room, an open window, curtains that waved in a breeze. He went to the door, grasped the knob, opened it. The woman's eyes tracked his every move.

"Good night," she said.

"Good night," said Toby.

He closed the door behind himself, and ran like hell for the stairs.

The girls' Hebrew classes at the Asylum were taught by Miss Pearl and Miss Franck, a pair of young women so alike in both appearance and temperament that even Miss Levy had difficulty telling them apart. She found them in the teachers' lounge, discussing their lesson plans over coffee. "I was wondering," she said, "about Kreindel Altschul."

The women winced as one. "Did she cause a disruption?" asked Miss Pearl.

"Not as such. But I was . . . surprised by her vehemence."

"I'm afraid it's our fault you've been stuck with her," said Miss Franck, her tone rueful. "She's a brilliant girl, but one of the most stubborn I've ever met. I wish she'd taken to the new curriculum—she simply *refused* to adjust. She even called it blasphemy, if you can believe it!"

"Her upbringing *was* rather strict. She's a true orphan, you know," said Miss Pearl, as though this fact explained much—and perhaps it did. "No mother since birth, and her father died when she was eight. He was a rabbi, and *very* traditional, from what we understand."

"Then she was eight, when she came here?" said Miss Levy.

"Yes, which was far too old, of course. But the state insisted, and there was little to be done."

"Does she have plans, for after the Asylum?"

They both shook their heads. Miss Franck said, "We suggested college, but she wouldn't hear of it. If I had to guess, I'd say she'll probably end up on the Lower East Side again."

"Such a shame," Miss Pearl said with a sigh. "She could be an incredible scholar. I think she *wants* to be—but she just won't let herself."

Wryly Miss Franck said, "For that to happen, she'd have to move on from her father's way of thinking."

Miss Levy thanked them and left, stopping first at the office, where the key for the large-item repository was waiting for her. She pocketed it, wondering idly when she might fit the task into her schedule, and made her way home.

In her apartment, she drew her bath and undressed, unclasped the locket and laid it upon its shelf. She sank beneath the surface and closed her eyes, breathed the water in and out.

Kreindel had taken her by surprise, that was all. The girl was angry; she felt that something she loved had been stolen from her. It was only natural that she considered Culinary Science a punishment of some kind. But slowly, Charlotte would win her over.

She doesn't want to be won over.

She frowned. The thought had arrived in a voice not her own.

Chava, you cannot control others for your own comfort.

That's not my name, she told him.

He snorted. He was standing at the edge of the Amherst rooftop, snow blowing around him like dust.

I don't want to control anyone, she said. *I only want—*

To help them. Yes, I know. And if she refuses your help?

Then we will simply endure each other, for as long as we must.

And what about the next girl who refuses your help? And the one after that?

Stop it, Ahmad.

Or what? He climbed the small ledge and stood facing her, his back to the alley.

Go ahead, she told him. *It's what you wanted.*

And you're certain of that?

She paused. *No. I could never be certain, with you.*

He smiled, and began to rock back and forth on his heels. The motion sent a strange vertigo through her, as though she herself were about to fall. *Don't do that,* she said.

You can't change those who don't want you to, he told her, tipping ever farther.

Ahmad, don't!

Come and get me, he said—and he closed his eyes, and went over.

She surfaced, spitting bathwater.

The room was spinning—no, it was merely the water, sloshing around her. She gripped the rim of the tub until the water stilled, then climbed out carefully and dried herself.

The locket gleamed upon the shelf, condensation beading its surface.

She picked it up and stared at it, wishing for a moment she could throw it out the window—but then fastened it about her neck as usual. She donned her housecoat, made her evening cup of tea, set it upon her desk, readied her work for the evening. Today had been an aberration. Tomorrow she'd be better prepared.

"He noticed *something*, the poor boy. But I suppose it can't be helped. Thank you, in any case. For not . . . appearing."

Sophia was on the settee braiding her hair, the blanket still wrapped around her. The jinniyeh watched from a corner and wondered why the woman still bothered with the braids, knowing the jinniyeh was immune to steel. Perhaps the defense had merely grown into habit.

Sophia said, "Dima, would you bring me my hairpins? They're in my valise, in a silver case."

The jinniyeh turned toward her with a retort on her lips—*I'm not your bound servant*—but then saw the woman's pallor, the bruised-looking hollows beneath her eyes. She warred with herself a moment before sullenly going to the valise. She picked through its contents—and the word *Ahmad* appeared, written upon a thin piece of paper half tucked into something else.

She paused, then moved it to the side, found the silver case and took it to Sophia.

The woman pinned her braids in place, then said, "I'm going to call down to the desk and have some food sent up, and an extra blanket. I'm sorry, Dima—I know you must be impatient to find him. But I won't be any help at all until I've eaten something and had a good night's sleep."

"I understand," the jinniyeh said. "Here—I'll put that back for you."

"Oh. Thank you." Sophia handed her the silver case and wrapped the blanket more tightly around herself, then lifted a contraption from the desk and spoke into it: "Yes, this is Sophia Williams, in Room 812. Could you send a pot of tea to my room? And does the restaurant have a soup tonight? . . ."

The jinniyeh replaced the silver case in the valise, and pulled the thin piece of paper free of Sophia's passport.

Arbeely & Ahmad
116 Washington St. (at Carlisle)

She read it carefully, then replaced it in the valise as Sophia finished her conversation. The woman had said nothing at all to her about how she intended to find the iron-bound jinni. Had she known where he was all along? Why would she hide such a thing? She went to the map, still spread upon the bed, found Waverly Place with its tiny arch. So many streets, each with a different name . . .

Sophia had noticed her renewed interest in the map. "Would you like me to show you a few places?" she said.

"Yes."

The woman came to the bed and pointed at the long rectangle in the middle of the island. "This is Central Park. It was my favorite place in the city, when I was young. And I spent a good deal of time here, at the Metropolitan Museum of Art, though that might not interest you. This is Broadway, it runs the length of the island, or near enough . . . Here's Riverside Park, which is lovely in the spring. And, let's see . . ." She searched the map, seemingly at a loss, and after a moment she laughed sadly. "Do you know, I've seen so little of this city. First I was too young to explore on my own, and then I simply wasn't allowed."

"Where did you live?" the jinniyeh asked.

"Here." She pointed to a spot just east of Central Park, near its bottom edge. "The family mansion." She said it with a faintly bitter tone.

A noise made the jinniyeh jump: a clatter in the wall nearby, like whirring wheels, or something being dragged upward. It stopped; a bell pealed. Sophia went to a small door in the wall that the jinniyeh hadn't noticed, opened it, and withdrew a tray that held a covered bowl and a teapot. There was another blanket as well, and an envelope atop it. Sophia opened the envelope. "This is strange," she murmured.

"What?"

"There's no message inside. It's only a blank." She paused, thinking. "That messenger-boy—but he thought I was . . . Oh, I'm too tired to think properly." She rubbed her forehead, then sat at the desk and began to eat. When she was finished, she seemed at last to notice the silence. "Is everything all right?"

Nothing is all right, the jinniyeh thought. "Why wouldn't it be?"

"You seem . . . a little overwhelmed, I suppose."

Of course I am. You are everywhere. You are overwhelming. She said only, "This place is like a tale. You have magic boxes in your walls that bring you things."

Sophia chuckled. "Yes, they're awfully convenient. There were many nights, in the desert, when I would've traded everything I owned for a magic box with a blanket in it." She put the empty bowl back in the box, closed the door, pushed a button. The machinery whirred again.

"Yet you could've come back, if you'd wanted to," the jinniyeh said.

Sophia had gone to her trunk for her bottle of laudanum. "But I didn't want to," she said. "I was searching for something." She sat on the settee, measured out a spoonful, drank it down.

"No. You were hiding."

Sophia looked up, startled. "What do you mean?"

"I saw it in your mind. You traveled from place to place, you kept yourself apart, you made few acquaintances and took no lovers. Your illness was your secret, you carried it as I once carried mine—except that I was banished only once. You banished yourself over and over again."

Silence. Sophia took a shaking breath. "I didn't have much of a choice," she murmured.

"I know," said the jinniyeh.

The woman's eyes had begun to brim. She looked up at the jinniyeh. "Will you cure me?" she said. "Truly?"

"When it is time," the jinniyeh told her.

Sophia nodded, looked away. She wiped at her eyes; tears leaked from the corners. She leaned her head back upon the settee. The jinniyeh watched as her eyes drifted closed and her breathing evened.

The jinniyeh returned to the map. It took many minutes, but eventually she found Washington Street, and then Carlisle: the thinnest of intersecting lines. She placed a finger upon Waverly Place, then drew it to her destination. The street that most closely followed her path was called West Broadway, and it was decorated along its length with a hatched line that, if she was reading the map correctly, signified a railway track. She could follow it from the air, if she was careful enough. She memorized the turnings and landmarks, then folded the map away.

Sophia was still asleep on the settee, trembling but not waking. The jinniyeh took the blanket from around her shoulders and laid it upon the bed, then spread the second blanket atop it and folded the bedclothes aside. She lifted the woman easily and carried her to the bed, tucking her in. Sophia turned over once beneath the blankets, then settled.

The jinniyeh turned out the lamps and waited until she was certain Sophia was deeply asleep. The woman's hair shone in the light from the window, the braids a series of hills and valleys that curved about her head. Very like the tales of Mount Qaf, the jinniyeh thought, were it not for the steel among the strands.

Carefully she cracked the window open, just wide enough for escape. Then she cast a final glance at the figure in the bed, loosed her form, and flew.

West Broadway was easy to find; she stayed high above it, mindful of the trains. One soon passed beneath her, smaller than its desert cousins but just as noisy. She matched its speed, then shot ahead when it braked at a platform. Soon the streets began to converge as the island narrowed. The ship-dotted bay glittered beyond, as wide and forbidding as the ocean at Jaffa. At last West Broadway angled into Greenwich Avenue, the track turning to follow. One intersection, two, three—and there it was, the corner of Washington and Carlisle.

It was evening now, and there were fewer people about. She descended and hovered, looking around until she found the number 116 painted upon a building that sat slightly taller than its neighbors. She thought, *They have so many boxes that they must number them to keep track.*

She floated up to the roof and looked around. On one corner was a squat, pointed tower, mounted upon spindly legs. In another corner, a doorway led down into the building itself. Warm air rose from the gap beneath the door.

She hovered, gathering courage.

The Jinni stood at his forge, a breeze tickling the back of his neck.

The shout in Yiddish, the shattering glass. His mind couldn't let it go. It all felt like a human's dream now, except that those were rumored to fade upon waking; and instead his remorseless memory brought him detail after detail, showing him each of his missteps. And where had he seen that messenger-boy before? His face, his look of startlement . . .

He frowned, straightened, steadied himself. He hadn't worked for years without cease simply to let the world best him in an instant. The message and its messenger were gone; what mattered now was the Amherst. If something essential was indeed missing, if some instinct was trying to warn him of a fundamental flaw, then he would listen to it.

He inhaled the smoldering air, pressed burning hands to his eyes, as though it might help him look past what was and see what ought to be. It wasn't just the cursed glass panes; it was something else . . .

The breeze on the back of his neck grew stronger.

What is it, what's missing? he thought. *Why can't I see it?*

She slipped beneath the door and drifted downward, riding against the heat.

From the ordinary exterior, she'd expected rooms, corridors, furniture—but this was entirely different. She was inside an open metal lattice, a sculpture of some kind. The smell of iron was everywhere. She descended farther and passed through an iron arch that stretched away to either side, undulating oddly. And below it—

A steel moon, hanging in midair.

She halted, pulled back. Other steel circles were arrayed beneath it, each lower than the one before—not floating, she saw now, but attached like leaves to a central pole that ran from the roof to the ground. Was it a kind of human weapon, like the ship at Jaffa? She descended past the rim of the first gigantic circle, then the next and the next, waiting for some purpose to reveal itself. She saw no one, human or otherwise—only steel and more steel.

Something glowed in the darkness below her—and now she heard the muted rumble, the familiar noise of conflagration. A red rectangle appeared, a bed of coals, its surface rippling with flame. Next to it stood a man. He wore a leather garment that hung about his neck, and tattered trousers. He stood with his hands pressed to his eyes. At one wrist, a wide iron cuff glowed with heat.

It was him! The iron-bound jinni! But—

Doubt seized her. She'd known he was trapped and unchanging; she'd seen his exact likeness in Sophia's mind—and yet, like the building, this was not what she'd expected. He seemed . . . small, to her eyes. Worn, tired. *Human.* And if this was his building, did that mean that he lived here, with an ominous steel tree looming over him?

"Why can't I see it?" he muttered.

She must have made some noise, or moved in the air. He put a hand to the back of his neck, absently, as though he'd felt a breeze—and then he stiffened.

Slowly the iron-bound jinni turned his head—

—And he saw a formless apparition, beautiful and blazing.

His senses knew the truth before his mind could understand it. It was impossible—and yet she couldn't be anything but what she was. No memory could cast such warmth; no delusion would stare back with such apprehension. *This was a jinniyeh.*

"Who," he said—and then once again, "*Who,*" not a question but an exhalation, as though from a blow to his stomach. His body's long-dormant instincts were roaring to life, urging him: *Change shape! Match her, rise into the air, and fly!*

His body shuddered against the iron's grip. He staggered, took a step toward her—and went sprawling.

She reared back in surprise as he tumbled to the floor.

What had happened? Was he injured? His eyes were squeezed shut—against the sight of her? Six directions, could he no longer stand even to look at his own kind? No, this wasn't what she'd wanted! She backed away through the air.

He lurched to his feet again. "No, wait!" he called—but she was rising quickly now, fleeing him as he stumbled toward the column and its staircase. "*Wait!*" He was climbing, but she was quicker; she dodged the edge of a steel moon and kept going, up through the arches to the door, slipping herself beneath the crack—

—And by the time he climbed through the arches and threw open the door to the roof she was only a glimmer in the air, flying away north.

The jinniyeh flew back to Washington Square Arch and then hung above it, berating herself as the sun rose. *What had she done?*

Yes, she'd thought he'd be different; and she certainly hadn't imagined him living inside that horrible iron building, with its moons and arches and spirals. But had she come all this way, risked everything, only to find him and then fly away again?

His story gave me so much strength, she realized, *that I never imagined he might be weaker than me.*

But that was unfair of her! After all, what tale had *he* been told during his years of hiding in this terrible human city, thinking himself utterly alone in the world? And now that she was here, now that she understood . . .

Perhaps she could tell a story that would give *him* strength.

Once, there was a jinniyeh who feared no iron. Banished from her tribe, she decided to seek out the iron-bound jinni, and rescue him. Alone, without aid, she braved oceans and ships and cities, searching for his hiding-place in the human world, so that she might teach him how to be a jinni again.

It was a good beginning. She would return, and start over again. But first . . .

She looked out above the treetops, at the Hotel Earle.

Sophia woke slowly. Was it morning? How long had she been asleep? She was in her hotel room, but she couldn't remember going to bed . . .

She squinted against the light trickling through the curtains. The jinniyeh was perched upon the settee, her knees drawn to her chin, watching her. "Are you awake?" the jinniyeh said.

"Yes, I am." Sophia stretched, and sat up. She felt immeasurably better, though she could do with breakfast . . .

"Here." The jinniyeh lifted a cup and saucer from the desk and brought them to Sophia. "I heated it for you." She pointed to the metal teapot on the desk, the one the kitchen had sent up the night before. Steam was rising from its spout.

Sophia smiled. "Thank you, Dima. I doubt I would've thought of that." She sipped at the tea, trying not to wince; it had gone bitter from sitting all night in the pot. But the jinniyeh seemed happy that she was drinking it, so she finished the cup. "We ought to plan the day," she said.

The jinniyeh poured more tea. "What do you propose?"

"First I'll go to Little Syria and see what I can find. I don't want to raise your hopes, but I found an address for him in an old directory. He might still be there. Or, if he isn't, perhaps I can find someone who'll help us."

The jinniyeh was listening, nervous, expectant. Sophia sipped the tea, thinking. "I'll need a story to tell, a reason why I'm looking for him. I *do* wish you'd reconsider wearing clothes—you might be a cousin of his, or . . ."

She blinked, slowly. The teacup was drooping in her hand. She tried to raise it, but her hand felt too far away. And she was suddenly so *tired* . . .

The jinniyeh came to her side and lifted the cup from her hand before it could spill.

"Dima?" The word slurred in her mouth. Something was wrong; the jinniyeh had done something to her . . . She lurched to the side, trying to get away, but only succeeded in falling out of the bed and knocking over her trunk. Shawls, underclothes, her pistol all spilled out— along with her laudanum bottle, uncapped and empty.

Warm hands lifted her back onto the bed, placed her head upon the pillow. Sophia tried to fight her, but could barely clench her fists. Her head was swimming; she was nearly gone . . . *Why?* she tried to say, but it was only a whisper of air.

"This is your cure," the jinniyeh told her gently. "Sleep. I'll be there soon."

She was in her parents' ballroom, dressed in her wine-colored gown.

Every friend and acquaintance of her youth was there around her, every important personage her parents had ever ordered her to impress. She tried to smile, but she was terrified. She was hiding a secret, something they could never know. They'd send her away, call her mad; she must keep herself from shaking, so they couldn't see . . .

In the crowd, a childhood friend turned to her and said, It's all right, Sophia. We know it already. And we don't think any less of you for it, not one bit.

Sophia stared. You don't?

One of her mother's acquaintances, a woman who'd always frightened Sophia with her narrow-eyed stares, now smiled at her in kind sympathy and said, Of course not! How could we possibly? It might have happened to any one of us!

They all nodded as they surrounded her, murmuring agreement and support. They ushered her to the fireplace, sat her in a well-appointed sofa, its cushions soft as clouds. Someone brought her a shawl, another a hot cup of tea. They arranged themselves around her, as though hoping she might tell them a tale. For a moment, Sophia glimpsed someone moving at the back of the crowd—a flash of bare skin and long dark hair—

What was Damascus like? said her brother in the front row. He was holding the carved wooden sword she'd sent him.

Tell us about the Pyramids, said her father next to him.

She looked to her mother, uncertain, but beginning to hope. Her mother nodded in encouragement and said, We're so proud of you, darling. We want to hear everything.

Hesitantly she began to talk, telling them the stories she'd always wanted to tell: her journeys and searches and struggles, her triumphs and her losses. All of it the truth, without amendment or alteration. Daniel Benbassa and Ned Lawrence sat with their chins in their hands as she talked, utterly absorbed. Abu Alim and Umm Sahir nodded at every word. They'd never known the true Sophia—and now that she could tell them, how much better they all felt! There were no secrets anymore, and no judgments, either. She could be herself, she could be Sophia Winston again, and it didn't mean rejection, or shame, or tragedy—only wholeness.

Behind the crowd, the jinniyeh went on building. It was easy work; Sophia's thoughts were slow and thick, her defenses stilled. No hand came to grab at the jinniyeh as she searched out the woman's deepest yearnings and molded them into being, like a house full of beautiful rooms for her to enjoy, all free *of secrecy and strife. Once she'd finished her creation, the jinniyeh enclosed it inside a curving wall, a soap-bubble sphere that would hold the dream in place and keep its occupant from traveling. She sealed it behind herself—*

—And peered down at Sophia as she lay asleep in the hotel bed. The woman was breathing evenly, her forehead smoothed of worry. She was barely even shaking.

Satisfied, the jinniyeh went to the contraption on the desk, studied it for a moment, then picked it up and held it to her ear as Sophia had.

"Front desk," said a man's voice.

"This is Sophia Winston in Room 812," she said, in what she hoped was an approximation of the woman's voice. "I am very tired and I need to sleep. Don't disturb me. Please."

"Would you like for the maid to—"

"No! Send no one. I am to be alone."

"Okay, miss. No disturbances." The man seemed taken aback; perhaps she'd said it wrong. It hardly mattered, so long as he complied.

She replaced the receiver, opened the window, and was gone.

17.

Charlotte Levy capped her pen and put it down with a sigh.

It was nearly five in the morning. The day's lessons were before her, organized and reviewed. For the beginners' class, she'd planned an introduction to the properties of eggs; for the intermediate class, the different types of oils. For the advanced class, a lesson in pie-making—and for Miss Altschul, a budgeting exercise, from earlier in the term. She hoped it would appeal to the girl's sense of exactitude.

The midterm student evaluations sat in a neat pile at the corner of her desk, waiting to be finished. She considered them, then remembered the basement storage room, the key in her bag. She oughtn't put it off; at the very least, she should assess the state of the place and draw up a plan of attack.

Outside, the sky was turning to sapphire. Not quite a respectable hour to be out walking; but it was barely half a block to the side gate on 136th, and the local roundsmen all knew her by name. Here, she could come and go as she pleased.

The Asylum basement was dark, and full of small noises: dripping water, the clanking of pipes. She rarely ever came here, save for her weekly trip to the laundry room, to oversee the washing and bleaching of the cook's whites. She disliked the basement and its pervasive air of decay, its ineffective half-measures taken against the damp and the pests. She felt something scurry past her foot and reflected that, although the headmistress's "spring cleaning" might be a step toward improving matters, more drastic action would be called for at some point.

The corridor grew warmer as she went; she could hear the rumble of the boiler in its closet. She reached the door and tried the key before realizing it was unnecessary: a hard turn of the knob, and the door creaked open on ancient hinges. A wash of warm air brought her the scents of paper, must, and decay. She found the light-switch—and was rewarded with a *ping* and a tinkle of glass from a distant bulb. Hastily she switched it off again. The brief flash had shown her the state of the place: overflowing shelves, boxes in heaps, chairs stacked like precarious sculpture, stage backdrops of crumpled papier-mâché. Her irritation grew. Would there be *anything* worth salvaging in this mess? Better, surely, to clear it all away, and begin again—

who

She froze, listening.

who
who was it

It couldn't be his master, for she lay asleep upstairs, dreaming of a classroom quiz whose words scrambled themselves when she wasn't looking. Was it a teacher? A janitor? Whoever it was, they stood beside the door, utterly silent, not even breathing.

He held still, listening.

who

A touch, upon her senses. Not one of the sleeping minds above her—those were restless, full of complicated dreams. This was nearby, and simple, like a single note that threaded through a symphony. The barest of questions, quiet yet urgent. It felt . . . familiar.

The intruder wasn't leaving. They merely stood there, in the dark.

This had never happened before, and he didn't know what it meant. His master was still asleep; he couldn't look to her mind for answers. But he mustn't be discovered; he must hide, and stay hidden.

Worry filled him. Who? Who was it?

The note—

who

—grew in force. Now it was a need, an urgent need to know who this visitor was. Who *she* was. The need coiled around her, thin as gossamer but impossibly strong, a lure made to her measure—as though she'd been created for nothing other than to feel this particular need, in this particular room.

She took a step forward. Another step. The stacks and boxes loomed before her, blocking her way—no, there was a narrow opening, a path through the maze. She slipped inside, unable to stop herself. A thicket of cot-frames jutted toward her, legs and springs dotted with rust. A hat-stand hooked itself to her jacket, and she righted it before it could fall, listening all the while to that urgent note—

who

—as it guided her into a narrow passageway.

A new scent reached her then, carried through the warm air. A dock-lands note, clean and sharp, riding above the musty paper and rotting wood. The smell of salt and sediment, the clay at the city's edge.

She knew, in her body, in that moment.

Stop, she thought. *Turn around. Go home.* But she might as well have told herself to fall asleep.

She rounded the final corner. Before her was a cluttered alcove lit only by a grimy window-well. At its far end, a human figure sat beneath a curtain of burlap, like an old, discarded statue.

Through the curtain Yossele saw a woman emerge into the alcove. She was tall, and wore a dark dress, its skirt streaked with dust from the maze. She was walking directly toward him. She was staring straight at him.

He tensed in alarm—and immediately the woman stopped. She said nothing, only slowly, very slowly, lowered herself to sit an arm's length away, the rough lattice of the burlap between them.

Confusion roiled him. Was this . . . discovery? If so, it felt nothing like the terror and anger that his master had expected.

The woman lifted a hand—

—and moved the burlap aside.

He was enormous: far taller than herself and twice as wide, with a barrel chest and shoulders that stretched half the width of the alcove. His face was roughly carved, with a slab for a forehead, a jagged nose, and uneven lips. His eyes were globes of blue glass, one clear and the other clouded. The imprints of fingertips decorated the hollows of his cheeks.

His urgency had turned to confusion. He was watching her, studying her; she could see her face in his thoughts. She felt no violence, not yet; no true intelligence, either. Only instinct and obedience, devotion to his master—and now, dimly, she sensed the echoes of a human mind, one of the sleepers above them, dreaming of a classroom and a test unstudied for.

His master was a child. An Asylum child!

There was something strange about the woman's face.

He peered at her as though compelled, not knowing why—

Some hidden instinct made his marble eyes shift their focus past her appearance, into her essence. The perfectly molded face. The unblinking eyes, the unmoving chest. She was—

golem

—the same as him.

She saw herself, in his thoughts. Felt him realize her nature—

the same

—and recoiled. *No.*

She let go of the burlap, stood, stepped backward. He didn't move, only watched, his glass eyes in shadow.

She backed into the corridor, then turned and stumbled through the maze, past the hat-stand, the cot-frames, the boxes that scraped at her shins, and emerged at last at the threshold. She wrenched the door open, shut it behind herself—just as the rising bell sounded through the Asylum, announcing the start of a new day.

Maryam Faddoul swept through her coffee-shop, smiling, listening, uprooting whispers, knowing in her heart that it wouldn't be enough.

The neighborhood was in a black and anxious mood. The situation in Lebanon was worsening; the news that made it past the censors spoke of scarce food, black market thievery, warehouses full of rotting silk. Worse, the money they sent home to their families was failing to reach them more often than not. *Why doesn't the U.S. enter the war?* people had begun to ask. *Can't Wilson see what's happening? Don't Syrian children matter, in American eyes?* All would shake their heads, and cast about for something to distract them—while Maryam swept from table to table, pouring rounds of coffee, searching desperately for a new bit of gossip, some alchemy she might perform—

The bell jingled. All heads turned as Sam Hosseini stepped through the door.

Maryam wanted to cry with relief. Sam was a friendly, boisterous man, and a natural storyteller; when he entered a room, ears bent and heads tilted. Moreover, his general store had long been a destination for eccentric Manhattanites who liked to go about in fanciful "Oriental" dress and who were willing to buy the most outlandish items at the most outrageous prices. Sam would have tales of his customers enough to last the morning, and no one would talk of anything else for a week.

Maryam ushered him to a table, its occupants eagerly moving aside to make room. Sayeed, too, came out of the kitchen, and greeted his friend, the two embracing like brothers. Maryam poured his coffee, and asked after his children's health. "Oh, well enough, well enough," he said, and spoke briefly of the calamities his sons and daughter liked to visit upon him: pranks and truancy, afternoons spent at the pictures instead of helping at the store. All smiled and nodded: yes, their own children did this too, and if Sam found it maddening, then they might be excused for feeling the same. And dear Lulu, his wife?

Sam's face clouded. "She's well, but—worried." In a moment the mood had lowered. All nodded, thinking of Lulu Hosseini, a sweet and gentle soul. Of course the war would weigh especially heavily upon her. Maryam resolved to visit her as soon as possible, and chided herself for not thinking of it before. Her attention had been elsewhere for far too long.

She was about to ask Sam if he'd been blessed with any interesting customers lately when the man brightened and said, "But now, here is a bit of news, a thing I saw with my own eyes, if you can believe it."

All drew in to hear him.

"I was at Ramzi's yesterday, for some digestive tablets—"

Lucas Ramzi owned the chemist's shop that sat opposite the Amherst. An alarm sounded deep in Maryam's bones.

"—and as I was leaving, whom should I see but the Bedouin himself! He was towering over a messenger-boy who'd had the misfortune to knock upon his door. I thought I might have to intervene and protect the poor lad—"

An astonished murmur began among the assembly.

"—but then he retreated back into his cave and slammed the door in the boy's face. Oh, and here is the most astounding part! What do you suppose our friend was wearing?"

No one could even begin to guess.

"A leather apron around his neck, a pair of trousers fit for the ragbin—and that was all! In full view of the entire neighborhood, no less. What do you think of *that*?"

At once the entire shop was exclaiming upon it. This went too far, certainly! Wasn't it time that something was done about the man? As a matter of public decency, if nothing else?

"What do *you* think, Maryam?" asked one of the men at Sam's table. "Something strange must be going on in that building."

The shop quieted, waiting for Maryam to give the blessing that would unleash them. And give it she must—for to protect the Jinni now would be to drag herself down, to risk her credibility, even her good name. And to what end? Even if she sacrificed everything she had, it wouldn't stop them from breaking down the Amherst door and dragging its owner's secrets into the daylight. She had lost the battle; it was over.

Her hand on the coffee-pot went slack. The crash reverberated throughout the shop—and Sam Hosseini jumped up with a grimace, his trouser-legs dripping with coffee.

Maryam gasped and bent to pick up the pot. "Sam, I'm so sorry!"

"No harm done, no harm done," he said, stepping away gingerly.

Sayeed went to fetch the mop, and Maryam escaped to the kitchen, where she stood at the sink and let a few tears fall. Then she gathered herself and refilled the coffee-pot. A long, puckered indentation now adorned its side. She wished that she could take it to her tinsmith friend Boutros, who'd have mended it beautifully and charged her far less than he ought. Once, she'd given him her mother's old copper flask, to see if he might remove the dents and repair the scrollwork. She wondered, sometimes, what she would've done if she'd known what was hidden inside it, waiting to be set loose among them.

The Jinni sat with his back to the forge, his head in his hands.

A jinniyeh. Here, impossibly *here*, in the Amherst. And she'd flown from him, in—fear? Horror? He'd seen both, in her features. He wished that he could believe he'd imagined it all, that he hadn't driven away the only one of his kind he'd seen in fifteen years—

A glimmer, from above.

He looked up, then slowly got to his feet as she descended through the arches and past the platforms. She didn't touch the iron—but she was utterly surrounded by it; she ought to have flown in terror regard-less.

Was she unaffected by iron, somehow? Was she like *him*?

He stood perfectly still as she approached, terrified that he'd frighten her away again. Her body glowed like a jewel in the thin morning light. She came to hover in front of him, only a few feet away. He stared at her, not daring to speak.

—*I apologize*, said the jinniyeh.

He wanted to cry out at the sound of her voice, at the wind-borne language unheard for so long.

—*I was afraid*, she said. *But I shouldn't have flown away like that.*

"Afraid . . . of me?" His own words seemed flat and clumsy in com-parison.

—*A little, I suppose. And this place was . . . unexpected. But I was also afraid of what you might think of me.*

"You're immune to iron," he said, not quite daring to believe it.

—*Yes. I always have been.*

He felt dazed, giddy. "Is such a thing . . . common now, among our kind?"

—*Not at all. I thought I was the only one—until I heard the tale of the iron-bound jinni.*

"The . . . what?"

She smiled at his blank confusion.—*Did you think we wouldn't tell your story, once you were gone? There isn't a creature along the desert's curve that hasn't heard of the iron-bound jinni, who buried the wizard's flask and then returned to his exile among humankind.*

His story? They had made a *story* of him?

—*It was said*, she said, drifting a touch closer, *that he could only be found by another such exile. From the first time I heard the tale, I knew that I was the one it meant.*

His mind struggled to take this in. "Another exile . . . You were exiled from your tribe?"

—*Yes, when my secret was discovered. They banished me, to the City of Sulayman.*

He gaped at this. "And you *survived*?"

She laughed then, and it was the most beautiful sound he'd ever heard.—*Then you remember the tales?*

"*Remember* them? They haunted my childhood! I was terrified of them—of Sulayman's bound ghuls, and the ravenous demons who'd hunt for jinn and tear them apart, flame by flame—"

—*The tales were all false*, she said gently, as though afraid of disappointing him. *There's nothing in the Cursed City except for stones, and Bedu. I lived in fear there for entire seasons before I accepted the truth. Then the Cursed City became my home, while I plotted a way to reach you.*

The world itself was changing shape beneath him. Disoriented, he shook his head. "But how could you possibly have come here? How did you find me on the strength of a tale and nothing more?"

—*It was easier than I thought it would be*, she told him. *First, I had to escape through the jinn lands, so I hid myself in a Bedouin's saddle-bag next to his sword, and traveled with him to the outskirts of Homs. There, a farmer*

*in a wheat-field told me of a healer in the Damascus souk who had the power
to find anyone alive beneath the heavens, be they flesh or flame. I followed the
railway from Homs to Damascus, and found the healer in the souk. I entered
her dreams, and told her, 'Find me the iron-bound jinni.'*

He listened, enraptured, picturing it all: the saddle-bag, the wheat-
field, the sleeping healer.

—*The healer said, 'He calls himself Ahmad al-Hadid. He is across a sea
and an ocean, hiding in a city where shining boxes rise as high as Mount Qaf,
and an arch of Palmyra stands among green trees.' I searched through many
sleeping minds before I understood what city she meant by this. Then, because
of the war, and the blockade—*

"War?" he said, startled. "There's a war?"

—*Yes, one of the humans' usual fights, only very large and inconvenient.
I flew to the city of Port Said, and hid inside a ship that crossed the sea, and
another ship that crossed the ocean. I arrived here—and then—*She paused.

And then? he wanted to say, like an eager jinn-child to a story-teller.

—*I found you in an old—*She frowned, at a loss. Then, a slow, shining smile. *An old . . .* directory.

She'd spoken the word in English, using the nearest sounds that
jinn language could muster, and the effect was so startling and strange
that he burst out laughing. At once he was afraid she'd take it wrongly—
but she, too, was laughing now, the sound melding with the flames behind him.

"By the six directions," he said, "that is an astonishing tale."

—*You swear in the old way, as I do,* she said, still smiling.

"I haven't in years," he said, surprised at himself. The words had come
to him naturally, easily, as though drawn out by her presence, without
the need to comment or explain. Was this all really happening? It still
seemed impossible. But she floated before him regardless, her heat upon
his skin; and something was waking, coming to life, inside him.

She was watching him now, a new thoughtfulness in her expression.
She twisted in the air and took form: a young woman, dark-haired, tall
and lithe. Her face burned from within, the features like the thinnest of
masks laid upon the flame.

"You truly came here just to find me," he said, still not quite believing.

"I had to," she said. "Once I realized that I alone could reach you, I knew that I must try, for both of us. To live alone, in exile from jinn-kind—it was like a small part of me was extinguished every single day."

"Yes," he said, startled. "Yes, that's exactly how it was."

She smiled. "You see? And this is our reward."

She stepped closer, a blazing sun only inches away. One shining hand reached out and took his wrist, the one that wore the cuff. He watched as she examined the iron, tentatively brushing her fingers across the chain and the pin—as though, if she treated it too roughly, it might ensnare her as well.

"Now that I've found you, I want to see all of you," she said, and reached up and took the leather apron from around his neck. Her fingers went to the waist of his trousers; and they, too, were gone.

A promise, he thought distantly. *I made a promise, once.* But that had been a different life. Here, there was only the forge at his back, and the fire before him. He closed his eyes, afraid his knees might buckle, suddenly certain that he'd disappoint her, that she'd find him inadequate—how could she not, considering—

A hand slipped into his. He realized that she, too, was trembling.

"*Please,*" she whispered; and the promise was broken.

"Miss Levy," a girl said, "I think something's burning."

Charlotte Levy hurried across the kitchen and pulled the tray of dinner-rolls from the oven, fanning a hand over their blackened tops. "Open the windows, please," she called.

The girls of her intermediate class all rushed to comply, pushing the wide sashes as high as they could reach. Gusts of spring air blew through the room; the smoke began to dissipate.

"Let that be a lesson, girls," Miss Levy said, straining to add cheer to her voice. "A woman might consider herself an accomplished baker, but if she forgets to check the clock, her rolls will burn all the same."

"Yes, Miss Levy," the girls chorused. There were a few scattered giggles.

The bell rang, and they left their cook's whites behind and filed out to the noisy hallway. Miss Levy carried the tray of ruined rolls to an open window and set it on the ledge to cool. If the birds ate them, so much the better.

She leaned out the window and took a deep, calming breath. Her advanced class would arrive in moments. She must be their teacher, and give them her undivided attention—but—*how on earth had this happened?* A golem, here at the Asylum! Had he been down there in the storage room this entire time, only two floors beneath her classroom? Who could have put him there? And . . . what did she intend to do about it?

She frowned, trying to think clearly. The truth was that it didn't matter how long he'd been there, or the circumstances of his creation. A golem such as this one—without true intelligence, clearly built for brute strength—had no place inside an orphanage. And to be bound to a child! It was a miracle that he'd managed to remain hidden, that he hadn't burst from his hiding-place to avenge some playground slight. And now that she knew, she couldn't simply ignore the danger and allow it to continue. She would have to destroy him.

She pulled the locket from beneath her collar, the steel cold between her fingers. She'd go to the basement that night and do it quickly, before he could realize what was happening. Her conscience would remain clear. And as for his master . . . Well, perhaps they didn't even know he existed. A child could hardly bind a golem on their own, after all. She imagined the desperate, impoverished parent creating an unseen guardian for their baby, as a way to protect them from afar. An understandable act, if deeply misguided. She would correct their mistake, and it would be as if the golem had never existed.

The advanced class began to file in behind her. Quickly she tucked the locket back into her dress and turned around. "Good afternoon, ladies. Today I have a treat for you all. Together, we will construct a lemon meringue pie. A pie such as this requires the mastery of multiple techniques, and we shall divide into teams to accomplish it. Ah, Kreindel—"

She smiled at the girl. "I have a separate lesson for you, if you'll meet me at my desk."

In the basement, Yossele watched the cooking class through Kreindel's eyes, the other golem distant from his thoughts.

This was not at all by choice, for the morning's encounter was the most startling thing ever to happen to him. But his master was awake, which meant that he must observe her, protect her. That night, once Kreindel was safely asleep, he'd review the morning, and make what sense of it he could.

He watched as Kreindel sullenly read through the assignment, felt her wish that she could study Hebrew instead. Her teacher, Miss Levy, came to her side, asking if she had any questions; Kreindel looked up at her—

And something inside the morning's memory clamored for Yossele's attention. He peered at her, and saw—and recognized—

The golem. Miss Levy, his master's cooking instructor, was the very same golem who'd come to his alcove! There could be no mistaking her—yet when he looked at her through Kreindel's eyes, he saw only an ordinary woman, with no hint of her true nature.

Miss Levy was a golem . . . and his master didn't know.

The engine of Yossele's mind was a slow and lumbering thing, but here was a problem that refused to be ignored. All of Yossele's knowledge, all of his experience, came to him through Kreindel. She was his life, his purpose. He could not exist without her. Yet Miss Levy had come to the basement and sat with him—not Kreindel, but *him*—and he had learned what she was. Kreindel looked at the same woman, and saw . . . merely a woman.

Over and over the problem turned. He knew that Miss Levy was a golem, and that what Kreindel saw was incorrect. What did it mean—it meant that—

The realization spread through him. It meant that he was not simply an extension of Kreindel. He was *other* than Kreindel. A servant to her will, yet separate and distinct, with his own thoughts, his own knowledge.

He didn't know what to do with this information. It made little sense, and yet it was the truth. But his attention had been divided for too long; he was growing restless, anxious. So he released his thoughts and returned to the task of watching Kreindel—while the day's revelations crammed themselves into the corners of his mind, awaiting their chance to be examined further.

BUDGETING EXERCISE

Your household budget allows $10 a week for food expenditures. Using the included recipe-book and price list, you must devise a week's worth of meals for yourself and your family: Husband, Son (12), and Daughter (9). In addition, you are hosting a Sunday luncheon for six women in your congregation's Sisterhood Club, and must set a menu of at least three courses. The club has allotted you $15 for the luncheon. Any additional expense must come from your household budget—but you may not use the Sisterhood money for your own family.

A headache gathered at Kreindel's temples. She picked up the recipe-book, hoping for guidance—but the recipes were unlike anything she'd ever eaten. She turned past fish quenelles and layered terrines, almond crescents and Franconia potatoes. And, yes, here were sauces: a vinaigrette for lettuce, and something called a Sauce Figaro, meant to be eaten over fish. She flipped through to the end, frowning. Where were the simpler recipes, for everyday meals? Why not substitute chopped liver for the terrine, and gefilte fish for the quenelles? And was the parsley garnish for the quenelles optional, or must she buy it? To Kreindel, parsley meant Passover: the herb dipped in salt-water, its sharp green taste. Why waste money on parsley if it wasn't meant for a Seder plate?

She looked up from the desk. At the island, the rest of the class was hard at work, whipping meringues and mixing fillings, rolling out lumps of dough. Their teacher circled around them slowly—as Kreindel now suspected was her habit—observing their progress and making small suggestions. One of the girls tasked with the meringue was beating her egg-whites with a vengeful hand. Mrs. Levy murmured a few words into her ear, and the girl lightened her stroke at once. They exchanged a smile, and Mrs. Levy moved on.

Kreindel suppressed a shiver. Seen from a distance in this way, the woman's effect on her students was almost sinister. That low murmur, as though gentling a skittish horse; the way each girl wore the same expression of admiring gratitude . . .

Miss Levy's head turned toward Kreindel.

Kreindel reddened and looked down. She'd spent too long ruminating; she was losing time. She'd serve soft-boiled eggs to the children for breakfast, and at one egg per child per day that equaled a dozen eggs plus two . . .

Footsteps; and her teacher was at her side. "How are you managing, Kreindel? Is the assignment clear?"

Don't argue, she told herself. *Just say yes.* But instead she asked, "Are the garnishes necessary, or may I leave them out?"

"It's quite possible to complete the assignment without omitting the garnishes."

"But . . . these dishes are so expensive. Why can't I make herring and kugel for the Sisterhood luncheon, and donate the rest of the money to the congregation?"

Miss Levy smiled. "If this was truly your budget and your luncheon, then of course you could do so, if you wished. For the purpose of this exercise, though, you've decided differently." She paused. "But I commend you for the question, Kreindel. You have the mind of a scholar."

Startled by the compliment, Kreindel felt herself blush. "Thank you," she murmured.

"I took the opportunity to speak with your Hebrew teachers, and they told me how proficient you are. Your father was a rabbi, I believe?"

She nodded.

"And he raised you on his own?"

"Our neighbors looked after me, when I was little. Then I looked after myself." She couldn't keep from adding: "And I taught myself to cook, too. Cabbage and potatoes, mostly. Chicken livers, if I could get them cheap enough." She smiled a bit, remembering. "My father called them yeshiva meals, because it was the sort of food he ate when he was a student."

"You took on quite a burden, for a young girl," said Miss Levy.

Kreindel shrugged. "Not really. It wasn't hard."

"Perhaps not the work itself. But you made yourself responsible for your father's welfare, at an age when most children must be goaded into their chores."

She blushed again, embarrassed and gratified. "I just wanted to help him," she murmured.

"You must have loved him very much."

Unexpected tears gathered in Kreindel's eyes. How long had she been waiting for someone, *anyone*, to say these things to her? She gazed up at the woman in her starched white jacket—and suddenly she was in a tenement hallway again, watching the settlement ladies in their white dresses, with their baskets of milk and eggs. *Better to starve*, her father said in her ear, *than to accept the worm that dangles on their hook.*

Her teacher's eyes widened—and for a panicked moment Kreindel worried that she'd said her thought aloud.

"Miss Levy?" A girl at the island raised a pleading hand. "My filling don't look right."

The woman excused herself and left Kreindel's side, and Kreindel forced her attention back to her assignment. Before too long she'd put together the week's meals, and the luncheon besides. She hadn't thought cooking classes would require so much arithmetic, but she supposed she could see the point of it.

She left the assignment on the desk and joined the rest of the class at the island just as Miss Levy said, "And now, the finished product. I took the liberty of baking a few in advance, so we'd have enough time to taste them."

Out of the refrigerator came three perfect pies, one by one. The girls gazed at them in open-mouthed ecstasy. The meringues had been piped in concentric circles atop the filling; they gleamed softly, each dollop of white touched with golden brown at its edges. The girls gathered closer as their teacher cut the pies into even slices, dipping the knife briefly in water between each stroke so that the meringues separated as neatly as clouds. Each girl took a slice of pie and stared in reverence at the gleaming peaks, the sunny yellow filling, the flaking crust. "It's too pretty to eat," one whispered.

"Nonsense," their teacher said with a smile. "It's meant to be eaten. So, please do."

They took their first bites, sighing in blissful appreciation—all except for Kreindel, who stared down at her plate. She'd have to say the proper blessing first.

The rest of the room had gone quiet. She looked up at a ring of smirking, expectant faces. They were all waiting for her to say the blessing. To make a spectacle of herself.

Slowly, deliberately, Kreindel pushed the pie away. The plate scraped harshly upon the countertop. For a moment no one said a word. Then, "You dummy," Sarah Rosen muttered next to her, "it ain't even *treyf.*"

Snickers all around. Kreindel felt herself turn hot. Had anyone ever teased her in class before? In the dining hall, yes, they chortled behind their hands—but never in a classroom. Would Miss Levy step in and reprimand her acolytes? But their instructor was silent, her face unreadable.

The bell rang, but no one moved. At last Miss Levy seemed to rouse herself. "Miss Altschul," she said, "a word, please, before you leave." And she set to work carrying the dirty dishes and measuring bowls to the sink in the corner.

The others hid their smug smiles as they hung their whites away and filed into the hall. Kreindel waited until they'd all left, not wanting an audience for whatever might happen next. When at last they were alone, she approached her teacher at the sink. "Yes, Miss Levy?"

"I apologize," the woman said. "I didn't realize your predicament. In the future, you may be excused into the hallway to say the blessing in private. Would that be suitable?"

No, it wouldn't, Kreindel thought. To slink off and say a furtive prayer out of others' sight, as though it were a shameful act—how was that suitable? But then, Miss Levy didn't have to make the offer at all. By the Asylum's standards, she was being exceedingly generous.

"I suppose," she muttered. At least it was better than everyone watching her.

"Thank you, Kreindel," Miss Levy said. "You're dismissed."

Kreindel went to her peg and took off the white jacket and cap and hung them away, resisting the petulant urge to wad them in a ball and throw them into a corner. Hot tears pricked at her eyes—but she wouldn't let them fall; she *wouldn't*. She turned inward, and pictured him there in his alcove, finding her resolve in his strength, his patience. Her constant companion, her beloved Yossele.

A sudden shattering of glass.

She jumped, startled. Miss Levy stood over the sink, head down, bracing herself against the porcelain.

"Miss Levy?" she said. "Are you all right?"

"Yes! A bowl slipped from my hand. That's all." The woman turned and gave her an apologetic smile. "Clumsy of me."

"Can I help—"

"No! No, don't risk cutting yourself. I'm going to fetch a pair of rubber gloves. Please, go now. You don't want to be late." And with that, Miss Levy strode from the room.

Sophia . . . Winston.

The desk-clerk at the Hotel Earle had been mulling it over all day long. The woman in 812 had reserved her room under the name Sophia Williams; the Western Union boy had said Williams, too. But the clerk had distinctly heard her say *Winston* that morning, when she'd called down to say she oughtn't be disturbed.

Of course, it wasn't unusual for a guest at the Earle to stay under an assumed name. No one gave a hoot in hell about it, so long as they didn't cause trouble and paid their bills in full. But the desk-clerk had a sweetheart, Maisie—and Maisie was a nut for the *Titanic*. She knew everything about the sinking, and even owned a box full of keepsakes: newspapers, sheet music, books of commemorative verse, a cheap lace fan that she said was just like Madeleine Astor's. But Maisie's most ardent obsession was reserved for George Winston, *the gallant young heir*, as the songs had called him. Maisie had discovered that she and George had been born a day apart, which to her suggested a mystical connection of some kind, or even a thwarted romance—never mind that George Winston had sprung from a millionaire's loins, while Maisie's father was a steamfitter with the Local 638.

But what the clerk remembered now was something Maisie had told him about George Winston's sister Sophia, and how she'd vanished years before the sinking. *She used to be in the society pages, but then she went overseas and never came back. She ain't even mentioned in the obituaries. It's a mystery to this day.* He'd snorted at this, sore at Maisie for mooning over a dead boy. *Probably ran off with a traveling salesman*, he'd said. *Some mystery.*

Now the clerk turned the register around and squinted again at the woman's signature. Williams, Winston: it might've been either. She'd cabled from Egypt to reserve the room, which certainly counted as overseas. And the high-handed tone she'd used on the telephone that morning had been exactly how he'd imagined a Fifth Avenue heiress to sound.

He went to the back office, opened the city directory, and found the number for the *New York Herald*.

18.

"Will you tell me your name?"

He was lying upon the forge, stretched his full length, the coals whispering in his ears. She hovered over him, facing him, all but touching. Flames below him, flames above. He didn't think he'd ever been so deliriously happy.

—*I don't have a name,* she said. *Not anymore.*

"You were banished," he said, remembering.

—*Yes.*

"And I can't tell you my own name, either."

—*Then we'll be nameless together,* she said, smiling.

He grinned back. Again he wanted to ask, *Is this truly happening?* How had everything changed in a single moment? And yet—wasn't that how jinn lived their lives? A sudden encounter, an impulse acted upon, and all was new again. He'd merely forgotten.

She turned slightly in the air, gazing up at the steel above them.—*Jinni,* she said, *what is this place?*

"It's my home," he said. "I built it."

A hint of doubt touched her features.—*But . . . why?*

"To pass the time. And to prove to myself that I could."

He felt her shudder slightly.—*I don't understand. To touch all that iron . . .*

"It doesn't hurt me."

—*I know that. Still, it feels . . .*

He smiled. "Obscene?"

—*Yes.*

"I've worked with iron for years. A metalsmith released me from the flask by accident, and I needed a skill to survive. It was a convenient choice."

—But—why do you say you needed a skill to survive? Even bound as you are, you're more powerful than any of them.

It was a simple question, asked in a language that tugged at his deepest instincts. Why *had* he chosen to be a metalsmith, to hide his nature behind something that his own kind counted as obscenity? "I didn't feel powerful at the time," he said. "A thousand years had passed. I had no idea where I was, and I couldn't remember what had happened to me. I was . . . afraid."

—So they took advantage of your fear, she said, as though finishing the story for him.

Had that been the case? He, not Arbeely, had been the one to propose a partnership—but the man had quickly agreed, and grown rich in the bargain. And the Golem, too, had encouraged his hiding. They had influenced him, the both of them.

He shook his head, the coals rustling at his scalp. He wanted to justify his choices to her, but he sensed that any attempt at an explanation would only turn into a litany of his own weaknesses. Why *had* he tied himself so strongly to Arbeely, and put himself at the man's service?

Because Arbeely was kind to me, he thought distantly.

As though bored with his silence, the jinniyeh pulled away from him and began to float about the remnants of the workshop. He propped his elbows on the coals, watching as she examined the anvil and hammer, the racks of tools with their wooden handles. "Careful," he called, as she drifted toward the forge's exhaust hood. "You'll end up on the roof."

She shot him a surprised look, then peered up inside the hood.—*Would it hurt me?*

"I doubt it—but you'd come out filthier than a ghul in spring." He grinned.

She laughed—the sound was like sunlight—and moved on, studying the hose that was fastened to the wall.

"That *would* hurt you," he told her. "It goes up to the water tower."

She backed away as though it might snap at her.—*Is that the smaller building, on top of this one?*

He nodded. "It's a reservoir."

—Why do you need such a thing? Is it for defense?

"No, it came with the Amherst."

—*What is an . . . Amherst?*

The sound of the word made him smile. "This building is the Amherst. I wasn't the one who named it."

She made a derisive sound.—*They name their boxes as well as number them?*

He raised an eyebrow. "'Boxes'?"

—*Yes, the boxes they so adore. They live in them, they put things inside them, they would turn the entire world into walls and corners if they could. I am heartily sick of boxes.*

He thought of his river-pebble model. "I feel the same. It's part of why I built this." He gestured upward, at his work. "To show that there's another way."

—*But it's still inside a box,* she said, dubious.

"That's true." He didn't want to think about it, though, didn't want to argue or scrutinize. He only wanted to be happy in her presence.

She floated back and settled above him, warm and beautiful. He reached up, and flames caressed his fingers.

—*Shall I tell you a story?* she whispered.

"I would like that."

—*An old story, or a new one?*

He smiled. "Will you tell me of the iron-bound jinni?"

—*Oh, but there are many versions of that story.*

"Then tell me all of them."

She laughed in approval.—*Of course. And afterward—if we cannot think of anything else that might occupy us—*

Another caress; the Amherst blurred above him—

—*you can tell me which one comes closest to the truth.*

Toby stood on the corner of Allen and Delancey, peering into the Radzin's Bakery window.

He'd never been inside Radzin's, not even once. His ma had always made a point of hurrying past it on errand days, her eyes dark with the grudge she still carried. Just to be here at all felt like a sin and a betrayal. Even knowing his ma was at the laundry, he found himself checking over his shoulder—but then, he'd been checking over his shoulder all day, thanks to his trip to the Hotel Earle. The memory of that room made his skin crawl; it had dogged him through his rounds, turning his smile nervous and false, cutting his usual tips in half. In a different life, he might've come home and said, *Ma, I delivered a telegram at the Hotel Earle and I think the place is haunted!* But he hadn't said a word to her about the hotel, or the man in Little Syria, or any of it. She would only tell him it was all nonsense, a hard edge of fear in her voice.

The pieces were gathering in his hands, one by one. The Syrian boy who'd spoken of Missus Chava like a sailor who'd glimpsed a mermaid. Her former lover, now holed up in an empty building, drawn staggering out into the sunlight by the lure of a Yiddish curse. The phantom presence at the Hotel Earle. His own mother rushing to slam the hallway door. His missing father. The grinning man in his dreams. Taken together, they pointed to something that he could neither see nor name but whose presence he'd felt his entire life, something that lay beyond the reasoned world and shadowed his life with its cobweb traces. And if he stopped looking for it now, he'd lose his chance to learn the truth. So he'd come to Radzin's, to the beginning of the story, to find out whatever he could.

He went inside and joined the long line that snaked back and forth inside the shop. It was a Friday afternoon, and everyone wanted a challah for the Sabbath; the refrain *With raisins or without?* rose from the girls at every register. The line moved quickly even so, and before long he reached the counter. The girl on the other side looked to be maybe two or three years older than himself. Going by her placid expression, she was long accustomed to these busy Friday afternoons. "A dozen cookies, please," he told her.

"What kind?"

"Huh. I don't know." He squinted at the gleaming glass, the endless stretch of trays. "Which ones do *you* like?"

She pursed her lips. "The hamantaschen ain't bad," she allowed.

"Then I'll have four of the poppy-seed ones, and two tea cookies"—he was pointing more or less at random—"And two of those almond maca-roons, and a couple of rugelach."

"That's ten," she said. "You got two left."

"Uh, two more tea cookies." He was beginning to wonder what he'd do with it all.

The girl pulled a bakery box from a stack by the register and started gathering his order. "Say, my ma used to work here," he said, as though he'd just remembered the fact himself. "Anna Blumberg?"

The girl frowned as she bent for the macaroons. "Never heard of her."

"Never heard of who, dear?" A middle-aged woman had appeared next to the girl, carrying a tray of walnut streusel and a near-palpable air of entitled presumption. This, Toby assumed, could only be Thea Radzin.

"Lady named Anna Blumberg," the girl told her.

Thea's eyes darkened at once. "Anna? That girl hasn't worked for us in years." She peered at Toby. "Is she in trouble again? Never learns, that one."

Toby felt himself go red.

"That's her son," said the girl, nodding at him.

Thea's face went slack with shock. She stared at him. "No," she said, "that can't be right, you're simply too old—that would've been, let's see—"

"Fifteen years ago," he said, forcing himself to smile.

The woman recovered quickly. "Fifteen *years*! Is it so long as that? My goodness, I'll be an old woman soon. Well, and how *is* your mother?"

She's exhausted. She nearly died. "She's well," he said. "She works at a laundry, she's in charge of a dozen girls."

"A laundry, really!" There was a bright, false note in Mrs. Radzin's tone that made him picture her telling the story to her friends. *She's still a washerwoman, after all these years. Yes, I heard it from the boy himself.*

A customer behind him shuffled impatiently. Toby said, "I was won-dering about a friend of hers who used to work here. Chava Levy?"

"Oh, yes!" The name kindled a new light of reverence in the woman's face. "Chava was the best baker we ever had. Why, she could braid a challah twice as fast as any of *these* girls—"

The girl tying Toby's box of cookies paused to glare at her.

"—but she left us in, let's see, that must have been in '08, after we expanded the store. We were devastated, we begged her to stay—but she went off to college, and I can't blame her. *Such* a smart girl."

Toby pounced upon the new information. "Do you know which college?"

"Of course I do! It was Teachers College—that's up at Columbia, of course—for their Domestic Sciences program." She spoke with such pride that Missus Chava might've been her own daughter. "But she must have graduated by now. We heard from her last in . . . Do you know, I'm not certain. So hard to keep track, with all the comings and goings." She sighed, but then said, "Wait here. I'll show you something."

She went to the far wall, lifted a framed photograph from its nail, and presented it for his inspection. It had been taken on the sidewalk outside; the year *1901* was penciled in a corner. Standing by the bakery window were a younger version of Thea and her husband, a boy and a girl who must have been their own children, and three women, one of whom was—

"There's Chava," Mrs. Radzin said, pointing at the woman who stood slightly hunched, as though embarrassed to have her picture taken. She was exactly the same as Toby remembered, not a line of her face different.

Nineteen-oh-one, he read again. His brow furrowed in confusion. If anyone had asked, he would've said that Missus Chava was younger than his mother—and yet . . .

Someone behind him coughed in protest. The girl handed him his box of cookies—and Mrs. Radzin, in a display of the blithe effrontery for which she'd grown so famous, told Toby to give his mother her best regards.

The Asylum hallways seethed with children rushing for the synagogue, their thoughts flying past Miss Levy as she navigated a hasty path to the side door.

I can't be late again, the monitor'll smack me . . .
I'm so hungry, why do they make us sit through services . . .
Wouldn't it be wonderful if the rabbi skipped the sermon . . .

Yossele, the girl had called him. Her father, the rabbi, must have built him. She thought of Kreindel's stubborn will, her clear refusal to change an iota of herself to suit the Asylum's conventions. *She'd have to move on from her father's way of thinking,* Miss Franck had said—but why would she, when her father had given Kreindel her only friend and companion?

"Charlotte, *there* you are. Do you have a moment?" It was the headmistress, cutting off her escape. She drew Miss Levy to one side of the hallway and said, "I was wondering how Miss Altschul handled her first few days of Culinary Science. I know that it was a rather abrupt transition."

With effort Miss Levy corralled her panicked thoughts into a reasonable answer. "To tell the truth, it hasn't been quite what I'd expected. Although, as you said, she's a very smart and determined young woman."

"She is indeed," the headmistress said wryly.

"I'm afraid that I haven't impressed her yet, but I'm hopeful that we can reach an understanding." Would that be enough for the headmistress? The children had filled the nearby synagogue, and the combined weight of their bored and hungry minds was an unwelcome pressure, like a sick headache.

"I know you'll do your best, Charlotte. But don't be surprised if she never warms to you. The girl is bound and determined to spite us all." The woman sighed, then eyed Miss Levy. "Have you heard how she arrived here?"

"I know that she's a true orphan," Miss Levy said cautiously, "and that her father was a rabbi."

"Yes, in a very traditional mold. She came to us in '08 when their tenement burned, an awful tragedy. Kreindel herself barely made it out alive. Her father led a congregation on Forsyth, across from their building. I don't think Kreindel ever left that street for the first eight years of her—Charlotte? Is something the matter?"

"No," she said faintly, "only a bit of a headache. Well. I'll try to do my best with the girl."

"That's all that any of us can do. Oh—I nearly forgot, I'd like to look over the basement storage room with you next week. As early as possible, considering the state of the place. Would Monday afternoon be suitable, after your classes?"

What ought she to say? What commitments might she have on a Monday afternoon that would keep her from accepting? In the moment, she could think of none. "Yes, that'll do," she said.

"Then I'll put it in the calendar. But for now, if you don't mind me saying so, you ought to go home and put your feet up. You look a little done in."

The jinniyeh watched her lover dress himself.

It wasn't much in the way of clothing, only the trousers and the leather apron. Fewer garments than the Bedu wore, and certainly fewer than Sophia, with her endless layers—but it still made her uneasy. Why did he wear anything at all?

He noticed her gaze, an obvious question in itself. "Habit, I suppose," he said with a shrug. "The apron pocket comes in han—" He paused. "—is useful, sometimes."

She smiled, though the answer made her feel no better. For a little while, lust had removed her doubts, but now she felt them creeping back again. Hiding, it was clear, had damaged his spirit; she sensed she must be careful not to ask too many judging questions, or pressure him to change his ways all at once. She remembered how weak she'd grown in her cave, how she'd come alive again once she'd left it behind. The same would happen to him; she only needed patience.

She looked up at the faraway ceiling, the iron that spread outward from the central trunk like a sinister wave.—*Those arches*, she said. *Did they come with the building, like the water tower?*

"No, I added them," he said.

—*Oh.*

"They hold up the roof, but they're also meant as decoration. I'm fitting them with glass, but it's slow going."

He pointed to an arch in the corner, and she saw the squares of opaque blue glass. It looked as though he'd trapped a portion of the sky and dragged it indoors. She suppressed a shudder.—*Is it . . . difficult?*

"Extremely. I've had poor luck with glass-making. And yesterday, I lost nearly four days of—" He paused, frowning in thought, and then said, "Jinniyeh, did you send me a cable, by chance? A message," he said to her confused look, "sent over a long distance, and then delivered on a piece of paper."

She tried to think. Was this something Sophia had done? The woman had told her nothing about a message. And if she said yes, she might become trapped in the lie.—*No, jinni. I sent no message, I only came myself.*

He nodded, a frown still on his forehead.

—*Tell me more about this glass,* she said.

He seemed to brighten at her interest. "I have to form it one sheet at a time, in an iron mold—here, I'll show you."

She followed him to a corner of the shop, where a large quantity of blue rocks lay heaped beside a large, shallow iron trough. She took human form and picked up one of the rocks, turning it over in her hands while he explained to her where it had come from, using words like *smelt* and *slag* and *by-product*. A distant corner of her mind whispered, *This is unnatural.* She ignored it. She, too, was unnatural. She would try to understand.

"But it's difficult to lift the pane from the mold without breaking it," he was saying. "I need to find some way to convince it to lift free, to float—" He stopped suddenly, his mouth half open.

She peered at him, uncertain. "Jinni?"

"*Float* it," he said—and abruptly he turned from her and strode away, toward a row of wooden boxes that sat the corner of the shop, doors hinged to their fronts. He opened them all, rummaged quickly through their contents. "Did I keep any—I could order more—no, all the catalogs are gone—yes, *here!*"

He extracted a large crate, and set it upon the floor. Inside were stacks of long metal bricks that gleamed a strange silver-white. She reached inside and picked one up—and at once her hand grew unpleasantly slick. She dropped the brick, and frowned at the grayish smears on her fingers.

"It won't hurt you," he told her. "It's only tin. Metal, not water."

"I know enough to hide from the rain," she snapped.

"Of course. I apologize. I'm only excited, this problem has been plaguing me for days—" He dug into a drawer and found a set of gloves—leather, like the apron—then filled the shallow iron trough with the silver bricks and lifted it above the forge. At once they began to slump and melt; within moments they were entirely liquid. He set it back on the floor and crouched over it, staring intently. "The glass is lighter than the tin, it should float on top—Arbeely, can you hand me a—"

His voice stopped.

She stood there, not knowing what to do. He'd gone still; she couldn't see his face. "Jinni?" she said, her voice small in the echoing space.

Slowly he sat back, away from the melted tin, his head in his hands. "Why am I doing this?" he muttered.

She crouched down next to him, gently lifted his face to look at her. "Because you've been alone among them for far too long," she told him. "But that's over now. Come back with me."

His eyes were glazed with confusion. "Back—where?"

"The Cursed City." A spasm of fear passed across his face, and she said, "No, remember, there is nothing to be afraid of. It's my own habitation now, and it can be yours, too."

He seemed to hear this. "But—what would I do there?"

"Explore. Lie with me. Whatever you wish."

He took this in, then looked up at the spiraling steel above them, the tree and its many moons. "I wished for this, for so long," he said.

Did he mean her offer, or his own metal creation? She didn't want to ask. Outside, the sunlight was nearly gone. Perhaps it was best to give him time. She said, "I'll go away, for a little while, so you may consider it."

He looked puzzled. "Where will you go?"

"The arch, the one that the healer spoke of. It feels a little like home, to me."

He nodded. "More so than here, I suppose."

She smiled at that, but said only, "I'll return tomorrow." Then she changed and flew up, watching as he diminished, and was gone again.

In their apartment above the coffee-house, Maryam spooned helpings of fattoush and mujaddara onto Sayeed's plate. Then she sat at the table, clasped her hands together, and asked the Father, Son, and Holy Spirit to bless their meal. For a few minutes they ate in heavy silence.

"I can go to Sam's tomorrow," Sayeed said at last. "I'll talk with him. Ask him not to spread rumors."

Maryam had no appetite; she'd done little more than push the food about with a fork, and was hoping Sayeed wouldn't notice. "Perhaps we should let it happen," she said. "Everyone will disagree on what ought to be done about him. Maybe they'll tire themselves out with talking, and move on to something else."

Sayeed shook his head in clear doubt—and in her heart she doubted it too. Perhaps she'd only made matters worse, in the end. Her neighbors' curiosity had been bottled for far too long. Now it would be unleashed— and what might he unleash in return? She thought of the patch in the alley, and shivered.

"Maryam?"

The room swam for a moment; she shivered again, suddenly chilled. Sayeed put a hand to her forehead and frowned; she realized that she was sweating. "You must go to bed, beloved," he said firmly. "No, leave the dishes, I'll do them."

She allowed him to shepherd her to the bedroom, fighting dizziness. "I don't think you're going to Mass in the morning," Sayeed told her.

Her head touched the pillow, and at once her fatigue began to swallow her. "I told Father Stephen I'd lead the rosary," she murmured as Sayeed turned down the lamp.

"I'll explain to Father Stephen."

What a nuisance, to be ill at such a time, she thought—and then, she was asleep.

Anna returned from her suffrage meeting that night to find the light burning in their apartment window.

That's strange, she thought. Toby was usually out at this hour, on one of his joy-rides. Sometimes she wanted to curse the day she'd ever let the Golem buy him that bicycle. She limped slowly up the stairs and opened the door.

Toby sat at the kitchen table, occupied with his gears and parts and polish. He'd spread a cloth over the table first, she saw. And he'd picked up his clothing from the parlor floor, too.

"Hi, Ma," he said, without looking up.

Anna hung up her coat and looked around. A pot full of beefsteak tomato soup sat upon the kitchen stove. Steam rose from the teapot on its trivet. At her usual spot at the table lay a plate of sardines on toast, a bowl of the soup, a cup and saucer, and her latest issue of *The Woman Voter.* The kitchen smelled delicious: fish and toast and tomatoes, and something else, something sweet.

Warily she eyed the tableau. "All right, boychik. What's going on?"

"Nothing, Ma."

"Did you break something? Did Julius fire you?"

"No!" His face reddened. "I just thought it would be nice for you, that's all. Honest to God."

Anna looked at the supper, and then at her son, who still wouldn't meet her eyes. She could interrogate him, extract the secret from him, whatever it was. Or, just this once, she could leave him alone.

She went to the cabinet above the sink—the sweet smell was stronger, here—and found her bottle of schnapps. She poured a healthy splash into the waiting teacup, and topped it with tea. Then she fetched another cup and saucer, poured more tea, and carried the two brimming cups to the table. She set his cup among his things, then sat down across from him, opened the magazine, and took a bite of the toast. Toby hesitated a moment, then took his own deliberate sip and went back to work, dotting the length of the bicycle chain with something out of a metal syringe. He could've been a doctor, Anna thought, watching him. Or a scientist, in a laboratory. Her eyes caught on the dark mist of stubble on his jawline, and she realized with a start that he'd begun shaving in earnest. When had that happened? How had she missed it?

"Toby," she said.

He looked up. "Yeah, Ma?"

"You're careful out there, aren't you?"

He peered at her, and then said, "Yeah, Ma. I am."

"Good." She took a long sip of tea, swallowing hard past the lump in her throat.

For an hour they sat at the table together, while she ate and he worked. At last she stood, washed her dishes, and said, "Thank you for the supper, boychik. I'm off to bed. Good night."

"Good night, Ma."

She went to the bedroom, changed into her nightgown, and turned out the light, then sat waiting in the dark until Toby had rolled out his pallet. She cracked open her door, listened to his light snores—and then carefully crept to the kitchen and removed the trash-can from beneath the sink. The sweet smell grew as she opened the lid, but she saw only the usual remnants: soup cans, wet tea-leaves and greasy butcher paper, the slimy eyes of potatoes. Wincing, she reached into the can, down past the scraps, until her hand found something large and sharp-cornered.

Slowly she unearthed it. It was a bakery box, deeply dented to fit inside the can. Inside were tea cookies and macaroons and hamantaschen—a full dozen by the look of it, all mashed and broken from the rough treatment. The box bore no name or stamp, but Anna still knew a cookie from Radzin's when she smelled it. She broke off a corner of a hamantaschen and tasted it, to remove any doubt. It was Radzin's, all right. Thea always put too much lemon zest in the dough.

She replaced the box, heaped the peelings over it again, and went

back to bed, wondering what had compelled her son to visit Radzin's—
and what, exactly, he'd learned there.

The window at the Hotel Earle was still open.

The jinniyeh flew inside, and surveyed the room. Nothing appeared
to have been disturbed: there was the woman's trunk and its spilled
contents, and the cold metal teapot upon the desk. And Sophia, asleep in
the bed, sunk inside the dream the jinniyeh had made for her.

The jinniyeh eyed the woman, and the smile that touched her
mouth, and felt a stab of jealousy. She gathered herself, and went inside.

*It was a perfectly warm afternoon in Jerusalem, as all the afternoons had been
lately. Sophia and Daniel were strolling together through the Jewish Quarter,
talking of history—when suddenly a naked woman appeared in the middle of
the street.*

*Dima! Sophia called, and waved. We were just going to a café. Will you
join us?*

Thank you, I will, the woman said.

*A waiter led them to a table in a sunny corner of the café, beside a pot-
ted palm. They ordered bread and za'atar, and sliced figs with honey. Sophia
turned to Daniel to ask if he wanted coffee—but where was he? Oh, yes—he
had that meeting, for his charity. She shook her head at herself for forgetting,
then bit into a ripe, honey-drenched fig.*

You seem happy, Dima said.

*Sophia smiled. I am. I think I'm happier now than I've ever been in my
life. Sometimes I think it can't be real. I keep waiting for something bad to happen, for my luck to change. Is that ungrateful of me?*

Perhaps, the woman said.

*Sophia laughed. Oh, I'm talking nonsense. But how are you? The last time
I saw you, you were looking for something—or someone . . . Sophia frowned,
trying to jog the memory loose.*

I found him, Dima said. But he isn't what I expected.

How so? Sophia sat forward, listening.

I thought he would be stronger, Dima said. None of the stories said how changed he would be by his hiding. But then, maybe they thought it was too obvious to mention. Maybe I'm the only one who didn't understand.

Oh, Dima, I'm sorry, Sophia said—but she was unnerved by something in her friend's words, and the bitter tone in her voice. It would help if she could remember who they were talking about, but the name simply refused to come to her.

Dima said, And you misled me, too, though I realize now that you didn't mean to.

Sophia frowned. I misled you? How?

I saw him, in your memories. And he was everything I wanted him to be—because he was everything that you had wanted him to be. I never saw how young you were then, how weak and trusting, the same way that I'd been myself once. And then you nearly destroyed your own mind trying to get rid of me—and I thought, she is only human, yet here is a strong and worthy enemy.

A creeping fear took hold of Sophia. Why was Dima talking like this, when they'd been friends for years? Or—wait. Had they been?

The words came to her as though whispered across an ocean: *Jinn do not have friends. We may be allies, or enemies, or lovers, but not friends.*

Sophia stood from the table. No, none of this was right—not the sunny day, or the ripe figs, or her friend Dima, beautiful and naked in a Jerusalem café. And Daniel—he'd married someone else, she'd seen them walking together in the marketplace . . . She wasn't in Jerusalem at all.

You see? Dima was smiling. You fight me even now.

Let me out, Sophia said. You promised to cure me! You swore by—

Yes, by Mount Qaf, the jinniyeh said. But, Sophia, Mount Qaf is just an old children's story. I never truly believed in it.

The café vanished—

The jinniyeh floated free, and took form. Sophia still lay asleep, but her expression was now deeply troubled. Her shaking, too, had returned.

The jinniyeh smoothed back a lock of the woman's hair that had escaped its braid, and replaced the pin that held it. *And still you fight*, she thought. *I only wish that you had been the one I was searching for.*

In her bed on Washington Street, Maryam Faddoul, too, was dreaming.

She stood upon the pier at Beirut Harbor, where a ship waited to take her to America. Her mother was there, too, but her back was to the sun, and Maryam could barely see her face. In her mother's hand was her parting gift to her daughter. It was an ordinary-looking copper flask, decorated with scroll-work. The air around it shimmered with heat.

Keep it, Mama, Maryam pleaded.

That is cowardice, her mother told her gently.

But I'm so tired, Maryam said. And my fever's returned.

She wondered at her own words—returned?—and then recalled, there in the dream, the story that her mother had told her so many times, of the terrible fever Maryam had suffered as a baby.

Her mother nodded and said, I took you to Jounieh Bay, to the Cave of Saint George, where the spear was washed clean of the dragon's blood. I plunged you into the healing waters, and you were cured. Remember that.

But to what end, Mama? Maryam cried. I am no saint, and he is no monster for me to slay—

She stopped short, and then said again, more slowly, He is no monster.

And you are no saint, said her mother, smiling.

Then what should I do?

You must keep your vigil, her mother said—

And Maryam woke.

The mug of tea on the corner of Charlotte Levy's desk had long since cooled. In the middle of the blotter was a pile of student evaluations, waiting for her attention.

The smoke-filled hallway. The girl ahead of her, somewhere in the darkness. Words cried out, lost in the noise of the flames. The feeling of something coming to life nearby, something waking.

She shook herself. Those were someone else's memories. She was Charlotte Levy, a cooking teacher at the Asylum for Orphaned Hebrews. Her students adored her, and she improved their lives daily, in little ways. She taught them to read recipes, clarify broths, separate eggs. She kept a predictable and ordinary life, and she had never once been late with her student evaluations.

She removed the first paper in the stack, picked up her pen.

Miss Bernstein has made considerable progress this semester. She is still easily distractible, but I am convinced she is trying her best. More to the point, she has been, so far as I can tell, completely truthful with me since last term's unfortanate

She frowned at the misspelling.

~~unfortanate~~ unfortunate incident, and I suspect the lesson has been lea

Her hand twitched, too tense on the pen—and the *a* grew an ugly and elongated tail.

"*Porca miseria!*" she growled—and then, horrified at herself, tossed the pen on the desk and pressed her hands to her eyes, pushing back against the memories. Why should it matter if Chava Levy had chased a girl into a burning tenement, or felt a golem come to life? What difference could it make when the bare facts were still the same? He was a threat to the children, regardless of his master's attachment to him. And if she ignored the danger—if she allowed it to continue—it would be her own fault if the worst happened.

Nothing had changed. She had to destroy him.

19.

I could go home.

The Jinni lifted a heavy pane of glass from the molten tin. To his genuine astonishment, his idea had worked, and not a single pane had broken since. Even so, it was still a delicate operation; he had to stand the panes on end to wipe the tin away, a nerve-racking process in itself. Already he'd begun to imagine a moving bath of some sort, the glass poured atop it at one end and then cooling as it went. Perhaps he could convert the forge, somehow . . .

Or, he thought again, *I could go home.*

But what would that mean, exactly? His memories of the desert were from a different life entirely. The jinniyeh seemed to think it would be easy for him—yet could he truly live there as her *iron-bound jinni?* Walking among the Cursed City's columns instead of flying high above, avoiding the Bedu for fear that they'd think him one of their own?

The Cursed City, the fabled land of monsters. It had a certain defiant appeal, he supposed. Would it only be the two of them? Perhaps there were others who would come and join them, if only they knew. He let himself imagine it: a city of outcasts, united in exile. Would it be enough to hold them together, or would they tear themselves apart in squabbling? How long could it possibly last? Already he sensed that the jinniyeh only barely tolerated him, that he'd have to change himself to suit her. But then, perhaps she was right about him. Perhaps he'd strayed too far from his nature, gone beyond mere difference, and into perversion, obscenity.

He stood the pane on its end, steadied it with a careful hand while he wiped away the streaks of tin. What about the Amherst? What would happen to it, if he left? He'd only just solved the problem of the glass, and there were still so many panes to make . . . In his old life, he'd have thought nothing of abandoning such an undertaking, usually at the moment it grew too demanding to hold his interest. Now, he balked at the notion. Perhaps he could ask the jinniyeh to wait here, with him, until the Amherst was done—but—

Something's missing. The thought prickled at him like fog. He'd forgotten something, it was staring him in the face, and he couldn't even see it—

Chava would know. The thought rose unbidden, but at once he knew it was correct. She would take one look at his imperfect creation, and she'd know. And if he left, if he went to the desert, he'd never see her again . . .

The world swayed suddenly; he closed his eyes.

You said we weren't good for each other, she told him as they fell from the roof together. *Was that a lie?*

No. A pause. *Perhaps. I don't know.*

You wanted to hurt me, she said.

Yes.

So I would hurt you back. So I'd be the one to end it.

Something was always bound to end us, Chava. Another burning building, perhaps.

She shook her head. *That's cowardice, Ahmad.*

It doesn't matter. I broke the promise we made.

He waited for her anger, but she only glanced sideways as the Amherst's windows flashed by, taking in the arches, the platforms. *It's nearly perfect,* she said. *There's just one thing missing.*

He frowned. *What is it?*

She said nothing, only smiled. The alley reached up to them, gathering them close—

The pane slipped from his hands.

It was long past midnight when a sleepless Maryam Faddoul rose from her bed, buttoned her coat over her nightgown, and walked up Washington Street to the Amherst.

Never in her life had Maryam been out alone this late, on an empty street. Nervously she glanced around the shuttered storefronts and curtained bedroom windows, feeling as though the entire neighborhood were staring at her. And in truth, she didn't even know what she meant to do at the Amherst. She only knew that she had to go there.

As always, the Amherst's paper-covered windows made her want to shudder, as though the building itself had been blinded. She considered knocking on the door, but then decided against it. She didn't want to confront the man, or berate him. Whatever instinct had brought her here, it wanted something else.

She stood in the doorway for a moment, feeling awkward and unsure, and then sat down in the corner, with the door beside her and her back to the wall. Hopefully anyone who noticed her there would mistake her for a vagrant. It was more comfortable than she'd expected—and considerably warmer, too, the sort of heat that brought to mind sleepless summer nights, and bricks that had baked for hours in the sun. Could it be from the forge?

The hinged brass door to the letterbox was only a few inches from her hand. Cautiously she lifted it. Sure enough, she could hear the forge nearby, its strange, voice-like murmur. The air, too, seemed a good deal warmer inside than out.

Then, from the depths, there came a man's strangled curse—
Crash.

A fusillade of breaking glass; the skittering hiss of shards upon the floor. A deep groan, of frustration and anger. A long pause. Then, footsteps, growing nearer—and he was sitting down next to her on the other side of the door, only inches away, his back against the wall.

Maryam froze, not knowing what to do. She was still holding the letterbox open. If she closed it, he'd likely hear it; if she didn't, it would be a sin.

She heard him rub at his face and let out a long and weary sigh. She began to grow ashamed. It felt wrong, to spy upon him like this. At last she took a deep breath and said, "Ahmad?"

He yelped in surprise and scrambled away. Then he stopped and crouched down, peering at her through the narrow opening. "Maryam," he said. His face darkened with anger. "What do you want?"

"I don't know," Maryam said.

He stared at her, baffled. Then he snorted, stood, and walked away.

She sat there holding the letterbox open, listening to him sweep up the broken glass. "Go away, Maryam," he called.

She smiled at that, but didn't move. A few more minutes passed; then he came back and crouched down again. "I cannot work," he told her with exaggerated patience, "if I know that you're here."

"Why? You worked for years behind these windows, in front of the whole neighborhood."

"That was different. That was before—"

Abruptly he went silent. She peered through the letterbox—she was certain he'd been about to say, *That was before Arbeely died*—and saw him bent in on himself, head in his hands, like someone on the verge of fainting. She was about to ask if he was all right—but then all at once he unfolded, and walked away again.

For perhaps ten minutes there was nothing. Once or twice she thought she heard him muttering to himself, though it might have been only the forge. She leaned her head against the door, one arm outstretched to keep the letterbox from shutting. She wished she had a stick, to prop it open with.

She'd nearly drifted asleep when he spoke next to her ear. "Maryam," he said, his voice a murmur of insinuation. "Does Sayeed know you're here? Ought I to telephone him, and let him know?"

She chuckled. "If you did, he'd suggest that you listen to whatever I had to say, and then he'd hang up and go back to sleep."

"Is he so very trusting, then?"

"This won't work, Ahmad. You can't shame me away from your door."

He made a noise of frustration. "All I want is to be left alone. Is it truly so much to ask?"

"Yes, it is," she told him. "And I'm afraid that you've been left alone for far too long."

A suspicious pause. "What do you mean?"

"The neighborhood is talking about you, Ahmad. You, and the Amherst. They want to know what you're doing in here, alone in an empty building. Soon they'll form committees, and hold meetings, to discuss what ought to be done. And then, they'll come knocking."

A short, angry laugh. "And what business is it of theirs? Of *anyone's*? Did *you* put them up to this?"

"Ahmad, I've spent the last three years keeping Little Syria away from your door."

A surprised silence from the other side.

"But I can't do it anymore," she said. "You're simply too large of a mystery. They've convinced themselves that you're a threat, that anyone who hides from sight as you do must have a reason."

"I'm not *hiding*, Maryam. I'm—" He stopped, and then sighed deeply, and leaned his head back against the wall with a *thump* that reverberated next to her ear. "These committees," he said, his voice weary. "What will they say, in their meetings?"

"They'll make much out of little," she told him. "They'll say that, aside from the briefest of glimpses, no one has seen the Amherst's owner in years. They'll lament that he refuses to rent out the factory floors when so many Syrian businesses are looking to expand. They'll ask why all the windows are papered over when the building is supposedly empty. They'll discuss his character in general, and recall that he once used to walk the rooftops with a strange woman who wasn't his wife."

He snorted, annoyed. "So that's all? I'm to be painted as a scoundrel and a misanthrope?"

"No. There's also Boutros."

"What about him?" The edge in his voice had sharpened.

"They'll question his choice of business partners."

"Sensible enough."

"They'll point out that you weren't seen at his funeral, and that his death made you the sole remaining owner of the Amherst."

She paused, trying to gauge if he understood yet. He was silent, thinking. She went on. "But they might go further than that. We all thought that Boutros had made it through the worst of his illness before it returned. It's possible that some will ask whether his doctors truly tried their utmost—or whether someone gave them a reason not to."

A pause. "Maryam," he said slowly, "are you telling me that I'll be accused of murdering Arbeely?"

She sighed. "I truly don't know. It's happened before. An unscrupulous person whispers a bit of slander, and others repeat it as gossip. Before long, the newspapers report it as 'rumors overheard in the neighborhood.' If I had to guess . . . yes, I'd say it will happen, eventually. People are frightened, and they want a distraction."

"Frightened—of what?"

"Of the war." Then, at his silence: "Do you know about it?"

"No. Not really. Tell me, please."

"All of Europe is in flames. And it's spreading outward. Every day, it seems, some new country joins the fighting. America hasn't declared yet, but few doubt that it'll happen. And back home, in Lebanon, the fields are stripped bare, and everything goes to the soldiers. The villages are on the edge of famine. Our families . . . Not everyone will survive."

A long pause, as he took this in. "And you can't simply . . . bring them here?"

She shook her head. "It's too dangerous. There's fighting at sea, and the ports are all under blockade. We send money instead, but it doesn't always arrive. So we wait, and we worry, and we look for something else to occupy us."

"Such as myself," he said.

"Do you blame us? For being curious, and afraid? For wondering what exactly you're doing in there?"

"I suppose not," he muttered. Then, "What I'm doing . . . I had an idea, a vision. And I've come so close. But there's something missing, I don't know what . . ." His voice trailed away; he sighed. "I just wanted a home of my own. Something that would last."

They sat there in silence, the door solid between them.

"Ahmad," she said, "have you ever heard of a place called Mount Qaf?"

He turned his head, startled. "You know of it?"

"Yes, the emerald mountain, where the jinn come from." She paused. "Forgive me, but—have you been there?"

He chuckled. "Of course not. It's a story, a legend. Like your garden, of Adam and Eve."

"Oh. What a shame. It always sounded so beautiful."

"Will you tell me what you've heard?"

She thought back. "There was a storyteller in my village who loved to talk about Mount Qaf. He never described it the same way twice. Once he said that it had eight peaks, and that each was home to a different city of jinn. Another time, he said it was possible for us to reach it, but we must walk barefoot for four months, in utter darkness. Oh—and that a fabulous phoenix lived there, but it only laid its eggs on the highest tip of the mountain."

"The *roc*," he muttered, as though in correction.

"Once," she said, "he told us that the earth itself balanced upon the peaks of Mount Qaf, like a plate held on one's fingertips. We asked him how that could be possible, since men have crossed the world and sailed every ocean, and no one has ever seen such a thing. He told us, quite seriously, that it was because Mount Qaf was not only a mountain, but a doorway between two different worlds, one visible and the other hidden. And that to pass through, from one world to the other, was a kind of transformation."

He frowned. "A transformation . . . into what?"

"He left that part unclear."

"How inconsiderate of him."

"Does any of that sound like your own legends?"

"Some of it," he said—but he sounded doubtful, and didn't elaborate.

They fell silent again. Maryam listened to the whisper of the breeze in the street, the rumble of the forge through the letterbox. Nighttime noises came from open windows: coughs and bed-creaks, the groans of water-closet pipes, infants' cries that were quickly hushed. Was this, she wondered, what it was like to be him? Eternally awake among the sleepers, watching from rooftops and doorways? The wall was growing uncomfortable against her back, but she stayed where she was, alert in the quiet.

"We aren't friends now, Maryam," he said at last. "I don't want to be your friend."

She smiled. "And I don't want to be yours. But I don't want to be your enemy, either. I told myself I'd never understand you, so I never tried. I set myself against you, I turned everyone's attention away . . . I thought I was protecting them. I'm ashamed of that now." She sighed. "I'm sorry, Ahmad. I ought to have helped you instead."

"I don't want help," he muttered. "I told you, I just want to be left alone."

"You've tried that. It doesn't seem to be working."

He pondered this, then snorted, half amusement and half acknowledgment.

She said, "Would it be an option, when they come knocking, to simply . . . let them in?"

"No," he said, his voice sharp in the quiet. And then, less forcefully: "No. The door stays closed." There was a heaviness to the words that made her think this was, somehow, not entirely his choice.

She said, "Then you'll need to decide what to do, very soon. It's in your hands. But know that I'm here, too. And I'll help in any way I can."

With that, she stood and brushed the threshold's dust from her clothing, and went home to her bed, where sleep embraced her.

The jinniyeh hovered above the Arch.

She'd resolved not to return to the Amherst until dawn; she wanted to give her lover enough time to contemplate her offer, as well as miss her presence. But the wait was growing tedious, and the wind was damp and uncomfortable. Irritated, she left the Arch and floated about the park, searching for currents more to her liking. The buildings at the perimeter of the square were silent and mostly dark, with a few lit windows here and there. She flew toward one of them, and peered inside to see a man sitting at a table, a bottle at his elbow and an empty glass in his hand. He stared outward at nothing for long moments, then picked up the bottle, filled the glass, and drank. When the glass was empty, he resumed his staring.

She peered into other windows. In one, two men sat together upon a couch, one resting his head upon the other's shoulder. In another, a man was hunched before a boxlike contraption, his fingers dancing over its many round buttons, each one making a *clack* that she could hear through the glass. She watched children sleeping, and in the next room saw a woman who lay awake, tears rolling slowly down her cheeks for no reason that the jinniyeh could discern.

It ought to have been like watching the Bedu in their half-crumbled citadel—and yet it wasn't. In the Cursed City, she might float in and out of their lives and be a nuisance as she liked. Here, the humans were sealed away from her reach. She supposed that if she wanted to, she could find a way inside, and cause trouble—but what would be the point? None of them would shout, *Iron, O unlucky one*, or raise an amulet against her, or set out a ball of wool in hopes of appeasing her. There was no place for her here, not even as their adversary.

Unsettled, she flew upward, away from the windows. Below, the streetlights resolved into lines that stretched down and across, and one wide, bright river that cut through them at an angle. *That must be Broadway*, she thought, remembering Sophia's map—and then felt irritated by her own knowledge, as though the woman had planted the name in her mind to annoy her. But there was little else for her to do—and before long she was following Broadway north. Rooftop spires reached toward her as the wide street drifted westward, crossing avenue after avenue. A huge, unlit space appeared, its straight-edged borders holding back a textured murk. Dimly she picked out trees, hills, paths, water. *Central Park*, she thought. One of Sophia's favorite places. She thought of the Ghouta, with its jinn-eating creatures, and decided to avoid the park for the moment. But it called to mind something else that Sophia had shown her: the box where the woman had once lived, the *mansion*, as she'd called it.

She left Broadway behind and flew to the south-east corner of the park, counting the cross-streets, circumnavigating each building in turn, unsure how she would tell Sophia's from the rest—

There. The balcony with its curving marble balustrade, the twin doors set with glass, the bedroom beyond. All of it exactly as it had been in Sophia's dream.

There were still hours left until dawn. Here, she thought, she might cause enough mischief to pass the time.

Julia Hamilton Winston lay in her bed, wide awake.

This sleeplessness was nothing new. She only slept in brief spells nowadays, with interminable hours between them. *Insomnia often comes with grief*, her doctors had told her when first she'd asked if there was something they could do, something they might give her. Now, though, they seemed to think she ought to be past such things. They spoke of mental hardiness, of learning to soothe and regulate her own mind, as though she merely wasn't giving it the proper effort. *Do emotional fancies tend to dominate your thoughts?* one specialist had asked her. *Do you find yourself susceptible to suggestions?* She'd suggested in return that, should he dare to label her a hysteric, she'd drag him before the Board of Health and have his license revoked. She was still Julia Winston; her grief hadn't sapped her completely.

On this night, though, her unquiet mind was full of more immediate matters. A sympathetic editor at the *New York Herald* had telephoned that afternoon to say that a woman calling herself Sophia Winston had been spotted at a Washington Square hotel. *I can't keep them from printing it if it's true*, he'd warned her. *There's still too much public interest.*

It made her seethe with anger. Once, the Winston name had meant industry, society, influence. Now it only meant *the disaster*. There were no more soirées in the ballroom, no more luncheons for worthy causes. Most of the servants had left, not wanting their own names chained to a sunken ship. Even Francis' corporation no longer bore his name. Without a Winston left to run it, the controlling parties had broken it apart, assigned each piece its own petty ruler. Each of them sent a portion of their annual profits to the family coffers, a burnt offering for the departed gods. And now some dimwitted girl dared to call herself Sophia Winston, and drag the name into scandal! Would anyone have attempted such a thing when Francis was alive?

She turned over in her bed, peered at the clock. *Three thirty.* She turned over again, her mind churning. Locked away in her writing-desk was a stack of Syrian postcards, dozens of them, each one blank save for the address. Many of Julia's sleepless nights were spent trying to imagine the life behind those silent messages: where Sophia was and whose company she kept, what she'd done in order to survive.

She won't come back while I'm still alive, Julia told herself. *She'd rather starve than be my daughter again.*

There was a noise in the dark.

Julia sat up. The heavy curtains let in only a little street-light; but at the far end of the room she could see a figure, a woman, standing in shadow.

"Sophia?" she said, ridiculously.

The figure vanished. It had been there; now it was gone. Julia was certain she hadn't blinked. She switched on the bedside lamp, saw only her room. Everything was as it should be.

She turned the lamp off again, lay back down, thought of Francis and the man in the fireplace. *Do you find yourself susceptible to suggestions?* Not long after the disaster, one of Julia's friends had suggested that she hold a séance, so she might talk with Francis and George again. Julia hadn't spoken to the woman since.

She lay in the dark. She turned over. Her eyes slowly closed.

Julia was in the ballroom, where the dead had gathered.

All of them were there, fifteen hundred and more, their faces blue and frost-rimed. Sea-water drenched their gowns and dinner-jackets. They stood, they talked; a few danced. Julia walked among them, forcing herself to smile, trying to remember whether she'd invited them, or whether they'd simply arrived. Sophia—where was Sophia?

She caught a flash of a wine-red gown amid the finery. Her daughter was dancing with a man, tall and dark-haired, dressed only in a ragged pair of trousers and a tradesman's leather apron. Julia recognized him at once. As she watched, he gathered Sophia close, and whispered into her ear; his eyes cut to Julia as he spoke. Sophia smiled, and turned her face to his.

Julia, furious, tried to push through the crowd—but the dead were too cold to touch, and they gathered around her, chilling her through; she was shaking, she would never be warm again—

Go away! she shrieked.

The dead vanished; the room changed. She was in a bedroom—no, a hotel room. Behind her, sheer curtains billowed in a breeze from a half-open window. Sophia trembled upon the bed, her face contorted. The man was bent over her as though examining her. He straightened and became a woman, naked, with long, dark hair.

What have you done to her? Julia cried.

The woman only smiled—

Julia woke, her head pounding. She sat up, one trembling hand to her mouth, wondering if she was about to be ill. A warm breeze trailed across her skin—and then it was gone.

In her coat and hat Charlotte Levy hurried the half block to the gate on 136th.

The night was cool and windy, the Asylum a weight of dreaming minds. She felt ahead for patrolmen, or runaways looking to jump the fence, but all was quiet. She unlocked the gate and slipped through, walked the path to the stairwell. The dark of the basement greeted her. At the end of the south wing, she placed a hand on the doorknob—*You are Charlotte Levy,* she told herself, *do not forget*—and turned it sharply to the left.

Yossele sat in his alcove, slowly examining each of the day's revelations while Kreindel dreamt above him.

Miss Levy was a cooking instructor. Miss Levy was a golem, too. His master didn't like her—but his master didn't know what she was. He, Yossele, was separate from Kreindel. He, not Kreindel, knew the truth of Miss Levy's nature.

These thoughts were large and unwieldy. He tried to hold them all together, so he could see the larger picture they made, but they slipped from his grasp. He didn't know how Miss Levy could be both a cooking teacher *and* a golem. He didn't know why she had left him so suddenly that morning, though he'd recognized her expression as dismay.

He didn't know how Kreindel's knowledge of her could be so incomplete. It felt wrong that he knew, and she didn't.

Distantly, through the maze, came the sound of the doorknob turning.

Yossele came alert. Only now, as the door opened, did he realize that a part of himself had been waiting, hoping that she'd return.

She closed the door behind herself and pulled the locket from around her neck. There was just enough light to read by—she'd be quick, she'd read the words into the air and then forget that anything had ever—

Miss Levy?

The thought, and its hope, pierced her like a spear.

is it Miss Levy?

Her finger shook on the locket's catch. Of course he'd know her name. He saw Kreindel's entire life; he would've seen her, too. She wanted to cry out, to sob. Everything she had was at risk if he lived, she had to do it, she *had* to—but—

Miss Levy?

golem?

But here, in this room, she couldn't pretend. Every buried impulse, every hint of otherness that she'd concealed beneath the polished veneer of *Charlotte Levy*—everything she'd tried so desperately to leave behind—all of it was rushing to the surface. He was the only other golem she'd ever known, and he sat only a few feet away. She wanted to see him again. Suddenly, she *needed* to.

She knew the way now, knew the worst of the obstacles: the thicket of cot-legs, the corner that threatened her shins. It must have been Kreindel who'd carved this path. She pictured the small, determined girl hauling at furniture in a pitch-black room, to make a home for her protector.

He was in the alcove, behind the hanging burlap, exactly where she'd left him. She sat, lifted the curtain away, tucked it up into a crevice between stacks of boxes.

"Hello, Yossele," she said quietly.

His eyes couldn't widen, but she felt his surprise: How could she know—?

"I heard it in Kreindel's mind," she told him.

But—how? *He* was Kreindel's golem, so how could Miss Levy . . .

"It's an ability that I have," she said. "My master died, soon after I was brought to life. I can't feel him anymore, so I feel everyone else instead."

His confusion only deepened. A master could die? But that made no sense! The world itself, vanishing! He struggled to imagine it; he reached out for Kreindel for reassurance—and felt her asleep, safe above him. But for how long? Yes; humans died. He knew this. He pictured Kreindel's father on the parlor floor, his unseeing eyes. The memory disturbed him. He wouldn't think about it.

That surprised her. His mind seemed stronger now than it had been that morning, his thoughts more conscious of themselves. Had she underestimated him? Or had something changed? She focused upon his mind, and saw herself in his thoughts: an inhuman woman, her face carved from clay, her nature clear and unmistakable. It was what she herself saw, when she allowed herself to look—except that he thought she was—

beautiful

She pulled back, startled by the thought. He saw her as she truly was; he thought that she was beautiful. *Am I?* she thought, dazed. She never would've said so, not even to herself. She returned his marble gaze, examining his rough-hewn features, the whorls pressed into his skin— two sets of fingerprints, she realized, one large and one small. Kreindel's, and her father's. How different his creation had been! Not an illicit purchase made by a scoundrel, but a task shared between father and daughter. He wasn't beautiful—she couldn't think of him that way—but in the marks of his makers she saw the work of love and care. In that sense, there was nothing sinister about him.

She felt his impulse to touch her, and thus wasn't surprised when he reached out, slowly, and took her hand in his.

She closed her eyes, strangely overwhelmed by the feel of rough and solid earth. She lifted her other hand, touched his cheek—and the sensation redoubled. A blissful strength was waking in her, spreading through her. She could feel him now, not just his thoughts but *him*, every particle of his body coming alive in her mind. She was herself, and she was him, too; they were merging together like layers of sediment. She gripped his hand harder, willing the boundary between them to grow thinner, to disappear—

She gasped, and fell inside him—and found Kreindel.

Kreindel's dream had changed.

She was in a forest, walking barefoot on the warm, needle-strewn ground. A river ran nearby, its waters clear and musical. On its bank stood an ancient, slanted shack. Flowering vines threaded themselves through the gaps in the timbers. Above her rose the anchoring tower for a new bridge, its roadway hanging unfinished in a net of cables. Or perhaps the bridge had been finished long ago, and now, like the shack, was returning to the forest.

The door to the shack hung from a single hinge. Inside was a cot, streaked with mud; and upon that cot lay the man she'd seen on the night of the fire, the man she'd never forgotten. He held a woman's cloak, bunched in his hands.

She spread the cloak over him, as she always did. I'm sorry that your friend is gone, she told him. May her memory be for a blessing.

She isn't gone, a voice said.

It was Miss Levy. She stood at a table nearby, dressed in her cook's whites, rolling out a pie-crust with quick, even motions.

Kreindel frowned. What do you mean?

Miss Levy didn't reply. Her fingers lifted the dough, braiding it. It wasn't a pie-crust, Kreindel realized, but a challah. The starched white jacket and hat had disappeared; she wore a shirtwaist and a dark skirt made of rough cotton, the sort that the mothers in the tenement had worn. A golden chain glinted around her neck. She put the challah in the oven, and when she straightened again, there was a piece of cloth in her hand.

Here, the woman said. Give him this, when he wakes.

It was a square of muslin, embroidered in golden cord with the outline of a woman—no, a girl, in a knee-length shift. A fire spread behind her, reaching to the heavens.

Is this me? Kreindel asked—but Miss Levy was fading, confusion on her face—

—as the sound of the rising bell pierced through the dream.

Kreindel struggled to remember it, to hold onto the dream before it faded. There'd been a shack in a forest, and Miss Levy had been inside it, and Kreindel was supposed to give someone a . . . piece of cloth? It had seemed so important; already it was nearly gone.

Sighing, she stood from her cot, grabbed her soap and toothbrush, and joined the line for the lavatory.

Charlotte Levy blinked up at a tower of boxes.

She was sprawled upon the alcove floor, lying there as though she'd fallen. For a moment she thought it was snowing—but it was only motes of dust, drifting through the watery sunlight.

She sat up. Yossele was immobile in his usual spot, his mind upon Kreindel. The whole Asylum was awake, the children yawning and rising from their cots above.

What had happened? How long had she been there, in the basement? Yossele had taken her hand, and . . . What was it, that they'd done together? What could she even call it? She hadn't meant to enter Kreindel's dreams, hadn't known that such a thing was possible. She'd acted on impulse and desire, without considering where it might lead—and it had simply . . . happened. She wasn't even certain whether she ought to be ashamed.

She stood slowly, straightened her dress, picked up her hat from the floor. "Yossele?" she said quietly—but he barely noticed her. Kreindel was awake, and he must be vigilant. For a moment she envied him deeply.

She navigated through the maze—an easier journey in the morning light—and met no one in the hallway. She left the Asylum, and walked home.

The nightmare propelled Toby awake.

He jumped up from his pallet, ready to grab his bicycle—and saw his mother sitting on the sofa behind him, dressed for work. Her eyes had a sleepless, haunted look.

"Ma? Aren't you going to be late?" He needed motion, he was about to jump out of his skin—but it was clear that something was wrong.

"Sit down, boychik," she said, her voice strange. He did so, trying not to twitch—and without preamble his mother said, "Your father's name is Irving Wasserman. We started courting when I was seventeen."

For a moment Toby didn't understand what was happening. Then his heart began to pound.

"He lived in the building next to mine," she said. "I'd see him on the stoop with his friends, in the afternoons. All the girls were sweet on him. I was so proud of myself, that I'd been the one to catch him. We fought all the time, but I didn't know any better. I thought that was what you were supposed to do when you were in love." A bitter, wistful note had crept into her voice. She hadn't looked up once, only stared at her hands as though reading her own story in their lines. "I fell pregnant," she said. "When I worked up the courage to tell him, he proposed. I was shocked, but there he was, full of plans for us—for all of us. A family." She paused. "A few nights later, we were supposed to meet at a dance hall, to tell our friends the news."

A dance hall? Toby pictured his nightmare: the tall windows, the mirrored columns.

"He didn't show up for hours. When I finally found him, he was roaring drunk, and his arm was around another girl. I marched him out back to the alley, and we had it out. He said I was trying to trap him, that—that you weren't really his. I called him a liar, and all sorts of other names. He hit me then, hard enough to knock me down. He'd never hit me before. He'd threatened to, once or twice. But I thought that was all it was—just threats." She swallowed, took a deep breath. "Someone passing by the alley must've seen him hit me. They attacked Irving, and beat him nearly to death. The police never found out who it was . . . I was on the ground, half out of my mind. I didn't know what was happening until it was over." She was trembling now. He wanted to lean over and take her hand, but he kept himself still, afraid that if he moved, she'd stop talking. "He was in the hospital for a long time, and then he left the city. I never saw him again after that night. You could try looking in Boston, if you want. He had family there."

She fell silent, then looked up at him searchingly, as though expecting some outburst. But he only sat there, absorbing what she'd said. She dropped her eyes again. "I just thought it was time you knew," she said, a murmur.

He'd never seen her look so vulnerable before, so small. Tears burned in his eyes. He leaned over, kissed her cheek. "Thanks, Ma," he mumbled. "I appreciate it."

She watched him a moment. Then she wiped her eyes, sniffed once, and stood. "Well," she said, uncertain, "I'd better be off. We can talk later. Or, stop by, if you want. The girls ask about you."

"Okay, Ma. I love you."

"I love you too, boychik." And the door closed behind her.

He sat there a little while longer, thinking. *Irving Wasserman.* His father's name, his story, the very thing Toby had wanted for so long. He held it in his hand, waiting to feel the *click* as his own life slid into place around it . . . but nothing happened. And now he realized that he hadn't truly expected it to. Maybe his father was a piece of the puzzle, but he wasn't the whole picture. He never had been.

She knows I went to Radzin's, he thought suddenly. *That's why she told me. She's trying to distract me, to give me just enough, so I'll stop looking.* The thought sent a chill through him. Somewhere in his mother's story, Missus Chava lurked, and Mister Ahmad, and Sophia Williams, and the evil old man from his nightmare. *They,* not Irving Wasserman, were the secret his mother couldn't name. He'd just have to learn the rest for himself.

He went to the 'phone on his mother's desk—he was forbidden to use it, except in emergencies—and picked up the handset. "Operator," a woman said.

"May I have the number for Teachers College, please?"

A pause. "That's Morningside four five eight five. Shall I put you through?"

"No, thank you." He replaced the handset, and put on his uniform.

From the alley, Anna watched her son pedal by.

He was dressed in his uniform, even though it was a Saturday, his day off. His messenger bag was over his shoulder, too. Either he'd taken on more shifts without telling her—which would be bad enough—or he was up to something.

She went back up the stairs to their apartment, shoved the couch aside, and pried up the loose floorboard. His cigar-roll of dollar bills was still there, much the same as before. But the golden Liberty head that winked up at her—that was new, and frightening.

She plucked the coin from its hiding-place, turned it over in her hand. Her boy wasn't one for card games or pawnshops. There was no good explanation for it, just as there'd been no good explanation for the box of pastries. What would she find next, one of Baba Yaga's iron teeth? A cup of water from Miriam's well?

Stay here, with me, she pleaded silently, to the empty air. *Stop searching for the things that no one can explain. Isn't this world cruel enough as it is?*

The old sewing basket sat in the back of the wardrobe, untouched since the day Charlotte Levy had arrived in Hamilton Heights.

She unearthed it, brought it to her desk, and unpacked all the little boxes, lining them up in neat rows. The stork scissors she held a moment, gazing at the clawed feet and elegant beak, and then put them aside. At the bottom were the folded squares of fabric. She sorted through them until she found the one she was looking for.

She lifted it out, unfolded it—and saw at once that Kreindel had been right. Not a winged woman, not a woman at all, but a thin-limbed girl, her smock hanging loose upon her frame. The flames weren't a part of her, they only rose to either side: her tenement, burning behind her. And now that she'd discovered what the portrait was truly meant to be, she wondered how she ever could've thought it otherwise.

Well, they'd fought, hadn't they? *If you were a jinniyeh* . . . In the aftermath of those words, she'd seen an image of the woman she'd thought he wanted, not the girl she'd tried to save. If she hadn't buried it at the bottom of her sewing basket, if she'd asked him about it instead . . . But perhaps he hadn't even realized what he'd made. His mind had been elsewhere, telling her the story of Mount Qaf. The emerald mountain, the paradise he'd wished he could believe in.

She smoothed out the fabric, traced the cord with her finger. He'd given her his silences, and she'd filled them with her fears. And perhaps it was true, what he'd said on the rooftop—they simply weren't good for each other, and never had been.

But we could've tried harder, she thought. *Both of us.*

20.

Toby rode his bicycle through the Columbia campus, feeling as though he'd barged into a garden party.

Well-dressed young men and women walked past him on the paths, trailing conversation and laughter. All around were tall, vine-covered buildings of red brick and white granite, weathered bronze statues and marble benches. The central plaza was laid out with geometric precision, the bricks arranged in concentric squares of light and dark. Even the cheers from a nearby field seemed orderly and genteel. He braked at the top of the library steps, expecting the ground to heave beneath him and eject him onto Broadway, like a spat seed. But not a single head turned his way. His uniform and bicycle made him invisible here, just like everywhere else.

He wheeled his bicycle down the steps and past a lush green lawn where a group of young men played a lazy, peacocking game of football, and at last reached the Teachers College quadrangle. *Administrative Office*, a wooden sign said, with an arrow pointing to a building that faced 120th. Would anyone be here, on a Saturday? He knew that secretaries and clerks often had Saturdays *and* Sundays off, which felt like the very definition of luxury. He locked his bicycle to the rack, then mentally rehearsed his story, took a deep breath, and opened the door.

The hallway was framed in dark wood above and marble tile below. Portraits of patrician-looking men in dark robes frowned at him as he passed by. The door labeled *Admissions Office* stood ajar; he peered around it and saw a woman at a secretary's desk. She was squinting at a ledger and taking notes, humming tunelessly. On the wall beside her were framed photographs in a neat grid: rows of young men and women, all wearing those same dark robes. The woman paused in her work to blow her nose, indelicately. It was clear she thought herself alone.

Well, nothing for it. He tucked his cap beneath his arm to hide the badge number and strode into the office. "Message, miss?"

The woman screeched so loudly that Toby nearly yelped, too.

"My *word!*" the woman gasped, one hand to her bosom. "For *heaven's* sake—"

"I'm sorry," he said quickly, "I didn't mean to—it's just, I'm here for your message, miss. I was sent to collect one, at this number." He looked to the corner of her desk, as though expecting to see a telegram blank waiting in its envelope.

The woman frowned. "There's no message, young man."

"There isn't?" He glanced around in confusion. "Isn't this Morning-side four five eight five?"

"Yes, but no one rang the call-box. I'm the only one here." Her tone was wary, and she examined him as though he might bite her. At once he realized: she thought he was pestering her deliberately, in the hopes that she'd give him a coin to go away.

"Well, that's odd," he said. He wanted to slink out of the room and vanish. "Wires got crossed, I guess. Sorry to bother you, miss."

He half turned from the desk—but then hesitated. This was his one chance. If he didn't take it, he might as well go home. He looked up at the photographs in their frames. "I don't mean to be a pest," he said, "but a friend of my ma's went to college here."

Her eyes narrowed. "Is that so."

"For Domestic Sciences, I think? Her name's Chava Levy."

And once again, the name worked its magic. The woman came alive, her suspicion falling away at once. "Oh! *Do* you know Mrs. Levy? Young man, I've been trying to contact her for *months!* We're publish-ing a new alumni directory, and we simply have no information for her at all. I tried her landlady, but apparently she moved years ago and never left an address. Do you know how I can reach her?" Eagerly she took up a pen.

Caught out, Toby shook his head. "I'm afraid I don't, miss. My ma hasn't heard from her in a while."

The woman deflated slightly. "Oh, what a shame."

"But I can tell my ma you're looking for her, in case she comes to visit."

"Well, thank you, young man. We were *so* impressed with her achievements here." Like Thea Radzin, the woman was apparently unable to help herself. "*Such* an intelligent, well-spoken young woman. And—well, perhaps I pulled a few strings in her favor, but she certainly proved herself worthy of them." She smiled at Toby. "You're standing next to her, in fact."

She pointed to a photograph on the wall beside him—and sure enough, there in the top row was Missus Chava, in robe and cap. Again, she was stooping slightly, not quite looking at the camera; again, every line of her face was exactly as he remembered. And even though the brass plaque on the frame read *Culinary Science Class of 1912*, she looked no older than the other women in the photo—none of whom, he'd wager, were over the age of twenty-five.

"Huh," he said, and shivered deeply.

"Is something wrong?"

Toby reaffixed his smile. "I'll be sure to tell my ma," he told her. "And I'm sorry about that mix-up, with the call-box. Won't happen again."

She pursed her lips. "Well, I *was* going to send a telegram this afternoon, as a matter of fact. But since you're here . . ." She opened a drawer, extracted a pad of blanks, scribbled a message, and handed it to him, along with a nickel. "Day letter, if you please."

Toby wheeled his bicycle back to Broadway, thinking hard.

In January of 1912, Missus Chava had disappeared from the Lower East Side. A few months later, she'd graduated college—and then disappeared *again*. No address left with her landlady, or the employer who'd been so proud of her, or the university that had educated her. Nothing left behind, except those photographs.

His stomach rumbled, reminding him that he hadn't eaten breakfast. But first things first: he had the secretary's telegram to deliver. Where was the nearest branch office? There'd be one on Broadway . . .

He pedaled north, scanning for the familiar sign. It appeared at 134th, tucked between a grocer's and a tobacconist's. He coasted to a stop at the corner. He couldn't just walk in and announce himself, or the manager would call Julius and demand to know why a Midtown boy was poaching telegrams up in Morningside Heights. He'd have to get another boy to turn it in for him. It shouldn't be too hard to find one; it was a sunny Saturday morning, and if the uptown bench-babies were anything like the ones back home, they'd be finding excuses to loiter out of doors instead of sitting in the office. Sometimes the managers let them play in the alley between calls, just to get them out from underfoot.

He wheeled his bicycle down 134th, to the alley behind the Western Union. Sure enough, a young boy in uniform was leaning against a wall, a half-eaten frankfurter in one hand and an issue of *All-Story Cavalier Weekly* in the other.

"Hey there," Toby said.

Startled, the boy looked up at Toby, his mouth full.

"For you," Toby said, and handed him the telegram and the nickel. "Morningside four five eight five. In good time, too, if you turn it in quick."

The boy swallowed. "Thanks, uh . . ."

"Toby." His empty stomach was alerting him to the boy's frankfurter. "Say, that looks good."

The boy wrinkled his nose. "I've had better."

Toby grinned. "That so? What's the best around?"

"The cart at 145th and Saint Nicholas, easy."

"Eleven blocks north, for a frankfurter? There's got to be a dozen carts between here and there."

The boy shrugged. "Suit yourself."

"Huh." Well, what else did he have to do? Maybe the ride would help him think. "Thanks, I'll give it a try," he said, and pedaled off.

The Asylum's Sabbath service was even more interminable than usual that morning. The rabbi droned on, reciting prayer after prayer. The little children kicked and elbowed one another, while their monitors hissed warnings and slapped fingers away from noses. Kreindel sat among her dormitory-mates, her mind wandering. What *had* that dream been about? She'd forgotten it all, but it still pulled at her. She wished she could ask Yossele, wished that he could tell her.

She looked up. A small commotion had begun in the front pew. Heads were bending together, exchanging quick whispers, murmurs of excitement:

It's an Excursion Day!

Wait, who said so? Who'd heard first? It was a boy seated next to the headmaster; he'd spied the clipboard in the man's hand, had read the glorious words *Excursion Roster* at the top of the page. An Excursion Day, the first of the season!

The news swept from row to row, and within moments the synagogue was churning with excitement. The rabbi floundered momentarily, then recovered enough to finish the service at near to a shout. With a glare of irritation he ceded the podium to the headmaster, who'd risen to rescue him.

"*Quiet, please,*" the headmaster called in his most thunderous voice.

The noise lowered to an electric hum.

"Since it seems that spring has arrived at last—"

The hum swelled in expectation—

"—we have decided that today will be an Excursion Day."

Pandemonium! The synagogue erupted in cheers and stamping. The Asylum youngsters all prized these days spent at the local parks and beaches, where they ate crullers and drank bottled sodas until they grew giddy and unmanageable, and had to be herded back to the Asylum by force. The older residents, however, gritted their teeth in unison. For them, an Excursion Day was a terrifying exercise in adulthood—for there were never enough monitors to watch all the children, and so they, too, were pressed into the role, and made responsible for their charges' welfare. All knew the stories of boys who'd run off on Excursion Days and had never come back, or girls who'd gotten separated from their groups and disappeared into certain ruin. Likely the stories were just stories; nevertheless it set their nerves on edge.

"Your monitors have the lists," the headmaster said. "And I will remind you all that it is incumbent upon you to comport yourselves respectfully, as representatives of—"

His admonishments were lost as the synagogue emptied in record speed, the children all rushing to learn where fate had placed them. Kreindel's dormitory clustered around their monitor with dread as she called out the assignments.

"Altschul and Winkelman, you're taking Dormitory 2, Room 3 to Colonial Park."

Kreindel groaned inwardly. Of all the rotten luck! Nearby, Rachel was likewise rolling her eyes in disgust. Kreindel wondered if they'd been paired deliberately. Was she expected to keep Rachel in line, along with the children? At once she felt punished, taken advantage of.

In the hallway, the girls of Dormitory 2, Room 3 already stood waiting in their pairs, quivering with excitement. Kreindel and Rachel took their places at the head of the column, Rachel fixing the yellow ribbon in her hair.

"Don't you wander off with some boy and stick me with all the work," Kreindel muttered.

"Why don't you go and pray about it, Altschul," Rachel muttered back.

One by one the dormitories were released through the Amsterdam gate, each group peeling off toward its particular destination: south and west to Riverside Park and Grant's Tomb, or to the nearest streetcar stop for adventures farther afield. Kreindel supposed she'd gotten off lightly, all things considered. There was little to tempt the girls between the Asylum and Colonial Park, only ten blocks of apartments and storefronts. She pictured Yossele watching her in his alcove, fretting at her departure.

It's not far, she thought to him. *Don't worry. I'll be back soon.*

The frankfurter cart was right where the boy had said it would be. Toby bought two, heaped the buns with mustard and sauerkraut, and took the first bite. Sure enough, the sausages were darned good, even worth the ride.

He leaned his bicycle on its kickstand, looking around while he chewed. Had he ever been this far north before? The tenements here didn't look any more spacious than his, but they still felt different—as though they'd been allotted more sunlight in their windows, more sky above their roofs. The day was growing warmer, and children streamed past him on the sidewalk, the boys in short pants and the girls in ging-ham one-pieces, all heading toward Colonial Park with nickels for shave ice and Coca-Cola. They didn't look as dirty as the kids at home, maybe; but a few hours at the park would set matters right.

He finished the frankfurters just as a small procession approached on the sidewalk. At its head were two girls roughly his age, one taller and light-haired, the other small and dark. Behind them, like ducklings, came twelve younger girls walking two by two. All wore the same uni-form: grayish-white blouses and stiff brown skirts, threadbare stockings, scuffed shoes. There was no badge or insignia, but none was needed: they had to be from an orphanage.

A distant bell rang at the back of Toby's mind. Had someone men-tioned an orphanage, once? He tried to remember, but it evaded him. One of the girls in front, the taller one, wore a lemon-yellow ribbon in her hair, garishly bright against her drab uniform. As they passed the frank-furter cart, the girl with the ribbon caught sight of Toby watching—and flashed him a smile so baldly flirtatious, complete with eye-batting and hair-tossing, that he couldn't help but grin.

At once the girl with the ribbon reddened and turned away. Beside her, the dark-haired girl shot her partner a look of exasperation—and then, as they went past, turned back and directed at Toby a glare of pure, withering anger.

At once Toby felt as small as a mouse. He hadn't meant anything by it, just that the girl with the ribbon was trying awfully hard. But maybe she thought he was looking down on the lot of them. He watched as they marched on toward the park, wanting to go after them and apologize, but that would probably make it worse—

From the direction of the park there came a loud, wet *splat* and an outraged shriek.

The tenements just west of Colonial Park were home to a group of young boys known throughout the neighborhood for their unparalleled skill at making trouble. The boys had been playing in the alley at 145th, growing ever more bored and restless, until someone spied the twin lines of Asylum girls, heading directly their way.

At once the plan took shape. They ran to the garbage bin behind the grocer's on Edgecombe and returned with crates full of ammunition: wilted cabbages and mushy potatoes, onions gone dark with mold. Snickering, they stacked the crates, chose their weapons, and hunkered down, a shooting gallery awaiting its ducks.

Rachel, in front and the tallest, was an easy target. The first volley, a cabbage, hit her square in the cheek and exploded, covering her hair and its ribbon with shreds of muck. She staggered sideways, screaming in horror.

The barrage began, a fusillade of rot. The girls fled in all directions, tripping and crying, arms over their heads. Crowing with glee, the boys came out from behind their crates and advanced toward the mouth of the alley, ready to chase the girls back the way they'd come.

Kreindel alone did not panic. She had no reason to; for she had Yossele. She only needed to call him forth. She turned to face the boys, fists clenched in righteous fury—

In the basement, Yossele came alert and rose to a crouch, clay muscles bunched and ready—

—just as a boy on a bicycle raced past her into the alley.

The assailants scrambled back behind their crates as he swept his bicycle into a skid, blocking their exit. He leapt off the bicycle and stalked toward them, pushing up his uniform sleeves. Kreindel realized it was the messenger-boy, the one who'd grinned so rudely at Rachel.

It wasn't much of a scrap. The other boys were younger and smaller;

most of them ran off, rather than fight. Only the two biggest stayed behind—and Kreindel watched, stunned, as the messenger-boy pummeled them both and then chased them down the alley, disappearing behind a corner.

His bicycle lay in the alley before her, abandoned.

Yossele hesitated, confused.

His master had nearly called him. He'd been ready, so ready—but then someone else had arrived at her side instead. This irritated him, though he wasn't certain why. Kreindel was safe, nothing else ought to matter—and yet he felt resentful, neglected. He sank back, watching.

Kreindel bent down and lifted the bicycle carefully by the handlebars. She'd never touched a bicycle before; it was heavier than she'd expected. The rubber grips on the bars were still warm from the boy's hands.

Footsteps, in the alley. It was the messenger-boy, sporting a cut on one eyebrow. He seemed surprised to see Kreindel there, waiting with his bicycle.

"I wasn't stealing it," she said quickly. "Just moving it out of the way. In case they came back." She felt a blush creeping up her cheeks.

"Thanks." He took the handlebars from her.

Flustered, Kreindel looked around. A silent, staring crowd of Asylum girls and neighborhood children had gathered at the alley entrance. Even the frankfurter vendor had come to investigate.

"You okay?" the boy asked her.

"I think so." She brushed ineffectually at the slime on her uniform, then went to her charges and counted them. There were many tearstained faces, and a few scraped knees—but the worst injury was the blow to Rachel's cheek, already swelling and turning purple. "I want to go back," she said, sniffling.

Kreindel sighed. "I suppose we ought to."

"What if they follow us?" one of the little girls said.

"I'll come with you," the boy said at once.

And so the Asylum procession reversed its course, this time with the boy wheeling his bicycle next to Kreindel as they walked. "Thank you," Kreindel said belatedly, wondering why she felt so tongue-tied. "For helping us."

"You're welcome." A pause. "I'm Toby."

"I'm Kreindel."

"I'm Rachel," Rachel said from Kreindel's other side.

"Kreindel," Toby said, surprised by the old-fashioned name. "You're Jewish?"

"Well, yes," Kreindel said, a touch warily. "We're from the A.O.H."

"What's that?"

"The Asylum for Orphaned Hebrews. On 136th."

"Oh. I've heard of it," he said.

"You must not be from around here."

"Nah, I'm Lower East Side. Born on Chrystie Street." He paused. "When I was little, there was a boy down the hall from us who disappeared one day. I asked my ma what happened, and she said, 'He went to the orphanage.' I bet that was your Asylum."

"What was his name?"

Toby thought. "Can't remember."

"They probably changed it anyway," Kreindel said, a bitter edge in her voice.

"Is that what happens when you get there? They change your name?"

"If they think it ain't—it isn't American enough."

"Huh." He wondered if *Toby* would've passed muster.

"I didn't let them change mine," Kreindel said.

"I wouldn't, either," he said at once.

Was he making fun of her? "Why not?"

"Well, names are important. You can't just go around *changing* them."

"Women do, all the time," Kreindel pointed out.

He considered it. "But that's different. That's for a family."

"You have to change your name when you marry, it's the law," Rachel put in, feeling ignored.

"No, it isn't," Kreindel said.

"Sure it is. Everyone does it," Rachel retorted.

"But that's custom, not law," Kreindel said. "There's a difference.

Everyone puts salt on their potatoes, but no one goes around making *laws* about it."

Toby grinned.

"What?" Kreindel said, frowning.

"I just like the way you talk. You sound like a rabbi."

It was a compliment; pleased, she took it as such. "That's from my father, I guess. He was a rabbi."

Rachel rolled her eyes heavenward. "And she won't shut up about it, either."

"Did you know him?" Toby asked, ignoring Rachel.

Kreindel nodded. "I was eight when he died," she said, wishing she could tell the truth for once.

"So it was your ma who took you . . ." He wasn't certain how one spoke of these things.

"No, she died when I was born. I didn't have anyone else, so I was sent to the Asylum."

"Oh. I'm sorry."

"Thank you," Kreindel said quietly.

On they walked down Amsterdam, the younger girls gathering as close as they dared behind their elders, the better to hear every word. By the Asylum's standards, this was shaping up to be a legendary incident, something to be talked about for months. Already Kreindel could imagine the tale passing from mouth to mouth: the attack from the alley, the young man riding to their rescue. And she'd be part of the story, too. She could feel it with every moment of attention he paid her, every step they took side by side, separated only by the bicycle.

"It's nice that you knew your father," Toby said on impulse, feeling as though he had to level the field between them. "I never met mine. I've got my ma's name, not his." He trailed off, thinking. *Toby Wasserman.* Who the hell was that, anyhow? Who would he have been with that man's name?

"Would you change it?" Kreindel ventured. "If she married someone?"

"No," he said at once. "I like my name as it is."

She nodded, pleased by this.

"How old are you?" he asked.

"Nearly sixteen," she said, remembering to lie.

"Oh. I'm fifteen," he said, stretching the truth.

"Really? You look older."

"I know. People say that a lot."

"But you don't like it?" she guessed.

"Ah, it's fine. It's just that everyone expects a bicycle messenger to be a little kid." He sighed. "I figure I'll give it another year, tops. Then I've got to find something else."

"Is it fun, being a messenger?" she asked.

"I used to think so. I still do, sometimes. This"—he pointed to his cap—"It's like a key that gets me through any door in the city. Fifth Avenue, City Hall, wherever. And no one looks at me twice."

"Huh," said Kreindel. She tried to imagine what that would be like, to slip through the world unnoticed.

He glanced at her. "What about you? When do they let you leave?"

"When we're eighteen," she said, morose. "We're supposed to learn a trade by then. So we can support ourselves."

"What'll yours be?"

"I don't know. I don't want a trade at all, not like they mean it. I just want . . ." She trailed off. She'd nearly said, *I just want to be a rabbi, like my father.* But that was absurd. A woman could no more be a rabbi than a man could be a mother. "I just want to study Hebrew," she said instead.

"Really?" said Toby. He'd never thought of Hebrew as something a girl might study.

"So she can pray more," Rachel put in. "She prays all the time, it's ridiculous." Rachel's resentment had been building with every word the two exchanged. They'd paid almost no attention to her hurt cheek—and *she'd* been the one to notice Toby first, not Kreindel. "She wanted an independent study for Hebrew, but they made her take Culinary Science instead. And I heard she's *awful* at it."

Culinary Science? Toby thought.

"Shut up, Rachel," Kreindel muttered.

"Well, you *are*. I bet Miss Levy kicks you out of the class."

Toby stumbled off the curb. The bicycle bumped into Kreindel, who joggled sideways; he reached out, put a hand on her arm to steady her. "Sorry," he muttered. "Wasn't looking."

"That's all right," she said, near to a whisper. Behind them, the girls giggled.

The Asylum crept into view along Amsterdam, looking like the biggest, oldest school Toby'd ever seen, or maybe a penitentiary. He'd thought to leave them at the main gate, but now the younger girls sensed their moment. They clustered around the bicycle and all but pushed him through the gate, clamoring questions: How long did it take to learn to ride? Would he teach them? Oh—he had a cut on his forehead, did he know? They'd find someone to help, they'd fetch a nurse! In their excitement, they raced up the drive, ready to tell their story to the first adult they saw.

As it happened, that adult was the headmistress herself, who'd been enjoying a cup of tea in the front office, blessedly free of duties for an hour. The girls burst into her sanctum, the story tumbling from a dozen mouths at once—*Headmistress, they threw vegetables at us, but then a boy with a bicycle made them run away, his name's Toby and he's a messenger and he's Jewish!* Confused, she turned to the window: and there, walking up the drive, was a Western Union boy wheeling his bicycle beside a decidedly blushing Kreindel Altschul.

The headmistress hurried to the door and ushered them inside, exclaiming over the girls' soiled clothing and Toby's injuries. Toby was invited to wash up in the office lavatory, an honor heretofore unheard of. Rachel presented herself for inspection, hoping to be fretted over; instead she was sent to the infirmary to fetch bandages and ice.

Toby came out of the office a few minutes later, with a scrubbed face and hastily combed hair. More of the Asylum staff appeared, drawn by the commotion, and thus the story had to be told all over again. Matron arrived, too, with a sullen Rachel in tow, and bandaged Toby's wounds herself.

Never before had Toby been the focus of so much female attention at once. He liked it, though it was a bit of a confusing whirl, what with the little girls all talking over one another and the matron dabbing at his forehead. Kreindel was standing at the edge of his vision, quietly answering the headmistress's questions about what had happened. He wondered, would he get to talk to her again? It seemed important, suddenly, that he be allowed to talk to her again.

Kreindel finished her report to the headmistress and tried to disappear into the crowd, but it was impossible. The crowd merely re-formed around her, maneuvering her next to Toby, the center of their attention. But—why should that be so terrible? She liked Toby. She'd never talked to a boy before, not like that. She'd never realized that one *could* talk to a boy like that: in honest conversation, about things that mattered. She watched him kneel down for one of the little girls, so she could better see his cap with its bronze badge, and heard Matron say, "How lucky that you came along when you did—or who knows what might've happened!"

But Kreindel knew. She could picture it: Yossele racing the blocks to her side, the velvet curtain around his shoulders rippling like a banner, righteous thunder in his footfalls. The boys in the alley, screaming and scattering in terror. If Toby hadn't come, if he'd delayed even a few moments more . . . Yes, she would have done it. And would it have been wrong of her? Yossele had been created to protect; he'd been given to her for that purpose. He was a gift of the Almighty, the source of all her strength, and he asked for so little in return. And if she told Toby, or any boy, about Yossele . . . would he understand? Or would she have to choose between them?

But—choose, how? Yossele was hers, forever. There wasn't any choice to make.

The spectacle was drawing toward its conclusion. Matron patted Toby's cheek and then departed. Rachel was deputized to lead the younger girls to their dormitory; she obeyed, fuming. The headmistress shook Toby's hand and disappeared back into her office.

Finally, Kreindel and Toby stood alone in the entrance hall.

"Well," Toby said, a grin pulling at his mouth, "that was an awful lot of fuss."

She wanted to smile back, to laugh and agree. She said nothing, only hugged herself and stared at the floor.

"Kreindel," he said, "would you—"

"Thank you, Toby," she said, cutting across him. "For helping us." And without looking at him, she walked past him to the staircase, tears rising in her eyes.

For a long minute Toby stood abandoned in the empty hallway, trying to figure out how he'd blundered. No answer came.

Outside, his bicycle was where he'd left it, leaning against a wall. He retrieved it and pedaled down the curving drive, and back along 136th. He crossed Broadway, then stopped on the sidewalk. From his satchel he pulled a sheet of paper he'd stolen from a file cabinet marked *Staff Information*, when he was thought to be in the lavatory:

> Levy, Charlotte
> 3352 Broadway Ave #508
> Manhattan, NYC

He peered back across the street, to the apartment building on the corner. There, above the lobby door, was the number 3352.

A chill spread outward from his stomach. Well, *now* what should he do? *I found Missus Chava*, he imagined telling his mother over supper, just to watch her spit out her tea. If he shouted it through the letterbox in Little Syria, would he be rewarded with another gold coin? The Teachers College secretary would sing his praises. Thea Radzin would shower him with hamantaschen.

But none of it made *sense*. Certainly a woman might vanish for her own good reasons, and leave a hated past behind. But there was more at work here. He thought of the photographs, the burning envelope. The fear in his mother's eyes as she'd braced the door, as though she meant to hold back certain death.

He pulled a pencil and a fresh blank from his satchel, thought hard, and wrote his message.

The contents of the old sewing-basket were still piled atop Charlotte Levy's desk, the embroidered muslin held loosely in her hands.

Get up, she told herself. *Put all of this away. It's Saturday. You have lists to make, errands to run.*

But the command could find no purchase. All that she wanted to do—all that she longed for, in body and mind—was to go back to the storage room, and sit with Yossele, and feel whole again.

You were supposed to destroy him, the voice within her chided. *You barely even tried.*

But was he truly such a risk? After all, he'd been in that room for years with no one the wiser. And now that she knew, she could watch over him like a guardian, perhaps even visit him regularly. She smiled, picturing it: days spent with her classes and students, and nights in the alcove, in the bliss of that union . . .

And what about Kreindel? Will you invade her dreams every night, perhaps even destroy her sanity, just to satisfy your desires? After all the times you accused Ahmad of arrogance, heedlessness?

That was Chava Levy's life. Not mine.

And this is who you would be instead?

She stared down at the muslin, the girl, the flames. Her hand went to the chain around her neck; she took a deep and shuddering breath. Why couldn't she think clearly? Why didn't her own arguments seem to matter anymore? She needed help, needed—

She froze. Someone was approaching in the hallway, the words *Chava Levy* fluttering from their mind like a flag.

A small piece of paper slid itself beneath her door.

She waited, tense, until the footsteps had receded again, before retrieving it. It was a Western Union telegram blank, with a message written in pencil:

JUST WANT TO TALK. WILL BE AT 136TH & RIVERSIDE UNTIL 1PM. WON'T TELL MA.

—TB

This far north, Riverside Park was little more than a steep green hill-side that separated the genteel brownstones above from the train-tracks and coal-yards far below. Toby sat on a bench at the park's edge, watching the river, the shimmering wakes left by the barges. He wouldn't look around for her, he decided. He'd wait, cool and patient, as if he did this sort of thing all the time. The bench was cold, and he resisted the urge to jiggle his leg. How, he wondered, would he know when it was one o'clock? He didn't have a pocket-watch. Maybe he ought to buy one, with his rolled-up hoard. No, his ma would wonder how he'd gotten it. He supposed he could ask a passerby for the time. They'd all have pocket-watches, a neighborhood like this. Had he ever sat still for this long in his life?

"Hello, Toby."

She sat down on the other end of the bench, not quite beside him, and stared out at the river, something like nervousness in her eyes. She looked different now. A navy wool coat instead of the cloak, kid leather gloves, a nicer hat. She looked like she belonged here, uptown.

She glanced down at her skirt, picked away a bit of lint, folded her hands in her lap. "How is your mother?"

Toby swallowed past a dry throat. "She's okay. Still at the laundry, still goes to her suffrage meetings. Still limps, a little."

She nodded, as though this was what she'd expected. "And you?"

"I'm all right. I finished school, last year."

She raised an eyebrow at that. "You didn't want to keep going?"

"Didn't see the point of it, at the time." He paused, and then said, "What should I call you, anyway?"

She smiled, sad and a little wry. "To be honest, I'm not entirely sure." She looked down at her hands, then up at him. "How did you find me?"

"Luck, mostly."

"But not entirely. You were looking for me." She said it as though to confirm what she already knew. "Why?"

He considered telling her that his curiosity had gotten the better of him, or that he'd done it just to see if he could. But she was regarding him with that seriousness he remembered, the sort that adults rarely ever showed him. "Because for my whole life," he said, "there's been this . . . this *thing* I'm not supposed to know. I thought it was about my father, but it isn't—it's more like a secret about the world itself. I can see pieces of it now and then, but I have no idea what I'm looking at." He glanced at her. "I came to find you because I'm pretty sure you know what I'm talking about."

Her sharp eyes turned back toward the river; she seemed to be wrestling with his answer. "And does your mother know you've been looking for me?"

He thought of their conversation that morning, the worry in Anna's face. "I haven't told her—but she might know anyway."

The woman looked troubled. Eventually she said, "Toby, I can't tell you everything that you want to know. I need to respect your mother's wishes, and some secrets aren't mine to reveal. But if you ask me your questions, I'll give you what answers I can. Is that fair enough?"

He considered this, then nodded. It was a start, if nothing else.

"Good." The woman sat straighter on the bench, waiting.

The sun was high above them, lifting the mist from the New Jersey hills and warming Toby's neck. He sat forward, elbows on his knees, frowning in thought. "First question," he said. "Who is Ahmad al-Hadid, exactly?"

She sighed as though she'd been holding her breath. "He was my friend, and more than my friend, for a long time."

He waited for more, but she'd gone silent. Was that all? Was everything else about him not *hers to reveal*? All right, he'd move on. "The night you came to our apartment and my ma slammed the door in your face—was that the same night that Mr. Arbeely died?" He was pretty sure he'd said it correctly.

She glanced at him, frowning. "How did—" She stopped herself, sighed again. "Yes."

"So why did my ma slam the door?"

She picked another imaginary bit of lint from her skirt. "She thought that I'd . . . lost control of myself. And that I would hurt you, or both of you, by accident."

"Why would she think that?"

"It's happened before." And then, before he could ask: "I won't give you the details, Toby. Just know that your mother acted sensibly."

That made him pause, but only for a moment. "*Would* you have hurt us?"

"No. I was upset, but not . . . dangerous. But she couldn't have known that."

"Then why'd you disappear?"

"Because I promised your mother a long time ago that I'd protect you. That night, it seemed to me that I'd become exactly the threat that your mother feared. I decided that the best way to protect you was to leave. To cut all ties, for your sake."

Toby mulled this over. On the one hand, it sounded like a reasonable, well-argued decision. On the other, it struck him as the sort of thing that adults liked to say when what they meant was *I was terrified, so I ran for it.* For now, he decided, he'd keep that opinion to himself.

A slightly rueful expression had passed across her face; he had the oddest sense that she'd guessed what he was thinking. "Next question, please," she said.

He decided to take the plunge. "Why don't you ever get older?"

She closed her eyes and laughed once, helplessly. "*Toby.*"

"Don't tell me I'm imagining it."

"I won't. I promise. It's only . . . I worked very hard to hide all of this, you know." She thought a moment, and then said, "I don't age because I simply don't. It's . . . not something that I can do."

"Why *not?*"

Silence. He let it stretch, but she only stared uncomfortably at her lap. He was reminded of the photographs: her hunched shoulders, her uneasy expression. "Fine," he muttered. "Next question, I guess. Who's the evil old man in the dance hall?"

At that she looked up—startled, even alarmed. He had the unsettling sense that she was trying to peer inside him. "You used to have nightmares," she said, "when you were little."

"Still do," he said.

"Is *that* what they're about? The evil old man?"

He nodded. "It's the same thing every time. He's holding my wrists, and I can't move. He doesn't say anything, just grins at me. It goes on and on." Just thinking about it had made his knee start to bounce; he stopped it with his hand.

"Are you yourself, in this dream?" she asked. "Or are you someone else?"

Toby frowned. He was himself in the dream, wasn't he? It had always been such a part of his life that he'd never considered. . . And then another puzzle-piece slid into place, with a *click* he felt in his bones. It wasn't a dream at all. Dreams *changed*, even just in little details here and there. They weren't exactly the same, every single night. So if it wasn't a dream, then what was it? A memory? Whose?

The realization made his heart pound. *It's Ma's memory. It happened to her.*

She was watching him carefully—but he decided to say nothing of his suspicions. She'd never confirm them; and besides, it felt too awful to say aloud. He might just end up crying. "So who is he?" he asked instead.

"He was . . . an evil old man, exactly as you said."

"Is he still alive?"

She considered. "Not in any sense that matters."

"What does *that* mean?" But she only shook her head.

"Look," he said, irritated, "maybe it happened to—to someone else, but he's been in my mind for as long as I can remember. Doesn't that count for something?"

"Toby, I'm sorry. I truly wish I could tell you."

He took off his cap, ran a frustrated hand through his hair. These answers weren't much better than nothing at all, but he was certain that if he pressed her too hard, she'd get up and leave. "Fine. Who's Sophia Williams?"

That seemed to confuse her. "Sophia . . . *Williams*?"

"That's what she called herself."

"Can you describe her?"

"A lady in her thirties. Shorter than me, blue eyes, brown hair braided like this." He drew a circle around his own head. "She's got a sickness of some kind. Anemia, she said it was. And there was a ghost in her hotel room."

Her eyes went wide. "A . . . *what?*"

He described it: the open window, the pressure in his ears, his certainty that something was behind him and that Miss Williams knew it too. "If it wasn't a ghost, then I don't know what to call it."

"Where was this?"

"The Hotel Earle on Washington Square, yesterday evening. I think she'd just arrived. She sent a shipboard cable to your friend Ahmad, a few days ago."

She considered this. "A ship . . . across the Atlantic?"

"I think so. The name sounded like a merchant ship's, and they're mostly the ones making the crossing, these days."

She nodded. There was a strange look on her face: troubled, but also . . . hurt? Jealous? "I could hazard a guess about the nature of this 'ghost.' But only a guess," she said firmly, "and I won't say it aloud."

"But," he said, "whatever it is—could it be a danger to your friend?"

She frowned. "Why do you ask?"

"In the cable, Miss Williams said that she had to see him, but that you weren't supposed to know about it. It said, *Chava Levy must not know.* It made me wonder why she didn't want you around. I thought maybe she didn't want you protecting him. And seeing as how he hasn't left that building ever since Mr. Arbeely died . . ." He broke off at the look on her face, suddenly certain that he'd said too much. "I'm sorry," he said, wanting to kick himself. "But it's true. He just doesn't come out. I think . . . I think he's in a bad way."

She sat there, utterly stricken. For a moment he thought she was about to cry. "Oh, Ahmad," she whispered. She stared out at the water, then gathered herself and said, "Toby, I won't ask how you've learned all of this. I won't scold you for spying, or meddling, or being terribly indiscreet. You were right to do all of it, and it's my own fault that you felt you needed to." She shook her head. "I thought that if I disappeared from your life, that all of this would disappear along with me. I didn't think . . . " She trailed off, her eyes troubled. Then she said, "As it happens, you've come at exactly the right time. Will you deliver a message to Ahmad for me? I need his help, I think."

Wordlessly he pulled a telegram blank and a pencil from his satchel and handed them to her. She wrote her message, then folded it in half, and in half again—he'd never seen anyone fold a blank like that before; it seemed oddly deliberate—and handed it to him. He was puzzled at what to do with the small, tightly folded square of paper, but then stuck it in his shirt-pocket.

"I think we'd better stop here," she said. "For the time being."

He wanted to object, to say that he'd barely learned anything, that he had ten new questions for each of the grudging half-answers she'd given him—but the look on her face told him the effort would be wasted. He nodded, accepting his dismissal.

"Toby," she said suddenly, "I know how difficult this must be. Just know that your mother has her reasons, and they're very good ones."

"I know," he muttered. "It's just hard to swallow, is all."

She nodded—and then peered at his face. "Ought I to ask about that cut on your forehead? Or would that be too meddlesome?"

He grinned, suddenly self-conscious; he'd forgotten all about the scrape in the alley. "Oh, it's nothing. Some idiots were making trouble for a bunch of girls from your Asylum, up by Colonial Park. I chased them off, and then I got to talking with one of the girls. That's how I found you, actually. She's in your cooking class."

She'd been listening with a quizzical half smile; suddenly it faded. "Kreindel," she said. "You met Kreindel."

"Yeah—wait, how'd you know—"

But she shook her head, impatient. "Tell me exactly what happened," she said. "Did somebody attack her?"

"Just some kids throwing rotten vegetables," he said, confused by her intensity. "They didn't really hurt her, it was the other one who got the worst of it. Rachel, I think."

"And that was it?" she said, searching his face. "No one else came and . . . and fought the boys?"

"Only me," he said, a little bewildered.

She nodded, looking relieved. Then she stood; after a moment he did likewise. "I'm afraid I have to go," she said. "But I'm glad you found me, Toby."

"Me too," he said.

They shook hands; he was unsurprised, somehow, by her cool, firm grip. Then he swung a leg over his bike and rode south along the Drive, off to deliver her message.

21.

The Jinni sat on the uppermost of the Amherst's platforms, his legs folded, gazing out over the edge.

He'd spent the hours since Maryam's departure in unaccustomed stillness, all sense of urgency vanished. What had made the change? he wondered. Was it because, one way or another, his years of seclusion were about to end? Or was it the knowledge that Maryam herself had made that seclusion possible? Yes, he'd shut the doors and covered the windows, but it was Maryam who'd turned their eyes away. *It shouldn't make a difference,* he told himself. And yet it did. It meant that everything he'd built was her gift to him, as well as his own creation.

What might she have said, he wondered, if he'd told her about the jinniyeh's offer? What advice would she have given him? He tried to imagine himself at her coffee-house, unburdening his troubles among the backgammon players and narghile smokers. Ought he to stay and face whatever happened when his neighbors wrenched the doors open? Or should he go to the desert, and the Cursed City?

But the Maryam in his mind remained silent. Perhaps he didn't know her well enough to imagine what she might say. Or perhaps she'd already given him all the advice that she could.

He looked up. A glow had appeared, beyond the arches.

He was waiting for her at the edge of the uppermost platform.

—Jinni, she greeted him, *did you miss me?*

"Yes," he said.

She hovered near him, just over the edge.—*I see why you like it here. The currents are exquisite. Well, lover, will you come back to the desert with me, as the story says?*

He put out a hand; she curled herself around it. "You'll tire of me," he said, smiling slightly.

She took form beside him, drew him close. "Perhaps," she murmured in his ear. "Or you'll tire of me first, and lie with all the Bedu in turn."

He shook his head. "I wouldn't."

Her fingers tugged at the leather apron-string. "You might change your mind when you see them. Some of the women are quite—"

He moved her hand away. "That's not what I meant."

Startled, she pulled back. He appeared to debate with himself, then said, "I took a human lover once, not long after I arrived here. I saw her in a park one day, and decided to seduce her. I didn't think . . . I wasn't careful enough. I made her ill, permanently. I'm not certain how it happened, I only know that I was the cause. She left the country, after that. I don't even know if she's still alive. But I swore to myself that it could never happen again."

"Then—you've never had another human lover, after all this time?"

"No. And I never will."

She watched him, schooling her expression to the mildest interest. "But surely this is too extreme a punishment. You felt no malice towards this woman, it was merely an unfortunate accident. And besides, if you don't know what's happened to her, then how can you be certain of the outcome? You might have changed her life for the better, in the end."

He frowned. "How could I possibly?"

"The illness might've strengthened her will, even as it weakened her body."

He seemed to consider this—but then shook his head. "She was barely more than a child, and I tore her life apart. Even if I somehow 'strengthened her will,' I can't believe she'd thank me for it." He was gazing past her, as though expecting to see Sophia floating beyond the platform, shivering in the updraft.

The jinniyeh stepped closer, drawing his attention back. "You've denied yourself so much pleasure, all because of a single unhappy experience. Have you always been so . . . severe?"

He smiled, and ran an idle hand through her hair. "Not always. There was a time when I wouldn't have cared in the least. Sometimes I wish I still didn't."

"The desert will help you," she whispered. "*I* will help you. You can be what you were again, once you're gone from this place."

A frown touched his forehead. "In some ways, yes. But I'll still be bound."

"Yes, of course—but your hiding cripples you twice over! There's no blame in this, I of all jinn understand. But imagine the freedom, the relief, not to wonder with each sunrise, *Is this the day that one of them learns what I am?*"

He'd been drawing her toward him, his hands sliding around her waist; now he paused. "There were a few who learned my secret, over the years. They helped me stay hidden, in fact."

"Arbeely," she said, remembering the name from Sophia's scrap of paper. "He was the tinsmith?"

"Yes. And . . . there was a woman. A baker. Her name was Chava."

She frowned, thinking. "The tinsmith had reason to protect you, you were his livelihood—but what about the woman? Why did *she* keep your secret?"

He smiled, uncomfortably. "Must there be a reason?"

"There is always a reason." Was he so very naive?

"Perhaps we were merely friends."

She chuckled at that. "I see. 'Friends.' And where are they now, these friends of yours?"

"Arbeely is dead," he said. "And Chava is . . . gone. We argued, and parted company, years ago. I wasn't a particularly good friend to her. To either of them."

"Of course you weren't," she told him. "You were attempting the impossible. Humans and jinn . . . we aren't meant to be 'friends.' We aren't meant to be anything at all."

He looked up. "But you and I are?"

"Yes! Can't you see it?" She grasped him by the wrist, her fingers around the cuff.

He was silent a moment, his eyes upon his wrist, where she held him. Then he said, "Jinniyeh, you must know that if I go back with you, then yes, I will change. But you will change, too."

She frowned at this. "What do you mean? Change, how?"

"I'll influence you, without even meaning to. I'll use some ridiculous human figure of speech, perhaps, and it'll take root in your mind even as you curse me for it—and one day, instead of telling me that you're *angrier than a ghul's mother*, out will come, *It makes my blood boil*. It can't help but happen."

She laughed, uneasy. "But that makes no sense. I would never say such a thing."

"No, not at first. But as time goes on . . ."

"Then simply *don't*," she said, growing irritated. "Forget these 'ridiculous human figures of speech,' and I needn't change. All will be well."

He shook his head. "But then I'd only be hiding again."

She bristled at that. "*Hiding?* Merely because I ask that you speak like a jinni, as much as you're able?"

"I understand your anger," he said. "I, too, used to think that I could live in this body, among these people, and not be changed by it. That I could, as they say, swim in the water and not get wet." She shuddered at the image; he smiled and said, "You see?"

"And you're *comfortable* saying such things?"

"No, but I've learned to live with the discomfort."

"And now," she said, "instead of returning to how you ought to be, you will demand that I do the same?"

"Jinniyeh, you may think that all my learned humanity can simply melt away—but it can't. I'll never be the same as I was. And if I try, the only thing I'll achieve is misery. So yes, I will come back to the desert with you. But you must accept that I'll always be just a little bit human—and that you will be too, in time."

For a long moment she only stared at him. Then: "No." She took a step back—his hands slipped from her waist—and then loosed her form and floated away from him, beyond the platform's edge.—*You're wrong. I didn't come all this way merely to weaken and debase myself, to grow as fearful of my own nature as you seem to be. I'm no cowering changeling! If I'd known when I first saw—*

Her voice stopped; she flinched. She'd used the form of *see* that implied both a woman and an adversary, as one spies an opponent across a battlefield.

He frowned. "First saw *who,* jinniyeh?"

—*The healer-woman in the souk,* she said. *The one who told me where to find you.*

But her hesitation had been too plain; he was watching her intently now. "Yes," he said, "the healer-woman, the one who spoke of shining boxes as high as Mount Qaf, and an arch of Palmyra among the trees. It was a beautiful story, jinniyeh. Will you tell me more of it?"

—*More of what? I don't know—*

"The story of how you came to find me. Your earlier version was lacking in detail. You said you had to enter many sleeping minds, before you learned which city the healer meant. Whose minds were they? What did they dream of?"

—*They were humans, old and young,* she said, making a dismissive gesture. *They dreamt nonsense, and I understood little of it.*

"And what of the ships? You said that you flew to Port Said, and then took a ship across the sea and another across the ocean. But how? Did you read the sailing schedules in the newspapers? Visit the ticket offices in the docklands?"

—*No, of course not!*

"Then how did you find your way?"

—*There were men near each of the ships. I changed into a bird and perched nearby, and listened to their conversations.* She said it defiantly, to make up for her earlier hesitation. *Now will you continue to interrogate me, or have I passed your test?*

He folded his arms. "Tell me, jinniyeh. What is a directory?"

She quailed, for she had no idea. What had Sophia said? *I found an address in an old directory. That was all.*—*It's a place where they keep addresses,* she said.

He smiled at that, but his eyes were sharp as flint. "What did the directory look like? Was it big, or small? Round? Flat? Carved from stone? Written in blood?"

—*You're insulting me,* she hissed.

"And you, my lover, are lying. You never came here on your own."

—*Oh? Do you think me too stupid, or too helpless?*

"Neither. You're too contemptuous of humans, and too afraid of polluting yourself to learn their ways."

—*I, afraid? You are the one who has locked yourself away, like a mole that fears the sun! And all the while the woman you*—She froze.

For a moment he stared blankly—and then his face darkened. "Sophia," he said. "Of course. She came to Palmyra, didn't she? You saw her there, you saw what I'd done to her . . . It was *Sophia's* dreams that you entered, not some healer's. Oh, I'm a thrice-cursed fool. Have you hurt her, jinniyeh?"

—*Of course not!*

"Where is she now?"

The jinniyeh said nothing.

His eyes narrowed. He turned from her and descended the staircase. After a moment she followed, spiraling alongside him.—*But this is ridiculous! You're no longer her lover, and you're neither her ally nor her kin. Why does it matter to you?*

"Because I'm the one who sent her into your path."

He reached the bottom and began a search of the workshop cabinets, at last pulling a stained work-shirt from their depths. He frowned at it, then yanked off the leather apron and donned the shirt in its place, tucking it into his ragged trousers.

—*What are you doing?* she said. *Are you leaving?*

"Yes. And so are you. You're going to take me to Sophia." He looked down at his feet, bent and rummaged in the cabinet again.

She made a scoffing sound.—*And why would I?*

"Because I won't go to the Cursed City if you don't." He emerged with a pair of heavy work-boots and put them on.

—*Perhaps I don't want you there anymore,* she told him.

"Oh, yes, you do," he said, tying up the laces. "I'm the iron-bound jinni, remember? I'm part of your precious story. You'll drag me back like an imp in a gourd if you have to."

She made a derisive noise.—*You might be grateful that I'm offering you a home, when all you have is this . . . this monstrosity in a box!*

That made him stop. He stood then and looked past her, gazing at the climbing metalwork with a strange look on his face. "A monstrosity in a box," he repeated—and then, to her bewilderment, began to chuckle.

—*You dare laugh at me?*

"No, jinniyeh, at *me*. I never truly noticed until now—but here, look." He gestured to the Amherst's corners, sketching a sharp-sided cube in the air. "Inside one unchanging, earthbound form . . ." And now he pointed to the central staircase, fingers spiraling upward—". . . is the memory of flight." He smiled at her confusion. "Don't you see? I thought I was creating something the world had never seen before, but I only built myself again. Ahmad al-Hadid, the not-quite jinni. The monstrosity in the box." He grinned, shaking his head. "They can have it, when they come," he said, as though to himself. "They'll find some use for it. A playground for the children, perhaps."

Had he gone mad?—*What children? Who are 'they'?*

"My neighbors, the others who live here. Apparently I've been hiding away for too long, and they're about to break down the Amherst door. Imagine their faces." He grinned.

—*And you'll simply . . . let them? You won't fight for your home?*

His smile faded. "No," he said, "I won't. I don't want to fight them, not for this. You were right. It's just a box."

She flew closer.—*And if the Cursed City should be threatened—if the humans and our kin should push eastward, against its borders—will you push back? Will you fight then?*

"Jinniyeh," he said, "I know what you want me to say. But—"

She didn't let him finish.

She grabbed the updraft from the forge and fashioned it into a cyclone that lifted him off his feet. Dust and cinders whirled around him as he struggled to break free. She raised him high in the air, so she could look him in the face. There it was: the fear she'd wanted to see.

—*You wish to fly?* she said, and threw him against a platform.

The entire building seemed to vibrate. He fell; she caught him in the wind again, lifted him. He was grimacing, his eyes half closed. She smiled. She wouldn't hurt him, not truly. She only wanted to remind him.

She spun him around and hurled him against the wall behind the forge. Brick and mortar shuddered—and the pipe that led to the water tower snapped in two.

A cataract of water burst from the wall and struck the burning forge, which exploded in a clap of steam that shook the air itself. The jinniyeh tumbled from her wind, half stunned. What had happened? The air was full of water, she couldn't find her bearings, there wasn't any sky—*where was the sky*—

Blinded, terrified, she flew straight into the torrent.

The pain brought the Jinni to his senses.

He lay beside the wall in a pool of water, shallow but growing. He hauled himself to standing, thankful for the boots. Water still poured from the burst pipe, a dozen feet above his head. The break was above the valve; the water would run until the tower was dry.

At the far end of the forge drifted the jinniyeh, stunned and injured, caught in the spray.

"*Jinniyeh!*" he shouted. He could see through her in places, her formless body flickering around the wounds. He wanted to run to her side—but what good would that do, when he couldn't even touch her?

He looked up at the fountaining water, then clenched his teeth, grabbed the pipe, and climbed.

Up he went like a cat-burglar, gripping with feet and fingers, hoping against hope that the pipe would bear his weight. Water gushed above him, drowning him in mist. His entire body glowed with pain.

He climbed the last few feet, braced himself for a moment—and then lunged and grabbed the pipe above the break.

Water poured over him as he twisted the pipe back upon itself. His legs shook; his hands grew numb. He could barely see, but he was almost there, just a few more inches—

The pipe below him buckled. The world turned gray.

The jinniyeh hung in tatters.

She drifted upward, trying to focus. Every part of her shrieked in pain. The forge below her was a dark pool of ash—but the pipe had been twisted shut. A thin stream of water ran from its bent lip.

The iron-bound jinni lay on the floor below it.

She dropped to his side, keening in horror. Was he alive? This was all her fault, she hadn't meant to—oh, it had all gone so terribly wrong—

She jumped at a sound nearby: a fist, knocking upon a door. "Hello?" a voice called. "Mister Ahm—Uh, Mister al-Hadid?"

She looked to her lover, then flew to the door and took form, nearly screaming with the pain of it. She turned the lock with shaking fingers, twisted the knob and pulled.

On the other side of the door was a boy—a man?—who wore a cap with a shining metal badge. He stood staring at her, his mouth open in shock.

"Help him," she pleaded, and vanished into the air.

It wasn't long before the entire Asylum knew the story of Kreindel Altschul and her bicycle messenger.

The tale greeted the children as they returned from their adventures, group by reluctant group. They traded it back and forth in the dormitories along with the contraband they'd gathered: chocolates and chewing gum, tobacco cards, pairs of dice, stolen oranges. With each retelling the tale grew more impressive and elaborate, until Toby had fought off a dozen Irishmen single-handed, and Kreindel had pledged her eternal love to him at the Amsterdam gate.

The girls of Dormitory 2, Room 3 talked of nothing else; all swore, with deep solemnity, that they'd marry a Western Union boy someday. They were clustered together in their room, in the midst of a dramatic reenactment, when the door opened and Rachel Winkelman strode in. She smiled into the silence, and held up a shining quarter.

"Who wants to earn this?" she said.

Charlotte Levy walked along Twelfth Avenue beneath the Riverside Drive Viaduct, listening to the thrum of tires on the pavement above. She hadn't been able to face returning to her apartment, not after watching Toby ride away with her message in his pocket. She needed to walk, to think.

Toby Blumberg. Older, taller, stubble upon his chin, his thoughts full of everything she'd tried to leave behind. And Kreindel! Her image shining in his mind: a small, dark-haired girl, walking beside his bicycle. Would Yossele have attacked those boys, if Toby hadn't intervened? How many lives might Toby have saved that morning, without even realizing it?

The Viaduct ended at 129th, the roadway merging into the park above her. A drift of decaying leaves lay at the base of the embankment, left over from the autumn. On impulse she took off her gloves and scooped a few damp handfuls into her coat pockets, then climbed the steps that curved around the hill, past Grant's Tomb and the Claremont Inn and into the park itself.

The river to her right was a flow of silver, seen in glimpses. The park turned from lawn to trees: maples and elms, cherries, maidenhairs, their leaves still young and freshly green. She walked among them, staring up into their canopies, then reached out a hand to one of them, marveling at its rough bark. Charlotte Levy had never once allowed herself to do this. She'd made a new life for herself, but it had been a rootless, undernourished thing, and now she could feel it withering away again. She wondered what she'd be left with, when it was gone.

She crouched down at the base of the tree, emptied the mulch from her pockets, and worked it into the soil with her fingers. A girl on the path stopped to watch her quizzically. She smiled at the girl, then stood and brushed the dirt from her hands. She would have to go back to the basement, she realized; there was still the matter of Monday's inspection. She couldn't simply hope that the headmistress would fail to notice its hidden inhabitant. If she could rearrange the room, she might disguise the alcove entirely. Perhaps that would gain them all enough time to arrive at a better solution, once her message reached its destination.

Chava Levy must not know. Was her guess about the "ghost" correct? She had no right at all to the jealousy that had filled her at the thought; no right, either, to ask for his help, after everything that had happened. But she feared that she'd never be able to open the locket herself, not for Yossele. She'd hesitate, make excuses, forgive him for everything that she would abhor in herself. The locket was useless to her—she needed the man who'd made it.

It was just a dream, Julia Winston thought.

Despite the headache that had dogged her since the morning, she was in her study, attempting the usual motions of a Saturday afternoon: a review of the household ledgers, as well as correspondence with those distant family members who wrote her dutifully in hopes of an eventual bequeathment. Make-work, all of it, designed to fill her superfluous hours, her superfluous life.

With each scratch of her pen the headache grew worse. She longed to lie down, but the thought of returning to her dream of the night before was too dreadful to contemplate. The dream had accompanied her through the day, with its image of the woman bending over Sophia like some vampiric spirit, ready to drain the life from her veins.

It was just a dream, she told herself again. *It wasn't real, for God's sake.*

A knock came at the door; a maid appeared, bearing an envelope. "This just arrived, ma'am. They said it was urgent, but didn't wait for an answer."

She took it, and read:

Dear Mrs. Winston:

My apologies for writing to you in such a fashion. The manager of the Hotel Earle on Waverly Place tells me that one of his guests is using your daughter's name. She is locked inside her room, and has not been heard from in some time. The manager is within his rights to enter, and plans to do so by 4 o'clock this afternoon, accompanied by myself. It's possible that this is all a misunderstanding, but the newspapers have all sent their men to the premises, and they will do whatever they can to stir up trouble. My aim is only to inform you, so that you might take any actions that you feel are warranted.

> *Very sincerely,*
> *Lieutenant Oscar Galloway, 15th Precinct Station-House*

Julia glanced at the clock. It was a quarter after three.

"Have the car brought around," she told the maid. "I must leave as soon as possible—and in full mourning, not half." Startled, the maid rushed away.

Perhaps, Julia thought, the newspaper-men would grin at the sight of the famed widow parading in her ghoulish finery. But if she was to walk into enemy territory, she wanted her best suit of armor. Let this girl, whoever she was, stare Julia Winston in the eye and explain herself.

In his alcove, Yossele struggled to watch his master as the day's events buzzed inside him, refusing to be ignored.

His master had been attacked. She'd nearly called him to defend her, only to be interrupted by the boy on the bicycle. Even now, as Kreindel sat alone in her dormitory room, a part of him was still poised at the end of his tether, listening for that summons. Then there was the fact of Miss Levy's nature, which thrilled him even as his master's ignorance of it distressed him; the confusion this caused added its own, distinct ache.

The knowledge that he was a separate being from his master had become a gulf, a resentment. *Why* didn't Kreindel know that Miss Levy was a golem? *Why* couldn't he tell her? *Why* had she spent the hours since her return to the Asylum thinking about the boy on the bicycle, the one who'd stolen Yossele's place? She was thinking about the boy even now. He didn't want to see. He couldn't look away.

A sound made him turn his head: a quiet knock, upon the storage room door.

Hope grew inside him as the doorknob turned. Yes; it was she. He'd begun to learn her patterns, her motions. Two steps inside, the door closing behind her. A deep breath at the threshold, even though she didn't need to breathe. Would she come to where he sat? Would she hold his hand again?

"I'm sorry," she said quietly, from outside the maze. "I can't come to you. I truly wish I could. I'm only here because I have to rearrange—"

But already his hope had turned to bitter frustration. Why must she come at all, if not to sit with him? He was beset by so many questions! He had no idea what to do with them all, and if this went on for much longer something would happen—he didn't know what, but he could feel it building—

"Oh, Yossele," she whispered; and then she was coming toward him, through the maze.

Desks, cots, hat-stand, final corner. She rushed through them as quickly as she could. He was hurting, dangerously so, and she must do what she could to help him.

He sat in the slanting afternoon light from the high window, fidgeting like a man plagued by a swarm of insects. As she approached, he reached out, took her hand, and pulled her to him.

Their connection came roaring back. She felt his mind aching beneath its burden of knowledge. It was all too large for him, it made no sense, he didn't want any of it—

It's all right, she told him. *I'm here. We can manage it together.*

She set to work among the seething tangle of his thoughts, gathering them one by one, holding them carefully in her arms. Some were incomplete, with pieces missing; these she patched with new knowledge and made whole. *Kreindel is a young woman now. It's natural that she should feel this way about a boy. She doesn't love you any less because of it. I'll tell Kreindel about myself as soon as I can. We'll find a way forward, together.* Then, once his thoughts had all been calmed, she slowly put them back again, finding neat and orderly places for each part of him, like a well-organized pantry where he could see everything at once. At last she stepped back, examining her work.

There, she said. *Is that any better?*

Kreindel sat alone upon her cot, knees to her chest.

Toby's face had haunted her all through the afternoon. She recalled each moment of their walk together, as though deliberately pressing on a bruise: the way her tongue-tied awkwardness had given way to easy conversation; how he'd seemed to fill her field of vision, even though they were walking side by side. The warmth of his hand on her arm, as he'd steadied her. He didn't know about true orphans. He'd talked to her, even touched her, as though she were an ordinary girl.

She looked up at a creak from the hallway door. It was one of the girls from Dormitory 2, Room 3. The girl darted into the room, running toward her between the cots. A folded note, dropped into Kreindel's hand—and the girl was gone again, giggling as the door closed behind her.

Kreindel opened the note.

I liked talking to you. I'm in the marching band room. Will you meet me there?—Toby

It was a prank; it had to be. How would he even know about the Marching Band room, or how to find it? Yes, the handwriting looked like a boy's, with its stick-straight letters. But any girl could write like that, if she wanted to.

Nevertheless, a small, stubborn hope had been kindled. She recalled what he'd said about his uniform, the key that opened every door in the city. He could get inside easily—maybe even through the gate on 136th, which would lead him straight to the basement. The Marching Band room was practically across the hall from the stairwell. It might even be the first door he'd try.

What if it actually *was* Toby?

She'd never snuck into the basement during daylight hours; it would be far too easy to get caught by a janitor, or even a teacher. But on Excursion Days the bell was silenced, the rules relaxed. If she went now, she'd be just another resident in a hallway, taking advantage of her temporary freedom. And if she took the time to think about it, she would lose her nerve.

Is that any better? Miss Levy asked.

It was as though Yossele had spent his entire life hunched over in a cramped room, and then Miss Levy had raised the ceiling so he could stand upright. He turned about in surprise, rejoicing at his quiet, orderly mind. He could see everything, could examine his own thoughts at his leisure. Nothing lurked just out of sight, clamoring to be noticed. And in the middle of it all was his beloved Kreindel, his connection to her stronger than ever.

Thank you, he told Miss Levy.

She was still there among his thoughts, a golden presence. He reached out to her, and she flowed around him like dust in sunlight, each mote a separate part of her. He gazed at them as they passed, saw flashes of people, places, memories. A Brooklyn cemetery; a burning building. Her own hands, braiding a challah. The tall man that Kreindel had dreamt about, lying not upon a bed but in a freezing alley, the ground broken beneath him. A silver chain, and a steel locket—and inside it—inside it was—

death, around her neck—

She'd tried to destroy him. She'd stood in this room, only feet away from him, and she had tried.

His mind darkened with anger.

Wait, she said, pulling away. *Yossele, please. I only meant to be careful, to—*

He surrounded her, instincts flaring to life, all thought obliterated by the urge to protect himself. But she, too, was strong; she pushed back against his anger, holding it at bay so that it wouldn't ignite her own. Within moments they were balanced at a standstill, his connection to Kreindel shining between them. And Kreindel—

Wait. What was Kreindel doing?

The basement's familiar scent of mildew greeted Kreindel as she descended.

The laundry room was empty, the shoe-shop dark and locked. She could hear shouts from the playground, where a few of the younger residents were spending their last minutes of freedom—but the basement seemed deserted. If Toby was truly here, then they'd be alone. She would tell him that he shouldn't have come, that she couldn't see him in secret like this. That it could only be just the once.

No light came from the Marching Band room, but someone had cracked the door open. She edged up to it, put a hand on the knob. "Toby?" she whispered.

There was a rustle of movement, deep in the room—and then an answering whisper: "Kreindel?"

The door creaked as she slowly pushed it open—

In the alcove, in their stalemate, the golems could only watch—

—as a deluge of water struck Kreindel in the face, filthy with salt and the stink of sweat.

Kreindel staggered backward into the hallway, blinded and choking, her stomach heaving. She heard shrieks of laughter, and the *clang* of a metal bucket dropping to the floor. Dimly she recognized Rachel Winkelman, Harriet Loeb, a few others. Her eyes burned; the world was a red haze. She fell to her knees, retched, vomited. Rage overwhelmed her.

Yossele, she thought. *Get them*—

—and the Golem fled Yossele's mind as it lit up like a bonfire behind her.

The others didn't notice at first, over their own laughter. Then, "Shhh," Rachel hissed, and all the girls heard it: a series of cascading crashes at the far end of the hallway, shelves falling over like dominoes, their spilled contents shoved aside to make a path.

"What the hell is that?" said Rachel.

On her hands and knees below her, Kreindel smiled grimly. "That's Yossele."

A door burst open in the murky distance—but what emerged wasn't Yossele. It was a woman, running toward them faster than anyone Kreindel had ever seen.

Miss Levy? she thought, dumbfounded—

And then the wall behind the woman exploded.

Pounding toward them through the dust came an enormous gray figure, its stride filling the hallway. It had a craggy, misshapen head that hung like a bull's between mountainous shoulders, and club-like fists that swung at the ends of thickly bunched arms. Its mouth was a cavernous maw surrounded by grotesquely raised lips that now opened in a silent roar, as though it meant to swallow them whole.

The girls all stood frozen—and then Kreindel shrieked in terror.

"Go, all of you!" Miss Levy cried.

The spell broke. Screaming, Rachel and the others fled up the staircase—but Kreindel stayed where she was, staring, aghast. How could this thing be her Yossele, who'd cradled her in his arms while she cried? It couldn't be—but of course it was. This was the creature her father had meant to build. She'd brought him to life and hidden him among children, and now he'd paint the walls with their blood—

Miss Levy placed herself in front of Kreindel, like a barrier. "Kreindel, tell him to stop," she said, her voice straining.

The girl let out a sob. Behind her, there was a commotion on the staircase, and then a scream.

"*Kreindel!*" Miss Levy shouted. "You're his master, he might still listen to you! Tell him to stop!"

My God, she *knew*? Everything bad was happening at once! "Yossele," she whispered. "Stop."

He barely slowed.

She tried again, her voice quavering. "Don't hurt them, Yossele. Stop. *Please.*"

His brow furrowed; he paused, still eyeing the staircase where the girls had vanished.

"It's not enough," Miss Levy said. She pulled something from around her neck, and held it out: a locket, on a chain. "Yossele!" she shouted.

The enormous head swiveled toward her. The marble eyes tracked the locket.

"Come and take it from me!" Miss Levy yelled—and then she ran for the door.

It was growing late in the day, the spring warmth leaching from the asphalt. The children on the Asylum playground were contemplating an end to their games, a retreat inside—when suddenly the stairwell door slammed open and their Culinary Science instructor burst out of the basement, navy skirts flying as she ran for the gate at 136th. And behind her, rising like a mountain out of the earth—was it an animal? A prankster in a costume? Or, most unthinkably, a man? None of the spectators would later agree, but all would remember the sound of its feet striking the path, like the crack of sledgehammers.

She reached the gate, wrenched off the lock, and ran toward Broadway, Yossele's fury a tide at her back. The intersection approached, a Saturday evening tangle of taxicabs and wagons. She dodged through them without pause, not looking back for fear that she might turn and fight him, there in the middle of the avenue. Was he gaining on her? She heard a shout, a woman's scream, the screech of tires. She kept going.

She crossed Riverside, ran past the benches, then jumped the balustrade and slid down the grassy slope to the retaining wall. Twelfth Avenue and the freight tracks lay twenty feet below her, a straight drop; beyond were the coal-yards and freight sheds, and then the river. Above her, onlookers on the sidewalk squinted down in horror at the madwoman standing on the wall. She had just enough time to reflect that there'd be no coming back from this, that Charlotte Levy would be gone forever—and then there was a shriek, and Yossele was at the balustrade, his anger rolling toward her down the hill. His body blotted out the sky.

The Golem smiled, and fell from the wall.

Yossele didn't so much as break stride. He vaulted the balustrade, sprinted down the slope, and leapt after her.

His arc took him across Twelfth and the tracks entirely, and into a coal-yard on the other side, landing with a concussion that shook the ground. He clambered out of the pulverized coal, his anger undiminished, and looked about. There she was, running toward a nearby pier.

He took off after her, ignoring the shouts from the park above. Only his anger mattered now. The world was a tunnel with Miss Levy at its end; even his master had receded to a pinprick in his mind. He wove between the coal-heaps and up onto the pier, the wood cracking beneath his feet as he followed, seeing only her, gaining, gaining, until suddenly she was gone and the pier had dwindled to its final plank—

He struck the water, and fell into a greenish gloom that deepened within moments to black.

22.

"Remember . . . you," the dying man murmured. "The messenger boy."

Toby was climbing a spiraling staircase, one hand upon the central column. With the other he supported Mister Ahmad, whose arm was slung over Toby's back. He concentrated, placing one foot and then the other upon the narrow steps, half dragging Mister Ahmad as they went. The man was lighter than he looked—disturbingly so, as though he were hollow inside. His head had lolled on his neck when Toby had hauled him out of the water, and he'd groaned at the sight of the flooded forge. *Up*, he'd told Toby, and then collapsed. So now they were going up. Toby would've liked to stop and take a look around, if he weren't so worried that the man was about to die. He felt as though he were climbing a giant steel treehouse.

"Mister Ahmad?" Was he still alive? "Did you build this place?"

The man was silent for long enough that Toby began to grow worried, but then: "Yes."

"It's amazing. What's it for?"

"Don't . . . know anymore."

That was definitely odd, but he decided not to ask. "Who was the naked lady?" he said instead. "Friend of yours?"

A weak chuckle. "Not . . . friend."

"Well, she disappeared. In front of me."

"Ah."

"She do that often?"

"When . . . necessary."

Around and around they went, Toby climbing as quickly as he could, though he still didn't know *why* they were going up, or what was at the top. He wished he could just sling the man over his shoulder, but the staircase wasn't very wide, and God forbid either of them should fall. He hadn't looked down yet; it seemed like a bad idea. Another platform came slowly into view beside them, glowing a soft silver in the filtered light.

"Sure is a lot of steps," he said, for no reason other than to keep talking. "Ever think about getting an elevator?"

Another chuckle. "Used to climb . . . every day. With Arbeely. For . . . exercise."

"Arbeely. He was your partner, right?"

He felt the man tense. "How . . . you know?"

"Oh, I asked around about you." They were nearing the top. Was there a catwalk up there, past the arches? "Also—I ought to confess something."

". . . Yes?"

"I peeked. At your cable."

"Oh. Who . . . from?"

"Sophia Williams."

A dubious pause. ". . . Williams?"

Toby huffed a laugh. "That's just what Missus Chava said."

The head lifted; he squinted at Toby. "Who . . . *are* you?"

"Toby Blumberg. I'm Anna's son."

The man took this in, then chuckled. "Gotten . . . older."

"Yeah, I know. It's a trick I play on people."

They passed through the undulating iron at the top of the column— and indeed there was a catwalk, stretching toward what looked to be an old stairwell door. "That way?" Toby said.

"That . . . way."

He hitched his passenger higher and went for the door, doing his best to ignore the fact that there weren't railings as such, only guy-wires at waist height. *Don't look down, don't look down . . .*

To his slight disappointment, the door opened onto an ordinary roof, covered in tar-paper and pigeon droppings. "Where to?" he asked.

"Anywhere. In the sun."

Toby chose a spot at the eastern edge of the roof, and sat Mister Ahmad against the wall. The sun was beginning to sink over the river, red-gold behind a veil of clouds. The man's eyes were closed; he'd gone completely still. Was he breathing? *Did* he breathe? Toby watched him warily until—"You've seen Chava," the man said, startling him.

Toby nodded—and then, remembering why he'd come, he pulled the message from his pocket. "She asked me to give you this," he said, and handed it over.

Mister Ahmad looked down at the small square of paper—first with alarm, and then confusion. He struggled to sit up higher, and unfolded it. Whatever was there made his eyes go wide. He looked up at Toby. "Did she show you?"

"No. And I didn't peek, either."

The man folded it again, closed a fist around it. Toby watched as a tiny wisp of smoke rose from his clenched hand. He felt himself grow resentful. Yes, they'd been lovers, and it was a private message—but it was also another piece hidden from his sight.

Mister Ahmad was watching him. "How much do you know?"

Was it going to be another guessing-game? "How about this," he said. "You tell me everything *you* know, and I'll tell you what surprised me."

A rueful smile. "I think not. Your mother wouldn't thank me for it. And neither would Chava." His voice was getting stronger, Toby was sure of it. The man stared at the setting sun for a moment, then said, "The cable you peeked at. I never read it. What did it say?"

Toby recited it word for word, finishing with *Chava Levy must not know*. The man considered this, then said, "You saw Sophia, didn't you?"

Toby nodded, slightly abashed. Somehow it had been easier to tell Missus Chava about his spying. "I went to the hotel," he said. "And there was a—Wait." He paused, thinking. "Someone else was there in the room, but I couldn't see them. Felt like a ghost. Was that your disappearing lady?"

"Yes, almost certainly." He frowned, thinking. "Was Sophia acting on her own? Not . . . controlled, or coerced?"

"I'd guess so—but I can't say for sure. She was sick and shivering, though. Nearly fainted in front of me. Did the disappearing lady do that to her?"

Mister Ahmad glanced away. "No. Someone else did." For a moment the man looked unutterably sad. Then he said, "Will you deliver a message for me?"

Toby pulled out a blank and a pencil, and handed them over. "Where am I taking it?"

The man wrote, and handed them back. "Just down the street. The coffee-house between Rector and Morris. I don't know the address."

"I'll find it."

"Give it to Maryam Faddoul, or her husband, Sayeed. No one else. And then go home, Toby."

"What, and just leave you here?"

"I'll be better soon."

Toby snorted. "Like hell you will. Your forge is broken, and the sun's going down." And then, at the man's surprise: "Look, you lit an envelope on fire in front of me, remember? I can put two and two together. You need warmth, or light, or maybe both." He paused. "Are you a demon?"

The man smiled. "No. I'm not a demon. And no, I can't tell you. Your mother would never forgive me. Now, will you promise to go to the Faddouls' and then straight home?"

Toby put the blank in his pocket, stood. Looked uneasily at the man.

"Deliver that message," Mister Ahmad said, "and I'll be fine."

In agony the injured jinniyeh flew slowly north.

She fought against the currents, barely holding herself together, picturing Washington Square, the Hotel Earle, the open window. She could heal there, if she managed to reach it—but then what? The iron-bound jinni was dying, perhaps already dead. And even if he survived, he'd never go to the Cursed City with her now. Why would he agree to stay with a lover who'd delivered such punishment?

She kept on. The sun helped, though it was growing low in the sky. At last, the park and its arch appeared, and she shuddered with relief. She imagined Sophia asleep in the bed, fighting to escape—and felt a new and disturbing pang of remorse. Perhaps she'd treated the woman too harshly. She would release her, the jinniyeh decided—and then, when Sophia returned across the ocean, the jinniyeh could follow her in secret. With Sophia to lead her, she would find her way back to the Cursed City, and survive.

Alone, Sophia wandered the desert.

How long had she been here, searching for a way out? Days, weeks? She'd drunk the last of her water ages ago. Sometimes the desert was her parents' ballroom, its parquet buried beneath the sand; sometimes it was the remains of the Damascus souk, the stalls empty and crumbling. Sometimes she remembered that she was dreaming, that Dima had trapped her here, inside her mind—but then the landscape would cloud over, and she would think herself to be waking, only to realize she was somewhere else, still searching, there was no end to it, she would certainly die here—

A naked woman appeared before her, holding a hand to her side as though injured. Wincing, the woman reached up, grabbed hold of the sky, and ripped downward. The entire landscape began to peel away like an orange rind—

In the last twenty-four hours, the lobby of the Hotel Earle had taken on a considerable air of intrigue.

The desk-clerk was gone, fired by the outraged manager for his thoughtless and indiscreet call to the *Herald*. But word had spread nevertheless, and the *Herald*'s man in the lobby had since been joined by half a dozen other newspaper-men, all looking for the scoop. There was no real evidence that the woman in Room 812 had used the name Winston at all—but this had been set aside as immaterial. She was either the heiress herself, or was pretending to be; both were stories fit for the papers.

The manager wrung his hands and watched the clock, smiling weakly at passing guests. The lieutenant from the precinct-house sat nearby, dusting his hat with his sleeve. Only he and the manager would be allowed to enter Room 812, and confront its occupant, before returning to the lobby to give a full and truthful account of what had transpired. The newspaper-men had objected, but to no avail. Now they perched on the sofas, penciling their drafts, leaving spaces for the details yet to come.

The lobby door opened—and the widow herself appeared.

The manager nearly fell over himself to reach her side, casting apologies like lilies at her feet. She eyed him coldly from beneath her wide black crown of *crepe anglaise*. The jet beads that lined its band glittered as bright and sharp as diamonds.

"Now, if we may," she said.

Someone was gripping Sophia roughly by her shoulders, trying to shake her awake.

What was happening? Was she still dreaming? She tried to bat her attacker away, but her limbs were cramped with cold. With effort she opened her eyes, and saw a woman, bare-skinned, frowning with impatience.

Dima.

Sophia gathered what strength she had, and shoved her—and was shocked when the jinniyeh stumbled backward, wincing and holding her side. Sophia tried to sit up, to escape, but the sheets were tangled around her—

The jinniyeh pushed Sophia back down on the bed, anger and annoyance on her face—

There was the sound of a key turning in a lock, the squeak of a doorknob—

—and the world swayed around Julia Winston as she walked straight into her own nightmare.

"Get away from her!"

On the bed, Sophia watched as her mother, dressed in an extravagant mourning cloak and hat, launched herself at the naked jinniyeh and grabbed her around the throat. Two men stood frozen in the doorway, one dressed in a policeman's uniform; their faces were a comedy of shock.

I'm still dreaming after all, Sophia thought.

She extricated herself from the sheets and slid out of the bed. She tried to stand, but stumbled over her upended trunk and fell to the floor—just as the jinniyeh broke from her mother's grip and knocked the woman down. The mourning hat rolled onto the carpet, jet beads spilling from its band.

The effort seemed to have cost the jinniyeh: she bent over, grimacing. Sophia's mother lay beyond her, one liver-spotted hand pressed to her bruised and sagging cheek. Her hair, loosed from its tightly scraped knot, rose in a thin cotton cloud about her head—and Sophia realized that she couldn't be asleep after all. Never, not even in her dreams, had she imagined that her mother could look so frail, so old.

She reached out with both hands, grabbed the jinniyeh's ankle, and yanked with all her might. The jinniyeh fell atop the trunk, cursing.

Julia struggled to her feet. "*Do something!*" she shouted at the men still gawping in the doorway, then turned to help her daughter—

Only to stare into the narrowed yellow eyes of a full-grown tiger that stood where the naked woman had been.

She froze in terror. The tiger panted its hot breath into her face, then bared its fangs and roared to rattle the windows.

Shouts; screams. Julia fell and scrambled backward, hampered by her cloak. A lamp smashed; a nightstand tipped onto the floor. Where was Sophia? She would not lose another child, she would *not*—

Something flashed silver on the carpet beside her. A lady's pistol, small and pearl-handled.

Julia grabbed it up with shaking hands, aimed into the tiger's mouth, and fired.

The noise was shocking, deafening. The tiger looked startled—and then disappeared.

Julia dropped the gun. Sophia lay on the floor beyond, a look of confusion upon her face, a bloom of red spreading across her stomach.

Toby sped up Greene Street, toward the Waverly Steam Laundry.

As promised, he'd delivered the message to Maryam Faddoul, who'd turned out to be a lady with brown eyes and a kind smile, holding a coffee-pot. She'd taken the message from him with a look of surprise, but then read it and nodded, as though she'd been waiting for it all along.

He reached the laundry and swerved into the long, narrow alley that led to the delivery entrance. One of the girls must've seen him coming because his mother was at the back door almost before he'd dismounted, concern on her face. "Toby? What's wrong?"

He looked past her at the girls in the shop, then drew her farther into the alley, away from the door. "Ma," he said, "I have to ask you something. It's about my nightmare."

Her concern turned to wary confusion. "Your *nightmare*? Toby, this isn't—"

"Ma, just listen. I'm in a huge room, with sunlight and brass chandeliers and mirrors everywhere. There's an old man standing in front of me. He's got this horrible grin, and he's holding my wrists, and I can't move. I can't even breathe."

The color had drained from his mother's face.

"I've had that dream my entire life," he said. "But it's your memory, isn't it? It happened to you."

She put a hand to her mouth, stifling a sob. Tears ran down her steam-reddened cheeks. "Oh, Toby, I'm so sorry—my sweet boy—"

"It's okay, Ma. It's not your fault." He swallowed, his own throat thick with tears. "But I need to know the rest of it, too. All of it. Because I found Missus Chava."

At once she glanced him up and down, newly alarmed, as though checking him for injury.

"And Mister Ahmad, too. He's in trouble. I don't know what it's all about, but there's a lady who disappears, and another who's sick—and something nearly killed him, I had to carry him up to his roof—"

"You did *what*? Toby—"

"But they won't tell me anything," he went on, determined to get it all out before she could stop him. "Like who they are, or . . . or *what* they are, I guess. They're trying to keep me out of it, and they know you'd be furious if they didn't. But they need help, and I have no idea what to do." He took her hands. "So, please. I'm begging you. *Tell* me."

She'd been staring at him in shock, but now her expression hardened. "Toby," she said, "they're right. Listen to them. To *me*. Go home, boychik. They're dangerous people, all of them."

"Ma, didn't you hear me? It's all a mess, and something awful's going to—"

"Something awful *did* happen," she snapped, pulling her hands from his. "I watched your Missus Chava nearly kill a man."

He stared at her—and the puzzle piece slid into place. "My father," he said. "In the alley."

She nodded tightly. "Ahmad was there, too. He pulled her off Irving, but he was barely strong enough. He had to hurt her—to burn her, with his bare hands—"

"Was she trying to protect you?"

Anger flared in her eyes. "What difference does it make? She's a monster, Toby! She's a *golem*!"

The word seemed to surprise her, even as she said it. She shut her mouth tightly, glared at him.

A golem? He knew what they were, of course, though mostly from insults. *Sammy's dumb as a golem. Don't just stand there like a golem.* He'd always pictured them as huge, lumbering things. His mother had never told him folktales about golems—but then, she'd never told him any tales at all.

"She can't be just a monster," he said. "She saved my life. And yours, too."

"And she could kill us both, as easy as breathing."

He shook his head. "You told me once that if I was ever in trouble, I should go to Missus Chava. So I did. Were you wrong?"

"No—but I wasn't smart, either. Protection comes with a cost, Toby, and this, right here, is the cost. It's you riding all over creation, poking your nose into the sort of trouble that'll get you killed."

"No, it's going to get *them* killed," he said, growing angry. "*They're* trying to keep me out of it!"

"So maybe you should *listen* to them!"

He crossed his arms. "Yell at me all you want—but I thought Missus Chava was your friend."

He braced for an outburst, and for a moment he thought she'd oblige him. But then she merely shook her head. "They aren't the sort of people you can be friends with, boychik."

"Fine," he muttered, turning away. "You tell yourself that. I'm going to help them."

"Don't you dare!" she shouted after him. "You think I'm saying all this for my health? This isn't some fairy-tale! It's all *real!*"

He turned back, peered at her in confusion. "I know that, Ma. Every night I go to sleep, and the old man's there, waiting for me. I've known my whole life that it's real."

A pause—and then she looked away, her face stricken. "Toby. Oh, how I wish I'd never set foot in that bakery."

They stood together, tense and uncomfortable. Then he said, "So how'd you get away from him?"

She was silent a moment, and then said grudgingly, "It was Chava. She came for me—no, they both did. I don't remember it very well. But the old man wanted her, not me. So he took her, and let me go."

"You mean, she traded places with you?"

His mother nodded—and then, seeing his expression, "But it was her fault I was there in the first place! If she hadn't . . ." Her voice trailed away; she sighed. "Oh, I don't know anymore. I was young, I got tangled up in their lives. Nothing was the same after that." Tears welled in her eyes. "I just wanted something better for you, sweetheart."

"I know, Ma," he said quietly. "But I think it's a part of me now. I can't just ignore it."

Silence. Then Anna wiped her face and said, "Now you tell *me* something, as long as we're having it all out. What's that gold coin doing beneath our sofa, with your hidden money?"

She'd known, this whole time? His face burned in embarrassment. "I got it from—well, Mister Ahmad, actually. It was just a tip for a cable!" he said as her eyes went wide. "That's how all of this started! I delivered him a cable, and he tipped me the coin. He didn't even know who I was. And I don't think he knew what he was giving me, either."

She snorted. "That sounds like him." And then, at his pleading look: "Yes, all right, boychik. So where *is* Chava?"

Relief flooded him; he wanted to grin, to kiss her. "She's teaching cooking lessons at an orphanage, up in Hamilton Heights. But she calls herself Charlotte now."

She made a face at that. "What was wrong with Chava? Well, never mind. And Ahmad—he's still in Little Syria?"

He nodded. "He's got a whole building he lives in. The Amherst. You wouldn't believe what he's done to it."

"I just might." She paused, eyed him. "When you were with Chava—did you think about anything that you didn't want her to know?"

He felt himself go pale. "You mean—she can . . ." He tapped his forehead with a finger.

"Yes, and it takes some getting used to." She sighed, thinking. "You can get uptown faster than I can. Find her, and tell her what's happened. But for God's sake, be *careful*. I'll go to Little Syria and make sure Ahmad's still alive, and you can meet me there. Walk me to a taxicab—I'll tell you the rest on the way."

Come to the roof. Bring fire. The door's open.—A.

It would be too risky for Maryam to be seen entering the Amherst alone, in broad daylight—and so Sayeed went instead, carrying a stack of seltzer-bottle crates as though returning them to the grocer's. He reached the Amherst, ducked quickly inside—and then, once he'd recovered from the sight before him, carried the crates up the staircase to the man who sat on the roof, in the sun's last fading rays.

The Jinni watched as Sayeed set down the crates. Inside one of them was a large stoneware bowl from Maryam's kitchen. Wordlessly Sayeed placed this upon the tar-paper, then broke one of the crates into kindling. He pulled a piece of paper from his pocket—it was, the Jinni saw, his telegram blank—and crumpled it, placed it inside the bowl, arranged the kindling around it, and set a match to the paper. A whiff of carbon, and the tinder began to burn.

The Jinni put his hands to the flames, and felt better at once. "Thank you," he said.

Sayeed nodded, and the Jinni thought he would leave—but he only sat back, staring into the fire. Suddenly the Jinni realized he'd never been alone with the man before. Had they ever so much as traded words?

A few minutes passed in silence—and then Sayeed said, "I've been trying to convince Maryam that we should move to Brooklyn."

The Jinni looked up, surprised. "Why?"

"Because of you," Sayeed said.

The Jinni took this in. Then: "But she refuses?"

A slow nod.

"Because of me?"

"Because of you."

The Jinni said, "Sayeed, will you tell me something? How does she do . . . what she does? How does she make it happen?"

Sayeed rubbed his chin, considering. "She listens to people," he said. "She remembers what they tell her. She prays, often. She puts her faith in Christ, and His salvation."

The Jinni sighed. "Yes, I was afraid you'd say something like that."

"It's not magic, if that's what you're asking. There's no trick to it. It's her own virtue. Nothing more."

"Is it ever difficult for you," the Jinni said, "to be married to someone like that?"

He'd expected the man to be offended, to scoff at him. Instead Sayeed looked thoughtful. "Sometimes," he said. "She challenges me, constantly, to be better than I am."

"And are there times when you resent the challenge?" the Jinni asked. "When you wish that, just this once, she'd let you be a little bit worse than you are?"

"Of course." Sayeed glanced at him, a hint of amusement in his eyes. "But we're not the same, you and I."

"I never said we were."

The last of the daylight was disappearing; the wood snapped in the flames. It occurred to the Jinni that this might've been the Bedouin life that he'd pretended to have lived: a fire at sunset, a conversation.

"What you've built down there," Sayeed said. "It's astonishing."

The Jinni smiled wryly. "*But?*"

"But what will you tell people when they see it?"

"I don't know. I never meant for it to be seen."

At that, Sayeed looked genuinely puzzled. "Why not?"

The Jinni shrugged, uncomfortable. "Arbeely was dead," he said. "And Chava was gone. Who else was there to show it to?"

The man had no reply to that.

For long minutes they sat in silence, their conversation run dry. Sayeed added more wood to the fire. The Jinni debated with himself, then said, "Chava sent me a message, today."

"I'd wondered what became of her," Sayeed said.

"We haven't spoken in years. I didn't know if she was still in the city. And then today, the very day when . . ." He paused, remembering that the man didn't know about the jinniyeh, or what had caused the catastrophe downstairs. "The message said, *I'm not alone. Must ask for your help.*"

Sayeed contemplated this. "What do you think it means?"

He frowned, staring at his hands in the fire. "That she needs me to do something she can't bring herself to do."

"And will you?"

"Yes, if I decide that I must. But—is this what I am to her? An executioner, to be summoned when needed? Does she think me so callous?"

"You just said it yourself. 'If I decide that I must.' Would you do this without question, simply because she wished it?"

"No, of course not!"

"Then perhaps that's why."

The Jinni fell silent, considering this—and then cringed as a shout in Yiddish rose up from the sidewalk:

"*Ahmad al-Hadid! If you're still alive, then get down here and explain yourself this instant!*"

Sayeed looked up. "What was that?"

The Jinni sighed. "Oh, just another woman who's never liked me. Help me up, would you?"

The sidewalk at Riverside Park was still crowded with onlookers.

Out on the river, a pair of fishing-boats searched the shoreline for bodies. The policemen who'd been summoned to investigate the incident read over their witness reports, shaking their heads. *A man in a gray suit. A man covered in mud. An enormous animal. A fraternity prank, or I'll eat my hat.*

Out in the river, Yossele sank through the currents and touched bottom.

He was at the edge of the shipping channel, and here the riverbed was littered with fallen freight: oil tanks, timber spars, an entire rusted boxcar. He tried to search through it all for Miss Levy, but after a few blind and stumbling minutes, his anger began to cool. Where was his master? Was she still in the Asylum? Yes, there—sitting on the floor in the lavatory, the stink of the water still in her hair and clothes. Tears were leaking from her eyes. She was crying, and he wasn't there. He wasn't in the basement, waiting to hold her.

Despondent, he sat down upon a rotten plank. Kreindel was his entire purpose. She'd called upon him to protect her—and then, when he'd obeyed, she'd rejected him. Once, this would've merely saddened him, as it saddened Kreindel. Now, he had the capacity to wonder how they would possibly go on from here. He was her bound golem; he *must* protect her, regardless of her wishes—and yet the memory of her horror was a crushing weight. What was he supposed to do?

A current pushed against him, from something moving nearby. He peered out, wiping muck and oil from his eyes. A figure was coming toward him through the water, walking along the river-bottom, stepping carefully around the debris. It was Miss Levy.

He wanted to still be angry at her—for trying to destroy him, for making him into what he'd become. But his anger seemed out of reach now, somewhere beyond his sadness. She stopped a few meters away from him, watching him carefully. The locket floated before her, on its chain. He looked at it, then up at her.

She held out a hand to him.

The policemen left Riverside Park and their fruitless interviews, and arrived at the Asylum.

They were shown to the basement, and the origin of the incident: the broken wall, the demolished storage room, its hidden alcove. They went up to the office, where Rachel Winkelman sat sobbing in a chair, and asked the girl to describe what she'd seen. She told them, and they sighed and disregarded it.

A vagrant, most likely, they told the headmistress. *Seen it before. They hole up somewhere warm, start mucking about with the boilers. Probably a boy-friend of that teacher you mentioned—Levy, was it?*

The image of Charlotte Levy nesting with a vagrant lover in the storage room was not one that came easily to the headmistress's mind—but then, what other explanation was there? She'd heard Rachel's account, and Harriet's, too, neither of which made a jot of sense. The pair had also flatly denied responsibility for Kreindel Altschul's sorry state, which didn't help them in the least. Even worse, the news of the incident had spread so quickly that it was now impossible to tell who'd truly witnessed it. From the talk in the hallways, one might think that half the Asylum had been in the basement with Kreindel, and the other half listening upon the stairs.

It was time, she decided, to reassert order. She thanked the men for their help, and began ushering them toward the front door. It was growing late, the children's supper was waiting, she'd let them know if they discovered anything new . . . Yes, of course the precinct-house would be invited to the Marching Band Revue, they were welcome every year . . . She saw them out, and then went upstairs.

Kreindel was still in the lavatory; sobs rose now and again from one of the stalls. A group of whispering girls lurked outside, clearly waiting to waylay her with questions. The headmistress told them in no uncertain terms to go downstairs for supper, then knocked gently upon the stall door. "Kreindel? Do you need anything?"

The sobs were tamed to sniffles. "No, thank you," Kreindel whispered.

The headmistress sighed. She, too, wanted to ask Kreindel what she'd seen in the basement—no more of these outlandish stories, only the honest truth—and what role, if any, Charlotte Levy had played. But the girl had gone through enough for one day. They could resume their questioning in the morning.

"Why don't you take a nice, long shower," she told Kreindel. "And then you can have your supper in the infirmary, if you like. I'll tell Matron to expect you."

The shower helped, somewhat.

Kreindel had only ever bathed in the mornings, when every faucet in the Asylum was open and the water ran at a lukewarm trickle. But now there was plenty, and steaming hot. Her matted hair unstuck itself from her neck; the film of salt dissolved from her skin. Her head throbbed from crying. Her stomach felt hollow, but she knew she couldn't eat. She'd just lost her only friend. He'd terrified her, and she'd driven him away. She wanted him back. She hoped she'd never see him again.

She sniffed back more tears, closed her eyes, tilted her face into the spray . . . and for a moment felt a different set of sensations. Water, but colder, and more of it, not just a shower's worth . . . There, again. She concentrated, seeking it out. Not quite knowing how, she reached out into the darkness—

—and grabbed his hand.

He was walking along a murky river-bottom, the currents curling around him, warm and cool, fresh and salt. He felt oddly at home here, in the quiet. He looked up, and saw faraway glimmers of light, filtering through the depths. Miss Levy was beside him, holding his hand: a hand like his own, not flesh and bone but clay, cool and strong. She, too, had lived in hiding, and had been hurt by it, deeply. Despite everything, he was glad, at this moment, to be walking beside her. She was taking him south toward the river's end, to a place that she knew of . . .

Kreindel gasped, and jolted back to herself.

Miss Levy was a golem, too.

The Hotel Earle was in chaos.

Guests roamed the hallways, asking each other if they'd heard the gunshot. In Room 812, they found a scene out of a dime novel: a blood-soaked carpet, a pearl-handled pistol, and an empty bottle of laudanum. It was everything that the newspaper-men could've wished for—but they were all out on Waverly Place, following after the lieutenant who'd fled white-faced through the lobby, babbling something about a tiger.

Sophia, meanwhile, only knew that someone was carrying her down a flight of stairs.

Where was she? She turned her head, saw a man's fleshy cheek and bristling mustache. The hotel manager. He'd come to her room, just before . . . What had happened? Her stomach hurt terribly. She tried to lift her head, but didn't have the strength. The walls were pale and unpainted, and the manager's shoes rang on bare risers. It must be a ser-vice staircase, she realized. Someone was behind them; she heard heeled boots, a woman's labored, half-sobbing breaths. Her mother.

The world was dimming; she saw a shimmer in the air, above her. Was it Dima? She tried to squint, to focus, but the pain was growing worse. She was warm, though. Why was she so warm?

I must be dying, she thought.

Above her, the jinniyeh kept pace unseen, watching as Sophia's face grew ever paler and her blood leaked from her stomach to drip upon the stairs. She had little knowledge of human injury, but this seemed alarming. Would the woman die? She shuddered at the memory of the bullet passing through her own body; even now she felt a horrible *wrong-ness* inside herself, as though it were still there somehow.

They reached the bottom of the stairwell, and emerged in an alley. The chauffeur had been idling the limousine nearby, for discretion's sake; he saw them coming, and rushed to help. Together they bundled Sophia into the back, her head in Julia's lap, Julia's cloak pressed upon the wound. There was a brief argument about their destination—Saint Vincent's was closest, but the House of Relief was the best—and the Oldsmobile sped out of the alley.

They drove south on West Broadway toward the House of Relief, the chauffeur leaning on the horn and speeding through the intersections while Julia gazed down at her now-unconscious daughter. A grown woman, all childhood softness gone, her hair plaited about her head like a Viking queen's. The first gray hairs were at her temples; the first fine wrinkles gathered at the corners of her eyes. *Dear God,* Julia thought, *let me not have killed her.*

Still battling her own injuries, the jinniyeh struggled to keep the Oldsmobile in sight, terrified that if she lost track of the woman, she might never find her again. *Don't die,* the jinniyeh thought. *Don't leave me alone in this terrible place.* It ought not to matter—merely one human life, vanished from among a seething sea of them—and yet the thought of Sophia dying made the jinniyeh's stomach twist with agony. . . .

Wait.

She slowed in the air as the sense of wrongness grew.

The Oldsmobile turned onto Jay Street, tires screeching, and arrived at the House of Relief.

The attendants lifted Sophia from her mother's lap, laid her carefully upon a stretcher, and carried her inside. Doctors were alerted, the surgery prepared. The bullet was lodged in the patient's abdomen; it would need to be removed, and the internal bleeding stanched. A nurse peeled aside Sophia's clothing to probe the wound—

—and in the air above West Broadway, the jinniyeh cried out in pain. She shook herself, tried to take a deep breath, and then remembered that she didn't breathe.

Six directions, what was *happening* to her?

The bullet had indeed lodged itself in Sophia's abdomen—but first, it had passed through the jinniyeh.

The jinniyeh's body ought to have parted easily around it, like a fingertip passing through a candle-flame. But her injuries had weakened her deeply; and instead the bullet had torn away a tiny scrap of her substance and carried it straight into Sophia, coming to rest beside her womb. The flame ought to have guttered and died there, overwhelmed by its human host. Were that anyone but Sophia, it would have.

But Sophia's body had harbored jinn-flame before.

A cinder, a bit of ash, left behind.

In the years since, Sophia's body had scarred itself deeply around this tiny cinder, enclosing it like an oyster's grain of sand. Now, the new flame thrashed about, desperate to survive—and in its throes it sensed the cold cinder nearby, safe inside its hollow. A place where it could live.

With its last strength, the flame gathered itself and broke through.

The cinder ignited—and a tiny thread of fire climbed its way up Sophia's spine.

The jinniyeh turned about blindly in the air. Something was happening far away, but also inside her. Below her was West Broadway, and the Elevated—and there on the next block was a man with a shave ice cart, like the ones she'd seen on walks in Central Park with her aunt. She'd always begged for a shave ice, but Auntie had said—

The jinniyeh stumbled in midair. Spasmed. *Changed.*

For the briefest of moments, a naked woman fell through the sky.

She loosed her form at once, found the wind again, flew higher. She looked down, saw Union Square and Madison Square, with Gramercy Park between them. The East River to one side, the Hudson to the other. Streets and avenues, city blocks, ferries, frankfurter carts. Peanut vendors. Rag-pickers. Astor Place, Washington Mews, billboards, marquees, Chinese lanterns, pretzel sellers, newsboys, tobacconists—

The jinniyeh shrieked in rage.

Dear Headmistress:

*I'm not really running away, because I should have left already.
I'm eighteen, not fifteen, which means I'm no longer a ward of the
state. My mother's death certificate will tell you that Malke Altschul
died after childbirth in January of 1897. I shouldn't have lied to you,
but then the lie grew too big to correct.*

*You warned me recently that the world will fail to meet my
standards. You're probably right. Still I hope to find a small corner of
it where I can be myself.*

Respectfully,
Kreindel Altschul

She left the note on her pillow.

Supper would be over soon; she didn't have much time. She opened
her footlocker, removed her Asylum-issue coat and her small drawstring
bag, and filled the bag with the two dollars in hoarded coins that was the
sum of her worldly wealth. After a moment she grabbed her composition
notebook, tore out her Psalm translations, and stuffed them inside as
well.

The residents were in the dining hall and the staff had all gone home,
leaving the hallways empty. She left the Asylum by the side door, as
though she were merely going to the infirmary—but then went past it,
opened the broken gate, and walked out into the evening.

She expected shouts, bells, truancy officers. None came. She'd left
the Asylum, and not a single soul had stopped her. With every step it
became more real. She was leaving at last! Where would she go? She'd
follow the pair in the river, try to find them somehow . . .

She rounded the corner onto Broadway—and at once was overwhelmed by the sight of the avenue, with its rushing traffic and hurrying crowds. Suddenly she felt lost and mouse-like. She had no idea how
to navigate the subway or the Elevated; she'd never so much as ridden a
streetcar by herself. She was a runaway, no matter what she'd written,
a frightened girl out alone after sunset. Already she was drawing atten-

tion, the passersby staring at her Asylum-issue clothing, clearly wondering if they should intervene . . .

As she looked around in growing panic, her gaze nearly passed over a boy in a Western Union uniform. He stood in front of an apartment building on the corner, his bicycle beside him, watching the passersby as though hoping that someone would appear. He saw her; his eyes widened in surprise. "Kreindel?"

"Toby?" she said. "What are *you* doing here?" And then, mortified at her own bluntness: "I didn't mean—I just thought you'd be downtown by now. Are you making deliveries?"

He gave her an oddly nervous smile, as though she'd caught him at something. "No, I just have to find someone," he said. "Say, you haven't seen your cooking teacher around lately, have you?"

"Miss Levy?" she said, confused. "That's who you have to find?"

"Yeah, she's a friend of my ma's. I wasn't sure if you were talking about the same lady, before. But it turns out you were."

"Miss Levy . . . is a friend of your mother's," she said slowly.

"Sort of, I guess. I just wanted to talk to her, about something. But she isn't home. You haven't, have you? Seen her, I mean?" Then he paused, looking Kreindel over, seeming to register at last that she was alone on the street, in her uniform. "Hey—are you running away?"

She eyed him. "What if I am?"

He grinned. "Good. I'm glad. That place sounded awful. You got somewhere to go?"

"Not really," she admitted.

"Don't worry, my ma will take you in. Once I've explained. Except, um—" He glanced back at the door. "I have to find Missus—Miss Levy first. It's kind of important." The sickly smile had returned.

With careful nonchalance Kreindel said, "Would you say that Miss Levy is made of stronger stuff than most women?"

The smile faded; he stared at her. "Yeah. Yeah, I would. Feet of clay, though, don't you think?"

Kreindel laughed in relief. "Oh, absolutely."

"Holy cats. How did you find out—"

"Toby," she cut over him, "is your mother really her friend?" Was such a thing possible? Could someone like Miss Levy have a friend—a regular, ordinary friend?

He eyed her, uncertain. "She used to be. Though I don't know if she'd say so in those words, exactly. Why?"

"Because I know where Miss Levy is." She took a quick, nervous breath. "And she isn't alone. There's another golem with her. His name is Yossele."

At the House of Relief, the damage to Sophia's body was repaired.

By luck or Providence, the bullet had missed the nearby artery, the surgeon explained to Julia. The loss of blood had been minimal. However, sepsis was still possible, and even if she recovered fully, she'd be weak with anemia for some time . . .

Julia, half listening at Sophia's bedside, wiped away her tears. She felt a sickening *déjà vu*, as though she'd never left the Paris hospital where they'd begun this terrible chapter in their lives. She watched as Sophia lay asleep—then peered down at the woman's twitching eyelids, her furrowed brow. "Is she in pain?" she asked.

The doctor, too, squinted at Sophia's face, then lifted her wrist and felt her pulse. "No, she's still anesthetized," he said. "Perhaps I'll increase the dosage." He replaced her wrist at her side and withdrew.

Sophia watched through the jinniyeh's eyes as she flew above the city, past newsstands, tailors, dray-carts, cobblestones, milk-wagons, factory lofts—

What did you do to me? the jinniyeh cried.

I did nothing, Sophia said. You're the one who broke our bargain.

I wish I'd never seen you, said the jinniyeh—and Sophia realized the language they spoke was the jinniyeh's, and that she understood every word. Seen: the female form, used for an adversary.

You thought of me as an enemy from the beginning, Sophia said. Perhaps that was your mistake.

Oh, so condescending, both you and the iron-bound one.

Then you found him? Sophia said—and at once she saw it all, their whole encounter from beginning to end, the jinniyeh's memories as clear to her as her own.

Get out! snarled the jinniyeh. Those are mine!

Oh, Dima, what have you done, Sophia whispered.

I didn't mean to! I swear to God—oh, what is happening to me, what are these words—

The doctor returned with the chloroform mask, and Sophia sank back into the depths.

23.

Kreindel held onto Toby's belt with both hands, and prayed that they wouldn't be killed.

She was perched upon the seat of his bicycle, her feet held awkwardly to either side of the rear tire. Toby stood on the pedals in front of her, steering them south along Riverside. She was terrified of losing her balance, but he kept them going fast enough that they didn't wobble, and before long she was leaning into the turns a little, like he did. Automobiles and wagons streamed by on one side, dusky trees and the river on the other—and in the middle was Toby, hunched over the handlebars, the brim of his cap angling to left and right as he watched the cross-streets. Her damp hair fluttered behind her; the breeze cut through her thin coat and stockings. She shivered, and tightened her grip upon his belt.

"You doing okay?" he called over his shoulder.

"I think so," she called back. She was, in fact, utterly exhilarated. The Asylum was behind her, she'd never go back—and oh, what a way to leave!

The river was dark now, all glimmers of sunlight gone.

The Golem held Yossele's hand, guiding him onward as he watched Kreindel. He felt her happiness at having left the Asylum at last, her joy at the bicycle ride. The pair on the street was gaining on the pair in the river; soon, Toby and Kreindel would overtake them, and pull ahead. To the Golem's relief, Yossele felt no rage at Toby's presence—only a bittersweet regret that the boy could be with his master in the open air while he, Yossele, could not.

They walked south along the shipping channel, the current at their backs, steamboats and barges cutting through the water above. The land held steady to either side of them, guiding them past ferry docks and freight depots, the oblique bend at Chelsea Piers. *This is where I first came ashore*, she told Yossele, and then showed him the memory: a shining summer day, the steamship coming into dock, her leap from the rail. How she'd pulled herself out of the water, and wandered the incomprehensible city.

And in return, he showed her the weeks he'd spent hiding in the shallows beneath the unfinished bridge, waiting for Kreindel's call. The thick scents of algae and engine grease, the whistle of the breeze through the cattails. The keening cries of migrating birds, the bite in the air as summer turned to autumn.

I wish I had known, she told him sadly. She pictured it, and he saw it, too: how she would've come to his hiding-place in the clay at the river's edge, how she would've sat beside him, sharing in his vigil while he waited—

And suddenly it was all too much for Yossele to bear.

He turned away, struggling against his inner vision. He didn't want this longing for something that hadn't happened and never would! What was the point of *if only*, when there was only the endless *now* of his watching, his servitude? What was the point of this new mind that she'd given him, if everything it showed him was beyond his reach?

Yossele, she said, *don't*—

He pulled his hand away, and the connection broke.

Yossele!

He was a spot of anguish in the dark, moving swiftly away from her. She cut across the current, climbing over oil-barrels and thickets of wire, trying desperately to keep pace—but his size and mass gave him the advantage. He sped away from her, and disappeared.

She stood alone in the debris, trying not to panic. There was little she could do. He might stay here, in the river; he might double back, and return to the Asylum. Now her only connection to him was through Kreindel—and Kreindel was with Toby, on her way to the Amherst.

She could only keep going.

"Well," Anna said, her arms folded, looking up at the Amherst's insides, "it's certainly big, whatever it is."

The Jinni sighed, and scooped another bucket of wet ash from the forge. Sayeed had gone to help Maryam close the coffee-house; Anna, however, seemed intent on not letting the Jinni out of her sight. *Toby will be here soon*, she'd informed him, her clipped tone matter-of-fact—and he'd been momentarily baffled by the speed with which his solitude had crumbled. Was this what it was like, he wondered, to have neighbors, acquaintances? To allow oneself to be talked about and watched over? It felt . . . disconcerting. Sayeed had even left Maryam's mixing bowl on the worktable nearby, full of kindling, *in case you need it*. The bowl was glazed in bands of white and yellow, with cheerful lemons painted about its middle; it felt utterly out of place on the scarred and pitted table, like a hack-saw in a bakery case. He wondered, would one of the Faddouls return for it? Or was he supposed to take it back on his own?

Anna watched as he cleaned out the forge. "So. Toby said you nearly died. Was he exaggerating?"

"Not at all. He saved my life."

"Well. We're all lucky, then."

He put down the bucket. "Anna, I had no intention of involving your son in any of this. I didn't even realize who he was."

"Oh, I know. He told me everything. He delivered you a cable, and it all went downhill from there."

"Then is there a specific reason you're angry at me? Or is it merely on principle?"

She pressed her lips together, looked away stonily. Then she said, "You know, I never told him tales when he was little. No golems, no *dybbuks*, no old witches in chicken-leg huts. I didn't want him believing in things that couldn't exist."

Confused, offended, he said, "Even though you knew we were real?"

She glared at him. "Let me tell you something, Ahmad. This is a cruel world for a boy like Toby. A good-hearted kid with no father, and a mother who's never home, with barely two nickels to rub together—a boy like that has to grow up learning certain truths. And one of them is that if someone shows you magic, it's a trick, and you're the mark. But you people—you and Chava and God knows who else—look what you can do." She pointed upward, at the shining steel. "You break all the rules and turn truth on its head, so now he starts to believe in the impossible. So what happens when he goes out into the world? Maybe he gets taken by the first confidence man he meets. And even if he doesn't, what then? Do you think he'll be satisfied working at some factory for the rest of his life? Or will he go running off after Mister Ahmad and Missus Chava—the woman I thought was going to—"

Her face tightened. Tears flooded her eyes. She turned away.

He stood there feeling helpless. "Anna. I'm sorry. You were trying to protect him."

She sniffed angrily, whisked her tears away. "And now he's uptown looking for a golem. Some job of it I did."

"Ma?"

They turned. Toby was standing in the doorway. Beside him was a stranger, a startled-looking girl in a shapeless gray coat.

"Ma, Mister Ahmad," Toby said, "this is Kreindel."

Kreindel didn't know where to look first.

She'd never seen a place so big, not even her father's synagogue. She stared up in fascination at the platforms hanging in midair, the spiraling column, the branching arches in the upper shadows—all of it gigantic yet delicate-looking, like an enormous whirligig that might come to life on a puff of wind.

"Kreindel," Toby whispered behind her, "tell them about Yossele."

She tore her gaze from the towering sculpture, took in the woman who stood with her hands on her hips, eyeing Kreindel with suspicion and curiosity. And then the man behind her, who was . . .

"My God," she whispered. "It's you."

It was the man from the tenement fire. Tall and striking, dark eyes, angular features. All this time, and not a day older, exactly the same as she'd dreamt him.

"You probably don't remember me," she said, her voice shaking. "But you were there when my building burned down. Your friend ran in after me, you were holding her cloak . . ." Her heart thudded as she realized. "Wait. Your friend. Was it Miss Levy? It was, wasn't it?"

"You're the girl from the fire," the man said, wonder in his voice.

"Ahmad, what's she talking about?" said Toby's mother.

Tears of relief sprang to Kreindel's eyes. "Oh, thank God. All this time I thought she'd died, that I'd killed her. I dreamt about you so often—"

She remembered, then. A portrait, sewn in golden thread. *Give him this, when he wakes.* She began to laugh, still crying. "I even dreamt that you'd sewn a picture of me, if you can believe it."

"But I did," the man said, puzzled. "I left it at her apartment, I'd forgotten all about it." He peered at her. "How could you possibly dream that?"

She thought. "Because of Miss Levy," she said. "And Yossele."

At the bottom of the river, huddled beneath a rust-cankered gantry crane, Yossele sat listening to his master.

There's another golem? said the mother of the boy on the bicycle, her tone wary.

He's not like Miss Levy, Kreindel said. *He's . . . different. My father built him because of the pogroms. We were supposed to go to Lithuania . . . but then the fire happened. It all went wrong.*

So he was made to be a weapon, said the man from the fire.

He's my protector, and my friend, his master said, in uneasy protest. *But . . . yes. That, too. He . . .* She winced; and in her mind Yossele saw the basement hallway, his own twisted face. *Something happened, today. Some girls played a prank on me, and—But he didn't hurt anyone!* she protested, at their dawning alarm. *He was going to, but Miss Levy stopped him. And it was my own fault anyway. I was so angry at them, I wanted him to—but I didn't think—*She began to cry again.

Yossele put his head in his hands. She blamed herself for what he'd nearly done!

Kreindel, the man said, *how did Miss Levy stop him?*

She had a . . . a necklace, Kreindel said. *She showed it to him and then ran away, and he ran after her.*

Her old locket, Toby's mother said, looking to the man in surprise.

A newer one, he muttered.

Beside Kreindel, Toby said, *What's so special about it? Did it hypnotize him or something?*

It has a command inside it, the man said. *It can destroy a golem.* He was watching Kreindel as he said it.

It can? Kreindel said, almost a whisper. Shock and relief burst inside her—followed by horror, guilt, and anguish—and suddenly she was sobbing. She turned and pressed her face to the boy's shoulder. Yossele felt him jump a bit, in surprise; then the boy's arms went around her, and he held Kreindel while she cried.

They sat Kreindel in a wooden swivel chair belonging to an old, incongruous rolltop desk, hidden beneath the lowest of the platforms. It was, it seemed, the only chair in the building. Toby gave her his pocket handkerchief—she wondered, briefly, if it had come with the uniform—and then went to help the man he'd called *Mister Ahmad* scoop buckets of murky water out of a long, high trough. Mister Ahmad seemed unsteady on his feet; at one point he stopped and leaned against the edge of the trough, the bucket sloshing in his hands. Seeing this, Toby's mother went to his side. "You should sit," she told him. "You won't feel any better if you spill that all over yourself."

"I will feel better," the man said, irritated, "when the forge is relit."

"Sit down, Ahmad," Toby's mother repeated, her voice firm. "Now. Keep Kreindel company. Toby and I will do the rest." And she took the bucket, not waiting for his assent.

He stood there a moment, clearly perplexed; and then, throwing up his hands, left them to their work and came to where Kreindel sat, just outside the shadow of the platform. She began to stand from the chair, but he shook his head and sat down on the floor beside her, his back against the wooden desk, an elbow on one knee. He was tall enough that they were nearly eye to eye. There was an awkward silence.

"So," he said after a moment, "when did you meet Toby?"

"This morning." Could it have only been that morning? How had so much happened in a single day?

The man glanced at her in surprise, as though he, too, thought it improbable. "And . . . Miss Levy?"

"A few days ago. They put me in her cooking class."

"I see. Is she a good teacher?" He said this with a studied nonchalance.

"I think she must be. Her students all love her."

A pause; he arched an eyebrow. "Except for you?"

Briefly she considered lying, but then shook her head. "No. But I didn't give her a chance, either. And I might like her better . . . now that I know."

He considered this, then nodded.

"Has she always been a teacher?" Kreindel said.

"Chava? No, she was a baker, for years," he said.

Kreindel frowned. "I thought her name was Charlotte."

"'Charlotte'?" She saw him wince, deeply. "That's . . . new."

Her hands fidgeted with Toby's handkerchief. After a moment she said, "May I ask you a question? It might be rude."

"Go ahead."

"What are you?"

A wry chuckle. "Must I be something?"

She glanced upward, at the hollow building and its steel creation.

"Well, yes, there is that." He seemed to debate with himself, and then said, "I am what you would call a jinni." He glanced across at her. "Here," he said, and took her hand in both of his. Within moments her skin was almost too warm to bear. He let go, quickly.

"Oh," she said, rubbing her hand in surprise. Her mind filled with questions; but seeing the look on his face, she bit them all back. "I'm sorry. I didn't mean to embarrass you."

He shook his head. "I've been hiding for years," he said quietly. "And now . . . perhaps I don't know how not to hide."

She nodded: that made sense. "I never told anyone about Yossele, until today."

"He watches you through your eyes?"

"Yes. And he knows what I'm thinking."

He thought a moment. "Even when it's about him?"

She nodded.

They fell silent, watching Toby and his mother work. She was aware of being hungry, and deeply tired. What time was it? Past lights-out, certainly. With a start she realized that this was the longest she'd gone in years without hearing the Asylum bell.

The front door opened, making both of them look up. A man and a woman slipped inside, both carrying wooden crates. The woman had large, dark eyes and curly hair streaked with gray. Something about the sight of her made Kreindel feel better at once, as though a kindly nurse had arrived at her bedside. The man closed the door quickly, as though afraid someone might see them.

Next to Kreindel, Mister Ahmad made a sound of minor outrage. "Yes, come in, why not," he said under his breath. His eyes looked pleased, though.

The pair set down the crates—and then the woman caught sight of the building's interior for what was clearly the first time. Her eyes widened; her mouth opened in shock.

Mister Ahmad, Kreindel saw, was smiling.

Sophia woke slowly.

She lay in a crisply made bed. The room was dark and empty save for a table and a chair, and smelled harshly of soap. A hospital, then.

She sat up, carefully. They'd dressed her in a thin cotton gown; her stomach was tightly bandaged. She touched the spot where the bullet had entered her, and felt a row of stitches beneath the fabric. It ached slightly, but not nearly as much as she'd expected.

She pulled the bedclothes aside, swung her legs over the edge. The tile floor was cool beneath her feet. She stood, half expecting a rush of pain, or for the stitches to tear open—but neither happened. She felt . . . alert. Strong. *Warm.*

A whisper, in her mind. *Sophia.*

The jinniyeh was nearby. Sophia felt along the connection between them, that thin line of fire, and oriented herself like a compass-needle, turning in place until she was facing the window. She reached out, pulled back the curtain.

On the other side of the window, the jinniyeh floated: a veil of flame, constantly moving, ever-changing.

Sophia put a hand to the pane. *Dima,* she said. She could see herself through the jinniyeh's eyes, like a second sight laid atop her own: a human face behind glass, faintly glimmering with new light.

They gazed at each other for long moments.

I ought to come in there, the jinniyeh said, *and tear myself out of you.*

For a moment Sophia was afraid that she might—but then she shook her head. *You'd still have my knowledge. My words, my memories. You can't unlearn what you've learned.*

Stop gloating! the jinniyeh cried.

I'm not, Dima. I'm only saying what's true.

A hitch in the air, like a sob. *You've destroyed my life.*

I'm sorry. I truly am. But you did this to yourself.

The jinniyeh sagged in the air. She turned, looking west to the river, only a block distant. *Then I will end it myself.*

Sophia said, *Dima*—

But already the jinniyeh had flown away.

The kind-eyed woman had brought supper to the Amherst.

Kreindel watched as she unpacked the crates and set their contents upon the worktable: loaves of flatbread, squares of baked meat mixed with grain and spices, a salad of crisp lettuces and cucumbers, a pot of coffee with cardamom. Kreindel recognized none of it, but it all smelled astonishingly good. Toby seemed to know the woman; he introduced his mother, and they shook hands. Then the woman's husband joined Toby at the forge, and the two women began to portion out the food onto plates the woman had brought.

Kreindel, meanwhile, sat in her chair in the shadows, not knowing what to do. Beside her, Mister Ahmad looked just as confused.

The kind-eyed woman approached, carrying two plates. "Would you like something to eat?" she said in accented English.

"Yes, thank you," Kreindel said.

The woman handed her a plate. "I'm Maryam," she said. "And that's my husband, Sayeed." She gestured to the man helping Toby at the forge.

"I'm Kreindel. It's nice to meet you." The words felt foreign on her tongue. How long had it been since she'd met so many new people at once?

Maryam smiled, and then turned to Mister Ahmad, a polite question on her face.

He looked unsure, uncomfortable; he put up a hand. "No, thank you," he said. Maryam nodded, unperturbed, and took the plate to Toby instead.

Kreindel murmured the proper blessings and then examined the flatbread. It was raised along its edges and dimpled in the middle, with a golden tinge to the crust. She tore off a corner, bit into it. The bread was still warm from the oven, and the crust yielded to a fragrant middle that tasted richly of yeast and salt. It was, quite possibly, the most delicious thing that Kreindel had ever eaten. Tears sprang to her eyes again, for no reason that she could see. She wiped them on her sleeve, ate more of the bread.

Mister Ahmad was watching her sidelong, his expression one of regret. Without a word, she tore a piece from her flatbread and handed it to him. He took a bite, chewed with interest.

"Is it as good as Miss Levy's bread?" she asked.

She'd thought it an innocent question—but he stopped chewing, then looked down at the bread in his hand. "I don't know," he said. "I never tried it."

"You didn't?" That was strange, wasn't it? He'd said she'd been a baker for years . . .

"No," he said. "I didn't. And she was known for her challah. But I never tried—" His mouth tightened. Suddenly he stood and walked away, behind the column and out of sight.

Nearby, Toby paused in wolfing down his plate of food and gave Kreindel a quizzical look, then cocked his head in the direction the man had gone. She shook her head, quickly. Better, she thought, to let the man alone. And indeed Mister Ahmad returned only a few minutes later, carrying a bucket of coal. He said nothing, only poured the coal into the newly cleaned forge and went back for more. Toby finished eating, and joined in. So did Toby's mother, and Sayeed—and soon the forge was filled. Then Mister Ahmad fetched a long-handled rake from a peg upon the wall and began to spread out the pieces to his liking. Intrigued, Kreindel set aside her plate and went to join the others, watching as he arranged the coal with quick strokes. Then he put down the rake and gazed around a moment, searching for something. "Kreindel," he said, "would you bring me that bowl?"

He pointed to a large, cheerful bowl painted with lemons that sat upon the worktable beside her. Inside the bowl was a handful of broken wooden slats, from a crate of some kind. She carried the bowl to him, and watched as he arranged the wood in a small pyramid atop the coals.

He looked up, then, and Kreindel followed his gaze. Toby and Anna and the Faddouls had gathered around the forge too, all standing a few feet back from its edge—cautious, expectant, not quite certain of what was about to happen. It felt like a held breath, the pause before a blessing.

Mister Ahmad put a hand to the kindling.

At once the wood began to crackle. He held his hand there a moment, then lifted it away and pressed a switch on the wall behind him. A fan began to whir, pulling the flames along the bed of coal. In moments the entire forge had come alive, its heat spreading outward.

Kreindel closed her eyes, and whispered the Havdalah prayers to herself, for the end of the Sabbath. It wasn't a proper ceremony; she had no spice-box, no braided candle, no cup of wine. But perhaps tonight, just this once, it didn't matter.

Yossele, she thought, *I know you're out there. I still love you.* And for a moment she could feel cold, dark water all around, and an answering pulse of love and sadness—and then the sensation faded.

In the river, Yossele sat beneath the rusted crane, thinking.

He'd never known—because neither had Kreindel—that there could be people like this in the world. Ordinary people, like Toby and

Anna and the Faddouls, who might learn her secrets and still accept her, understand her. Who could protect her when necessary, and hold her when she cried.

His master, it seemed, didn't have to hide anymore. He, Yossele, was separate from his master—and his master no longer required a golem.

It ought to have angered him. Instead, he only felt relief. He could make this decision for her; he could lift this weight from her shoulders.

He left the shelter of the crane, and began to walk south again, toward his master.

Night fell along the docklands.

In the pier-sheds, watchmen strolled between the stacked boxes, light spilling from their lanterns. Car-floats bumped up against the docks, their boxcars heavy with cargo. Stevedores whose shifts had ended strolled across West Street to the taverns, or took their week's pay to the back rooms of terminal houses, where men sat upon wooden crates and dealt out hands of rummy.

The Golem surfaced at the end of a freight pier.

She found a ladder nailed to the pilings and climbed upward, pausing at the top to make certain that she was alone. The pier-shed rose before her, a narrow walkway beside it. A pair of barges was tied to the pier, the river lapping at their hulls.

She pulled herself onto the wooden deck, sat and wiped the water from her face. Where was she? She squinted down the pier, and saw the words *Baltimore & Ohio Freight* painted in white on the terminal house. She must be at Jay Street, then. Only a few blocks from Carlisle, and the Amherst.

She wrung out her jacket, squeezed handfuls of muck from her skirt. Her boots and stockings were ruined, gashed to ribbons by the river's jetsam. She took them off and set them beside her, then looked out over the water, wondering where Yossele was. She wished she could've held on more tightly . . . She'd have to face Kreindel, and tell her what had happened. She and Toby must have reached the Amherst, by now.

She stood, keeping to the shadows, judging her options. She could go back into the water and walk the rest of the way to Carlisle, counting the piers as she went—but if she overshot she'd end up in the bay, where the currents might be difficult to navigate. Could she risk taking West Street instead? It was nighttime, but the streets weren't deserted by any means—and she was alone, wet, and bedraggled, not to mention barefoot.

The back of her neck prickled. Something was approaching—a mind, a presence . . .

She turned, and saw a light in the sky.

The Jinni stood beside the forge, his arms crossed, looking into its depths.

There'd been a brief discussion, verging on argument. Sayeed, they'd decided, would go to the Hotel Earle in the Jinni's stead, and look for Sophia. When the Jinni had insisted that he was recovered enough to make the trip, they'd reminded him that, according to Kreindel, there were two golems in the river heading toward Little Syria, and it might be best for all involved if he was there when they arrived. It all made very good sense—and yet it left the Jinni stuck in one place, waiting for others, which was exactly what he'd wished to avoid.

It's my own fault, he thought ruefully. *I opened the door, and they came in.*

He looked around. Kreindel was dozing in Arbeely's chair; Toby, sitting beside her on the floor, was likewise asleep, his head against the desk. Maryam was packing away her supper things, with help from Anna. He caught Maryam's eye; she came over, and he handed her the cream-and-yellow mixing bowl. "Thank you," he said.

She smiled—as always, it didn't quite reach her eyes—but then paused at his expression. "Is something wrong?"

"No, not wrong. I only wanted to tell you . . . I'm leaving New York."

To his surprise, she seemed neither glad nor relieved, only puzzled. "You are? But—where will you go?"

"Back to the desert. I've had . . . an offer, I suppose. From one of my kind, another exile. She wants me to come live with her, so that neither of us are alone."

"Oh. I see."

His mouth quirked. "Of course, that was before she nearly murdered me. But I don't think she meant it," he said to Maryam's shocked expression, "and I believe her offer still stands. And even if it doesn't . . . Maryam, I don't belong here anymore. Maybe I never did. Maybe it was just easier to pretend when Arbeely was still alive." He glanced over to the desk and chair, and their sleeping occupants. "I think Ahmad al-Hadid died too, that night," he said quietly. "I just didn't realize it at the time."

"If this is what you truly want, then I'm glad for you," she said. "But what will you do there, in the desert?"

He chuckled. "I have no idea. Perhaps I'll build the Amherst again, where no one can see it."

She looked slightly appalled. "But—Ahmad, talents such as yours are meant to be shared."

"I don't know what else I can do," he said. "I can't just wander the earth like an accursed spirit for the next six centuries. I'm only content when I'm making something new—but who'd ever look at the Amherst and believe that I'm human?"

Maryam's eyes had widened. "Six centuries? Is *that* how much longer you'll live?"

"Barring malice, accident, or my own idiocy, yes."

She began to laugh, one hand to her mouth, all wariness fallen away. "Oh, *Ahmad.* Forgive me, but—how long have you been here, with us?"

"It'll be sixteen years, this summer."

"And how many changes have there been, in those sixteen years? How many inventions, how many new marvels?"

He frowned. "I . . . don't understand."

"Do you remember the first automobiles? Or when the subway opened?"

"Of course I do," he said. "I remember all of it. The telephones. The Woolworth Building."

"Exactly. All in sixteen years. And you have another *six hundred* ahead of you. How long will it be, do you think, before we ordinary humans begin to make our own Amhersts? How long before there's an Amherst on every corner?"

He stared at her, and then looked upward.

"We're going to catch up to you," she told him, smiling. "And more quickly than you'd expect. If you're not careful, we'll pull ahead. All you have to do is wait."

The jinniyeh flew toward the river.

Some say, she told herself, *that the iron-bound jinni was last seen crossing into the Ghouta, perhaps to drown himself, and thus end his unhappy life.*

The river stretched north and south, its shoreline a sharp edge, the piers lying across it like fallen wheat. *Ferries, barges, freight terminals,* she thought. She could feel Sophia trying to grab her attention, pleading with her to stop; she ignored the woman and kept going, flying out over the nearest pier, aiming toward the middle of the river. *Jersey City,* she thought in despair, as she gazed toward the opposite shore. *Hoboken.* She didn't want to die—but she didn't want to live, either. Not like this. She gathered herself, shuddering in fear—

"*Wait!*" a woman's voice cried out.

Startled, she halted in the air, turned—and saw the figure at the end of the pier.

In her shock, the Golem could only think of the Jinni's golden embroidery. Never would she have mistaken it for a jinniyeh if she'd seen this creature first. This was no fire-winged girl, but a living, blazing aurora, a veil of flame that twisted in the air.

The jinniyeh descended and began to circle her slowly, examining her with a curiosity so intense that it was nearly unbearable. Her thoughts assailed the Golem, images and emotions bursting from her mind and vanishing again, too quickly for sense.

—*You aren't human*, the jinniyeh said. *You are something else. A creature of earth, made by human hands. What are you?*

The windblown language, too, was like nothing the Golem had ever heard. The words were brief, yet they held oceans of meaning: a language with depth enough to satisfy centuries of exploration, so one might describe a rock, a sunset, a lover, all to the final detail.

Oh, Ahmad, she thought, amazed. *I see what you lost. I understand.*

The jinniyeh was still circling her, studying her. Then, suddenly she pulled back.—*You're a wizard's automaton*, she said. *The tales of the Cursed City were full of monsters like you. Who controls you?*

But the Golem stayed warily silent. She could hardly bear the rush of images, both familiar and strange. A desert valley, littered with fallen ruins. The Washington Square Arch, seen from above. The Amherst's forge, and the Jinni lying atop it, beneath her—

The Golem flinched.

And in the hospital room, watching it all with that new second sight, Sophia thought in surprise, *Chava?*

—*Chava?* the jinniyeh said, incredulous. *The baker that the iron-bound one spoke of? His 'friend?' But he led me to believe that you were human, not some thrice-damned*—

Dima, Sophia thought quickly. *Be careful. Don't make an enemy of her.*

"Dima," the monster said.

The jinniyeh started in surprise.

"That's what Sophia Winston calls you."

—How could you know that? she snarled.

"I can see her in your thoughts," the monster said, her tone puzzled. "Though I don't know *how.*"

—Is my mind an open carcass now, to be picked over by passing jackals? Get out—

She broke off, shuddering in pain as the damp night air pressed against her injuries.

And Sophia winced too, one hand to her stomach, feeling Dima's pain as well as her own.

"You're hurt," the monster said. "Both of you."

—Stop that, the jinniyeh snapped. Why had he lied to her? Was it to protect the creature? But why would he do such a thing? Sophia had known her on sight . . .

The memory came to her, then.

A high-ceilinged dining-room, a roaring fireplace. The tall woman bursting through the door, an unconscious man carried in her arms, her face a mask of desperation, of—love?

—Six directions, the jinniyeh whispered. *You were—but he said, after Sophia, he swore—Ah. 'Never another human.' I failed to see the exception. He must have been lonely indeed, to have lowered himself so.*

Anger flared in the monster's eyes, was carefully tamped down. *Good,* the jinniyeh thought: she greatly preferred it to the concern and pity she'd seen there a moment ago. Why, she wondered, had the monster called out when she'd seen her? Why not simply let her drown herself?

"Because you were in pain," the monster said. "And this isn't a battlefield. We aren't enemies, even if you think we are."

—Of course we're enemies, said the jinniyeh. *How could we possibly be anything else?*

"We can simply choose not to be. I can help you, Dima. Whatever's happened to you and Sophia—we can navigate it together. You don't have to be alone."

Dima, please, Sophia thought. *Neither of us wanted this. But maybe she's right, and there's a way forward.*

What was Sophia saying? That they should all become allies? *Friends?*

I know, thought Sophia. *Jinn don't have friends. But perhaps, just this once, you could change that.*

But—*she doesn't know what I've done,* thought the jinniyeh.

The monster went still. "What did you do? What's happened?"

The jinniyeh hesitated—

—but in an overwhelming flash of her memory, the Golem saw it all: the battle, the broken pipe, the flooded forge. The Jinni, lying in the water.

The Golem staggered. "Ahmad," she whispered; then turned, and ran for the shore.

—*Stop!* the jinniyeh called—but the monster was already halfway down the pier, her bare feet shaking the boards.

Rage and shame overwhelmed the jinniyeh. She'd lost far too much—and the worst of it was that, for a moment, she'd allowed herself to weaken, and believe as they did. To become just a little bit human.

Enough of this. She'd decided to extinguish herself—and she would die like a jinniyeh. She'd make this pier into a battlefield, whether the monster wished it or not.

She flew higher, and gathered the winds.

A breeze began.

The hanging signs on the Jay Street establishments began to sway. Pedestrians clutched at their hats; dust and gravel skittered across the bricks.

The Golem stood motionless upon the pier, straining against the whirlwind that had trapped her.

The wind spread outward.

The tenement windows facing West Street began to rattle, the trash to stir in the gutters. Men up and down the docklands rushed to tie down stacks of cargo as the barges knocked against the pilings.

A dozen blocks south, on a car-float tied to a pier at the end of Carlisle Street, Yossele slipped between the boxcars.

He moved as quickly and quietly as he could, steadying himself as the float rocked on the waves. Soon he was crouched at the bow. It would be an easy leap to the wharf, but conspicuous; and then there was the wide expanse of West Street to cross, an open space overlooked by hundreds of tenement windows.

He thought a moment—and then turned back to the boxcars. All were empty; some stood open. In the second one he checked, he found a stack of gray canvas tarpaulins.

For the first time in his life, Yossele smiled.

Master, he thought, *I'm coming.*

In the Amherst, Kreindel stirred in her chair and sat up. "He's here," she said.

The waves on the river had turned to whitecaps. Out in the shipping channel, the buoys clanged like a carillon. Signs on the storefronts tore themselves from their hangers, and were sent whipping down the piers.

The Golem clenched her teeth and placed one foot in front of the other. *One step. Good. Now another step. Keep moving.* Spray flew about her face; the pier vibrated beneath her like a tuning-fork. The jinniyeh was far above, directing the gale—and so the Golem felt none of her opponent's anger and hatred, only the indifferent wind.

Another step. Shingles blew past from the pier-sheds. A billboard came loose from a rooftop and flew into the air like a kite. *Again. Again.* But it was growing more difficult. She stood now at the center of a hurricane, the boards slick beneath her bare feet. She slipped backward, fell to one knee.

The winds pressed down, crushing her.

The pain in Sophia's stomach was growing worse.

She braced herself against it and watched from the window as a cart overturned on West Street. All the pedestrians were gone, fled indoors.

Dima, she thought desperately. *Don't.*

But the jinniyeh ignored her, intent on the winds that threatened to rip her apart, pouring every last part of herself into the battle—

Including the part that was inside Sophia.

The woman doubled over in agony as the flame that sustained her began to waver. *Dima!* she thought, her teeth chattering with cold. *You'll kill me!*

Sophia!

The jinniyeh spasmed with Sophia's pain. A chill swept over her, worse than any mountain wind. *Six directions, the woman wouldn't survive this—*

It doesn't matter, the jinniyeh told herself. She was just a human! One among thousands, millions—

And yet suddenly she mattered greatly.

Sophia must have cried out, for women in white now gathered around her, talking in stern voices. They carried her to the bed, affixed tight straps to her arms and legs. Sophia tried to struggle against them, but she had no strength. Her vision dimmed.

Dima, please, she thought—

And with a cry of despair the jinniyeh let go.

The howling winds relented; the dreadful weight began to lift.

The Golem staggered to her feet in the quiet. The jinniyeh hung above her, torn, her light guttering. She wavered in the air, fell—

"*Dima!*" the Golem shouted—

Let her help you, thought Sophia weakly—

—and at the last moment twisted into human form and collapsed upon the deck.

The Golem scooped her up, and raced down the pier.

The Jinni opened the alley door and went out into the night, Kreindel following close behind.

The wind had picked up considerably; the streets seemed deserted. Kreindel wrapped her thin coat tightly around herself, shivering. Together they stood at the alley entrance, staring down Carlisle toward the river.

"Will I know him when I see him?" the Jinni murmured.

Just then a vast dark shape sped across West Street, moving from shadow to shadow. The Jinni felt a series of distant *thrums* beneath his feet. Six directions, were those *footsteps*?

"That's him," Kreindel whispered.

A moment later the shape was moving up Carlisle, draped in a voluminous cloak—no, a tarpaulin, the sort the dockworkers used. The shape drew nearer; it grew and grew, became an enormous human figure—

Kreindel sobbed once, and ran the last few steps to him.

The golem knelt, and took her in his arms. For a horrible moment the Jinni was certain the girl would be crushed; but Yossele only held her as she cried on his shoulder. Something in the Jinni twisted uneasily as he watched. *This* was the creature he was supposed to destroy? And— where was Chava?

"Kreindel," he whispered, "we must get back to the alley."

At once Yossele carried his master into the alley entrance and set her down by the door. The Jinni surveyed the street once, then followed.

"Yossele," Kreindel whispered, "this is Ahmad."

The Jinni stared up into a broad, lumpish face half hidden by the tarpaulin's folds. The glass eyes peered at him—and then Yossele seemed to start in surprise. He looked to Kreindel, and then to the Jinni again. The massive hands lifted—

The Jinni tensed—

—only to flutter in the air between them, the blunt fingers waving.

"Yossele?" Kreindel said, unsure.

"It's my face," the Jinni said, realizing. "He sees the flames. Chava—Miss Levy—can see them, too, when she looks at me. But others can't."

"Really?" said Kreindel.

The gigantic head nodded.

"I thought Miss Levy would be with you," the Jinni said.

In response Yossele bent and took Kreindel's hand, and then slowly let go. He looked up at the Jinni, to see if he understood.

The Jinni nodded, growing worried. Was she still in the water? Was she trapped somewhere?

"I'm sure she'll be here soon," Kreindel said, though her voice sounded less than certain.

"You should go inside," the Jinni told them. "I'll join you in a minute."

Yossele had to duck and angle sideways to fit through the alley door. On the other side, still out of sight of the others, Kreindel said, "Yossele, wait."

He looked down at her quizzically, head cocked, as though to say, *What is it?* She couldn't remember him ever being so expressive. Was it Miss Levy's influence? He still held the tarpaulin around himself; she pulled it from his shoulders. "That's better," she said. "You don't have to hide, here."

He looked past her, to where the others were.

"They might be scared of you at first," she said. "That's only natural. My father built you to be frightening. But he hoped that you'd be gentle, too." She cleared her throat, nervous. In truth she wasn't nearly so calm. What if something went wrong, what if she thought the wrong thing and made him attack—*No, don't think about it, don't remember how he looked in the hallway, don't!* Her chin wavered; her tired, reddened eyes filled again.

He stood sadly, watching her.

"I'm sorry," she whispered.

He shook his head, and put a hand to his chest. *No. I am.*

She smiled through her tears. "Did Miss Levy teach you to do that?"

He nodded.

"I'm glad." She wiped her eyes with Toby's handkerchief and said, "Let's introduce you to the others."

"Toby?"

The boy looked up from the workbench, where he'd been poking through a tool-box. Kreindel stood a few feet away—and behind her was the biggest creature Toby had ever seen.

"Toby, this is Yossele," Kreindel said.

Holy smokes, Toby thought.

Her golem stared at him with marble eyes. Toby stared back, terrified. His mother was nearby, with Maryam; her face had gone utterly white. She looked ready to attack Yossele herself, to grab Toby and run.

It's all right, Toby thought, pushing back his fright. *He's calm now. Kreindel's in control of him.* "Yossele," he said, fighting to keep his voice steady. "It's good to meet you. I'm Toby." And he stuck out a hand.

Behind him, Anna stifled a gasp.

Yossele stared down at Toby's hand. Then, very carefully, he closed his own around it, lifted once, twice, and let go.

"Huh," Toby said, startled.

Beside Yossele, Kreindel glowed like a proud mother.

Maryam squeezed Anna's arm in reassurance, then came to where Toby stood. "Hello, Yossele," she said, smiling up at the massive gray head. "I'm Maryam." And she, too, shook his hand.

Toby turned to look at his mother. She stood unmoving, her eyes hard with fear.

Yossele put up a hand: *It's all right.* Then, slowly, he bowed his head to Anna.

Please, Ma, Toby thought.

After a moment Anna nodded back, a small, stiff motion.

Toby cast her a look of fervent gratitude. The glare that she gave him in return promised him the worst tongue-lashing of his life.

The Jinni stood in the alley entrance on Carlisle, thinking.

An Amherst on every corner. Was Maryam right? Did he merely need to be patient and wait for humanity to catch up to him? He had to admit, it was an intriguing thought. His own hidden abilities turned commonplace. *Ordinary.* What would it be like, to be ordinary again?

The night air felt harsher than usual against his skin. He knew he ought to return to the forge before his injuries caught up with him—but he wanted to spend a few more minutes by himself, away from the unlikely community inside. After so long in solitude, he felt overwhelmed, exposed. He wondered what he'd regret having said aloud, when all of this was over.

Distantly, through the dying wind, came the sound of someone running.

He stepped out onto Carlisle, looked up and down the street. No one. But the footsteps were coming closer, and quickly.

He walked down the block to West Street and peered north. A figure was running toward him down the empty street. A woman, tall and fast, carrying someone.

He went still.

He was alive. Alive, and standing in the middle of West Street as though he'd been waiting there all this time.

In her relief she nearly careened into him, but then remembered the jinniyeh. She slowed, holding tight to her passenger—and saw him realize who it was that she carried.

She stopped a few feet away, his lover in her arms.

Chava, he nearly said; but his voice caught on the name.

She looked down at the jinniyeh, then came toward him. "She's badly hurt. She needs a fire."

Numbly he took the jinniyeh from her. Her features were far too dim, her eyes barely open. He wondered how all of this had come to pass, then put it aside for later. The Golem stood nervous, hesitant—as though unsure of her welcome now that she'd delivered her burden.

"You should come inside," he told her. "Yossele is here."

He saw her flinch—at his words, or Yossele's presence, or all of it, perhaps. "Kreindel, too?"

"And Toby, and Anna, and the Faddouls."

That surprised her. She peered at him, bemused—and he could sense the questions she would ask, the conversations that would surely follow, their shared ways and habits waiting to be donned like old, familiar garments. But then she said only, "Is the forge lit?"

He nodded, unable to speak.

"Then let's get her out of the cold."

Inside, there was a quick knock at the front door.

It was Sayeed, returned from the Hotel Earle. Maryam hurried to his side, murmured quickly; and Toby watched as Sayeed looked past her to Yossele, sitting on the floor beside Kreindel. Yossele saw the newcomer, and stood. Sayeed took several deep and steadying breaths before nodding hello. Yossele nodded back.

"Was there anything at the hotel?" Anna asked.

"Perhaps," Sayeed said, tearing his gaze from Yossele with difficulty. "The manager was in a state, he threatened to have me thrown out of the lobby—but I heard one of the guests say that—"

He broke off at the sound of the alley door opening, and a commotion of quick footsteps. From around the central column the Jinni appeared, along with the Golem, and—

"What on *earth?*" Anna murmured, staring at the naked woman in the Jinni's arms. She looked to Toby, wondering if she ought to make him close his eyes—but he was already at the Jinni's side, peering at the woman as though he knew her. "What happened?" said Toby. "Will she be okay?"

"I don't know," the Jinni muttered.

Carefully he placed the jinniyeh atop the burning coals. She lay there unmoving, surrounded by flames, a fairy-princess in her enchanted bower. Maryam crossed herself at the sight.

Behind them all, the Golem had stopped in the middle of the room, and now stared up at the Amherst in amazement. She turned to look for its creator—and saw him at the forge, surrounded by the others, all watching the woman on the coals. She hesitated, then walked to the other side of the forge and stood there, alone.

Something in her pained expression made Anna soften. It was the face of every Waverly Laundry girl who'd watched a former suitor stroll past the window with his new love, and who now had to work among her peers as though nothing had happened. Anna caught the Golem's eye, then looked to the Jinni, whose own face was dark with worry. The Golem nodded slightly. Anna sighed, and shook her head in disbelief.

Yossele, too, had noticed Miss Levy's sadness, and how she stood far away from the others. Kreindel, next to him, squeezed his hand. *It's all right*, she told him. *You can go to her.*

He looked down at her upturned face, and then let go of her hand and went to where Miss Levy stood. She glanced up at his approach—

Just as, in the coals, the jinniyeh stirred.

Slowly the world came into focus. She was in human form, lying atop a fire. An ominous steel moon floated above her. *The Amherst*, she realized, and shuddered. She'd fought the automaton, had nearly torn herself apart in the process, but then—

Sophia. Had the woman survived?

I'm still here, Dima, came the answer, weak but clear.

The jinniyeh sat up in the coals. A host of faces stared back at her. Her lover was among them, his expression wary but hopeful. The rest were humans, young and old. Dimly she recognized one as the boy from the hotel room, standing beside a girl of similar age. But where was the automaton? The jinniyeh wouldn't be comfortable until she knew . . .

Suddenly her lover said, "Wait. Don't turn around. You should know, there's someone—"

The jinniyeh turned around—and shrieked.

My God, Sophia cried in her mind, *what is that?*

The monster was gigantic, hideous, a demon risen from the depths of every terrifying story she'd ever heard. The jinniyeh scrabbled backwards in fright, then loosed her form and flew toward her lover, who stood with the children—

And Yossele roared.

It was an eruption, an avalanche of sound, as though years of fury had come unstuck from his throat all at once. The others scattered in fright as he strode toward them, his face dark with anger, his gaze fixed upon the glowing veil of flame that had come so dangerously close to his master.

The jinniyeh fled backward, towards the central column and its staircase. Yossele followed her, fists swinging.

"Yossele, wait!" Miss Levy cried behind him. "She's a jinniyeh, she's like Ahmad!"

But even with the faculties Miss Levy had given him, Yossele had no way to comprehend this. The fire was alive, it floated through the air; he could see it, but his master couldn't. It could only be a menace.

"Kreindel!" the Jinni shouted. "Stop him! You can't see her, but he can!"

"Yossele!" Kreindel cried. "Whatever it is, stop!"

It was no use. The jinniyeh had retreated between two of the steel platforms; he lunged toward her, landing a blow upon the lower one and denting it deeply. He grabbed its edge and pulled himself up, following her—and the stem that connected the platform to the column bent at once beneath his weight. He slid, recovered, ran up the now-tilting surface, and hurled himself at the jinniyeh.

His fist passed through her. Unbalanced, he crashed through the staircase and struck the central column with his shoulder.

There was a sound like the tolling of an enormous bell. The Amherst roof shook. Dust floated down from the arches.

"Get everybody out!" the Jinni shouted to Maryam.

Kreindel was on the floor, sobbing, her face in her hands. Toby ran to her, but Sayeed was quicker; he lifted the girl into his arms and sped toward the alley door, Maryam and Toby and Anna behind him.

The jinniyeh flew upward, out of Yossele's reach. Yossele followed, hauling himself up the broken staircase and jumping onto the next platform, which bent just as its sibling had, like a flower with a broken stem.

The Jinni watched, his mind racing.

It isn't strong enough, he thought. *It can't withstand the weight. I never accounted for the weight of others, of people. Of anything that wasn't itself. That's what was missing.*

He looked up at the beautiful secret he'd built, and remembered the neighbors, ready to come knocking. The children, who'd surely love to play upon such a creation.

He ran to the alley door, where Maryam was quickly ushering the others out. "Maryam," he said, "the Amherst—it's dangerous, and I never realized. It has to come down. Can you keep everyone away?"

Her eyes went wide with fright, but then she nodded. "Yes. Of course."

He shut the door behind them, ran back. The Golem was desperately calling for Yossele to stop, and for a moment his head turned toward her, as though he might listen . . .

But by now the jinniyeh's terror had subsided. The monster was powerful, but he couldn't hurt her, so long as she remained formless. She looked to her lover, and the creatures he'd aligned himself with; and then at the building she so hated, its bent and dented platforms.

Let it become another ruin, she thought.

She flew closer to Yossele and then darted backwards, taunting him. Again he chased after her.

"Stop!" the Golem shouted again, despairing.

"No, wait," said the Jinni, at her side. "Let them, Chava."

"*Let* them?" she said, bewildered.

"Maryam is warning the neighbors. It comes down tonight."

"But—" She looked up at the building she'd barely had a chance to see. *This took him years*, she thought. "Ahmad, are you sure?"

He nodded. "I'm sure."

She turned to him, a host of questions upon her lips—and then Yossele struck the column again.

Glass fell from the arches in a hail of blue shards as the jinniyeh dodged another fist. Yossele hurled himself at her—and this time, when he collided with the column, something shifted.

There was a screech of rending metal. The central column leaned to one side, dragging the arches with it, twisting them out of their alignment. With an ear-splitting shriek, the topmost section of the column broke free.

The arches gave way—and the roof collapsed.

Bricks and girders, tar-paper and cigarette butts all tumbled around them. The Jinni grabbed the Golem and brought her beneath the shelter of the column, which stood like a broken redwood, its branches bent. The night sky appeared above, moonlight shining through the dust.

With a slow, strange grandeur, one of the upper platforms crashed edge-first into the forge.

Coals scattered to the outer walls. The metal crumpled like tissue and began to melt. Flames climbed the window-paper, the showroom curtains. Beneath the column, the Golem and the Jinni held each other in the wreckage as, above them, Yossele and the jinniyeh kept on fighting: no longer out of fear or self-defense, but in matched exhilaration, a dark and destructive joy.

Another shudder; and the hole in the roof grew. A round-sided structure came into view, listing toward them—

The Jinni said, "Is that—"

The Golem grabbed him and ran out from beneath the column's shadow as the water tower toppled from its platform and burst apart.

A vast flood of water poured down the column. It missed the jinniyeh by inches—she screamed and flew to safer air—and struck Yossele like a battering ram. He tumbled backward, fell three stories, and crashed to the ground. The deluge covered him in an instant, a wave spreading outward. It reached the Golem, who picked up the Jinni and threw him onto the forge as the water knocked her off her feet. He landed in the coals, which hissed and spat as the wave broke around the forge's housing. The wave struck the outer wall, rebounded, rippled, stilled.

Silence.

The jinniyeh hung in the air.

Below her was a shallow sea full of broken, twisted metal. The two monsters lay in the water, submerged. Her lover stood atop the forge, gazing around at the wreckage. He looked up to her; his face was grim.

The woman-creature stood from the water, wiped her hair back from her face. She, too, looked around with chagrin, and saw her hideous counterpart trapped beneath one of the fallen girders. She went to him, lifted the girder away. He sat up, his anger apparently spent—but he wouldn't look at any of them, only sat there in the water.

Already the flood was receding, carried away by the drains in the floor. Gingerly her lover stepped down from the forge, and went to the woman. A quick murmur between them, words of concern. *Are you all right. I think so, and you.*

Watching, listening, the jinniyeh felt as though she was back at Washington Square Park, gazing through cold panes of glass into lives that she'd never comprehend. She had no place here; nor did she want one.

She looked up at the hole in the roof, the sky beyond. She would return to the desert, she decided. She could manage it herself, now. *The sailing schedules in the newspapers. The ticket offices in the docklands.* She'd use her accursed knowledge to go back—and then she'd find a way to cut the humanity out of herself, even if it took the rest of her life to do it.

Dima, Sophia pleaded—

"Dima," the Golem called—

Dima? the Jinni thought in confusion—

But the jinniyeh was already gone.

Below, the pair stood together, numb and unsure. Voices came from outside: a crowd murmuring, and Maryam telling them to wake their neighbors, to make certain that everyone was out—

"What do we do now?" the Golem said in dismay.

The Jinni looked around. Even now, the Amherst's wreckage had a certain splendor, as though it were the toppled city of some unimaginable race. Yossele and the jinniyeh had done much of the work for them—but it wasn't enough. Not yet.

He looked to the burning forge, and the wooden remains of the water tower, arranged conveniently around the column. He thought of the bucket of powdered magnesium in the workshop cabinet; he'd bought it long ago on a whim, meaning to experiment with alloys. The wood was damp, but the magnesium would help.

"We melt it down," he told her. "As much of it as we can."

The onlookers crowded Washington Street, all of them drawn outside by the news that something strange was happening inside the Amherst. They milled about, whispering and speculating, many in pajamas beneath their overcoats and slippers upon their feet. No one knew quite what was going on, only that the most horrible noises had been heard inside the building: crashes, shouts, inhuman shrieks. Maryam and Sayeed had recruited a handful of men to keep everyone back, away from the sidewalk. Murmurs ran through the crowd: ought they to knock? Break down the door? Could the Bedouin still be in there?

Suddenly, flames leapt behind the papered windows.

People cried out, pushed back. The flames were a strange, blinding white; they traveled through the building, floating between the floors, igniting whatever lay in their path. Before long it seemed that the entire interior was ablaze.

The crowd stood silent in shock, and not a little satisfaction. This was no accidental tenement fire. The outer walls refused to burn; no flames leapt from the roof, to endanger others. Later, it would be whispered that the Faddouls had been seen earlier that evening going into and out of the building, carrying something in a box. Whatever was inside the Amherst, whatever menace it had contained, it had been dealt with.

By the time the firemen arrived, there was little left for them to do. The fire had burned itself out. Inside, they found only a hollow shell littered with melted, twisted wreckage, its roof open to the stars. And no one saw Sayeed Faddoul slip around the corner onto Carlisle and then usher three figures—one enormous, and covered in a tarpaulin—out of the alley and down onto West Street, away from the commotion.

The storage room of the Faddouls' coffee-shop was small and dark, with barely enough room for the three people inside it. The Blumbergs sat together, dozing, their backs against the burlap sacks of roasted beans.

Kreindel sat across from them, awake despite her fatigue. She could still feel Yossele's rage in some distant part of her mind. It had felt horribly *right* to him, and thus to her as well: an avenging anger, its very existence its own justification.

The back door opened; footsteps, in the hallway. It was the Faddouls, followed by the three fugitives from the Amherst. Anna and Toby started awake to see the Jinni standing in the doorway, dressed in little more than singed rags. Anna's eyes widened. "Is it done? Was anyone hurt?"

"It's done," the Jinni said. "And no one was hurt."

"Thank God," Anna sighed. And then, guardedly: "Where is . . . the other one? Your friend?"

Not his friend, Toby thought.

"She's gone," the Jinni said quietly.

"Oh," said Anna.

Without another word the Jinni withdrew. More footsteps—and then Yossele was there, his glass eyes glinting beneath the tarpaulin.

The Blumbergs stiffened.

Yossele glanced at the doorway: too small for him, the room too tight. Everyone inside that room feared him, for good reason. He walked past, into the coffee-house.

Kreindel went out into the darkened hallway, and found Miss Levy. Soot covered her clothing and streaked her face, giving her a hollow-eyed look.

Kreindel had thought herself too exhausted for tears, but they filled her eyes again. "Miss Levy," she said, "I don't know how . . . I *can't*. I can't even think it, or . . ."

The Golem nodded. "I know, Kreindel. It's all right. I'll do it."

In the main room of the coffee-house, Yossele sat between the tables, his head in his hands.

The others had discussed what was about to happen. Sayeed and Maryam stood near the front door, Toby and Anna near the back hallway. All could run, escape, if they needed to. But it felt wrong to simply turn their backs and leave.

Kreindel stood beside the Jinni, trying to keep her mind steady. She pictured the maze, the alcove. Hands, reaching for each other in the dark.

Next to her, the Jinni watched, tense, as the Golem approached Yossele. The locket was in her hand. She looked to the Jinni—his face was unreadable—and put her thumb to the latch.

The locket sprang open. The paper inside was dry and undamaged; it fell into her hand, a tightly folded square. Her mind clamored at her: *He is the only other of your kind. Your time together was far too brief. There can be so much more.* With effort she pushed it all aside. This was her responsibility. She would put an end to the danger that Yossele had become, just as she would put an end to herself if she thought it necessary.

She opened the first fold of the square—and there on the paper, just before it opened completely, the Jinni had written:

But you deserve life.

She dropped the paper, put a hand to her mouth. A sound like a sob escaped her throat. Blindly she turned away—and he came to her and gathered her tightly in his arms. She closed her eyes, buried her face in his shoulder.

A giant hand plucked the paper from the floor.

For a moment, Kreindel thought Yossele would tear it to shreds. But he merely cupped the paper in his palm, like something precious: a blossom, an egg. He reached out, offered it to Kreindel.

"No, Yossele," she whispered. "Not me."

In the Jinni's arms, the Golem trembled as Yossele fought against his master's wishes. Slowly the giant, grave head nodded. *Yes. You.*

The girl wiped the tears from her face. She looked around the room: at Toby and his mother, at the Faddouls. People whom she barely knew, but who'd shown her more kindness in the last few hours than anyone had in years. And now, they were trusting her to make the right choice.

The girl lifted the paper from Yossele's hand. She opened the first fold, and then the second. She read the Hebrew letters there, the words that the Jinni remembered writing as though they'd been dragged from his soul. The Golem's face was still pressed to his shoulder—but he knew that she'd feel it all. She had no choice. She couldn't turn away from that weight. And so he decided that he wouldn't turn away, either. He'd learn to bear what he could.

Kreindel folded the paper again, slipped it into her pocket. Tears still dotted her lashes, but now her expression was composed, steady. All the sadness, it seemed, belonged to Yossele, who sat with his rough head bowed, staring at the floor. She stepped closer and embraced him, her arms around his shoulders. Her lips went to his ear; he tilted his head, as though listening to a secret.

With a sound like skittering leaves, Yossele came apart. Each piece of him crumbled bit by bit, dissolving into what it once had been. Within moments, there was only a mound of earth, rich and fragrant with spring.

Kreindel stood alone, weeping.

Epilogue

Friday, 7 May 1915
NARRAGANSETT, RHODE ISLAND

S *houts. Human voices. The sound of rushing water.*
The world lurched, listed sideways.

Panicking, the jinniyeh broke free from the box where she'd stowed herself and flew from the injured ship. The ocean air bit into her as she searched desperately for land, a horizon, anything at all. There—a green and rocky shoreline. She flew towards it, the ship foundering behind her—

Sophia gasped awake and sat up in bed, one hand over her mouth. Hot tears fell upon the bedclothes. Her heart pounded with the remnants of the jinniyeh's panic; she breathed deeply, trying to calm herself.

Dima? she called. But there was no answer. The jinniyeh had gotten better at shutting her out—but their connection was stronger when Sophia dreamt.

After a while she wiped her tears away and rose from her bed, wrapped a silk robe over her thin nightgown. She went to the writing-desk, found a fresh sheet of paper, and wrote:

Lusitania sunk near coast of Ireland. Torpedo to starboard side.

She folded this once, placed it in an envelope, wrote the date and time across the seal, and took it downstairs.

It was late morning; she'd been up until three, walking the low cliff along the ocean, listening to the waves. All her hated childhood summers had been spent here, enduring badminton lessons and lawn parties. Now, though, she appreciated the place far better; it reminded her of her father. *You were not meant to be tamed,* the crashing waves seemed to whisper to the clipped boxwoods, the manicured lawn. *You, too, would be free, if it were not for the work of men's hands.*

She found her mother in a chair in the solarium, watching the water, a cup of tea untouched beside her. She glanced up at Sophia as she entered, then away again. Sophia had flatly refused to speak to her mother—no polite small talk, no discussion of meals or her health—until Julia acknowledged the truth of what had happened to them. And thus silence had reigned since their arrival.

Sophia placed the envelope on the table. "Open this tomorrow night," she said. "And then tell me it's all mesmerism and suggestion."

At the Faddouls' coffee-house, the news arrived in a rush of murmurs and gasps that started at the door and swept to the back of the shop. All bowed their heads in prayer for the dead and the missing. Before long, their shock had progressed to speculation. Many swore that America would declare within a month; spirits rose at the thought of a swift end to the war, their families safe, the whole terrible ordeal behind them. And then who would rule Syria, when the Turks had gone? The French, the Russians, the English? *Why not ourselves?* a few voices said—and soon all were mired in debate.

Maryam walked among them, pouring coffee, saying little. It had been weeks since the Amherst burned—and yet still, in her dance between the tables, she occasionally caught the distracting, heartbreaking scent of springtime loam.

The customers argued and sighed and drank their coffee, and at last departed, leaving their newspapers behind. Maryam swept the shop and gathered the papers, and found among them a copy of the *Brooklyn Daily Eagle*. She hesitated—and then thought of all the friends and neighbors who'd come to her café looking for a bit of guidance, a small sign that pointed toward a more hopeful future. Perhaps, she thought, it was time to take her own advice.

She opened the newspaper, and found the listings for storefronts on Atlantic Avenue.

At the Asylum for Orphaned Hebrews, the announcement of the *Lusitania*'s torpedoing came during the Havdalah service. The children sat in uncharacteristic silence as the headmaster read the headline from the dais, his voice thick with tears. He spoke at length about the patriotism of America's Jews stretching back to the Revolution, and the duty of every good citizen to take a stand against brazen tyranny. The older boys shuddered, thinking of shells and trenchworks and U-boats.

The service ended, and the headmistress dried her eyes and went back to her office, where a dozen applications for the new Culinary Science position waited upon her desk. Idly she read them over, then put them down with a sigh. The wall in the basement had been patched over, Miss Altschul's cot and footlocker removed from her dormitory. The hiring of the new instructor was the final step in expunging all traces of what had happened that day—yet there was nothing to be done about the story itself, which now existed in a hundred different tellings, each more lurid and outlandish than the next. A few of the instructors had suggested disciplinary measures for those caught repeating it, but the headmistress knew better. Before long, the story would wear itself into mundanity; it would become merely another ghost in the Asylum halls, another bit of lore that the children absorbed with their morning toast and stewed prunes. *Be careful in the basement, or Miss Levy's monster will crawl out of its closet, hunt you down, and chew on your bones.*

The empty shell of the Amherst sat crumbling on its corner.

The building itself was now a source of some consternation. Its owner was presumed to have perished in the fire, and no one knew of any possible inheritors—which meant that, by law, it would become the property of New York State, a process that promised to take months. In the meantime, the structure continued to creak and decay. The children of Little Syria were warned away from it time and time again, yet still their mothers found strange new items in their pockets: shining lumps of steel, melted squares of opaque blue glass.

Then, news. An investment company had taken interest in the site, and was willing to purchase it from the state at a favorable price. The bureaucratic wheels were greased, and before long the wreck of the Amherst belonged to the Troy Investment Company of Wilmington, Delaware. No one had ever heard of Troy Investment, but that was nothing strange; half the buildings in Little Syria were owned by distant, unseen landlords. All the negotiations were handled by an intermediary. The owner's name appeared nowhere on the paperwork.

The ink had barely dried on the deed of transfer when the demolition crew arrived. They'd been given strict instructions to sift the rubble for steel, all of which was carted to a warehouse uptown. A wooden rolltop desk and its matching chair were also unearthed, whole and unharmed, save for a few scorch-marks.

Soon the Amherst was gone, vanished into memory. But now the Troy Investment Company seemed to lose interest in its acquisition. The empty lot was put up for auction and sold to an unremarkable firm, one that had built dozens of properties in lower Manhattan. Before long the corner was home to another square and ordinary factory loft, five stories high, so exactly like its predecessor that a casual observer might have passed it none the wiser.

Only the children mourned the loss. At night, they'd take their hoarded bits of steel and glass from their treasure-boxes, and make all sorts of wishes upon them, and try to convince themselves of a magic that they'd once believed in without question.

The Jinni sat at a sidewalk café, a cup of coffee untouched on the table before him.

A woman soon arrived, and sat in the chair opposite. He wouldn't have recognized her, had he not arranged the meeting himself. Instead of dark winter woolens, she wore a summer dress of pale blue cotton; the braided crown was gone, a fashionable bob in its place. Her cheeks were slightly flushed. She asked a waiter for a glass of iced tea, and then sat back, regarding him. "Ahmad."

"Sophia. You look . . . well."

She raised an eyebrow. "You see it too?"

He nodded, his eyes traveling over the new and subtle glow about her skin, like a sea creature's phosphorescence. He realized, with an embarrassed start, that he was staring at her. He looked away.

She removed an envelope from her purse, slid it across the table. He opened it, and read with surprise the amount on the cheque: the price of the Amherst's steel, melted down and sold for scrap. "That's more than I expected," he said.

"How long has it been since you purchased steel?"

"Over three years, I suppose—oh. The war."

She nodded. "It's a profitable business. Especially when one is 'too proud to fight,' as they say."

The bitter tone was hard to miss. "You disagree with Wilson?"

"I think," she said, "that neutrality is easier when one hasn't lived among the people who are about to be slaughtered." She sighed. "But, never mind. The money from the sale of the property will arrive soon. Are you sure . . . ?"

He nodded. "Half to the foreign aid services, whichever you recommend. The other half to Chava." Arbeely, he felt certain, would've wanted to help his countrymen with his share of the Amherst's worth. And as for his own portion, it only seemed fair. Both Charlotte Levy and Ahmad al-Hadid had perished that day; but the Golem's savings had been in a bank, not a building, and now lay beyond her reach. "Does she still mean to go on with her plan?"

She nodded. "We view the property tomorrow. Officially, she'll be the caretaker. The name on the title will be Troy Investment."

"But Troy Investment is Chava," he said, puzzled. "Funded by you."

"That's true. But she's also an unmarried woman, and therefore can't own property in her own name."

He sat back. "Ah. How inconvenient."

"That's one way of putting it."

A silence descended. Then, "How is she?" he asked.

Sophia sighed. "She's frightened, and miserable. She accuses me of stealing a part of her, and then shuts me out when I defend myself. She can only see what's happened as my gain and her loss. And when I sleep, I dream in words that I can never say when I'm awake." She looked at him then, a touch of sympathy in her eyes. "It's a beautiful language, Ahmad. You must miss it terribly."

He nodded; he felt suddenly, unutterably sad. *It's a beautiful language. I miss it terribly.* Why had he never spoken to the Golem in this way? Why had he never told her these plain and simple truths? He put his regrets aside and said only, "Did she reach Casablanca?"

"Yes, last week. She tried to go inland, to jinn territory—but the jinn that she met there . . . They know she's different. They see something— a glimmer of me, I suppose. It frightens them, and they fly from her. So for now she's staying nearer to the coast, rather than endure that."

Her gaze was elsewhere, and he wondered if she was trying to see the jinniyeh. He pictured her: a veil of fire drifting along the desert's edge, alone save for Sophia's thoughts.

Her eyes turned to his, a touch of flame in their depths. "What about you? Have you decided where you're going?"

"No. Not yet. But it has to be soon. I'm legally dead—I shouldn't even be in Manhattan."

She chuckled, at that. Then, sobering: "Have you seen Chava yet?"

He shook his head. "I will. Before I leave. For now . . . we decided it was better not to. She's trying to create something new. I might cause . . . distractions. Complications." He paused and then said, "Do you think she can truly do what she means to? It's a noble idea, certainly. It only seems . . . optimistic. Given recent events."

She nodded. "I know. But she feels she has to try. To be ready, in case Dima changes her mind. And she'll be looking for others, too. We can't be the only accidents of fate."

The house was in Brooklyn, to the east of Clinton Hill. It was built in the Queen Anne style, and had originally been a financier's present for his daughter, on the occasion of her marriage. Unimpressed with the size of the lots on offer, he'd purchased two and built the house on the border between them—set back from the street for privacy's sake, with a drive that curved around the front and led to a large carriage-house at the back.

As Brooklyn grew, and the middle classes began to encroach, the fashionable address had grown less appealing. Her children having grown and gone, the financier's daughter put the property up for sale. The house was in relatively good repair; it was the double lot that wanted attention. There were good, strong lindens and maples, and a large green ash that shaded the drive—but the lawn had gone sparse with neglect, and the kitchen garden was overrun with nettles and milkweed.

One morning, a taxicab pulled to the curb, and two women emerged. One was noticeably tall, the other smaller, her hair cut in a bob. Together the women toured the house's bedrooms and the front and back parlors, the kitchen with its double oven, the small glass conservatory. They inspected the carriage-house, and saw that it could easily be converted into living quarters. They walked back down the drive and stood beneath the green ash, and considered what they'd seen.

"What do you think?" Sophia asked.

The Golem gazed around at the house and the trees, the weed-littered lawn, the drive that she thought ought to be pea-gravel instead of asphalt. She bent to the base of the ash and sifted a handful of dirt between her fingers, then laid a palm upon the trunk and felt the life that hummed inside.

"I think I'll take it," she said.

The construction site in Midtown belonged to a steel-frame "skyscraper," one of the newer breed that had begun to appear across the city. The architect who'd designed it was often at the site, monitoring its progress—and soon he began to notice a tall and striking man who'd appear each day on the sidewalk, watching the construction as well. The man seemed especially interested in the problem of steel bracing, and the mechanics of loads and stresses. He'd track each beam as it was lifted into place, holding up a hand to mimic its position, trying to guess the angle at which it would be attached. Usually, his guess was correct. When he was wrong, he'd ponder the problem, often sketching it in the air with his hands until he found the answer. One afternoon, he seemed particularly stuck for an explanation—and at last the architect went to the fence and told him, "It's to do with the opposing forces on the beam. It needs cross-bracing at that point."

The man frowned at this. "But why? It's perpendicular to the ground. The compressive strength should be more than enough."

"Unless you're building on top of fill. Then you've got to account for the shear."

The man thought a moment, then grinned. "Thank you. That was bothering me."

"You in the construction trade?"

"Not like this," the man said, nodding to the building.

The two men watched the progress for a while, and then the man on the sidewalk said, "If someone told you that he wanted to learn to design buildings like these, and could go anywhere in the world to do it—what would you tell him?"

"I'd tell him to go to Chicago," the architect said at once. "That's the new frontier. The things they do with steel in that city, I don't understand the half of them."

"Chicago," the man said in mild surprise, as though he'd just been handed the key to a vexing mystery. "How interesting. Thank you." He smiled, and walked away—and the architect never saw him again.

Toby Blumberg stood frozen in the sunlit dance hall, his wrists held in the grip of a grinning old man.

I know your name, Toby told him.

The man's grin wavered.

It's Yehudah Schaalman. You aren't really here, you're in a flask buried on the other side of the world. All of this happened to my mother, before I was born. Say, do you want to know what comes next?

A touch of confusion, in the old man's eyes.

In just a minute, Chava Levy and Ahmad al-Hadid are going to come through the door and rescue me—and then they'll stick your sorry ass in that flask for good.

The man snarled, angered in defeat—

And Toby woke upon his pallet.

He took a deep breath and let it out slowly. Even now, months after his mother had told him everything, it still surprised him to wake without that desperate need for movement. He tended to laze about in the mornings now, until Anna yelled at him to quit loafing and eat his breakfast.

But this was a Sunday, and Anna had left for work already, so Toby was alone. He lay there for a few minutes more, mostly out of principle, then washed himself and found a clean shirt and a pair of dungarees. He'd quit his job at Western Union; the uniform was gone, to be worn upon the back of some other boy. He'd enrolled at Stuyvesant High instead, with an eye toward the Cooper Union entrance exam. All summer long he'd studied at the library: geometry, algebra, basic chemistry. It shocked him how long he could sit still and study, now that he didn't need to move around so much.

He wolfed down a few slices of raisin challah, slung a heavy rucksack across his back, and carried his bicycle downstairs.

By now, he could navigate the trip to Brooklyn without much thought. He crossed the columned plaza and climbed the Manhattan Bridge, feeling, as always, as though he were about to be launched into the air. At the exit, he circled around and rode the waterfront past Wallabout Channel and the Navy Yard, then turned south, pedaling past brownstones and frame houses, to the eastern edge of Clinton Hill and the house on the double lot.

He leaned the bicycle against the porch and rang the bell. The woman who opened it wore a housekeeper's dress and a clean white apron tied at her waist.

"Good morning, Chava," he said.

"Good morning, Toby," she said, smiling. "Kreindel's upstairs."

Kreindel sat at the desk in her bedroom, pencil in her hand, frowning at her composition book.

Her bedroom was the smallest in the house. She'd been offered one far larger, but had quailed at the idea of living in so much space, like a pea rattling in a can. Even her own little room had felt too big until the bookshelves had arrived and were nailed into place. She'd lined them with a motley collection of Hebrew and Yiddish volumes, all chosen from the book-carts of Williamsburg and Borough Park: Talmud and Maimonides and modern theology, Sephardic poetry, even a romance novel. She spent afternoons and evenings studying, pulling the languages apart and examining how they were made. Hesitantly she'd begun to think of going to college, or even someday to the Holy Land, to speak Hebrew with the settlers. Her father's words still rung in her ears: *abomination, desecration.* She wrestled with them daily. It was harder, somehow, to live by his strictures without the Asylum to set them against. Her landlady allowed Kreindel to come and go as she pleased, to pray as often as she liked, to take a job somewhere in town or live a life of indolence. Her hours were hers to fill—a terrifying freedom, after seven years of the Asylum bell.

She hadn't stopped reaching for Yossele. Sometimes, without thinking, she'd picture him in the alcove, and try to draw comfort from the image. There were days when she would bitterly regret what she'd done, and feel a dull anger towards the Golem for not having the strength to do it herself. Other times, she'd wake in the night with the memory of Yossele bursting from the storage room, ready to kill at her command— and remember the Golem standing before her in the hallway, the locket raised in her fist.

Absently she put her hand to the chain at her neck. Instead of asking Kreindel to return the paper, the Golem had given her the locket to keep it in. They watched over each other now, Kreindel and her landlady.

Downstairs, the doorbell rang. Soon Kreindel heard Toby's familiar footsteps on the stairs. A knock, and his head poked around the door-frame. "Hey there," he said. "How're the translations going?"

She tossed her pencil onto the desk. "It's useless," she said. "I have no idea why I'm doing it. No one will read them anyway."

"I will," he said. "And Miss—and Chava will, too."

She snorted. "She won't need to read them, she hears me thinking about them all the time."

"I bet she'll still read them."

"Because she wants to? Or because *I* want her to?"

Toby cringed, and glanced at the half-open door.

"Oh, stop it," Kreindel told him, annoyed. "She's not my monitor *or* my mother. Besides, she told me she asks herself the same thing."

Toby still thought it rude of her, but said nothing. The thorny na-ture of Kreindel and the Golem's relationship made him uneasy, and he was helpless to change matters. He believed Kreindel when she said he was too taken with his childhood memories of *Missus Chava* to see her clearly. He also believed the Golem when she said it was only natural, even preferable, for Kreindel to be angry for a while. *The important thing is that we talk to each other,* she'd said. *Arguments are uncomfortable, but silence is worse.*

"What's all that?" Kreindel asked, nodding at his rucksack. "Parts for the wireless?"

He nodded. "I'm going to finish it today. Want to help?"

"Sure," she said.

He grinned. "Really? Or do you only want to because *I* want you to want to?"

That made her roll her eyes, but she abandoned her translations and followed him up the stairs to the attic.

For all the house's comforts, the attic was the only room where Kreindel felt truly at home. Its dormer roof sloped nearly to the floor, creating two large, triangular walls, each set with a porthole window. She liked to sit against the low wall beneath the dormer, close her eyes, and inhale the attic's scents of dust and wood-polish. In her first weeks at the house, she'd come up to the attic late at night with a velveteen blanket she'd found, wrap it around her shoulders, and pretend she was with Yossele. But the pretending had begun to pale lately; it felt too simple, too superficial, for the fraught and complicated thing that was her grief.

She watched as Toby stood with one foot out the porthole window, fiddling with a wire he'd strung up to an aerial on the roof. In the same way that she no longer knew what to do with her hours, she no longer knew what she wanted from Toby, either. At eighteen to his fifteen, she couldn't help thinking of him as a child, an innocent; but she knew that was unfair. He, too, had been set apart from his peers by secrets and impossibilities. Perhaps they were destined to be a part of each other's lives, and were only free to choose what form that would take. Perhaps that was what it was like to have friends, or a family.

It was true, though, that she liked watching him build the wireless. He'd been at it for weeks now: hauling the parts to Brooklyn trip by trip, clamping the aerial onto the roof, littering the attic floor with instruction booklets and scribbled diagrams. She hadn't the faintest clue how any of it worked, but Toby could explain it clear as a bell. He'd learned how from library books, and trial and error; and when she complimented his skill, he'd say things like, *Oh, anybody could figure that out.* She doubted that greatly. She had to admit, he looked different out of his uniform, dressed in regular clothing. Like a real person. Someone she could get to know.

He glanced up from his work and caught her watching him. She glanced away, embarrassed. When she looked back, he'd returned to the wireless, but his cheeks shone a bright and fiery red.

Huh, she thought. *So boys can blush, too.*

In the kitchen downstairs, the Golem washed and shredded the carrots for a salad, while also taking note of the various emotions drifting down from the attic. She preferred to give the pair as much privacy as she could, knowing that her own presence was enough to, as Anna put it, "*keep them out of trouble.*" Still, she had to remind Kreindel occasionally that she'd only act on words, not thoughts—and that if Kreindel wanted something in particular for supper, she must come to the kitchen and ask, instead of thinking it as loudly as possible from the top of the stairs.

They were all still vulnerable to each other, still recovering from the events of the spring. Kreindel had made no secret of her night-time trips to the attic, nor did she even try. Rightly or wrongly, the girl had insisted that since her new landlady knew all of Kreindel's innermost fears and desires, she was entitled to know the Golem's in return. The resulting conversations had made the Golem feel as though she were spreading out her life upon a butcher's counter, pointing out the choicest bits. Now there was little that Kreindel didn't know about her. She supposed that to ask for her locket back would be beside the point: with or without it, Kreindel held her life in her hands.

She finished the salad, covered it with waxed paper, and put it in the refrigerator, then fetched her wicker basket and went out to the garden.

After a summer of enjoyable toil, the once-neglected kitchen garden was now twice as large as before. She made the rounds of the beds, filling her basket with ripe tomatoes and eggplants, fragrant basil, bell peppers and summer squash. The harvest was far too much for their small household; she would send much of it home with Toby, along with challah and stuffed cabbage rolls and jars of borscht.

She pulled a few weeds, then paused with her fingertips in the earth, feeling the life that traveled from the soil into the roots. Yossele was here, buried among the beds, his clay strengthening the Brooklyn loam. Sometimes, working in the garden, she'd turn over a fragrant spadeful of dirt and be transported back to the Asylum basement, and the bliss of their connection. Sometimes, she wondered if she'd broken her promise just as much as the Jinni had. Or perhaps *I will have only you* had been entirely the wrong promise to make.

I love you. She'd never said that to him, not once. They'd traded so many words in their countless arguments that it was hard to believe one small phrase, not even a breath's worth, might've changed matters. Perhaps it was the only thing that could have.

In the kitchen, she chopped the tomatoes and basil, sliced and salted the eggplant. There was ground sirloin in the refrigerator, and home-made pappardelle drying over a wooden dowel. She finished the prepara-tions quickly—she could work as quickly as she liked now—and put it all away for later, then untied her apron and went out back again, past the garden, to the newly renovated carriage-house behind it.

The carriage-house was hers alone. Downstairs was her sitting room, with a fireplace for the winter evenings. Upstairs, there was a small bedroom, used mainly for its wardrobe; a bathroom with a claw-foot tub deep enough to submerge herself completely; and a large, sunlit study with an old rolltop desk, newly sanded and refinished. She, like Kreindel, had begun to build a library, though her own was far more eclectic. Volumes of world history sat beside collections of folk-tales and fairy-stories. Investment books and housekeeping manuals kept com-pany with travel memoirs, anthropology journals, and a complete set of the *Encyclopaedia Britannica*. There were myths in a dozen languages, and explorers' dubious accounts of tribal superstitions and unexplained events. Her vast, flawless memory absorbed each tale and snippet, look-ing for hints, matches, threads. It was her own vigil: she would keep watch, and find whomever she could, and offer help, if they wanted it.

She sat at Arbeely's desk and reviewed the map spread before her, marked with arrows and *X*'s: the first on Ireland's southern coast, then Southampton, Casablanca, Fès, and Algiers. She traced her finger past the *X* at Algiers, to Tripoli, Alexandria, Cairo, Jerusalem, Damascus. *She stays near the cities now,* Sophia had told her the last time they spoke. *She doesn't want to admit it, but she's less lonely when she can hear human voices.* How long would it take the jinniyeh to reach Palmyra? the Golem wondered. Might she have changed, by then, into someone who could accept the company of those unlike herself? Despite all that had hap-pened, all the various wounds the jinniyeh had inflicted, the Golem hoped that she'd consent to become an ally someday, if not a friend. And for good or ill, even if she wanted nothing to do with any of them, she'd never be truly alone.

On a bright September morning, the Golem took the subway to Union Square and walked to a hotel on the corner of 15th Street. She counted the windows—over, up—and found the one she was looking for, then stood beneath it on the sidewalk, beside a lamp-post. She gazed around while she waited, taking in the theater marquees, the fashionable crowd. The balmy weather felt like summer's last gift before the arrival of autumn. She'd sensed it on the subway ride: the ground drawing into itself, banking its warmth.

She didn't have to wait long before the Jinni emerged from the lobby door and came to where she stood. He wore a new suit in navy pinstripe, and carried a suitcase in his hand. After a moment's pause, he offered her his arm: a formal gesture, almost shy. She took it, feeling a pang at the hint of distance. She wanted to object, to descend with him into the subway, to take him back to Brooklyn and her carriage-house—to hoard time with him against his absence, enough for a night, a week, a year. But this walk together was what they'd agreed to instead.

They said little as they went north along Broadway, side by side. They passed Madison Square Park, and the Jinni realized he was trying to look at each statue and elm tree and bend of the skyline, storing the sights like rare riches. He wondered when he'd see them next, and what would bring him back. He wondered who, exactly, he would be when he returned.

At 31st Street they turned west, and the soaring columns came into view. They passed between them and into the narrow, high Arcade, their reflections keeping pace in the shop windows. Then, down into the vaulted magnificence of the Waiting Room—and she slowed her steps, the better to take in the palatial expanse, the details in every carved inch of marble and travertine. And he smiled to see her upturned face, her wide eyes; glad, despite the occasion, to have brought her here at last.

They reached the Concourse—and now the Golem was struck by the notion that she knew this place, even though she'd never been here before. She knew it by the feel of its rising columns and steel arches, its scent of coal-smoke, its shining grandeur. And she knew the community of travelers, too: strangers, alone and separate, who'd nevertheless come together to share a moment of transition, a brief connection.

They descended to the waiting train. He set his suitcase on the platform, and at last took her in his arms.

"I wish that I had done so many things differently," he murmured.

"I wish that we both had," she replied. "Maybe we'll have a chance to try again, someday."

He nodded. "Until then," he said, "would you allow me to renew my promise?"

"No," she said. "I want to make a different one."

He pulled back and looked at her, puzzled.

"I love you," she told him. "And I always will."

He went still in surprise. Then he closed his eyes, and gathered her close.

"I love you," he whispered. "And I always will."

They stood together for a long moment. Then, slowly, they let go. He picked up his suitcase, lifted a hand in farewell, and boarded the train.

He found his seat, and placed his suitcase in the luggage rack above. The conductor came down the aisle, calling for tickets; the Jinni removed his own from his jacket pocket and presented it. A click of the ticket punch, and the conductor moved on.

The Jinni replaced the ticket in his pocket, snug beside the small notebook and pen that he'd begun to carry on his walks. Inside was a collection of sketches: architectural details and rough schematics, buildings that he saw and others that he imagined. Interspersed among them were brief sections of writing, a sentence or two at a time. *An unlucky jinni who'd been caught in the rain decided to warm himself inside a Bedu's cooking-fire.* Or, *Long ago there lived a jinni-child who found a wizard's trove of gold and silver, hidden deep in a cave.* Many of these lines had been crossed out, rewritten in other languages, crossed out again. He wasn't satisfied with any of his brief translations, and doubted he ever would be, not completely. He wasn't even certain who he was writing them for. The work compelled him, nevertheless.

He sat back and gazed out the window. The train jolted once, and then slowly pulled away from the station.

The Golem stood on the platform until the train had disappeared.

She returned to the Concourse's upper level, and spent a few more minutes admiring the glassed arches, the elegant ironwork. Then she walked through to the Waiting Room, and found an information booth tucked into the shadow of a marble pillar. The booth held a neatly ordered display of printed timetables, and she perused them row by row until her gloved finger landed upon the one labeled *New York to Chicago*. She plucked the paper from its stack, folded it into her purse, and walked out into the city.

Acknowledgments

First, I have to thank my readers. This book was a long time in coming, and I'm grateful to everyone who read *The Golem and the Jinni* and was willing to wait for more. And I'm especially thankful for all the booksellers, librarians, teachers, and book club members who helped *The Golem and the Jinni* find its audience.

My agent, Sam Stoloff, once again delivered much-needed guidance and reassurance in equal turns. Terry Karten, my editor, gave *The Hidden Palace* enough space and time to come into its own. Coralie Hunter provided stellar notes and advice. Huge thanks to the fantastic team at HarperCollins for all of their hard work, patience, and dedication.

Like its predecessor, this book required quite a lot of research before I could write it properly. My "Asylum for Orphaned Hebrews" is loosely based upon the real-life Hebrew Orphan Asylum, which housed many thousands of Manhattan's Jewish children from 1884 until it closed in 1941. Hyman Bogen's history of the H.O.A., *The Luckiest Orphans*, was invaluable reading as I created my own version. Everything I know about turn-of-the-century lessons in Modern Hebrew comes from Jonathan B. Krasner's *The Benderly Boys and American Jewish Education*. For Toby's escapades, I relied on Gregory J. Downey's research into the world of bicycle messengers, especially *Telegraph Messenger Boys: Labor, Technology, and Geography, 1850–1950*. Sophia's travels and encounters drew from numerous sources, including Jeremy Wilson's archive of T.E. Lawrence's documents at telstudies.org; Scott Anderson's *Lawrence in Arabia: War, Deceit, Imperial Folly and the Making of the Modern Middle East*; Janet Wallach's biography of Gertrude Bell, *Desert Queen*; and Bell's own *The Desert and the Sown*. Any errors, stretches, or unlikelihoods are, of course, my own.

Many thanks to Shaina Hammerman, Kara Levy, Ruth Galm, Michelle Adelman, Clare Beams, Julianne Douglas, Kim McCoy, Kelly Brooks, Todd Figlio, Rebecca McLaughlin, Melanie Grossheider, Adam

Monkowski, Kari Wilcox, and James Wilcox for their sustaining friendships. Jason Snell of *The Incomparable* was kind enough to let me join his merry band of podcasters, and they quickly became a treasured community. Kathy Campbell, Lisa Schmeiser, and Aleen Simms gave me world-class support and advice. Antony Johnston, Scott McNulty, and Dan Moren shared great conversations about fandoms, stories, and writing in general.

My family continues to be my life's greatest blessing. My gratitude to my parents is more than I can say; I hope to model their unwavering support for my own children. My brother and sister-in-law, my husband's family, our nieces and nephews, my extended relations near and far: I thank you for everything, especially the laughter when I needed it. My children, Maya and Gavin, make me proud every day, and I hope that when they're older they'll read this book and understand what all the "Shhh, Mommy's writing" was about.

Much of *The Hidden Palace* was written and edited in 2020, a year when all normalcy and routine were thrown out the window. If this book succeeds at all in its finished form, it's in no small part thanks to my husband, who took over the household and our kids' distance learning while I sequestered myself with the manuscript. Kareem, first and best reader of my heart, I am forever grateful for you.

About the Author

HELENE WECKER's debut novel, *The Golem and the Jinni*, was awarded the Mythopoeic Fantasy Award for Adult Literature, the VCU Cabell First Novelist Award, and the Harold U. Ribalow Prize, and was nominated for a Nebula Award and a World Fantasy Award. A Midwest native, she holds a BA in English from Carleton College and an MFA in fiction writing from Columbia University. Her work has appeared in literary journals such as *Joyland* and *Catamaran*, as well as in the fantasy anthology *The Djinn Falls in Love and Other Stories*. She lives in the San Francisco Bay area with her husband and children.